THE FIRE
WITNESS

LARS KEPLER

Translated from the Swedish by Neil Smith

HarperCollins*Publishers*

HarperCollins*Publishers*
1 London Bridge Street
London SE1 9GF

This paperback edition 2018
1

First published in Great Britain by HarperCollins*Publishers* 2013

Originally published in 2011 by Albert Bonniers Förlag, Sweden, as *Eldvittnet*

Lars Kepler assert the moral right to be identified as the author of this work

A catalogue record for this book is available from the British Library

ISBN: 978-0-00-824183-4

Typeset in Electra LT Std by Palimpsest Book Production Limited,
Falkirk, Stirlingshire

Printed and bound in Great Britain by
CPI Group (UK) Ltd, Croydon, CR0 4YY

MIX
Paper from
responsible sources
FSC
www.fsc.org **FSC™ C007454**

and all liars shall have their part in the lake
which burneth with fire and brimstone

Revelations 21:8

A medium is a person who claims to have a paranormal gift, an ability to see connections beyond accepted scientific parameters.

Some mediums offer contact with the dead through spiritualist seances, while others offer guidance with the help of Tarot cards, for instance.

Trying to contact the dead through a medium is a practice that reaches a long way back through human history. A thousand years before the birth of Christ, King Saul of Israel attempted to ask the spirit of the dead prophet Samuel for advice.

All over the world the police seek the help of mediums and spiritualists with complex cases. This happens many times every year, even though there isn't a single documented case of a medium contributing to solving a case.

1

Elisabet Grim is fifty-one years old and her hair is peppered with grey. She has cheerful eyes, and when she smiles you can see that one of her front teeth sticks out a bit further than the other.

Elisabet works as a nurse at the Birgitta Home, a children's care home north of Sundsvall. It's a privately-run home, and takes girls aged between twelve and seventeen who have been placed in care.

Many of the girls have problems with drugs when they arrive, almost all have a history of self-harm and eating disorders, and several of them are very violent.

There aren't really any alternatives to secure children's homes with alarmed doors, barred windows, and airlocks. The next step is usually adult prison and compulsory psychiatric care, but the Birgitta Home is one of the few exceptions, offering girls a path back to open care homes.

Elisabet likes to say that the Birgitta Home is where the good girls end up.

She picks up the last piece of dark chocolate, puts it in her mouth and feels its blend of sweetness and bitterness tingle on her tongue.

Slowly her shoulders start to relax. It's been a difficult evening, even though the day started so well: lessons in the morning, and swimming in the lake after lunch.

After supper the housekeeper went home, leaving her on her own at the home.

The number of night staff was cut four months after the Blancheford holding company bought the care business of which the Birgitta Home forms a part.

The residents were allowed to watch television until ten. She spent the evening in the nurses' office, and was trying to catch up with her journal entries when she heard angry shouting. She hurried to the TV room where she found Miranda attacking little Tuula. She was yelling that Tuula was a cunt and a whore, and dragged her off the sofa to kick her in the back.

Elisabet is starting to get used to Miranda's violent outbursts. She rushed in and pulled her away from Tuula, earning herself a blow on the cheek, and she had to shout at Miranda about this being clearly unacceptable behaviour. Without any discussion she led Miranda away to the isolation room along the corridor.

Elisabet said goodnight, but Miranda didn't answer. She just sat on the bed staring at the floor, and smiled to herself when Elisabet closed and locked the door.

The new girl, Vicky Bennet, was booked for an evening conversation, but there was no time because of the trouble with Miranda and Tuula. Vicky tentatively pointed out that it was her turn, and got upset when she was told it would have to be postponed, smashed a cup, then slashed her stomach and wrists with one of the fragments.

When Elisabet came in, Vicky was sitting with her hands in front of her face and blood running down her arms.

Elisabet bathed the cuts, which turned out to be superficial, put a plaster on her stomach, and bandaged her wrists, then sat and comforted her until she saw a little smile. For the third night in a row she gave the girl ten milligrams of Sonata so that she'd get some sleep.

All the residents are asleep now, and the Birgitta Home is quiet. There's a light on in the office window, making the world outside seem impenetrable and black.

With a deep frown on her face, Elisabet is sitting in front of the computer writing up the evening's events in the journal.

It's almost midnight, and she realises that she hasn't even found time to take her evening pill. Her little habit, she likes to joke. The combination of nights on call and exhausting day-shifts have ruined her sleep. She usually takes ten milligrams of Stilnoct at ten o'clock so that she can be asleep by eleven and get at least a few hours' rest.

The September darkness has settled on the forest, but the smooth surface of Himmelsjön is still visible, shining like mother-of-pearl.

At last she can switch the computer off and take her pill. She pulls her cardigan tighter around her and thinks how nice a glass of red wine would be. She's longing for a chance to sit in bed with a book and a glass of wine, reading and chatting with Daniel.

But she's on call tonight, and will be sleeping in the little overnight room.

She jumps when Buster suddenly starts barking out in the yard. He sounds so agitated that she gets goosebumps on her arms.

It's late, she should be in bed.

She's usually asleep by now.

The room turns darker when the computer shuts down. Suddenly everything seems incredibly quiet. Elisabet becomes aware of the sounds she herself is making. The sigh of the office chair when she stands up, the tiles creaking as she walks over to the window. She tries to see out, but the glass just reflects her own face, the office with its computer and phone, the yellow and green patterned walls.

Suddenly she sees the door slip open behind her.

Her heart starts to beat faster. The door was only just ajar, but now it's half-open. There must be a draught, she tries to tell herself. The wood-burning stove in the dining room always seems to pull in a lot of air.

Elisabet feels peculiarly anxious, and fear starts to creep through her veins. She daren't turn around, just stares into the dark window at the reflection of the door behind her back.

She listens to the silence, to the computer, which is still ticking.

In an attempt to shake off her unease, she reaches out her hand and switches off the lamp in the window, then turns around.

Now the door is wide open.

A shiver runs down her spine.

The lights are on in the corridor leading to the dining room and the girls' rooms. She leaves the office, intending to check that the vents on the stove are closed, when she suddenly hears whispers from one of the bedrooms.

Elisabet stands still, listening as she looks out into the corridor. At first she can't hear anything, then there it is again. A slight whisper, so faint that it's barely audible. 'It's your turn to close your eyes,' a voice whispers.

Elisabet stands perfectly still, staring off into the darkness. She blinks several times, but can't see anyone there.

She has time to think that it must be one of the girls talking in her sleep when she hears a strange noise. Like someone dropping an overripe peach on the floor. And then another one. Heavy and wet. A table leg scrapes as it moves, then another two peaches fall to the floor.

Elisabet catches a glimpse of movement from the corner of her eye. A shadow slipping past. She turns around, and sees that the door to the dining room is slowly swinging closed.

'Wait,' she says, even though she tells herself it was just the wind again.

She hurries over and grabs the handle, but meets a peculiar resistance. There's a brief tug-of-war before the door simply glides open.

Elisabet walks into the dining room, very warily, trying to scan the room with her eyes. The scratched table stands out in the darkness. She moves slowly towards the stove, sees her own movement reflected in its closed brass doors.

The flue is still radiating heat.

Suddenly there's a crackling, knocking sound behind the stove doors. She takes a step back and bumps into a chair.

It's only a piece of firewood falling against the inside of the doors. The room is completely empty.

She takes a deep breath and walks out of the dining room, closing the door behind her. She starts to head back towards the corridor where her overnight room is, but stops again and listens.

She can't hear anything from the girls' rooms. There's an acrid smell in the air, metallic, almost. She looks for movement in the dark corridor, but everything is still. Even so, she is drawn in that direction, towards the row of unlocked doors. Some of them seem to be ajar, while others are closed.

On the right-hand side of the corridor are the bathrooms, and then an alcove containing the locked door to the isolation room where Miranda is sleeping.

The peephole in the door glints gently.

Elisabet stops and holds her breath. A high voice is whispering something in one of the rooms, but falls abruptly silent when Elisabet starts to move again.

'Quiet, now,' she says.

Her heart starts to beat harder when she hears a series of rapid thuds. It's hard to localise them, but it sounds like Miranda is lying in bed kicking the wall with her bare feet. Elisabet is about to go and check on her through the peephole in the door when she sees that there's someone standing in the alcove. There's someone there.

She lets out a gasp and starts to back away, with a dream-like sense of wading through water.

She realises at once how dangerous the situation is, but fear makes her slow.

Only when the floor of the corridor creaks does the impulse to run for her life finally manifest itself.

The figure in the darkness suddenly moves very quickly.

She turns and starts to run, hearing footsteps behind her. She slips on the rag-rug, and knocks her shoulder against the wall, but keeps moving.

8

A soft voice is telling her to stop, but she doesn't, she runs, almost throwing herself along the corridor.

Doors fly open then bounce back.

In panic she rushes past the registration room, using the walls for support. The poster of the UN Convention on the Rights of the Child falls to the floor. She reaches the front door, fumbles, and manages to open it, shoves the door open and runs out into the cool night air, but slips on the porch steps. One of her legs folds beneath her as she lands awkwardly on her hip. The stabbing pain from her ankle makes her yell out loud. She slumps to the ground, then hears heavy steps in the porch, and starts to crawl away. She loses her indoor shoes as she struggles to her feet with a whimper.

4

The dog is barking at her as it runs about, panting and moaning. Elisabet limps away from the house, across the dark driveway. The dog barks again, ragged and anxious. Elisabet knows she won't be able to get through the forest – the nearest farm is half an hour's drive away. There's nowhere to go. She looks around in the darkness, then creeps behind the drying house. She reaches the old brew-house and opens the door with shaking hands, goes inside, and carefully closes the door.

Gasping, she sinks to the floor and tries to find her telephone. 'Oh God, oh God . . .'

Elisabet's hands are shaking so badly that she drops it on the floor. The back comes loose and the battery falls out. She starts to pick up the pieces as she hears footsteps crunching across the gravel.

She holds her breath.

Her pulse is thudding through her body. Her ears are roaring. She tries to look out through the low window.

The dog is barking right outside. Buster has followed her there. He's scratching at the door and whimpering.

She crawls further into the corner next to the brick fireplace, and tries to breathe quietly, hiding right at the back next to the wood basket, as she pushes the battery back into her mobile.

Elisabet lets out a scream when the door to the brew-house

opens. She tries to shuffle along the wall in panic, but there's nowhere to go.

She sees a pair of boots, then the shadowy figure, and then the terrible face, and the hand holding the dark, heavy hammer.

She nods, listens to the voice, and covers her face.

The shadow hesitates, then rushes across the floor, holds her down on the floor with one foot, and strikes hard. There's a flash of pain at the front of her head, just above her hairline. Her sight disappears completely. The pain is appalling, but she can still feel the warm blood running over her ears and down her neck like a soft caress.

The next blows hits the same place, her head lurches, and all she can feel is how air is being drawn down into her lungs.

Bewildered, she can't help thinking that the air is wonderfully sweet, then she loses consciousness.

Elisabet doesn't feel the rest of the blows and how they make her body flinch. She doesn't notice the keys to the office and the isolation room being taken from her pocket, and she isn't aware of being left on the floor, or how the dog slips into the brew-house and starts to lick the blood from her crushed head as life slowly leaves her.

5

Someone's left a big red apple on the table. It looks really lovely, all shiny. She decides to eat it and then pretend not to know anything about it. Ignore the questions and nagging, just sit there looking grumpy.

She reaches towards it, but when she's got it in her hand she realises that it's completely rotten.

Her fingers sink into the cold, wet flesh.

Nina Molander wakes up the moment she snatches her hand back. It's the middle of the night. She's lying in bed. The only sound is the dog barking out in the yard. Her new medication often wakes her at night, and she has to get up to pee. Her calves and feet have swollen up, but she needs the pills, otherwise her thoughts turn very dark and she stops caring about anything and just lies there with her eyes shut.

She feels she needs something bright, something to look forward to. Not just death, not just thinking about death.

Nina folds the covers back, sets her feet down on the warm wooden floor, and gets out of bed. She's fifteen years old, and has straight blonde hair. She's got a stocky build, with broad hips and big breasts. Her white flannel nightdress is stretched tight across her stomach.

The children's home is quiet, and the corridor is lit up by the green sign for the emergency exit.

She can hear strange whispering behind one door, and Nina wonders if the other girls are having a party without bothering to ask if she'd like to join in.

I don't want to anyway, she thinks.

There's the smell of a burned-out fire in the air. The dog starts barking again. The floor in the corridor is colder. She doesn't bother trying to be quiet. She feels like slamming the toilet door several times. She couldn't care less about Almira getting angry and throwing things at her.

The old tiles creak gently. Nina carries on towards the toilets, but stops when she feels something wet under her right foot. A dark puddle is seeping out from under the door to the isolation room where Miranda is sleeping. At first Nina just stands still, unsure of what to do, but then she notices that the key is in the lock.

Very odd.

She reaches out for the shiny handle, opens the door, goes inside and switches the light on.

There's blood everywhere – dripping, shining, oozing.

Miranda is lying on the bed.

Nina takes a few steps back, doesn't even notice that's she's wet herself. She reaches out to the wall for support as she sees the bloody shoeprints on the floor, and thinks she's going to faint.

She turns around and rushes out into the corridor, opens the door of the next room, turns the light on and goes over and shakes Caroline's shoulder.

'Miranda's hurt,' she whispers. 'I think she's been hurt.'

'What are you doing in my room?' Caroline asks, sitting up in bed. 'What the hell's the time?'

'There's blood on the floor!' Nina shouts.

'Just calm down.'

6

Nina is breathing far too fast as she looks into Caroline's eyes. She has to make her understand, but at the same time is surprised by her own voice, and the fact that she's dared to shout in the middle of the night.

'There's blood everywhere!'

'Be quiet,' Caroline hisses, and gets out of bed.

Nina's cries have woken the others; she can already hear voices from the other rooms.

'Come and look!' Nina says, scratching her arms anxiously. 'Miranda looks funny, you have to come and look at her, you . . .'

'Can you just calm down? I'll come and look, but I'm sure . . .'

They hear a scream from the corridor. It's little Tuula. Caroline hurries out. Tuula is staring into the isolation room, her eyes open wide. Indie comes out into the corridor, scratching one armpit.

Caroline pulls Tuula away, but still has time to see the blood on the walls and Miranda's white body. Her heart is beating fast. She stands in Indie's way, thinking that none of them need to see any more suicides.

'There's been an accident,' she explains quickly. 'Can you take everyone to the dining room, Indie?'

'Has something happened to Miranda?' Indie asks.

'Yes, we need to wake Elisabet.'

Lu Chu and Almira come out from the same room. Lu Chu is only wearing a pair of pyjama trousers, and Almira is wrapped in the duvet.

'Go to the dining room,' Indie says.

'Can I wash my face first?' Lu Chu asks.

'Take Tuula with you.'

'What the hell is going on?' Almira asks.

'We don't know,' Caroline replies curtly.

While Indie tries to get everyone into the dining room, Caroline hurries along the corridor to the staff's overnight room. She knows Elisabet takes sleeping pills and never hears when any of the girls are running about at night.

Caroline bangs on the door as hard as she can.

'Elisabet, you have to wake up,' she cries.

No response. Not a sound.

Caroline carries on, past the registration room to the nurses' office. The door is open, so she goes in, picks up the phone and calls Daniel, the first person she thinks of.

The line crackles.

Indie and Nina come into the office. Nina's lips are white, she's moving weirdly, and her body's shaking.

'Wait in the dining room,' Caroline snaps.

'What about the blood? Did you see the blood?' Nina screams, drawing blood as she scratches her right arm.

'Daniel Grim,' a tired voice says over the phone.

'It's me, Caroline – there's been an accident here, and Elisabet won't wake up, I can't wake her, so I called you, I don't know what to do.'

'I've got blood on my feet,' Nina yells. 'I've got blood on my feet . . .'

'Calm down,' Indie shouts, and tries to take Nina out of the room.

'What's going on?' Daniel asks in a voice that's suddenly very awake, and very focused.

'Miranda's in the cell, it's full of blood,' Caroline replies, then swallows hard. 'I don't know what we . . .'

'Is she badly hurt?' he asks.

'Yes, I think . . . well, I . . .'

15

'Caroline,' Daniel interrupts. 'I'm going to call an ambulance, then . . .'

'But what should I do? What should . . .'

'See if Miranda needs help, and try to wake Elisabet,' Daniel replies.

The emergency call centre in Sundsvall is located in a three-storey brick building on Björneborgsgatan, next to Bäckparken. Jasmin doesn't usually have any trouble with the night-shift, but she's feeling unusually tired now. It's four o'clock in the morning, and the worst part of the night has passed. She's sitting in front of the computer with her headset on, and blows on the mug of black coffee. In the staffroom they're still laughing and joking. The day before, the tabloids ran a story about one of the police's emergency operators earning a bit extra on the side, from telephone sex. It turned out that she just had an administrative job with a company that ran sex chat-lines, but the tabloids made it sound like she was dealing with both types of call in the emergency call centre.

Jasmin looks past the screen and out through the window. It hasn't started to get light yet. An articulated lorry rumbles past. There's a streetlamp further along the road. Its weak light illuminates a tree, a grey electricity box, and a stretch of empty pavement.

Jasmin puts her coffee cup down and takes an incoming call.

'SOS 112 . . . What's the nature of the emergency?'

'My name is Daniel Grim, I'm a counsellor at the Birgitta Home. One of the residents has just called me. It sounded extremely serious, you have to get out there.'

'Can you tell me what's happened?' Jasmin asks as she searches for the Birgitta Home on the computer.

'I don't know, one of the girls called. I didn't really understand what she was saying, there was a lot of shouting in the background, and she was crying and saying there was blood all over the room.'

Jasmin gestures to her colleague Ingrid Sandén that they need more operators.

'And are you at the scene yourself?' Jasmin says through the headset.

'No, I'm at home, I was asleep, but one of the girls called . . .'

'You're talking about the Birgitta Home, north of Sunnås?' Jasmin asks calmly.

'Please, hurry up,' he says in a shaky voice.

'We're sending police and an ambulance to the Birgitta Home, north of Sunnås,' Jasmin repeats, just to be sure.

She transfers the call to Ingrid, who goes on talking to Daniel while Jasmin alerts the police and paramedics.

'The Birgitta Home is a children's home, isn't it?'

'Yes, a secure children's home,' he replies.

'Shouldn't there be some staff there?'

'Yes, my wife Elisabet is on duty, I'm about to call her . . . I don't know what's happened, I don't know anything.'

'The police are on their way,' Ingrid says calmly, and from the corner of her eye sees the flashing blue lights of the first emergency vehicle sweep across the deserted street.

The narrow turning off Highway 86 leads straight into the dark forest, toward Himmelsjön and the Birgitta Home.

The grit crunches beneath the tyres of the police car. The headlights play across the tall trunks of the pines.

'You said you'd been out here before?' Rolf Wikner asks, changing up to fourth gear.

'Yes . . . a couple of years ago one of the girls tried to set light to one of the buildings,' Sonja Rask replies.

'Why the hell can't they get hold of the staff?' Rolf mutters.

'Probably got their hands full – regardless of what's happened,' Sonja says.

'It would be useful to know a bit more.'

'Yes,' she agrees calmly.

The two colleagues sit in silence next to each other, listening to the communications over the police radio. An ambulance is on its way, and another police car has set out from the station.

The road, like so many logging roads, is perfectly straight. The tyres thunder over potholes and dips. Tree trunks flit past as the flashing blue lights make their way far into the forest.

Sonja reports back to the station as they pull up into the yard in front of the dark red buildings of the Birgitta Home.

A girl in a nightdress is standing on the steps of the main building. Her eyes are wide open, but her face is pale and distant.

Rolf and Sonja get out of the car and hurry over to her in the flickering blue light, but the girl doesn't seem to notice them.

A dog starts to bark anxiously.

'Is anyone hurt?' Rolf says in a loud voice. 'Does anyone need help?'

The girl waves vaguely towards the edge of the forest, wobbles, and tries to take a step, but her legs buckle beneath her. She falls backwards and hits her head.

'Are you OK?' Sonja asks, rushing over to her.

The girl lies there on the steps staring up at the sky, breathing fast and shallow. Sonja notes that she's drawn blood from scratching her arms and neck.

'I'm going in,' Rolf says firmly.

Sonja stays with the shocked girl and waits for the ambulance while Rolf goes inside. He sees bloody marks left by boots and bare feet on the wooden floor, heading off in different directions, including long strides through the passageway towards the hall, then back again. Rolf feels adrenaline course through his body. He does his best not to stand on the footprints, but knows that his primary objective is to save lives.

He looks into a common room where all the lights are on, and sees four girls sitting on the two sofas.

'Is anyone hurt?' he calls.

'Maybe a bit,' a small, red-haired girl in a pink tracksuit smiles.

'Where is she?' he asks anxiously.

'Miranda's on her bed,' an older girl with straight dark hair says.

'In here?' he says, pointing towards the corridor with the bedrooms.

The older girl just nods in reply, and Rolf follows the bloody footprints past a dining room containing a large wooden table and tiled stove, and into a dark corridor lined with doors leading to the girls' private rooms. Shoes and bare feet have trodden through the blood. The old floor creaks beneath him. Rolf stops, pulls his torch from his belt, and shines it along the corridor. He quickly looks along the hand-painted maxims and ornate biblical quotations, then aims the beam at the floor.

The blood has seeped out across the floor from under the door in a dark alcove. The key is in the lock. He walks towards it, carefully moves the torch to his other hand, and reaches out towards the handle and touches it as gently as he can.

There's a click, the door slips open, and the handle pings back up.

'Hello? Miranda? My name is Rolf, I'm a police officer,' he says into the darkness as he steps closer. 'I'm coming in now . . .'

The only sound is his own breathing.

He carefully pushes the door open and sweeps the beam of the torch around the room. The sight that greets him is so brutal that he stumbles and has to reach out for the doorframe.

Instinctively he looks away, but his eyes have already seen what he didn't want to see. His ears register the rushing of his pulse as well as the drips hitting the puddle on the floor.

A young woman is lying on the bed, but large parts of her head seem to be missing. Blood is spattered up the walls, and is still dripping from the dark lampshade.

The door suddenly closes behind Rolf, and he's so startled that he drops the torch on the floor. The room goes completely black. He turns and fumbles in the darkness, and hears a girl's small hands hammering on the other side of the door.

'Now she can see you!' a high-pitched voice screams. 'Now she's looking!'

Rolf finds the handle and tries to open the door, but it won't budge. The little peephole glints at him in the darkness. With his hands shaking, he pushes the handle down and shoves with his shoulder.

The door flies open, and Rolf staggers into the corridor. He breathes in deeply. The little red-haired girl is standing a short distance away looking at him with big eyes.

9

Detective Superintendent Joona Linna is standing at the window in his hotel room in Sveg, four hundred and fifty kilometres north of Stockholm. The dawn light is cold, steamily blue. There are no lights lit along Älvgatan. It will be many hours yet before he finds out if he's found Rosa Bergman.

His light grey shirt is unbuttoned and hanging outside his black suit trousers. His blond hair is unkempt, as usual, and his pistol is lying on the bed in its shoulder holster.

Despite numerous approaches from various specialist groups, Joona has remained as an operative superintendent with the National Crime Unit. His habit of going his own way annoys a lot of people, but in less than fifteen years he has solved more complex cases in Scandinavia than any other police officer.

During the summer a complaint was filed against Joona with the Internal Investigations Committee, claiming that he had alerted an extreme left-wing group about a forthcoming raid by the Security Police. Since then, Joona has been relieved of certain duties without actually being formally suspended.

The head of Internal Investigations has made it very clear that he will contact the senior prosecutor at the National Police Cases Authority if he believes there are any grounds at all for prosecution.

The allegations are serious, but right now Joona hasn't got

time to worry about any potential suspension or reprimand.

His thoughts are focused on the old woman who had followed him outside Adolf Fredrik Church in Stockholm, and who gave him a message from Rosa Bergman. With thin hands she passed him two tattered cards from an old 'cuckoo' card game.

'This is you, isn't it?' the woman said uncertainly. 'And here's the crown, the bridal crown.'

'What do you want?' Joona asked.

'I don't want anything,' the old woman said. 'But I've got a message from Rosa Bergman.'

His heart began to thud. But he forced himself to shrug and explain kindly that there must be some mistake: 'Because I don't know anyone called . . .'

'She's wondering why you're pretending that your daughter's dead.'

'I'm sorry, but I don't know what you're talking about,' Joona replied with a smile.

He was smiling, but his voice sounded like a stranger's, distant and cold, as if it were coming from under a large rock. The woman's words swirled through him and he felt like grabbing her by her thin arms and demanding to know what she was talking about, but instead he remained calm.

'I have to go,' he explained, and was about to turn away when a migraine shot through his brain like the blade of a knife through his left eye. His field of vision shrank to a jagged, flickering halo.

When he regained fragments of his sight, he saw that people were standing in a circle around him. They moved aside to make way for the paramedics.

The old woman had vanished.

Joona had denied knowing Rosa Bergman, had said there must be some misunderstanding. But he had been lying.

Because he knows very well who Rosa Bergman is.

He thinks about her every day. He thinks about her, but she shouldn't know anything about him. Because if Rosa Bergman knows who he is, then something could have gone very badly wrong.

Joona left the hospital a few hours later and immediately set about trying to find Rosa Bergman.

He had no choice but to conduct the search alone, and requested a period of leave.

According to official records there was no one called Rosa Bergman living in Sweden, but there are more than two thousand people with the surname Bergman in Scandinavia.

Joona systematically checked through database after database. Two weeks ago the only option remaining to him was to start to search the physical archives of the Swedish Population Register. For centuries the maintenance of the register was the responsibility of the Church, but in 1991 the register was digitised and transferred to the Tax Office.

Joona started to work his way through the registers, beginning in the south of the country. He sat down in the National Archive in Lund with a paper cup of coffee in front of him, searching in the card files for a Rosa Bergman born at the right time and place. Then he travelled to Visby, Vadstena, and Gothenburg.

He went to Uppsala, and the vast archive in Härnösand. He searched through thousands of pages of births, locations, and family connections.

10

Joona spent the previous afternoon in the archive in Östersund. The sweet antiquarian smell of discoloured old paper and heavy bindings filled the room. Sunlight wandered slowly across the tall walls, glinting off the glass of the motionless clock before moving on.

Just before the archive closed, Joona found a girl who was born eighty-four years ago and who was christened Rosa Maja in the parish of Sveg in Härjedalen, in the province of Jämtland. The girl's parents were Kristina and Evert Bergman. Joona couldn't find any information about their marriage, but the mother, Kristina Stefanson, was born nineteen years before in the same parish.

It took Joona three hours to locate an eighty-four-year-old woman named Maja Stefanson in a care home in Sveg. It was already seven o'clock in the evening, but Joona still got in his car and drove to Sveg. It was late by the time he arrived, and he wasn't allowed into the home.

Joona booked into Lilla Hotellet and tried to get some sleep, but woke up at four o'clock, and has been standing at the window ever since, waiting for morning.

He's almost certain that he's found Rosa Bergman. She's adopted her mother's maiden name, and is using her middle name.

Joona looks at his watch and decides that it's time to go. He buttons his jacket, leaves the room, goes down to reception, and out into the small town.

The Blue Wings care home is a cluster of yellow-plastered houses around a neat lawn with footpaths and benches to rest on.

Joona opens the door to the main building and goes inside. He forces himself to walk slowly through the neon-lit corridor lined with closed doors leading to offices and the kitchen.

She wasn't supposed to be able to find me, he thinks once more. She wasn't supposed to know about me. Something's gone wrong.

Joona never talks about the reason why he's ended up alone, but it's with him every waking moment.

His life burned like magnesium, flared up and died away in an instant, from gleaming white to smouldering ash.

In the dayroom a thin man in his eighties is standing and staring at the bright screen of the television. A TV chef is heating sesame oil in a pan, and talking about various ways of updating traditional crayfish parties.

The old man turns to Joona and screws up his eyes.

'Anders?' the man says in an unsteady voice. 'Is that you, Anders?'

'My name is Joona,' he replies in his soft Finnish accent. 'I'm looking for Maja Stefanson.'

The man stares at him with moist, red-rimmed eyes.

'Anders, listen, lad. You've got to help me get out of here. It's full of old people.'

The man hits the arm of the sofa with a frail fist, but stops abruptly when a care assistant walks into the room.

'Good morning,' Joona says. 'I'm here to visit Maja Stefanson.'

'How lovely,' she says. 'But I should warn you, Maja's dementia has got worse. She tries to get out whenever she has a chance.'

'I understand,' Joona says.

'Back in the summer she managed to get all the way to Stockholm.'

The care assistant leads Joona through a freshly-mopped corridor with subdued lighting, and opens one of the doors.

'Maja?' she calls out warmly.

An old woman is making the bed. When she looks up, Joona recognises her at once. It's the woman who was following him outside Adolf Fredrik Church, the one who showed him the playing cards. The one who told him she had a message from Rosa Bergman.

Joona's heart is beating hard.

She's the only person who knows where his wife and daughter are, and she shouldn't be aware of his existence.

'Rosa Bergman?' Joona asks.

'Yes,' she replies, raising one of her hands like a schoolgirl.

'My name is Joona Linna.'

'Yes,' Rosa Bergman smiles, shuffling towards him.

'You had a message for me,' he says.

'Oh my, I don't remember that,' Rosa replies, and sits down on the sofa.

He swallows hard and takes a step towards her.

'You asked me why I was pretending my daughter is dead.'

'You shouldn't do that,' she says sternly. 'That's not nice at all.'

'What do you know about my daughter?' Joona asks, taking another step towards the woman. 'Have you heard anything?'

She merely smiles distractedly, and Joona lowers his gaze. He tries to think clearly, and notices that his hands are shaking as he goes over to the kitchenette in the corner and pours coffee into two cups.

'Rosa, this is important to me,' he says slowly, putting the cups on the table. 'Very important.'

She blinks a couple of times, then asks in a timid voice: 'Who are you? Has something happened to Mother?'

'Rosa, do you remember a little girl called Lumi? Her mother's name was Summa, and you helped them to . . .'

Joona falls silent when he sees the lost expression in the woman's eyes, clouded with cataracts.

'Why did you try to find me?' he asks, even though he knows there's no point.

Rosa Bergman drops her coffee cup on the floor and starts to cry. The care assistant comes in, and soothes her in a practised way.

'I'll show you out,' she says quietly to Joona.

They walk through the corridor.

'How long has she had dementia?' Joona asks.

'It happened quickly with Maja . . . We started to notice the first signs last summer, so about a year ago . . . people used to say it was like a second childhood, which is still pretty close to the truth for most sufferers.'

'If she . . . if she suddenly has a lucid period,' Joona says seriously, 'would you mind contacting me?'

'That does actually happen occasionally,' the woman nods.

'Call me at once,' he says, handing her his card.

'Detective Superintendent?' she says in surprise, and pins the card to the noticeboard behind the desk in the office.

12

When Joona emerges into the fresh air he breathes in deeply, as if he's been holding his breath. Perhaps Rosa Bergman had had something important to tell him, he thinks. It's possible that someone asked her to pass on a message. But she succumbed to dementia before she managed to tell him.

He's never going to know what it was.

Twelve years have passed since he lost Summa and Lumi.

The last traces of them have been erased along with Rosa Bergman's lost memories.

It's over now.

Joona sits in his car, wipes the tears from his cheeks, closes his eyes for a while, then turns the key in the ignition to drive back home to Stockholm.

He's driven thirty kilometres south along the E45 towards Mora when the head of the National Crime Unit, Carlos Eliasson, calls him.

'We've got a murder at a children's home up in Sundsvall,' Carlos says in a tense voice. 'The emergency call centre was alerted just after four this morning.'

'I'm on leave,' Joona says, almost inaudibly.

'You could still have come to the karaoke evening.'

'Another time,' Joona says, almost to himself.

The road runs straight through the forest. Far off between the trees a silvery lake is glinting.

'Joona? What's happened?'

'Nothing.'

Someone calls for Carlos in the background.

'I've got a meeting now, but I want . . . I just spoke to Susanne Öst, and she says the Västernorrland Police aren't going to make a formal request for help from National Crime.'

'So why are you calling me?'

'I said we'd send an observer.'

'We never send observers, do we?'

'We do now,' Carlos says, lowering his voice. 'I'm afraid this one's rather sensitive. You remember Janne Svensson, the captain of the national hockey team? The press never stopped talking about how incompetent the police were.'

'Because they never found . . .'

'Don't start . . . that was Susanne Öst's first big case as a prosecutor,' Carlos goes on. 'I don't want to say that the press were right, but the Västernorrland Police could have done with you on that occasion. They were too slow, they went by the book, and time passed . . . nothing unusual, of course, but sometimes the press picks up on it.'

'I can't talk any more,' Joona says by way of conclusion.

'You know I wouldn't ask you if it was just a straightforward murder,' Carlos says, and takes a deep breath. 'But there's going to be a lot of coverage, Joona . . . this one's very, very brutal, very bloody . . . and the girl's body has been arranged.'

'How? How has it been arranged?' Joona asks.

'Apparently she's lying on her bed with her hands over her face.'

Joona drives on in silence, his left hand on the wheel. The trees flit past on both sides of the car. He can hear Carlos breathing over the phone. There are other voices in the background. Without saying anything, Joona turns off the E45 towards Los, onto a road that will take him to the coast, and then up to Sundsvall.

'Please, Joona, just go up there . . . help them solve the case themselves, preferably before the press gets hold of it.'

'So now I'm not just an observer?'

'Yes, you are . . . just hang around, observe the investigation, make suggestions . . . As long as you realise that you have no official authority.'

'Because I'm the subject of an internal investigation?'

'It's important that you keep a low profile,' Carlos says.

13

North of Sundsvall Joona leaves the coast road and turns onto Highway 86, which heads up inland along the valley of Indalsälven.

After two hours of driving he's approaching the isolated children's home.

He slows down and turns onto a narrow gravel track. Sunlight filters through the tall pine trees.

A dead girl, Joona thinks.

While everyone was asleep, a girl was murdered and positioned on her bed. The violence was extreme and very aggressive, according to the local police. They have no immediate suspect, it's too late for roadblocks, but everyone in the local force has been informed, and Superintendent Olle Gunnarsson is leading the preliminary investigation.

It's just before ten o'clock by the time Joona parks and leaves the car beyond the police's outer cordon. The ditch is swarming with insects. The forest has opened up into a large clearing. Damp trees are sparkling in the sunlight on the slope down towards the lake, Himmelsjön. By the side of the road is a metal sign saying *The Birgitta Home, Specialist Children's Home*.

Joona walks towards the cluster of rust-red buildings, gathered around the central yard like a traditional farm. An ambulance, three police cars, a white Mercedes, and three other cars are parked in front of the buildings.

A dog is barking nonstop as it runs along a line between two trees to which it's tethered.

An older man with a walrus moustache, a pot-belly, and a crumpled linen suit is standing in front of the main building. He's spotted Joona, but shows no sign of saying hello. Instead he finishes rolling his cigarette and licks the paper. Joona steps over another cordon, and the man tucks the cigarette behind his ear.

'I'm the National Police observer,' Joona says.

'Gunnarsson,' the man says. 'Superintendent.'

'I'm supposed to follow your work here.'

'Yes, as long as you don't get in the way,' the man says, looking at him coolly.

Joona looks up at the main building. The forensics team is already at work. The rooms are illuminated by arc lights, lending all the windows an unnatural glow.

A police officer emerges from the door, his face almost white. He claps one hand to his mouth, stumbles down the steps, then leans against the wall, bends forward, and throws up onto the nettles beside the water butt.

'You'll do the same once you've been inside,' Gunnarsson says to Joona with a smile.

'What do you know so far?'

'Not a damn thing . . . We got the call in the middle of the night, from a counsellor at the home . . . Daniel Grim's his name. That was at four o'clock. He was at his home on Bruksgatan in Sundsvall, and had just received a call from here . . . he didn't know much when he called the emergency call centre, just that the girls were yelling about lots of blood.'

'So it was the girls themselves who made the call?' Joona asks.

'Yes.'

'But they called the counsellor in Sundsvall rather than the police?' Joona says.

'Exactly.'

'There must have been night staff here?'

'No.'

'Shouldn't there have been?'

'Presumably,' Gunnarsson says in a tired voice.

'Which one of the girls called the counsellor?' Joona asks.

'One of the older residents,' Gunnarsson says, looking in his notebook. 'A Caroline Forsgren . . . But as I understand it, she wasn't the one who found the body. That was . . . it's a hell of a mess, several of the girls have looked in the room. It's bloody nasty, I don't mind saying. We've taken one of them off to hospital. She was hysterical, and the paramedics thought that was the safest thing to do.'

'Who was first on the scene?' Joona asks.

'Two colleagues, Rolf Wikner and Sonja Rask,' Gunnarsson replies. 'I got here at around a quarter to six and called the prosecutor . . . and then she evidently wet herself and contacted Stockholm . . . so now we're lumbered with you.'

He smiles at Joona without any warmth.

'Do you have a suspect?' Joona asks.

Gunnarsson takes a deep breath and says in a didactic tone: 'Years of experience have taught me to let an investigation unfold at its own pace . . . we need to get people out here, start to interview the witnesses, secure the evidence . . .'

'Is it OK to go in and take a look?' Joona asks, looking up at the door.

'I wouldn't recommend it . . . we'll soon have pictures.'

'I need to look at the girl before she's moved,' Joona says.

'We're dealing with an attack with a blunt instrument, very brutal, very aggressive,' he says. 'The perpetrator's a strong guy. After her death the victim was laid out on her bed. No one noticed anything until one of the girls was going to the toilet and trod in the blood that was seeping under the door.'

'Was it still warm?'

'Look . . . these girls are pretty tricky to deal with,' Gunnarsson explains. 'They're frightened, and they're very angry, they object to everything we say, they don't listen, they scream at us, and . . . Earlier on they were determined to get through the cordon to fetch things from their rooms – iPods, Lypsyl, coats, and so on – and when we were going to move them to the other building, two of them escaped into the forest.'

'Escaped?'

'We've just managed to catch up with them . . . now we just need to get them to return voluntarily. They're lying on the ground demanding to be allowed to ride on Rolf's shoulders.'

14

Joona puts on protective clothing, goes up the steps to the main building and in through the door. Inside the porch the fans of the arc lights are working hard and the air is already warm. Every detail is visible in their strong glare. Dust is moving slowly through the air.

Joona walks carefully along the protective mats that have been laid out across the floor tiles. One picture has fallen to the floor, and the broken glass glints in the strong light. Bloody shoe prints lead off in different directions in the corridor, towards the front door, and back again.

The house has retained its original character from when it was a grand farmhouse. The painted panels have faded over the years, but are still colourful, and the traditional patterns made by itinerant painters curl across the walls and woodwork.

Further along the corridor a forensics officer named Jimi Sjöberg is shining a green lamp at a black chair, having already applied Hungarian red to it.

'Blood?' Joona asks.

'Not on this one,' Jimi mutters, and moves on with the green lamp.

'Have you found anything unexpected?'

'Erixon called from Stockholm and told us not to touch a

thing until Joona Linna had given the go-ahead,' he replies with a smile.

'I'm grateful.'

'So we haven't really got going yet,' Jimi goes on. 'We've laid out all these damn mats, and photographed and filmed everything, and . . . well, I took the liberty to get samples of the blood in the corridor so we could send something off to the lab.'

'Good.'

'And Siri lifted the prints in the hall before they got contaminated . . .'

The other forensics expert, Siri Karlsson, has just dismantled the brass handle from the door to the isolation room. She puts it carefully in a paper bag, then comes over to Joona and Jimi.

'He's here to take a look at the crime scene,' Jimi explains.

'It's pretty unpleasant,' Siri says through her mask. Her eyes look tired and troubled.

'So I understand,' Joona says.

'You can look at pictures instead if you'd rather,' she says.

'This is Joona Linna,' Jimi tells her.

'Sorry, I didn't realise.'

'I'm just an observer,' Joona says.

She looks down, and when she raises her eyes again there's a trace of a blush on her cheeks.

'Everyone's talking about you,' she says. 'I mean . . . I . . . I don't care about the internal investigation. I think it'll be interesting to work with you.'

'Same here,' Joona says.

He stands still and listens to the whirr of the lamps, and tries to focus, so that he'll be able to absorb the impressions of what he sees without giving in to the instinct to look away.

15

Joona goes over to the alcove and the door that no longer has a handle.

The lock and key are still in place.

He closes his eyes for a moment, then walks into the small room.

Everything is still, and brightly lit.

The warm air is heavy with the smell of blood and urine. He forces himself to inhale it to detect the other smells: damp wood, sweaty sheets, deodorant.

The hot metal of the lamps ticks. He can hear the muffled sound of barking through the walls.

Joona stands perfectly still and forces himself to look at the body on the bed. His eyes linger on every detail, even though he'd like nothing more than to hurry out, leave the building, and walk into the fresh air and shade of the forest.

Blood has run across the floor, and is spattered over the immoveable furniture and the pale biblical motifs on the walls. It's sprayed across the ceiling and over to the toilet. A thin girl in the early stages of puberty is lying on the bed. She has been laid out on her back, with her hands covering her face. She's wearing nothing but a pair of cotton pants. Her breasts are covered by her elbows, and her feet are crossed at the ankles.

Joona feels his heart beating, feels his own blood coursing through his veins to his brain, as his pulse roars in his temples.

He forces himself to look, register, and think.

The girl's face is hidden.

As if she's frightened, as if she doesn't want to see the perpetrator.

Before the girl was positioned on the bed she was subjected to extreme violence.

Repeated blows with a blunt object to her forehead and scalp.

She's only a young girl, and must have been horribly frightened.

A few short years ago she was just a child, but a chain of events has led her to this room, to this secure children's home. Maybe she was just unlucky with her parents and foster parents. Maybe she thought she'd be safe here.

Joona studies every terrible detail until it feels as if he can longer bear it. Then he shuts his eyes for a few moments and thinks about his daughter's face and the gravestone that isn't hers, before opening his eyes again and carrying on with the examination.

The evidence suggests that the victim was sitting on the chair at the little table when the attacker struck.

Joona tries to identify the movements that led to this spatter pattern.

Every drop of blood falling through the air naturally assumes a round shape, and has a diameter of five millimetres. If the drop is smaller, that means that the blood has been subjected to external force that's broken it into smaller drops.

And that's when spatter pattern analysis comes in.

Joona is now standing on two protective mats in front of the small table, probably exactly where the murderer stood a few hours before. The girl was sitting on the chair on the other side of the table. Joona looks at the spatter pattern, turns around, and sees blood sprayed high up the wall. The implement has been swung backwards several times to gain momentum, and every time it changed direction for another blow, blood sprayed back from it.

Joona has already stayed longer at this crime scene than any other superintendent would have. But he isn't finished yet. He goes back to the girl on the bed, stands in front of her, sees the stud in her navel, the lip-print on the glass of water, sees that she has had a birthmark removed below her right breast, sees the fine hairs on her shins, and a yellowed bruise on her thigh.

He leans cautiously over her. Her bare skin is emitting very faint heat now. He looks at the hands covering her face, and sees that she didn't manage to scratch the perpetrator, there's no skin under her fingernails.

He takes a few steps back, and then looks at her again. Her white skin. The hands over her face. There's hardly any blood on her body. Only the pillow is bloody.

Apart from that she's clean.

Joona looks around the room. Behind the door there's a small shelf with two hooks for clothes beneath it. On the floor beneath the shelf are a pair of trainers with white socks tucked inside them, and a pair of washed-out jeans is hanging from one of the hooks, along with a black college sweater and a denim jacket. There's a small white bra on the shelf.

Joona doesn't touch the clothes, but they don't appear to be bloody.

Presumably she got undressed and hung her clothes up before she was murdered.

So why isn't her whole body covered with blood? Something must have protected her. But what? There's nothing else here.

Joona is walking in the sunshine in the yard, thinking about the extreme level of violence that the girl was subjected to, and the fact that her body was as clean and white as a pebble in the sea.

Gunnarsson had said that violence inflicted on her had been aggressive.

Joona is thinking that it clearly required a lot of force, almost desperate force, but it wasn't aggressive in the sense of being uncontrolled. The blows were focused, the intention was to kill, but apart from that the body had been treated with care.

Gunnarsson is sitting on the bonnet of his Mercedes talking on his phone.

Unlike most other things, murder investigations don't tend to become chaotic if they're left without direction. They mostly sort themselves out, that's the usual way of things. But Joona has never waited, has never trusted that order would be restored by itself.

Of course he knows that the murderer is almost always someone close to the victim, and that they usually make contact with the police shortly afterwards to confess, but he's not counting on it.

She's lying on the bed now, he thinks. But was sitting at the table in just her underpants when she was murdered.

It's hard to believe that could have happened in complete silence.

There must be a witness in a place like this.

One of the girls has seen or heard something, Joona thinks, as he heads towards the smaller building. Someone probably had an idea of what was coming, identified some sort of threat or conflict.

The dog is whining under the tree, then bites at the leash tying it to the line, before starting to bark again.

Joona walks over to the two men standing talking outside the smaller building. He understands that one of them is the crime-scene coordinator, a man in his fifties with a side parting and a dark blue police sweater. The other one doesn't seem to be a police officer. He's unshaven, and has friendly, if tired, eyes.

'Joona Linna, observer from National Crime,' he says, shaking hands with them both.

'Åke,' the coordinator says.

'My name is Daniel,' the man with the tired eyes says. 'I work as a counsellor here at the home . . . I came as soon as I heard what had happened.'

'Have you got a minute?' Joona asks. 'I'd like to meet the girls, and it would probably be a good idea if you were there.'

'Now?' Daniel asks.

'If that's OK,' Joona replies.

The man blinks behind his glasses and says worriedly: 'It's just that two of the residents managed to run off into the forest . . .'

'They've been found,' Joona explains.

'Yes, I know, but I probably need to talk to them,' Daniel says, then suddenly gives an involuntary smile. 'They're saying they won't come back unless they're allowed to ride on one of the police officer's shoulders.'

'Gunnarsson would probably volunteer,' Joona replies, and walks on towards the small red cottage.

He's thinking that this first meeting will be his chance to try to study the girls, see how they interact, what sort of things are going on under the surface.

If anyone has seen something, the other members of a group tend to indicate it unconsciously, acting as compass needles.

Joona knows he doesn't have the authority to hold interviews, but he needs to know if there's a witness, he thinks, as he bends down to go through the low door.

The floor creaks as Joona walks into the small house, stepping over the threshold. There are three girls in the cramped room. The youngest of them can't be more than twelve years old. Her skin is pink, and her hair coppery red. She's sitting on the floor, leaning back against the wall watching television. She whispers to herself, then hits the back of her head against the wall several times, closes her eyes for a few seconds, then goes on watching the television.

The other two don't even seem to notice her. They're just sitting back on an old corduroy sofa leafing through old fashion magazines.

A psychologist from the regional hospital in Sundsvall is sitting on the floor next to the red-haired girl.

'My name is Lisa,' she says tentatively, in a warm voice. 'What's your name?'

The girl doesn't take her eyes off the television. It's a repeat of the series *Blue Water High*. The volume is turned up loud, and the screen is casting a chilly glow across the room.

'Have you heard the story of Thumbelina?' Lisa asks. 'I often feel like her. The size of someone's thumb . . . How are you feeling?'

'Like Jack the Ripper,' the girl replies in a high voice without taking her eyes from the screen.

Joona goes and sits in an armchair in front of the television. One of the girls on the sofa stares at him wide-eyed, but looks down with a smile when he says hello. She's got a stocky build, her fingernails are badly bitten, and she's wearing jeans and a black top with the words 'Razors cause less pain than life' on it. She's wearing blue eyeshadow, and has a sparkly hairband around her wrist. The other girl looks slightly older, and is wearing a ripped T-shirt with a horse on it, and a white pearl rosary necklace. She has old injection scars in the crook of her arm, and a khaki jacket rolled up to form a pillow behind her head.

'Indie?' the older girl asks in a subdued voice. 'Did you go in and look before the cops came?'

'I don't want nightmares,' the larger girl says languidly.

'Poor little Indie,' the older one teases.

'What?'

'You're scared of nightmares then . . .'

'Yes, I am.'

The other girl laughs: 'So fucking self—'

'Shut up, Caroline,' the red-haired girl cries.

'Miranda's been murdered,' Caroline goes on. 'That's probably a bit worse than—'

'I just think it's nice not to have to deal with her,' Indie says.

'You're so sick,' Caroline smiles.

'She was fucking sick, she burned me with a cigarette and—'

'Stop bitching!' the red-haired girl snaps.

'And she hit me with a skipping rope,' Indie goes on.

'You really are a bitch,' Caroline sighs.

'Sure, I'm happy to say it if it makes you feel better,' Indie teases. 'It's really sad that an idiot's dead, but I—'

The little red-haired girl hits her head against the wall again, then closes her eyes. The front door opens, and the two girls who ran off come in with Gunnarsson.

18

Joona leans back in the chair, his face is calm, his dark jacket has fallen open in gentle folds, his muscular body is relaxed, and his eyes are as grey as the frozen sea as he watches the girls walking in.

The others boo loudly and laugh. Lu Chu is swaying her hips exaggeratedly as she walks, flicking a V-sign with her fingers.

'Lesbian loser,' Indie calls.

'We could take a shower together,' Lu Chu replies.

The counsellor, Daniel Grim, comes into the cottage behind the girls. He's obviously trying to get Gunnarsson to listen.

'I'd just like you to take it a bit more gently with the girls,' Daniel says, then lowers his voice before he goes on. 'You're frightening them just by being here . . .'

'Don't worry,' Gunnarsson reassures him.

'But I am,' Daniel replies frankly.

'What?'

'I am actually worried,' he says.

'Well you can sod off, then,' Gunnarsson sighs. 'Just get out of the way and let me do my job.'

Joona notes that the counsellor hasn't shaved, and that the T-shirt under his jacket is inside out.

'I just want to point out that for these girls, the police don't represent security.'

'Yes they do!' Caroline jokes.

'That's good to hear,' Daniel says with a smile, then turns back to Gunnarsson. 'Seriously, though . . . for most of our residents, the police have only featured in their lives when things were going wrong.'

Joona can see that Daniel is well aware that the police officer regards him as a nuisance, but he still chooses to raise another matter: 'I was speaking to the coordinator outside about temporary accommodation for—'

'One thing at a time,' Gunnarsson interrupts.

'It's important, because—'

'Cunt,' Indie says irritably.

'Fuck you,' Lu Chu teases.

'Because it could be damaging,' Daniel goes on. 'It could be damaging for the girls to have to sleep here tonight.'

'Are they going to stay in a hotel, then?' Gunnarsson asks.

'You ought to be murdered!' Almira yells, and throws a glass at Indie.

It shatters against the wall, scattering water and jagged fragments across the floor. Daniel rushes over, Almira turns away, but Indie manages to punch her in the back several times before Daniel separates them.

'For God's sake, control yourselves!' he roars.

'Almira's a fucking cunt who—'

'Just calm down, Indie,' he says, blocking her hand. 'We've talked about this – haven't we?'

'Yes,' she replies in a calmer voice.

'You're a good girl really,' he says with a smile.

She nods and starts to pick up pieces of glass from the floor with Almira.

'I'll get the vacuum cleaner,' Daniel says, and leaves the cottage.

He pushes the door shut from outside, but it swings open again, so he slams it, making the framed Carl Larsson print rattle against the wall.

'Did Miranda have any enemies?' Gunnarsson asks the group.

'No,' Almira replies, and giggles.

Indie glances at Joona.

'OK, listen!' Gunnarsson says, raising his voice. 'I just want you to answer my questions, not start shrieking and messing about. It can't be that bloody difficult, can it?'

'That depends on the questions,' Caroline replies calmly.

'I'll probably stick to shrieking,' Lu Chu mutters.

'Truth or dare,' Indie says, pointing at Joona with a smile.

'Truth,' Joona replies.

'I'm asking the questions,' Gunnarsson protests.

'What does this mean?' Joona asks, and covers his face with his hands.

'What? I don't know,' Indie replies. 'Vicky and Miranda were the ones who did all that—'

'I can't handle this,' Caroline interrupts. 'You didn't see Miranda, that's how she was lying, there was so much blood, there was blood everywhere. And . . .'

Her voice collapses into sobs, and the psychologist goes over and tries to calm her down.

'Who's Vicky?' Joona asks, getting up from the armchair.

'She's the most recent arrival here.'

'So where the hell is she?' Lu Chu snaps.

'Which one's her room?' Joona asks quickly.

'She's probably sneaked out to see her fuck-buddy,' Tuula says.

'We usually store up Stesolid pills, then sleep like—'

'Who are we talking about now?' Gunnarsson asks in a loud voice.

'Vicky Bennet,' Caroline replies. 'I haven't seen her all—'

'Where the hell is she?'

'Vicky's just too fucking much,' Lu Chu laughs.

'Turn the television off,' Gunnarsson says, sounding stressed. 'I want everyone to calm down, and—'

'Stop shouting!' Tuula shouts, and turns the volume up.

Joona crouches down in front of Caroline, looks into her eyes, and holds her gaze with calm intensity.

'Which is Vicky's room?'

'The last one, at the end of the corridor,' Caroline replies.

19

Joona leaves the small house and hurries across the yard, passing the counsellor with the vacuum cleaner and saying hello to the forensics officers before running up the steps and going back into the main building. It's gloomy now, the lamps are switched off, but the mats on the floor stand out like stepping stones.

One girl is missing, Joona thinks. No one has seen her. Maybe she ran away in the chaos, maybe the others are trying to help her by withholding what they know.

The crime scene investigation has only just begun, and the rooms haven't been searched yet. The entire Birgitta Home should have been examined with a toothcomb, but there hasn't been time, too much has been happening all at once.

The girls are anxious and scared.

The victim support team should be here.

The police need reinforcements, more forensics officers, more resources.

Joona shudders at the thought that the missing girl might be hiding in her room. She could have seen something, and is now so terrified that she daren't come out.

He hurries into the corridor containing the girls' rooms.

The walls and timbers are creaking slightly, but otherwise the building is quiet. In the alcove the door with no handle is standing ajar. The dead girl is lying on the bed in there with her hands over her eyes.

Joona suddenly remembers that he saw three horizontal marks in the blood on the edge of the alcove. Blood from three fingers, but not fingerprints. Joona noticed the marks, but was so absorbed in structuring his impressions of the crime scene that only now does he realise that they were on the wrong side. The marks didn't lead away from the murder, but the other way, further along the corridor. There are faint prints from boots, shoes, and bare feet leading in all directions, but the three streaks of blood lead deeper into the building.

Whoever left the marks was planning to do something in one of the other girls' rooms.

No more dead bodies, Joona whispers to himself.

He pulls on a pair of latex gloves and walks to the last room. When he opens the door he hears a rustling sound, and stops abruptly, trying to see. The sound disappears. Joona carefully reaches in for the light switch with his hand.

He hears the noise again, it's an odd, metallic sound.

'Vicky?'

He feels across the wall, finds the switch, and turns the light on. Yellow light immediately fills the barely furnished room. There's a creak as the window swings open towards the forest and lake. A sudden noise in the corner draws Joona's attention, and he sees a birdcage lying on the floor. A yellow budgie is flapping its wings and climbing the roof of the cage.

The smell of blood is unmistakeable. A mixture of iron and something else, something cloying and rancid.

Joona lays out some plastic mats and walks slowly into the room.

There's blood around the window catch. Clear handprints show how someone climbed up onto the windowsill, took hold of the window frame, and then presumably jumped out onto the lawn below.

He goes over to the bed. An icy shiver runs down his neck when he pulls the covers back. The sheet is covered with dried blood. But whoever was lying in the bed hadn't been injured.

The blood has been wiped off onto the sheet, smeared across it.

Someone covered in blood has slept in these sheets.

Joona stands still for a while, trying to read the movements. She really did sleep, he thinks.

When he tries to pick up the pillow he discovers that it's stuck to the bottom sheet and mattress. Joona pulls it free, to find a bloodstained hammer with congealed brown matter and strands of hair stuck to it. Most of the blood has been absorbed by the sheet, but it's still glinting wetly around the head of the hammer.

20

The Birgitta Home is bathed in soft, beautiful light, and Himmelsjön is glinting magically between the tall old trees. But just a few hours ago Nina Mollander got up to go to the toilet and found Miranda dead on her bed. She woke the others, panic broke out, and they called counsellor Daniel Grim, who immediately alerted the police.

Nina Molander was so shocked that she'd had to be taken by ambulance to the regional hospital in Sundsvall.

Gunnarsson is standing in the yard with the counsellor, Daniel Grim, and Sonja Rask. Gunnarsson has opened the boot of his white Mercedes and has laid out the forensics officers' sketches of the crime scene in the back.

The dog is still barking excitedly, tugging at its leash.

When Joona stops behind the car and runs his hand through his tousled hair the other three have already turned to face him.

'The girl's escaped through her window,' he says.

'Escaped?' Daniel says in astonishment. 'Vicky's escaped? Why would—'

'There's blood on the window frame, there's blood in her bed, and—'

'Surely that doesn't necessarily mean—'

'There's a bloody hammer under her pillow,' Joona concludes.

'This doesn't make sense,' Gunnarsson says irritably. 'It's can't be right, because the level of violence was so damn extreme.'

Joona turns back to the counsellor, Daniel Grim. His face looks fragile and naked in the sunlight.

'What do you say?' Joona asks him.

'What? About the idea that Vicky might . . . It's insane,' Daniel replies.

'Why?'

'Just now,' the counsellor says, and smiles involuntarily, 'just now you were convinced this was the work of a grown man – Vicky's small, weighs less than fifty kilos, and her wrists are as thin as—'

'Is she violent?' Joona asks.

'Vicky didn't do this,' Daniel replies calmly. 'I've spent two months working with her, and I can tell you that she isn't.'

'Was she violent before she came here?'

'I have to obey the oath of confidentiality,' Daniel replies.

'And surely you can see that your bloody oath of confidentiality is costing us time,' Gunnarsson says.

'What I can say is that I coach some residents to adopt alternatives to aggressive responses . . . so that they don't react angrily when they feel disappointed or frightened, for instance,' Daniel says mildly.

'But not Vicky?' Joona says.

'No.'

'So why isn't she here?' Sonja asks.

'I can't discuss individual residents.'

'But you don't consider her violent?'

'She's a sweet girl,' he replies simply.

'So what do you think happened? Why is there a bloody hammer under her pillow?'

'I don't know, it doesn't make sense. Maybe she was helping someone? Hid the weapon?'

'Which of the girls are violent?' Gunnarsson asks angrily.

'I can't identify them individually – you must understand that.'

'We do,' Joona replies.

Daniel looks at him gratefully and tries to breathe more calmly.

'Try talking to them,' Daniel says. 'You'll soon see which girls I mean.'

'Thanks,' Joona says, and starts to walk off.

'Bear in mind that they've lost a friend,' Daniel says quickly.

Joona stops and walks back towards the counsellor.

'Do you know which room Miranda was found in?'

'No, but I assumed . . .'

Daniel falls silent and shakes his head.

'Because I'm having trouble thinking it's her room,' Joona says. 'It's almost bare, on the right, just past the toilets.'

'The isolation room,' Daniel replies.

'Why would someone end up there?' Joona asks.

'Because . . .' Daniel tails off and looks thoughtful.

'What are you thinking?'

'The door should have been locked,' he says.

'There's a key in the lock.'

'What key?' Daniel asks, raising his voice. 'Elisabet's the only person who's got a key to the isolation room.'

'Who's Elisabet?' Gunnarsson asks.

'My wife,' Daniel replies. 'She was on duty last night . . .'

'So where is she now?' Sonja asks.

'What?' Daniel says, looking at her in confusion.

'Is she at home?' she asks.

Daniel looks surprised and uncertain.

'I assumed Elisabet had gone with Nina in the ambulance,' he says slowly.

'No, Nina Molander went on her own,' Sonja replies.

'Of course Elisabet went with her to the hospital, she'd never let one of the—'

'I was the first officer on the scene,' Sonja interrupts.

Exhaustion is making her voice sound brusque and hoarse.

'There was no member of staff here,' she goes on. 'Just a load of frightened girls.'

'But my wife was—'

'Call her,' Sonja says.

'I've tried, her phone's switched off,' Daniel says quietly. 'I thought . . . I assumed . . .'

'God, this is a mess,' Gunnarsson says.

'My wife, Elisabet,' Daniel goes on in a voice that's getting increasingly unsteady. 'She's got a heart condition, it might, she might . . .'

'Try to talk calmly,' Joona says.

'My wife has an enlarged heart and . . . she was working last night, she should be here . . . her phone is switched off and . . .'

21

Daniel looks at them desperately, fumbles with the zipper on his jacket, and repeats that his wife has a heart condition. The dog is barking and pulling so hard at its leash that it's almost strangling itself. It coughs, then goes on barking.

Joona goes over to the barking dog beneath the tree. He tries to calm it down as he loosens the leash attached to its collar. As soon as Joona lets go, the dog runs across the yard to a small building. Joona hurries after it. The dog is scratching at the door, whimpering and panting.

Daniel Grim stares at Joona and the dog, and starts to walk towards them. Gunnarsson calls to him to stop, but he keeps moving. His body is stiff and his face full of despair. The gravel crunches beneath his feet. Joona tries to calm the dog, and grabs hold of its collar to pull it back, away from the door.

Gunnarsson runs across the yard and gets hold of Daniel's jacket, but he pulls free and falls to the ground, scrapes his hand, but gets back up again.

The dog is barking, tensing its body and pulling at its collar.

The uniformed police officer stops in front of the door. Daniel tries to push past, and calls out with a sob in his voice: 'Elisabet? Elisabet! I have to . . .'

The police officer tries to lead him aside while Gunnarsson hurries over to Joona and helps him with the dog.

'My wife,' Daniel whimpers. 'My wife could be . . .'

Gunnarsson pulls the dog back towards the tree again.

The dog is panting hard, kicking up grit with its paws and barking at the door.

Joona feels a sting of pain at the back of his eyes as he pulls on a latex glove.

A carved wooden sign beneath the low eaves of the building says 'Brew-house'.

Joona opens the door carefully and looks into the dimly-lit room. A small window is open, and hundreds of flies are buzzing about. There are bloody paw prints from the dog all over the worn floor tiles. Without going inside, Joona moves sideways to see around the brick fireplace.

He can see the back panel of a mobile phone next to a patch of blood.

As Joona leans forward through the door the buzzing of the flies gets louder. A woman in her fifties is lying in a pool of blood with her mouth open. She's dressed in jeans, pink socks and a grey cardigan. The woman evidently tried to shuffle away, but the upper part of her face and head have been caved in.

22

Pia Abrahamsson realises that she's driving a bit too fast.

She'd counted on getting away earlier, but the diocesan meeting in Östersund dragged on longer than expected.

Pia looks at her son in the mirror. His head is lolling against the edge of his child's seat. His eyes are closed behind his glasses. The morning sunlight flashes between the trees and across his calm little face.

She slows down to eighty kilometres an hour even though the road stretches out perfectly straight ahead of her through the forest.

The roads are eerily empty.

Twenty minutes ago she passed a truck loaded with logs, but since then she hasn't seen another vehicle.

She screws up her eyes to see better.

The animal-proof fencing on either side of the road flickers past monotonously.

Human beings must be the most frightened creatures on the planet, she thinks.

This country has eight thousand kilometres of animal-proof fencing. Not to protect the animals, but to protect human beings. Narrow roads run through these oceans of forest surrounded on both sides by high fences.

Pia Abrahamsson glances quickly at Dante in the back seat.

She got pregnant when she was working as a priest in Hässelby parish. The father was the editor of the *Church Times*. She stood there with the pregnancy test in her hand, thinking about the fact that she was thirty-six years old.

She kept the child, but not the father of the child. Her son is the best thing that's ever happened to her.

Dante is sitting asleep in his child's car seat. His head is hanging heavily on his chest and his comfort blanket has fallen onto the floor.

Before he fell asleep he was so tired that he was crying at everything. He cried because the car smelled nasty from his mum's perfume, and because Super Mario had been eaten.

There are over two hundred kilometres to go until Sundsvall, and another four hundred and sixty before Stockholm.

Pia Abrahamsson needs to go to the toilet – she drank far too much coffee at the meeting.

There must an open petrol station soon.

She tells herself that she shouldn't stop in the middle of the forest.

She shouldn't, but she's going to anyway.

Pia Abrahamsson, who every Sunday preaches that everything that happens, happens for a deeper purpose, is about to become the victim of blind, indifferent fate.

She pulls gently over to the side of the road by a logging track and stops by the locked barrier blocking the animal fence. Behind the barrier the stony track leads into the forest.

She thinks that she shouldn't go out of sight of the road, and leaves the car door open so she can hear if Dante wakes up.

'Mummy?'

'Try to go back to sleep.'

'Mummy, don't go.'

'Sweetheart,' Pia says. 'I just need to pee. I'll leave the door open, so I'll be able to see you the whole time.'

He looks at her sleepily.

'I don't want to be alone,' he whispers.

She smiles at him and pats his sweaty little cheek. She knows she's over-protective, that she's turning him into a mummy's boy, but she can't help it.

'It's only for a really short time,' she says cheerfully.

Dante clings onto her hand and tries to stop her going, but she pulls free and takes a wet-wipe from the packet.

Pia gets out of the car, ducks under the barrier, and walks up the track, then turns and waves to Dante.

Imagine if someone pulled in and filmed her on her their mobile phone while she was squatting with her backside exposed.

The images of the peeing priest would be all over YouTube, Facebook, forums, blogs and chat-rooms.

She shivers, steps off the track, and goes further into the trees. Heavy forestry machinery has churned up the ground.

When she's sure she can't be seen from the road, she pulls down her pants, steps out of them, then hoists up her skirt and squats down.

She can feel how tired she is, her thighs start to shake and she rests one hand on the moss that's growing on the tree trunks.

Relief courses through her and she closes her eyes.

When she looks up again she sees something incomprehensible. An animal has got up onto two legs and is walking along the logging track, staggering and hunched over.

A thick figure covered in dirt, blood, and mud.

Pia holds her breath.

It isn't an animal, it's as if part of the forest has broken free and come to life.

Like a small girl made of twigs.

The apparition stumbles, but keeps walking towards the barrier.

Pia gets up and follows it.

She tries to speak, but her voice has vanished.

A branch snaps beneath her foot.

Gentle rain has started to fall on the forest.

She moves slowly, as if in a nightmare: she doesn't seem to be able to run.

Between the trees she sees that the being has already reached the car. Dirty scraps of cloth are wrapped around the wrists of the bizarre girl.

Pia stumbles out onto the logging track and sees the creature sweep her handbag from the seat, get in, and close the door.

'Dante,' she gasps.

The car roars into life, drives over her mobile phone and keyring, pulls out into the road, hits the railing between the carriageways, straightens up, and vanishes into the distance.

Whimpering to herself, Pia runs to the barrier, feeling how her whole body is shaking.

It's incomprehensible. The mud creature came out of nowhere, suddenly it was just there, and now the car and her son are gone.

She ducks under the barrier and walks out into the big, empty road. She doesn't scream, she doesn't seem to be able to. The only sound is her ragged breathing.

23

The forest flickers past, and raindrops patter against the large windscreen. Danish lorry driver Mads Jensen can see a woman standing in the middle of the road two hundred metres away. He swears to himself and blows the horn. He sees her flinch at the noise, but she makes no attempt to get off the road. The driver sounds the horn again, and the woman takes a slow step forward, raises her chin, and looks up at the approaching lorry.

Mads Jensen brakes, and feels the heavy articulated trailer pushing against the old Fliegel cab. He presses the brake pedal harder, the drive-shaft creaks, and the whole vehicle shudders before finally coming to a stop.

The engine winds down, and the rumble from the pistons becomes more audible.

The woman just stands there, three metres from the front of the lorry. Only now does the driver see that she is dressed as a priest under her denim jacket. A small rectangle of her white collar stands out against her black shirt.

The woman's face is open and remarkably pale. When their eyes meet through the windscreen, tears start to run down her cheeks.

Mads Jensen puts the hazard lights on and gets out of the cab. The engine is radiating heat and a strong smell of diesel.

When he walks around to the front of the vehicle the woman is leaning against one of the headlamps, gasping for breath.

'What's happened?' Mads asks.

She looks up at him, wide-eyed. The amber glare of the hazard lights pulses over her.

'Do you need help?' he asks.

She nods, and he tries to lead her around the cab. The rain is getting harder, and it's quickly getting dark.

'Has someone hurt you?'

She resists, then goes with him and climbs into the passenger seat. He closes the door behind her and hurries around to get in the driver's seat.

'I can't stay here, I'm blocking the whole road,' he explains. 'I have to move, is that OK?'

She doesn't answer, but he sets the truck moving and switches on the windscreen wipers.

'Are you hurt?' he asks.

She shakes her head and claps one hand over her mouth.

'My son,' she whispers. 'My . . .'

'What are you saying?' he asks. 'What's happened?'

'She took my son . . .'

'I'll call the police. Is it OK if I call the police?'

'Oh, God,' she moans.

24

The rain is beating hard against the windscreen, the wiper blades are moving fast, and the road ahead of them looks as if it's boiling.

Pia is sitting in the warm cab high above the ground, shaking. She can't calm down. She realises that she's not making any sense, but now she can hear the lorry driver talk to the emergency call centre. He is advised to carry on along Highway 86, then the 330, where he'll meet an emergency vehicle at Timrå that will take her to Sundsvall Hospital.

'What? What are you talking about?' Pia asks. 'This isn't about me. They have to stop my car, that's the only thing that matters.'

The Danish driver gives her a confused look, and she realises that she needs to concentrate to make herself understood. She has to act calmly even though the ground has disappeared beneath her, even though she's in free-fall.

'My son has been kidnapped,' she says.

'She says her son's been kidnapped,' the driver repeats into his phone.

'The police have to stop the car,' she goes on. 'A Toyota . . . a red Toyota Auris. I can't remember the licence number, but . . .'

The driver asks the emergency operator to wait.

'It's ahead of us on this road . . . you have to stop it . . . my son's only four, he was sitting in the back when I . . .'

He repeats her words to the operator, explains that he's driving east along Highway 86, about forty kilometres from Timrå.

'They have to hurry . . .'

The truck slows down and passes a bent-over traffic light, and drives across a roundabout. The trailer judders as the wheels roll over the kerb, then the truck accelerates past a white brick building, driving parallel to the river.

The emergency call centre puts the Danish driver through to a female police officer in a patrol car. She introduces herself as Mirja Zlatnek, and says she's thirty kilometres away, on Highway 330 in Djupängen.

Pia Abrahamsson takes the phone, swallows hard to stifle the nausea she feels. She hears her own voice, calm but shaky.

'Listen,' she says. 'My son's been kidnapped, and the car is driving along . . . hang on . . .'

She turns to the driver.

'Where are we? What road are we on?'

'Highway 86,' the driver says.

'How much of a head start did they get?' the police officer asks.

'I don't know,' Pia says. 'Five minutes, maybe?'

'Have you passed Indal?'

'Indal,' Pia repeats.

'We're almost twenty kilometres from there,' the driver says loudly.

'Then we've got them,' the police officer says. 'There are no alternative routes . . .'

When Pia Abrahamsson hears those words her tears start to flow. She quickly wipes her cheeks and hears the police officer talk to a colleague. They're going to set up roadblocks on Highway 330 and on the bridge over the river. The second police officer is in Nordansjö, and says he can be in position in less than five minutes.

'That's good enough,' the policewoman says quickly.

The truck drives along the winding road as it follows the river through a sparsely populated part of Medelpad. Even though they can't see it, they're following the car with Pia Abrahamsson's four-year-old son in it: they know it must be ahead of them, because there are no other options. Highway 86 passes through a few isolated communities, but there are no side roads, just forest tracks that don't connect to other roads, and only lead into the forest, stretching many kilometres through boggy land to logging areas, but no further.

'I can't bear this,' Pia whispers.

The road they're on splits in two ten kilometres ahead of them. Just past the little town of Indal, one branch of the road crosses the river and carries on almost due south, while the other goes on following the river towards the coast.

Pia sits with her hands clasped tightly, praying to God. Up ahead, two police cars have set up roadblocks on the two branches of the road. One car is parked at the far end of the bridge, and the other is eight kilometres to the east.

The truck carrying the Danish truck driver and Pia Abrahamsson is passing through Indal. Through the heavy rain they see the empty bridge over the teeming water, and the blue lights of the lone police car rotating at the far end of the bridge.

25

Police Constable Mirja Zlatnek has parked her patrol car across the whole width of the road. If any car wanted to get past, it would have to pull off the road and drive with two wheels in the ditch.

In front of her is a long, straight stretch of road. The police car's blue lights flash across the wet tarmac and dark branches of the trees, in among the trunks.

The rain is beating hard on the car roof.

Mirja sits quietly for a while looking out through the windscreen and trying to think through the situation.

Visibility is poor because of the rain.

She had counted on having a very quiet day, seeing as almost all her colleagues in the whole district are busy with the case of the dead girl at the Birgitta Home. Even the National Crime Unit have been brought into the investigation.

Mirja has been developing a secret fear of the operational side of the job, without ever actually having been in any particularly traumatic situations. Perhaps it's because of that time she tried to mediate in a domestic drama that ended badly, but that was many years ago now.

The anxiety has crept up on her. She prefers administrative duties, and crime prevention work.

She spent the morning sitting at her desk looking at recipes online. Elk fillet wrapped in pastry, potato wedges, and cream sauce with penny bun mushrooms. And puréed artichoke hearts.

She was in the car heading to Djupängen to look at a stolen trailer when the call came through about the abducted boy.

Mirja tells herself that she's going to be able to solve the situation of the kidnapped boy. Because the car containing the woman's four-year-old son has nowhere else to go.

This stretch of road is like a long tunnel, a trap.

The lorry is following it from the other direction.

Either the car containing the boy crosses the bridge just after Indal, where her colleague Lasse Bengtsson has blocked the road.

Or it comes this way, and I'm waiting here, Mirja thinks.

And ten kilometres behind the car is the lorry.

Obviously it all depends how fast the car is driving, but within the next twenty minutes there'll be some sort of confrontation.

Mirja tells herself that the child almost certainly hasn't been kidnapped in the real sense of the word. Probably a custody dispute. The woman she spoke to was too upset to give her any coherent information, but from what she did say her car must be somewhere on the road this side of Nilsböle.

It'll soon be over, she tells herself.

It won't be long before she can go back to her room at the station, get a cup of coffee and a ham sandwich.

But at the same time there's something worrying her. The woman spoke about a girl with arms like twigs.

Mirja didn't ask her name. There hadn't been time. She assumed the emergency call centre had taken all the relevant details.

The fear in her voice had been alarming. She had been breathing fast, and described what she'd been through as incomprehensible, beyond logical explanation.

The rain is bouncing off the windscreen and bonnet. Mirja reaches for the radio, waits a moment, then calls Lasse Bengtsson.

'What's happening?' she asks.

'Torrential rain, but not much else. No cars, not a single damn . . . Hang on, I can see a truck, a bloody big articulated truck heading down Highway 330.'

'He's the guy who called,' Mirja says.

'So where the hell's the Toyota?' Lasse says. 'I've been here a quarter of an hour, so it'll have to reach you in the next five minutes, unless some UFO has—'

'Give me a moment,' Mirja says quickly and ends the call to her colleague when she sees the distant light from two car headlamps.

26

Mirja Zlatnek gets out of her patrol car and hunches in the downpour. She squints at the car approaching through the heavy rain.

With one hand on her holstered pistol she walks towards the car, simultaneously holding her left hand up to make the driver stop.

The water coursing across the road and into the ditches by the side of the carriageway looks as if it's bubbling.

Mirja sees the car slow down, and she sees her own shadow bounce along the road surrounded by the rotating blue light from behind her. She hears a call on the radio in the patrol car, but stays on the road. The voices on the comms radio are tinny, and there's a lot of crackling, but the words are still clearly audible.

'Hell of a lot of blood,' a younger colleague is saying as he describes the discovery of a second body at the Birgitta Home, a middle-aged woman.

The car comes closer, driving slowly, then pulls over to the edge of the road and stops. Mirja Zlatnek starts to walk towards it. It's a Mazda pickup with muddy tyres. The driver's door opens, and a large man in a green hunting jacket and a Helly Hansen sweater gets out. He has neatly combed shoulder-length hair, and a wide face with a large nose and narrow eyes.

'Are you alone in the car?' Mirja shouts, wiping the water from her face.

He nods, then looks over at the forest.

'Stay back,' she says as he walks closer.

He takes a tiny step back.

Mirja leans forward to look inside the car. Water trickles down the back of her neck.

It's hard to see anything through the rain and mud on the windscreen. There's a newspaper spread out on the driver's seat. He's been sitting on it while he was driving. She walks around and moves closer, trying to see what's lying on the narrow back seat. An old blanket and a thermos flask.

The radio in the car crackles again, but she can no longer hear the words.

The shoulders of the man's hunting jacket are already dark from the rain. There's a sound of something scraping against metal coming from the vehicle.

When she looks back at the man again she sees he's come closer. Just a little, one step, perhaps. Unless she's imagining it. She's no longer sure. He's staring at her, looks her up and down, and then frowns.

'Do you live here?' she asks.

She rubs the mud from the licence plate with her foot, makes a note of it, then carries on around the pickup.

There's a pink sports bag on the floor in front of the passenger seat. Mirja keeps moving around the vehicle, but keeps the big man in sight the whole time. There's something on the back of the pickup under a green tarpaulin, held down by thick straps.

'Where are you going?' she asks.

He's standing still, following her with his eyes. Suddenly some blood seeps out from under the tarpaulin, along the dirty grooves.

'What have you got here?' she asks.

When he doesn't answer, she reaches over the back of the pickup. It isn't easy to reach, she has to lean on the vehicle. The man moves sideways slightly. She managed to reach the tarpaulin with her fingertips without taking her eyes off the man. He licks his lips as she lifts it. She unfastens her pistol, then glances quickly at the back of the pickup, long enough to see the hoof of a young deer.

The man is standing completely still in the flashing blue light, but Mirja keeps her hand on her pistol as she steps back from the vehicle.

'Where did you shoot the deer?'

'It was lying on the road,' he says.

'Did you make a note of where?'

He spits slowly on the road, between his own feet.

'Can I see your driving licence?' she says.

He doesn't answer, and shows no sign of obeying her.

'Driving licence,' she repeats, aware of the uncertainty in her own voice.

'We're done here,' he says, and walks towards the pickup.

'You're legally obliged to report accidents involving wild animals . . .'

The man gets in the driver's seat, closes the door, starts the engine, and pulls away. She watches him pass the police car with two wheels in the ditch. When he drives up onto the road again Mirja tells herself she should have examined the pickup more closely, should have removed the whole tarpaulin, and looked under the blanket on the back seat.

The rain is lashing the trees around her, and in the distance a crow calls from a treetop.

Mirja starts when she hears the sound of a heavy vehicle behind her. She turns around and pulls out her pistol, but can't see anything except the rain.

27

Danish lorry driver Mads Jansen is being reprimanded over the phone by his transport manager. He blushes as he tries to explain the situation. Pia Abrahamsson can hear the angry voice through the phone, and the transport manager goes on yelling about coordinates and fucked-up logistics.

'But,' Mads Jensen tries to say, 'surely we have to help other—'

'This'll be deducted from your wages,' his boss snaps. 'That's all the help you're getting from me.'

'Thanks a lot,' Mads says, and ends the call.

Pia sits beside the driver in silence as the dense forest flies past on both sides. The heavy rain sounds deafening in the cab. In the split wing mirror Pia can see the swaying trailer and the trees they've just passed.

Mads pops some nicotine gum in his mouth and stares ahead at the road. The sound of the engine and the thud of the heavy wheels on the tarmac blur into one.

She looks at the calendar that sways with the motion of the cab. A curvaceous woman holding an inflatable swan in a swimming pool. At the bottom of the glossy photograph the date is given as August 1968.

The road slopes downward, and the weight of the cargo of iron bars increases the speed of the vehicle.

Far off in the groove between the trees a strong blue light

is flickering in the grey rain. A police car is blocking the road.

Pia Abrahamsson feels her heart start to beat hard and fast. She stares at the police car and the woman in the dark blue sweater waving her arm at them. Before the truck has stopped, Pia opens the door. The sound of the engine and the tyres becomes instantly much louder.

She feels dizzy as she clambers down and hurries over to the waiting police officer.

'Where's the car?' the police officer asks.

'What? What are you saying?'

Pia stares at the other woman and tries to read her face, but just gets more shaken by her serious expression. She feels as if her legs are going to give way beneath her.

'Did you see the car when you passed it?' the police woman clarifies.

'Passed it?' Pia says weakly.

Mads Jensen walks over to them.

'We haven't seen anything,' he tells the police officer. 'You must have set up the roadblock too late.'

'Too late? I drove up this road to get here . . .'

'So where the hell is the car?' he asks.

Mirja Zlatnek runs back to her car and calls her colleague.

'Lasse?' she says urgently.

'I've been trying to get you,' he says. 'You weren't answering.'

'No, I was—'

'Has everything gone OK?' he asks.

'Where the hell's the car?' she asks, almost shouting. 'The truck's here, but there's no sign of the car.'

'There aren't any other roads,' he says.

'We need to put an alert out and block the 86 in the other direction.'

'I'll get onto that at once,' he says, and ends the call.

Pia Abrahamsson has come over to the police car. The rain has soaked her clothes. Police Constable Mirja Zlatnek is sitting in the driver's seat with the door open.

'You told me you were going to get him,' Pia says.

'Yes, I—'

'You told me, I believed you when you said that.'

73

'I know, I don't understand this,' Mirja says. 'It doesn't make sense, you can't drive fast on these roads, there's no way the car could have got to the bridge before Lasse got there.'

'It has to be somewhere,' Pia says in a hard voice, pulling her priest's collar from her shirt.

'Hang on,' Mirja Zlatnek suddenly says.

She calls the command centre.

'This is patrol car 321,' she says quickly. 'We need another roadblock, at once . . . Before Aspen . . . There's a small road there, if you know the way, you can get from Kävsta up to Myckelsjö . . . Yes, exactly . . . Who? Good, he'll be there in eight, ten minutes . . .'

Mirja gets out of the car and looks along the straight road, as if she still expects the Toyota to appear.

'My boy – he's gone?' Pia asks her.

'There's nowhere they could have gone,' Mirja says, doing her best to sound patient. 'I understand that you're worried, but we'll get them – they must have turned off and stopped somewhere, but there's nowhere they can go . . .'

She falls silent and wipes the rain from her forehead, takes a deep breath, and goes on: 'We'll closing off the last roads, and we're calling in a helicopter . . .'

Pia undoes the top button of her shirt and leans one hand on the bonnet of the police car. She's breathing far too heavily, and tries to calm down, her chest is pounding. She knows she ought to be making demands, but she can't think clearly, can only feel a desperate fear and confusion.

28

Although the rain is still pouring from the sky, only a few drops manage to reach the ground between the trees in the forest.

A large white command vehicle is parked in the rain at the centre of the yard between the Birgitta Home's buildings. The bus contains a coordination centre, and a group of men and women are seated around a table covered with maps and computers.

Their discussion of the ongoing murder investigation is interrupted as they listen to the radio communication about a boy who's been abducted. Roadblocks have been set up on Highway 330, and at the bridge at Indal, as well as at Kävsta and further north on Highway 86. At first their colleagues sound confident of stopping the vehicle, but then everything goes quiet. No communication for ten minutes, until the radio suddenly crackles again and an officer reports breathlessly: 'It's gone, the car's gone . . . it should be here, but it hasn't turned up . . . We shut off every damn road there is, but it's still vanished . . . I don't know what to do,' Mirja says wearily. 'The mother's sitting in my car, I'll try and talk to her . . .'

The police officers have sat in silence as they listen to the exchanges. Now they gather around the map on the table, as Bosse Norling points out Highway 86 with his finger.

'If they blocked the road here and here, the car can't just disappear,' he says. 'Obviously it could have driven into a garage in Bäck or Bjällsta . . . or up one of the logging trails, but it's still bloody weird.'

'And they won't get anywhere,' Sonja Rask says.

'Am I the only one thinking that Vicky Bennet might have taken the car?' Bosse asks tentatively.

The pattering on the roof has grown quieter, but rain is still running down the bus's windows.

Sonja sits down at the computer and uses the police intranet to check the databases of people with a criminal record, people who've been suspected of committing a crime, and ongoing custody disputes.

'In nine times out of ten,' Gunnarsson says, leaning back and peeling a banana, 'problems like this sort themselves out of their own accord . . . I think she had her bloke in the car, they had an argument, and in the end he'd had enough and dumped her at the side of the road before taking off with the kid.'

'She's not married,' Sonja says.

'According to the statistics,' Gunnarsson goes on in the same lecturing tone, 'the majority of children in Sweden are now born out of wedlock.'

'Here it is,' Sonya says, interrupting. 'Pia Abrahamsson sought sole custody of her son Dante, and the father has tried to lodge an appeal . . .'

'So we're dropping any suggestion of a connection to Vicky Bennet?' Bosse asks.

'Try to get hold of the father first,' Joona says.

'I'll get onto that,' Sonya says, and goes to the back of the bus.

'Was there anything outside Vicky Bennet's window?' Joona asks.

'Nothing on the ground, but we found prints and some coagulated remains on the windowsill and the outside of the building,' one of the forensics officers says.

'How about the edge of the forest?'

'We didn't get that far before it started to rain.'

'But presumably Vicky Bennet ran straight into the forest,' Joona says thoughtfully.

He looks at Bosse Norling, who is doing things the old-fashioned way by leaning over the map with a compass, putting the point on the Birgitta Home, and drawing a circle.

'It wasn't her who took the car,' Gunnarsson says. 'Christ, it doesn't take three hours to walk through the forest to Highway 86 and then follow it to . . .'

'But it isn't easy to get your bearings at night . . . so she could very well have walked something like this,' Bosse says.

He points to a possible route to the east of an area of bog, then heading north.

'Then the timing would fit,' Joona says.

'Dante's father is in Tenerife at the moment,' Sonja calls from the back of the bus.

Olle Gunnarsson swears under his breath, then goes over to the radio and calls Police Constable Mirja Zlatnek.

'Gunnarsson here,' he says. 'Have you taken a witness statement from the mother?'

'Yes, I—'

'Have we got a description?'

'It's not easy, she's in a very emotional state, and the mother doesn't seem to have a coherent picture of events,' Mirja replies, and breathes through her nose. 'She's badly shaken, and keeps talking about a skeleton with wiry hands that came out of the forest. A girl with blood on her face, a girl with twig-like arms . . .'

'But she's talking about a girl?'

'I recorded her statement, but she says lots of weird stuff, she needs to calm down before we can question her properly . . .'

'But she keeps coming back to the idea that it was a girl?' Gunnarsson says slowly.

'Yes . . . several times.'

29

Joona stops the car at the roadblock on Highway 330, says hello to one of the police officers stationed there, shows his ID, then carries on along the road beside the river.

He's been told that the girls from the Birgitta Home are being temporarily housed in the Hotel Ibis. The counsellor, Daniel Grim, has been admitted to the acute psychiatric ward of the district hospital, the housekeeper, Margot Lundin, is at home in Timrå, and Faduumo Axmed, who works part-time as a care assistant, is off duty according to the rota, and down with her parents in Vänersborg.

When Police Constable Mirja Zlatnek said that Pia Abrahamsson kept coming back to the idea that it was a thin girl with bandages around her wrists, everyone realised that it was Vicky Bennet who had taken the car containing the little boy.

'It's a mystery that she hasn't been caught in the roadblocks,' Bosse Norling had said.

A helicopter was deployed, but there's no trace of the car, not in the small town, and not along any of the logging tracks.

It isn't really a mystery, Joona thinks. The most plausible explanation is that she managed to find somewhere to hide before she reached any of the roadblocks.

But where?

She must know someone who lives in Indal, someone who has a garage.

Joona has asked to speak to the girls in the company of a youth psychologist and a legally responsible adult from Victim Support, and is trying to remember the details of his first encounter with them in the small cottage at the home, when Gunnarsson came back with the two who had run off into the forest. The red-haired little girl had been watching television and banging her head against the wall. The girl called Indie had associated hands covering a face with Vicky, and then they had all started shouting and yelling at each other when they realised that she was missing. One of the girls claimed she was asleep, having taken Stesolid. Almira spat on the floor, and Indie rubbed her face and ended up with blue eyeshadow on her hand.

Joona can't help thinking that there's something about Tuula, the red-haired girl with white eyelashes and bright pink jogging bottoms. At first she yelled at them all to be quiet, but she had also said something when everyone was talking at the same time.

Tuula had said that Vicky had sneaked off to see her fuck-buddy.

30

The two-star Hotel Ibis is located on Trädgårdsgatan, not far
from the police station in Sundsvall. It's the sort of hotel that
smells of vacuum cleaners, rugs, and ingrained cigarette smoke.
The façade is covered with cream-coloured cladding. There's a
bowl of sweets on the reception desk. The police have put the
girls from the Birgitta Home in five adjacent rooms, and have
placed two uniformed officers in the corridor.

Joona walks purposefully across the worn floor.

The psychologist, Lisa Jern, is waiting for Joona outside one
of the doors. Her dark hair is streaked with grey at the front,
and her mouth is thin and nervous.

'Is Tuula already here?' Joona asks.

'Yes, she is . . . wait a moment, though,' the psychologist
says when he reaches for the door handle. 'As I understand
it, you're here as an observer from the National Crime Unit,
and—'

'A boy's life is in danger,' Joona interrupts.

'Tuula is barely speaking, and . . . I'm afraid my recommen-
dation as a child psychologist is to wait until she takes the
initiative herself and starts to talk about what's happened.'

'There isn't time for that,' Joona says, taking hold of the
handle.

'Wait, I . . . It's extremely important to be on the same

wavelength as the children, they absolutely mustn't feel that they're being regarded as unwell or . . .'

Joona opens the door and walks into the room. Tuula Lehti is sitting on a chair with her back to the row of windows. A little girl, just twelve years old, in a tracksuit and trainers.

The street outside, lined with parked cars, is visible between the wooden slats of the blind. All the tables are covered with beech veneer, and there's a fitted green carpet on the floor.

At the end of the room a man in a chequered blue flannel shirt with neatly combed hair is sitting looking at his phone. Joona realises that he's the girls' legally responsible adult.

Joona sits down in front of Tuula and looks at her. Her eyebrows are fair, her red hair straight and greasy.

'We met very briefly this morning,' he says.

She folds her freckled arms over her stomach. Her lips are thin and almost colourless.

'Fuck the police,' she mutters.

Lisa Jern walks around the table and sits down beside the hunched frame of the little girl.

'Tuula,' she says gently. 'Do you remember me saying that I sometimes used to feel like Thumbelina? There's nothing odd about that, because even as an adult you can feel really small sometimes.'

'Why is everyone talking such fucking shit?' Tuula asks, looking Joona in the eye. 'Is it because you're all thick, or because you think I'm thick?'

'Well, we probably think you're a bit thick,' Joona replies.

Tuula smiles in surprise, and is about to say something, when Lisa Jern assures her that it isn't true, that the superintendent was just joking.

Tuula folds her arms even tighter, stares at the table, and blows out her cheeks.

'You're definitely not thick,' Lisa Jern repeats after a while.

'Yes I am,' Tuula whispers.

She spits a gob of saliva onto the table, then sits there silently poking at it and making it into a star shape.

'Don't you want to talk?' Lisa whispers.

'Only to the Finn,' Tuula says almost inaudibly.

'What did you just say?' she asks with a smile.

'I'll only talk to the Finn,' Tuula says, raising her chin.

'How lovely,' the psychologist replies stiffly.

Joona starts the recording, then calmly goes through the formalities, time and location, the names of those present, and the purpose of the conversation.

'How did you end up at the Birgitta Home, Tuula?' he asks.

'I was at Lövsta . . . A few things happened that weren't that fucking great,' she says, and lowers her gaze. 'I got caught up with some kids who got locked up, even though I'm really too young . . . I kept my cool, watched television, and one year and four months later I got moved to the Birgitta Home.'

'What's the difference . . . compared with Lövsta?'

'It's . . . the Birgitta Home feels like a proper home . . . Rugs on the floor, the furniture's not screwed down . . . And there aren't locks and alarms everywhere . . . And you get left to sleep in peace, and have home-cooked food.'

Joona nods, and sees from the corner of his eye that the responsible adult is still fiddling with his phone. The psychologist, Lisa Jern, is breathing through her nose as she listens to them.

'What did you have to eat yesterday?'

'Tacos,' Tuula replies.

'Was everyone there for dinner?'

She shrugs.

'I think so.'

'Miranda too? She had tacos yesterday evening as well?'

'Can't you just cut her stomach open and check? Haven't you done that yet?'

'No, we haven't.'

'Why not?'

'We haven't had time.'

Tuula smiles, and starts to pull at a loose thread on her trousers. Her nails have been bitten ragged, and her cuticles are torn.

'I looked in the isolation room – it was pretty full-on,' Tuula says, and starts to rock backwards and forwards.

'Did you see the way Miranda was lying?' Joona asks after a while.

'Yes, like this,' Tuula says quickly, and puts her hands in front of her face.

'Why do you think she was doing that?'

Tuula kicks up the edge of the rug, then flattens it again.

'Maybe she was frightened.'

'Have you seen anyone else do that?' Joona asks lightly.

'No,' Tuula says, and scratches her neck.

'You don't get locked in your rooms, then?'

'It's kind of like an open prison,' Tuula smiles.

'Do people often sneak out at night?'

'I don't.'

Tuula's mouth becomes small and hard, and she pretends to fire her forefinger at the psychologist.

'Why not?' Joona asks.

She looks him in the eye and says quietly: 'I'm scared of the dark.'

'What about the others?'

Joona sees Lisa Jern standing there listening to them with an irritable frown between her eyebrows.

'Yes,' Tuula whispers.

'What do they do when they sneak out?'

The girl looks down and smiles to herself.

'They're older than you, aren't they?' Joona goes on.

'Yes,' she replies, and blushes.

'Do they meet boys?'

She nods.

'Does Vicky do that too?'

'Yes, she sneaks out at night,' Tuula says, and leans closer to Joona.

'Do you know who she goes to see?'

'Dennis.'

'Who's that?'

'I don't know,' she whispers, and licks her lips.

'But his name is Dennis? Do you know his surname?'

'No.'

'How long is she usually gone?'

Tuula shrugs her shoulders and picks at a piece of tape that's hanging from the seat of her chair.

31

The prosecutor, Susanne Öst, is waiting outside the Hotel Ibis beside a large Ford Fairlane. Her face is round and free from make-up. She's got her blonde hair in a ponytail, and is dressed in long grey trousers and a smart grey jacket. It looks as if she's been scratching her neck hard, and one wing of her shirt collar is sticking up.

'Do you have any objections to me pretending to be a police officer for a while?' she asks, and blushes.

'On the contrary,' Joona says, shaking her hand.

'We're busy knocking on doors, looking in garages, barns, car parks and so on,' she says seriously. 'We're closing the net, there aren't that many places you can hide a car . . .'

'No.'

'But obviously it'll go a bit quicker now we've got a name,' she smiles, and opens the front door of the big Ford. 'There are four men called Dennis in the area.'

'I'll follow you,' he says, and gets in his Volvo.

The American car sways as it pulls out and sets off towards Indal. Joona follows, thinking about Vicky.

Her mother, Susie Bennet, was an addict, and was homeless before her death last winter. Vicky has lived in various foster families and institutions from the age of six, and presumably quickly learned how to let old relationships go and how to make new ones.

If Vicky has been sneaking out to meet someone at night, he must live fairly close. Perhaps he waits for her in the forest or on the logging track. Perhaps she heads down Highway 86 to his home in Baggböle or Västloning.

The tarmac is drying now, the rainwater is settling in the ditches and shallow puddles. The sky is brighter now, but the forest is still dripping.

The prosecutor phones Joona, and he can see her looking in her rear-view mirror as she talks.

'We've just found one Dennis in Indal,' she says. 'He's seven years old. There's another one who lives out at Stige, but he's currently working in Leeds.'

'Which leaves two others,' Joona says.

'Yes. Dennis and Lovisa Karmstedt live in a house outside Tomming. We haven't been there yet. And there's a Dennis Rolando who lives with his parents just south of Indal. We've paid a visit to the parents, and there's nothing there. But he owns a large workshop on Kvarnåvägen that we can't get into . . . It's probably nothing, because they've spoken to him, and apparently he's in his car on the way to Sollefteå.'

'Break the door open.'

'OK,' she says, and ends the call.

The landscape opens up and the road is lined by fields on both sides, sparkling from the recent rain. Red-painted farms press up against the forest, which stretches off into the distance behind them.

As Joona is passing through the peaceful hamlet of Östanskär, two uniformed police officers are cutting through the heavy hinges of the workshop's steel door with an angle-grinder. A cascade of sparks sprays across the wall. The officers insert sturdy crowbars, break the door open, and go inside. The beams of their torches seek their way into the shadows. The workshop contains about fifty old-fashioned arcade games, Space Invaders, Asteroids, Street Fighter, all covered with dirty plastic sheeting.

Joona sees Susanne Öst talking on her phone, then she glances at him in the rear-view mirror. His phone rings. Susanne tells him quickly that there's only one address left. It's not far away. They ought to be there in ten minutes.

He slows down and follows her as she turns right onto a road between two waterlogged meadows, then on into the forest. They approach a yellow wooden house with closed blinds in all the windows. There are apple trees growing in the well-tended garden, and a blue-and-white-striped swing seat in the middle of the plot.

They pull up and walk together towards a parked police car.

Joona says hello to the two officers, then looks up at the house with the closed blinds.

'We don't know if Vicky took the car to abduct the child, or if she just wanted a car and there happened to be a child in the back seat,' he says. 'Either way, we have to regard the child as a hostage under current circumstances.'

'A hostage,' the prosecutor repeats quietly.

She walks over and rings the bell, then calls out that the police will force the door open if they're not let in. Someone moves inside the house. The floor creaks, and a heavy piece of furniture topples over.

'I'm going in,' Joona says.

One of the police officers keeps watch on the front door, the gable end facing the grass and the locked garage door, while the other one goes around to the rear of the house with Joona.

Their shoes and trousers get wet in the tall grass. At the back is a small flight of concrete steps leading down to a door with a mottled glass window. When Joona kicks the door in, the frame shatters and fragments of glass fly across the utility-room floor.

32

Broken glass crunches under Joona's shoes as he enters a neat utility room containing a hand-driven mangle.

Miranda was sitting on a chair when she was murdered, Joona thinks. Elisabet was chased across the yard in her stockinged feet and into the brew-house, tried to crawl away, but was beaten to death from the front.

He can feel the weight of the new pistol in its holster beneath his right arm. It's a semi-automatic Smith & Wesson, .45 calibre ACP. It's heavier than his old one, holds fewer bullets, but is quicker with the first shot.

Joona carefully opens a creaking door and looks into an old-fashioned kitchen. There's a large ceramic bowl of red apples on the round table, and the fine old stove smells of wood-smoke. A plate of frozen cinnamon buns is defrosting, and a drawer full of sharp knives is open.

He can see the wet greenery of the garden through the blinds.

Joona carries on into the hall and hears the ceiling light tinkle as its glass prisms knock against each other. Someone's walking across the floor upstairs, making the lamp sway.

He creeps up the stairs, and glances down between the treads. There are clothes hung up in the darkness beneath the stairs.

Joona reaches the first landing and moves almost without a

sound along the banister and into a bedroom containing a double bed. The blinds are drawn, and the ceiling light doesn't work.

Joona goes in, checks possible lines of fire, then moves sideways.

On top of the colourful bedspread is the telescopic sight of a hunting rifle.

He can hear someone breathing, very close to him. Joona steps further into the room and aims his pistol at the far corner. Behind the open wardrobe a round-shouldered man with light brown hair is standing staring at him.

The man is barefoot and wearing dark blue jeans and a white T-shirt with the name Stora Enso on it. He's hiding something behind his back as he moves slowly to his right, towards the bed.

'I'm from the National Crime Unit,' Joona says, lowering his pistol slightly.

'This is my house,' the man says in a subdued voice.

'You should have opened the door.'

Joona sees sweat running down the man's cheeks.

'Did you break my back door?' the man asks.

'Yes.'

'Can it be repaired?'

'I doubt it,' Joona replies.

There's a flicker in the smoked mirror on the sliding wardrobe door. Joona sees that the man is concealing a large kitchen knife behind his back.

'I need to look in your garage,' Joona says calmly.

'My car's in there.'

'Put the knife on the bed and show me the garage.'

The man takes out the knife and stares at it. The polished wooden handle is worn, and the blade has been sharpened many times.

'I haven't got time to wait,' Joona says.

'You shouldn't have broken my—'

Suddenly Joona detects movement behind him. Bare feet running across the floor. He only has time to move sideways slightly without taking his eyes off the knife. A shadow rushes towards him from behind. Joona twists his body, raises his arm, and follows through, adding force to the blow as he hits the rushing figure with his elbow.

Keeping the barrel of the pistol aimed at the man with the knife, he hits a boy in the chest with his elbow. The boy sighs, and all the air goes out of him, he reaches out for support, and sinks to his knees.

He breathes in deeply, curls up on the floor, crumpling the rag-rug beneath him, and lies there gasping on his side.

'They're from Afghanistan,' the man says quietly. 'They need help, and—'

'I'll shoot you in the leg if you don't put the knife down,' Joona says.

The man looks at the knife, then tosses it on the bed. Two smaller children suddenly appear in the doorway. They stare at Joona, wide-eyed.

'You're hiding refugees?' Joona asks. 'How much do you get for that?'

'As if I'd take money,' the man says indignantly.

'Do you?'

'No, I don't.'

Joona meets the boy's dark gaze.

'Do you pay him?' he asks in English.

The boy shakes his head.

'No human being is illegal,' the man says.

'You don't have to be afraid,' Joona tells the older boy. 'I promise I will help you if you are abused in any way.'

The boy looks into Joona's eyes for a long time, then shakes his head.

'Dennis is a good man,' he whispers.

'I'm glad,' Joona says, meets the man's gaze, then leaves the room.

Joona goes down the stairs, all the way to the garage. He stands for a while looking at the dusty Saab parked there, and thinks about the fact that Vicky and Dante have disappeared, and they have no more places to look.

33

Flora Hansen is mopping the shabby linoleum floor in the hall of the flat. Her left cheek still stings from the slap, and there's an odd buzzing sound in her ear. The floor has lost its shine over the years, but mopping it makes it look better for a little while at least.

The smell of detergent spreads through the rooms.

Flora has beaten all the mats, and has already mopped the living room, the cramped kitchen, and Hans-Gunnar's room, but she's waiting to do Ewa's bedroom until *Solsidan* starts on television.

Ewa and Hans-Gunnar both watch the series, and would never miss an episode.

Flora mops the floor energetically, the grey fabric of the mop-head keeps slapping into the skirting boards. She moves backwards, and bumps into the picture she made thirty years ago, when she was at preschool. All the children stuck different types of pasta to a piece of wood, then the whole thing was sprayed with gold paint.

The programme's theme tune comes on.

Now's her chance.

Flora feels a jolt of pain in her back as she picks up the heavy bucket and carries it into Ewa's room.

She shuts the door behind her and puts the bucket in the way to stop the door being pushed open easily.

Her heart is already beating hard as she dunks the mop in the bucket, squeezes out the excess water, and looks at the wedding photograph on the bedside table.

Ewa hides the key to the bureau in the back of the frame.

Flora takes care of all the housework in return for being allowed to live in the box room. She had to move back in with Ewa and Hans-Gunnar when her unemployment benefit ran out after she lost her job as an auxiliary nurse at Sankt Göran's Hospital.

When she was a child, Flora always thought her real parents were going to come and get her, but they were probably junkies, seeing as Ewa and Hans-Gunnar say they don't know anything about them. Flora arrived here when she was five years old, and has no memories from before then. Hans-Gunnar has always described her as a burden, and she's been desperate to get away ever since she was a teenager. When she was nineteen she got a job at the hospital and moved into her own flat in Kallhäll the same month.

The mop drips as Flora goes over to the window and starts mopping the floor. The linoleum is black under the radiator, from water damage. The old blinds are broken and hang crookedly between the inner and outer panes of glass. There is a wooden Dala horse from Rättvik on the windowsill between the pelargoniums.

Flora moves slowly towards the bedside table, stops and listens.

She can hear the television.

Ewa and Hans-Gunnar look young on the wedding photograph. She's wearing a white dress, him a suit with a silver-coloured tie. The sky is white. A black, onion-domed bell tower stands on a mound beside the church. The tower is sticking up behind Hans-Gunnar like a peculiar hat. Flora has never been able to put her finger on why she's always found the picture unsettling.

She tries to breathe calmly.

She gently leans the handle of the mop against the wall, but waits until she hears her aunt laugh at something on television, before picking up the photograph.

The ornate brass key is hanging from the back of the frame. Flora removes it from its hook, but her hands are shaking so much she drops it.

It hits the floor with a tinkle and bounces under the bed.

Flora has to reach out for support as she bends down.

She hears footsteps in the passageway, and lies still and waits. Her pulse is throbbing in her temples.

The floor outside the door creaks, then everything is quiet again.

The key is nestled among the dusty cables by the wall. She reaches in and picks it up, then gets to her feet and waits a few seconds before walking over to the bureau. She unlocks it, folds the heavy lid down, and pulls out one of the small drawers. Beneath the postcards from Paris and Mallorca is the envelope where Ewa keeps the money for the regular expenses. Flora opens the envelope containing the money for next month's bills, and takes half of it, puts the notes in her pocket, quickly puts the envelope back, and tries to slide the little drawer back in, but there's something stopping it.

'Flora,' Ewa calls.

She pulls out the drawer again, but can't see anything odd, and tries again, but her hands are shaking too much now.

She hears footsteps in the passageway again.

Flora pushes the drawer. It's slightly crooked, but it goes in, reluctantly. She closes the bureau but doesn't have time to lock it.

The door to her aunt's bedroom opens, hitting the bucket so hard that water sloshes out.

'Flora?'

She grabs the mop, mumbles something, and moves the bucket. She mops the spilled water, then carries on with the floor.

'I can't find my hand cream,' Ewa says.

There's a suspicious look in her eyes, and the wrinkles around her unhappy mouth are deeper than usual. She walks barefoot across the newly cleaned floor. Her yellow sweatpants are sagging and her white T-shirt is stretched tightly across her stomach and large bust.

'It . . . Maybe it's in the bathroom cabinet, I think that's where it is, next to the hair lotion,' Flora says, rinsing the mop again.

There's an advertising break on television, the volume is louder, and shrill voices are talking about athlete's foot. Ewa stops in the doorway and looks at her.

'Hans-Gunnar doesn't like the coffee,' she says.

'I'm sorry about that.'

Flora squeezes out the excess water.

'He says you're refilling the packet with cheaper stuff.'

'Why would I—'

'Don't lie,' Ewa snaps.

'I'm not,' Flora mumbles, and carries on mopping the floor.

'Well, you know you're going to have to go and get his cup, wash it up, and make some fresh coffee.'

Flora stops mopping the floor, leans the handle against the door, apologises, and goes into the living room. She can feel the key and money in her pocket. Hans-Gunnar doesn't even look at her when she picks up his cup next to the plate of biscuits.

'For fuck's sake, Ewa,' he cries. 'It's starting again!'

His voice makes Flora jump, and she hurries out. She passes Ewa in the hall, and catches her eye.

'Do you remember that I have to go on that jobseekers' course this evening?' Flora says.

'You still won't get a job.'

'No, but I have to go, it's the rules . . . I'll make some fresh coffee and try to finish the floor . . . then maybe I can get the curtains done tomorrow.'

34

Flora pays the man in the grey coat. Water drips onto her face from his umbrella. He gives her the door key and tells her to leave it in the antique shop's letterbox as usual when she's finished.

Flora thanks him and hurries on along the pavement. The seams in her old coat have started to come loose. She's forty years old, but her girlish face radiates loneliness.

The first block of Upplandsgatan closest to Odenplan is full of antique and curiosity shops. Their windows are full of chandeliers and glass-fronted cabinets, old tin toys, porcelain dolls, medals, and clocks.

Beside the mesh-covered door to Carlén Antiques is a narrower door leading to a small basement. Flora tapes a sheet of white paper to the dimpled glass.

SPIRITUALIST EVENING

A steep flight of steps leads down to the basement, where the pipes roar whenever someone above flushes a toilet or runs the taps. Flora has rented the room seven times to hold seances. She's had between four and six participants each time, which only just covers the cost of hiring the room. She's contacted a number of newspapers to see if they'd like to write about her ability to talk to the dead, but hasn't had any response. In advance of this evening's seance, she placed a larger advert in the new-age journal *Phenomena*.

Flora only has a few minutes before the participants arrive, but she knows what she has to do. She quickly moves the furniture and arranges twelve chairs in a circle.

On the table in the middle, she places the doll's house figures in nineteenth-century costume. A man and a woman with tiny, shiny porcelain faces. The idea is that they should help conjure up a sense of the past. Immediately after the seances, she hides them away again in the fuse-box, because she doesn't really like them.

She places twelve tea-lights in a circle around the dolls. She pushes some strontium chloride into the wax in one of the candles with a matchstick, then conceals the hole.

She hurries over to the dresser to set the alarm on the old clock. She tried that four sessions ago. The clapper is missing, so the only noise is a dry hacking sound from the cupboard. But, before she has time to wind the mechanism, the door opens from the street. The first participants are here. She hears umbrellas being shaken, then footsteps on the stairs.

Flora happens to see her own reflection in the rectangular mirror on the wall. She stops, takes a deep breath, and runs her hand across the grey dress she bought from the Salvation Army.

When she smiles, she instantly looks much calmer.

She lights some incense, then says hello quietly to Dina and Asker Sibelius. They hang up their coats and talk in subdued voices.

The participants are almost all old people who know they're approaching death. They're people who can't bear what they've lost, who can't accept the idea that death might be absolute.

The front door opens again and someone comes down the steps. It's an elderly couple she hasn't seen before.

'Welcome,' she says in a low voice.

Just as she's about to turn away, she stops and looks at the man as if she's seen something unusual, then pretends to shake off the feeling, and asks them to take a seat.

The door opens again and more participants arrive.

At ten past seven she has to accept that no one else is coming. Nine is still the most so far, but still too few for her to be able to replace the money she's borrowed from Ewa.

Flora tries to breathe calmly, but can feel her legs trembling as she returns to the large, windowless room. The participants are already sitting in a circle. They stop talking, and all eyes turn to look at her.

35

Flora Hansen lights the candles on the tray, and only when she's taken her seat does she allow herself to look around at the participants. She's seen five of them before, but the others are all new. Opposite her is a man who looks only thirty years old or so. His face is open and handsome in a boyish way.

'Welcome, all of you,' she says, and swallows hard. 'I think we should start at once . . .'

'Yes,' old Asker says in his creaking, friendly voice.

'Take hold of each other's hands to form the circle,' Flora says warmly.

The young man is looking straight at her. The look in his eyes is smiling and curious. A sense of excitement and expectation begins to flutter in Flora's stomach.

The silence that settles is black and imposing, ten people forming a circle and simultaneously feeling the dead gathering behind their backs.

'Don't break the circle,' she tells the group sternly. 'Don't break the circle, no matter what happens. That could mean that our visitors are unable to find their way back to the other side.'

Her guests are usually so old that they have lost far more people to death than they still have alive. For them death is a place full of familiar faces.

'You must never ask about the time of your own death,' Flora says. 'And you must never ask about the devil.'

'Why not?' the young man asks with a smile.

'Not all spirits are good, and the circle is only a portal to the other side . . .'

The young man's dark eyes glint.

'Demons?' he asks.

'I don't believe that,' Dina Sibelius smiles anxiously.

'I try to guard the portal,' Flora says seriously. 'But they . . . they can feel our warmth, they can see the candles burning.'

The room falls silent again. There's an odd, agitated buzzing sound, like a fly caught in a spider's web.

'Are you ready?' she asks slowly.

The participants mumble affirmatively, and Flora feels a shiver of pleasure when she realises that there's a whole new level of concentration in the room. She imagines she can hear their hearts beating, feel their pulses throbbing in the circle.

'I'm going to go into a trance now.'

Flora holds her breath and squeezes Asker Sibelius's and the new woman's hands. She shuts her eyes tightly, waits as long as she can, fights the instinct to breathe until she starts to shake, and then she inhales.

'We have so many visitors from the other side,' Flora says, after a pause.

Those who have been here before murmur supportively.

Flora can feel the young man looking at her, she can sense his alert, interested gaze on her cheeks, her hair, her neck.

She lowers her face and decides to start with Violet, to help convince the young man. Flora knows her background, but has made her wait. Violet Larsen is a terribly lonely person. She lost her only son fifty years ago. One evening the boy fell ill with meningitis, and no hospital would take him for fear of spreading the infection. Violet's husband drove the sick boy from hospital to hospital all night. When morning came his son died in his arms. The father was overcome by grief and died just a year later. One fateful night all her happiness died. Since then, Violet has been a childless widow. She has lived like that for half a century.

'Violet,' Flora whispers.

The old woman turns her moist eyes towards her.

'Yes?'

'There's a child here, a child who's holding a man by the hand.'

'What are their names?' Violet asks in a tremulous voice.

'Their names . . . the boy says you used to call him Jusse.'

Violet lets out a gasp.

'It's my little Jusse,' she whispers.

'And the man, he says you know who he is, you're his little flower.'

Violet nods and smiles.

'That's my Albert.'

'They have a message for you, Violet,' Flora goes on seriously. 'They say they're with you every day, every night, and that you're never alone.'

A large tear trickles down Violet's wrinkled cheek.

'The boy is telling you not to be sad. Mummy, he says, I'm fine. Daddy's with me all the time.'

'I miss you so much,' Violet sniffs.

'I can see the boy, he's standing right next to you, touching your cheek,' Flora whispers.

Violet is sobbing gently, and the room falls silent again. Flora waits for the heat of the candle to ignite the strontium chloride, but it takes a while.

She murmurs to herself and thinks about who to pick next. She closes her eyes and rocks back and forth slightly.

'There are so many here . . .' she mutters. 'There are so many . . . They're crowded at the narrow portal, I can feel their presence, they miss you, they're longing to talk to you . . .'

She falls silent as one of the candles on the tray starts to crackle.

'Don't squabble at the portal,' she mumbles.

The crackling candle suddenly flares bright red, and one member of the circle lets out a little scream.

'You haven't been invited, wait outside,' Flora says sternly, and waits until the red flame has gone. 'I want to speak to the man in the glasses,' she murmurs. 'Yes, come closer. What's your name?'

She listens.

'You want it the way you usually have it,' Flora says, looking up at the group. 'He says he wants it the way he usually has it. Exactly as usual, with faggots and boiled potatoes and . . .'

'That's my Stig!' the woman next to Flora exclaims.

'It's hard to hear what he's saying,' Flora goes on. 'There are so many here, they keep interrupting him.'

'Stig,' the woman whispers.

'He says he's sorry . . . he wants you to forgive him.'

Through the hand she's holding, Flora can feel the old woman shaking.

'I've forgiven you,' the old woman whispers.

36

After the seance is over Flora takes a very measured farewell. She knows that people usually want to be alone with their fantasies and memories.

She goes around the room slowly, blowing out the candles and rearranging the chairs. She can still feel a lingering satisfaction in her body from everything having gone so well.

She's left a box in the hall for the participants to leave their money in. She counts it and confirms that it isn't enough to pay back what she borrowed from Ewa's envelope. Next week she's got another spiritualist evening, and that's her last chance to earn the money back without being found out.

Despite the fact that she advertised in *Phenomena*, there still weren't enough participants. She's started waking up at night, staring dry-eyed into the darkness wondering what on earth she's going to do. Ewa usually pays the bills at the start of each month, and that's when she's going to realise that some of the money's missing.

The rain has stopped by the time she emerges into the street. The sky is black. Streetlamps and neon signs shimmer in the wet tarmac. Flora locks the door and drops the key through the letterbox of Carlén Antiques.

Just as she is removing the paper sign and putting it in her bag, she notices that there's someone standing in the next doorway. It's the young man from the seance. He takes a step towards her and smiles apologetically.

'Hi, I was wondering . . . can I offer you a glass of wine somewhere?'

'I can't,' she says with instinctive shyness.

'You're really great,' he says.

Flora doesn't know what to say, she can feel her face getting redder and redder the longer he looks at her.

'It's just that I'm going to Paris,' she lies.

'No time for me to ask a few questions?'

Now she realises that he must be a journalist from one of the newspapers she's been trying to contact.

'I'm leaving first thing tomorrow morning,' she says.

'Give me half an hour – can you manage that?'

As they hurry across the street to the nearest bistro, the young man tells her that his name is Julian Borg, and that he writes for the magazine *Close*.

A few minutes later Flora is sitting opposite him at a table covered by a white paper cloth. She takes a careful sip of the red wine. Sweet and sour blend in her mouth, and warmth spreads through her body. Julian Borg picks at a Caesar salad as he looks at her curiously.

'How did this start?' he asks. 'Have you always seen spirits?'

'When I was little I thought everyone could, it didn't seem at all odd to me,' she says, blushing because the lies come so easily.

'What did you see?'

'People I didn't know seemed to live with us . . . I just thought they were lonely people . . . and sometimes a child would come into my room and I'd try to play with her . . .'

'Did you tell your parents?'

'I learned very early to keep quiet,' Flora says, taking another sip of the wine. 'It's only fairly recently that I've realised that a lot of people actually need the spirits, even if they can't see them . . . and the spirits need people. I've finally found my purpose . . . I stand in the middle and help them to connect.'

She looks into Julian Borg's warm eyes for a few moments.

In fact it all started when Flora lost her job as an auxiliary nurse. She saw less and less of her old workmates, and in just one year she had lost touch with all her friends. When Flora's unemployment benefit ran out, she had to move back in with Ewa and Hans-Gunnar.

The job centre helped her get onto a course to become a nail technician, where she got to know one of the other participants, Jadranka from Slovakia. Jadranka went through low patches, but when she was feeling better she used to earn extra money by taking calls on a webpage called the Tarot Hotline.

They started to socialise, and Jadranka took Flora to a big seance held by the Society of Truth Seekers. Afterwards they talked about how it could be done much better, and just a few months later they found the basement room on Upplandsgatan. After two seances, Jadranka's depression got worse, and she was admitted to a clinic south of Stockholm. But Flora carried on holding the seances on her own.

She borrowed books from the library about healing, past lives, angels, auras, and astral bodies. She read about the Fox sisters, about the cabinet of mirrors, and Uri Geller, but the person she learned most from was the sceptic James Randi's attempts to uncover deceptions and tricks.

Flora has never seen any spirits or ghosts, but she's realised that she's good at saying the things people are desperate to hear.

'You use the word spirits rather than ghosts,' Julian says, putting his knife and fork together on the plate.

'They're the same thing,' she replies. 'But ghosts sound unpleasant and negative.'

Julian smiles, and there's a disarming honesty in his eyes when he says: 'I have to confess . . . I have a lot of trouble believing in spirits, but . . .'

'You just need to be open-minded,' Flora explains. 'Conan Doyle, for instance, he was a spiritualist . . . you know, the guy who wrote all those books about Sherlock Holmes . . .'

'Have you ever helped the police?'

'No, that . . .'

Flora blushes hard and doesn't know what to say, and looks at her watch.

'Sorry, you need to go,' he says, and takes hold of her hands across the table. 'I just want to say that I can tell you want to help people, and I think that's a good thing.'

His touch makes Flora's heart beat faster. She daren't meet his gaze again until he lets go, and they go their separate ways.

37

The red buildings that make up the Birgitta Home look idyllic in daylight. Joona is standing beside a huge silver birch talking to prosecutor Susanne Öst. Raindrops sparkle in the air as they fall from the branches.

'The police are still knocking on doors in Indal,' the prosecutor says. 'Someone drove into a traffic light, and there's a load of broken glass on the ground, but apart from that . . . nothing.'

'I need to talk to the girls again,' Joona says, thinking about the violence that played out inside the misted windows of the main building.

'I thought this business with Dennis would give us something,' Susanne says.

Joona thinks about the isolation room, and is seized by an unsettling suspicion. He tries to picture the sequence of brutal events, but can only make out shadows between the furniture. People's figures are transparent, like dusty glass, fluid, almost impossible to see.

He takes a deep breath, and suddenly the room where Miranda is lying with her hands over her face becomes perfectly clear. He can see the force behind the cascade of blood, the heavy blows. He can identify every impact, and sees how the angle changes after the third blow. The lamp starts to swing. Miranda's body is covered with blood.

'But there was no blood on her,' he whispers.

'What are you saying now?' the prosecutor whispers.

'I just need to check something,' Joona says as the door to the main building opens and a small man in tight protective clothing comes out.

He's Holger Jalmert, a professor of forensic science at Umeå University. He slowly removes his mask, to reveal a very sweaty face.

'I'll arrange an interview with the girls at the hotel in an hour,' Susanne says.

'Thanks,' Joona says, walking across the yard.

The professor is standing beside his van as he removes the protective clothing, places it in a rubbish bag and seals it carefully.

'The duvet's missing,' Joona says.

'So I finally get to meet Joona Linna,' the professor says, opening a fresh set of disposable overalls.

'Have you been in Miranda's room?'

'Yes, I'm finished in there.'

'There was no duvet.'

Holger stops with a frown.

'No, you're right about that.'

'Vicky must have hidden Miranda's duvet in the wardrobe or under the bed in her own room,' Joona says.

'I'm just about to start in there,' but Joona is already on his way towards the building.

The professor watches him go, and can't help thinking about what he's heard about Joona Linna: that he's so determined that he can stand and stare at a crime scene until it opens up like a book.

He puts the bag down, then hurries after the detective super-intendent, clutching the overalls.

They put the protective outfits on, the shoe covers and latex gloves, before they open the door to Vicky's bedroom.

'There's something under the bed,' Joona confirms.

'One thing at a time,' Holger murmurs, and puts a mask on.

Joona waits in the doorway while the professor photographs and measures the room with a laser so that he can locate anything he finds using a three-dimensional set of coordinates.

On the wall above the ornate Bible passages there's a poster of Robert Pattinson, with his pale face and dark eyeshadow, and there's a large bowl full of white plastic security tags from H&M on a shelf.

Joona watches Holger as he systematically covers the floor with foil, presses it down with a roller, then lifts it gently before photographing and packing it away. He moves slowly from the door to the bed, then across towards the window. As he lifts the foil from the floor, the imprint of a trainer is clearly visible on the layer of yellow gelatine.

'I need to go soon,' Joona says.

'But you'd like me to look under the bed first?'

Holger shakes his head at Joona's impatience, but carefully spreads a layer of plastic on the floor beside the bed. He kneels down and reaches one hand beneath the bed and takes hold of the object under there.

'It feels like a duvet,' he says, concentrating.

He carefully pulls the heavy duvet out onto the plastic. It's been twisted up, and is drenched in blood.

'I think Miranda had it around her shoulders when she was murdered,' Joona says in a low voice.

Harry folds the plastic over, then pulls a large sack over the wrapped duvet. Joona looks at his watch. He can stay another ten minutes. Holger goes on taking more samples. He uses moist cotton-buds on the dried blood, then lets them dry out before packing them.

'If you find anything that relates to either a person or a location, you must call me at once,' Joona says.

'Understood.'

For the hammer under the pillow the professor uses one hundred and twenty cotton-buds, which he wraps and labels individually. He collects strands of hair and textile fibres on adhesive plastic, wraps loose hairs in paper, and puts tissue samples and fragments of bone in test tubes so they can be chilled to prevent the growth of bacteria.

38

The conference room at the Hotel Ibis is busy, and Joona waits in the breakfast room while the prosecutor talks to the anxious staff about another room for the interviews. A television screen is shimmering from a metal frame near the ceiling.

Joona calls Anja and reaches her voicemail. He asks her to find out if there's a pathologist in Sundsvall.

The television news is starting to cover the murders at the Birgitta Home and the latest dramatic developments. They show pictures of the police cordon, the red buildings and the sign to the home. The perpetrator's suspected escape route is shown on a map, and a reporter stands in the middle of Highway 86 talking about the abduction and the police's unsuccessful roadblocks.

Joona gets to his feet and is walking towards the television as the voiceover reports that the mother of the missing boy has chosen to give the kidnapper a message in a live broadcast.

Pia Abrahamsson appears on the screen. Her face looks drawn as she sits at a kitchen table with a sheet of prompts in her hand.

'If you're hearing this,' she begins, 'I understand that you have been the victim of injustice, but Dante has nothing to do with that . . .'

Pia looks directly at the camera.

'You have to give him back,' she whispers, her chin trembling.

'I'm sure you're kind, but Dante is only four years old, and I know how frightened he is . . . he's so . . .'

She looks at the sheet of paper as tears run down her cheeks.

'You mustn't be mean to him, you mustn't hit my little . . .'

She bursts into racking sobs and turns her face away before they cut back to the studio in Stockholm.

A forensic psychiatrist from Säter Hospital is perched at a tall table, and explains just how serious the situation is to the newsreader: 'I haven't had access to the girl's medical records, of course, and I don't want to speculate as to whether she may have committed the two murders, but the fact that she's been living in this particular care home means that it's very possible that she's seriously mentally unstable, and even if—'

'What are the dangers?' the newsreader asks.

'It's possible that she doesn't care about the boy at all,' the psychiatrist explains. 'She might forget about him altogether at times . . . but he's only four years old, and if he suddenly starts to cry or call for his mother she could get angry and dangerous . . .'

Susanne Öst comes into the breakfast room to fetch Joona. With a small smile she offers him a cup of coffee and some cake. He thanks her and follows her to the lift, and they head up to the top floor. They walk into an uninspiring bridal suite, with a locked minibar and a Jacuzzi perched on battered gold paws.

Tuula Lehti is lying on the wide bed watching the Disney Channel. The responsible adult from the Victim Support Service nods to them. Susanne closes the door, and Joona pulls out a chair with a pink velvet seat and sits down.

'Why did you tell me that Vicky goes to see someone called Dennis?' Joona asks.

Tuula sits up and clutches a heart-shaped cushion to her stomach.

'I thought that's what she does,' she says simply.

'What made you think that?'

Tuula shrugs her shoulders and looks back at the television.

'Did she ever talk about someone called Dennis?'

'No,' she smiles.

'Tuula, I really do need to find Vicky.'

She kicks the bedspread and pink satin duvet onto the floor, then turns back to the television.

'Am I going to have to sit here all day?' she asks.

'No, you can go back to your room if you want,' the support person says.

'*Sinä olet vain pieni lapsi*,' Joona says in Finnish. You're only a small child.

'*Ei*,' she replies, and looks him in the eye.

'You shouldn't have to live in institutions.'

'I like it there,' she says blankly.

'Nothing bad ever happens to you?'

Her neck flushes and she blinks her white eyelashes.

'No,' she says bluntly.

'Miranda hit you yesterday.'

'Oh, yeah,' she mutters, and tries to squeeze the cushion.

'Why was she angry?'

'She thought I'd been poking about in her room.'

'Had you?'

Tuula licks the heart-shaped cushion.

'Yes, but I didn't take anything.'

'Why were you poking about in her room?'

'I poke about in everyone's rooms.'

'Why?'

'It's fun,' she replies.

'But Miranda thought you'd taken something from her?'

'Yeah, she was a bit cross . . .'

'What did she think you'd taken?'

'She didn't say,' Tuula smiles.

'What do you think it was?'

'I don't know, but it's usually pills . . . Lu Chu pushed me down the stairs once when she thought I'd taken her fucking benzos.'

'And if it wasn't drugs – what might she have thought you'd taken?'

'Who cares?' Tuula sighs. 'Make-up, jewellery . . .'

She sits on the edge of the bed again, leans back, and whispers something about a studded necklace.

'What about Vicky?' Joona asks. 'Does Vicky fight as well?'

'No,' Tuula smiles again.

'What does she do, then?'

'I shouldn't say, because I don't know her. I don't think she's ever spoken to me, but . . .'

The girl falls silent and shrugs.

'Why not?'

'Don't know.'

'But you must have seen her when she's angry?'

'She cuts herself, so you don't . . .'

Tuula stops and shakes her head.

'What were you going to say?'

'That you don't have to worry about her . . . she'll kill herself soon, then you'll have one less problem,' Tuula says without looking at Joona.

She stares at her fingers, mutters something to herself, then stands up abruptly and walks out of the room.

39

Caroline, the slightly older girl, comes into the room with the man from Victim Support. She's wearing a long, baggy T-shirt with a kitten on it. She has a runic tattoo, and the scars of old injections glint white in the crook of her arm.

She smiles shyly when she says hello to Joona. Then she sits down carefully on the armchair by the brown desk.

'Tuula says Vicky creeps out at nights to meet a boy,' Joona says.

'No,' Caroline laughs.

'What makes you say that?'

'She doesn't do that,' Caroline smiles.

'You sound very sure.'

'Tuula thinks everyone's a total whore,' she explains.

'So Vicky doesn't creep out?'

'Oh, she does that,' Caroline says, looking serious.

'What does she do when she gets out?' Joona asks, trying to hide his eagerness.

Caroline looks him in the eye briefly, then turns to gaze at the window.

'She sits behind the brew-house and phones her mother.'

Joona knows that Vicky's mother died before Vicky arrived at the Birgitta Home, but instead of confronting Caroline with this he asks calmly: 'What do they talk about?'

'Well . . . Vicky just leaves little messages on her mother's voicemail, but I think . . . if I've got this right, her mum never calls back.'

Joona nods, thinking that no one seems to have told Vicky that her mother is dead.

'Have you ever heard of someone called Dennis?' he asks.

'No,' Caroline says instantly.

'Think carefully.'

She looks him calmly in the eye, then jumps when Susanne Öst's phone buzzes as a text message arrives.

'Who would Vicky turn to?' Joona goes on, even though the energy has gone out of the conversation.

'Her mum – that's the only person I can think of.'

'Friends, boys?'

'No,' Caroline replies. 'But I don't know her . . . look, we're both doing ADL, so we see each other quite a bit, but she never talks about herself.'

'ADL?'

'Sounds like a condition, doesn't it?' Caroline laughs. 'It stands for All Day Lifestyle. Only for people who are really good. You get to try going out, you tag along to Sundsvall to get the groceries, exciting stuff like that . . .'

'You must have talked to each other when you were doing that?' Joona prompts.

'A bit, but not much.'

'So who else would she talk to, then?'

'No one,' she replies. 'Except Daniel, of course.'

'The counsellor?'

40

Joona and Susanne leave the bridal suite and walk back along the corridor to the lift. She laughs as they both reach for the button at the same time.

'When can we talk to Daniel Grim?' Joona asks.

'His doctor said it was too soon yesterday, which is understandable,' she says, glancing at him. 'This isn't easy. But I'll try prompting, and see what happens.'

They get out on the ground floor and head towards the front door, but stop at the reception desk when they see Gunnarsson standing there.

'Oh yes, I got a text message to let me know that the post-mortem's underway,' Susanne tells Joona.

'Good. When do you think we'll get the first results?' he asks.

'Go home,' Gunnarsson grunts. 'You shouldn't be here, you're not going to see any damn results, you . . .'

'OK, calm down,' Susanne interrupts, surprised.

'We're so damn stupid up here that we're happy to let some fucking observer take over the whole preliminary investigation just because he comes from Stockholm.'

'I'm trying to help,' Joona says. 'Seeing as—'

'Just shut up.'

'This is my preliminary investigation,' the prosecutor says, looking Gunnarsson hard in the eye.

'Then maybe you'd like to know that Joona Linna has got Internal Investigations on his back, and that senior prosecutor at National—'

'Are you under investigation?' Susanne Öst asks, taken aback.

'Yes,' Joona replies. 'But my role—'

'And here I am going about trusting you,' she says, her mouth contracting tightly. 'I've let you in on the investigation, listened to you. And it turns out you're just a liar.'

'I haven't got time for this,' Joona says seriously. 'I need to talk to Daniel Grim.'

'I'll do that,' Gunnarsson says with a snort.

'You do realise how serious this is,' Joona goes on. 'Daniel Grim could be the only person who—'

'I'm not prepared to work with you,' the prosecutor interrupts.

'You're suspended,' Gunnarsson says.

'I've lost all faith in you,' Susanne sighs, and starts to walk towards the door.

'Goodbye,' Gunnarsson says, and follows her.

'If you get a chance to talk to Daniel, you have to ask him about Dennis,' Joona calls after them. 'Ask Daniel if he knows who Dennis is, but above all ask him where Vicky might have gone. We need a name or a location. Daniel's the only person Vicky talked to, and—'

'Go home,' Gunnarsson laughs, then waves at him over his shoulder and walks out.

41

Counsellor Daniel Grim has worked part-time with the girls at the Birgitta Home for eleven years. He practises Cognitive Behavioural Therapy and Aggression Replacement Training, and talks to the residents individually at least once a week.

Daniel's wife Elisabet was a nurse, and had been working the night-shift when he thought she had gone with the badly shocked Nina Molander in the ambulance to the district hospital.

When Daniel realised that Elisabet was lying dead in the brew-house, he collapsed on the ground. He was talking confusedly about Elisabet's heart disease, but when he heard that she had been killed he fell completely silent. He had goosebumps on his arms, and sweat was running down his cheeks. He was breathing fast, and didn't say a word when he was lifted into the ambulance on a stretcher.

Superintendent Gunnarsson has already pulled out another cigarette when he gets out of the lift at Ward 52A in the psychiatric clinic at the West Norrland district hospital.

A young man in a white coat comes to meet him, they shake hands, then Gunnarsson follows him down a corridor with pale grey walls.

'Like I said on the phone, I don't think there's much point trying to interview him this soon . . .'

'No, but I can just have a little chat with him.'

The doctor stops and looks at Gunnarsson for a moment before he begins to explain: 'Daniel Grim is in a state of traumatised shock, which is commonly known as arousal. It's triggered by the hypothalamus and the limbic system, and—'

'I don't give a damn about that,' Gunnarsson interrupts. 'I just need to know if he's been stuffed with a load of drugs and is totally fucking out of it.'

'No, he's not out of it, but I wouldn't let you see him unless—'

'We've got a double murder—'

'You know full well whose decision is final here,' the doctor interrupts calmly. 'If I believe the patient's recovery might be adversely affected by talking to the police, then you'll just have to wait.'

'I understand,' Gunnarsson says, forcing himself to speak calmly.

'But seeing as the patient himself has repeatedly stated that he wants to help the police, I'm prepared to allow you to ask him a few questions in my presence.'

'I'm very grateful,' Gunnarsson smiles.

They set off down the corridor again, turn a corner, walk past a row of windows looking onto an internal courtyard full of skylights and ventilation units, before the doctor opens the door to one of the patients' rooms.

There are sheets and blankets lying on a small sofa, but Daniel Grim is sitting on the floor below the window with his back to the radiator. His face looks oddly relaxed, and he doesn't look up when they walk in.

Gunnarsson pulls up a chair and sits down in front of Daniel. After a while he swears, and crouches down next to the grieving man.

'I need to talk to you,' he says. 'We have to find Vicky Bennet . . . she's suspected of committing the murders at the Birgitta Home, and—'

'But I . . .'

Gunnarsson stops talking abruptly as Daniel whispers something, and waits for him to go on.

'I didn't hear what you said,' he says.

The doctor stands and watches them in silence.

'I don't think it was her,' Daniel whispers. 'She's a sweet girl, and . . .'

He raises his glasses and wipes the tears from his cheeks.

'I know you're governed by an oath of confidentiality,' Gunnarsson says. 'But is there any way you could help us find Vicky Bennet?'

'I'll try,' Daniel mumbles, then purses his lips together tightly.

'Does she know anyone who lives near the Birgitta Home?'

'Maybe . . . I'm having trouble sorting my thoughts out . . .'

Gunnarsson groans and shifts his position.

'You were Vicky's counsellor,' he says sternly. 'Where do you think she's gone? Let's ignore any question of guilt, because we really don't know. But we're fairly certain that she's kidnapped a child.'

'No,' he whispers.

'Who would she go to? Who would she get to help her?'

'She's frightened,' Daniel replies in a shaky voice. 'She curls up under a tree and hides, that's . . . that . . . What was the question?'

'Do you know of any particular hiding place?'

Daniel starts to mutter about Elisabet's heart, saying he was sure it was because of the problems with her heart.

'Daniel, you don't have to do this if it's too difficult,' the doctor says. 'I can ask the police to come back later if you need to rest.'

Daniel shakes his head quickly and tries to breathe calmly.

'Give me a few places,' Gunnarsson says,

'Stockholm.'

'Where?'

'I . . . I don't know about—'

'For fuck's sake!' Gunnarsson exclaims.

'Sorry, I'm sorry . . .'

Daniel's chin trembles, and the corners of his mouth droop as tears well up in his eyes, and he turns away and starts to sob loudly, his whole body shaking.

'She murdered your wife with a hammer and . . .'

Daniel hits the back of his head against the radiator so hard that his glasses fall into his lap.

'Get out of here,' the doctor says sharply. 'Not another word. This was a mistake, there won't be any further conversations.'

42

The car park outside the district hospital in Sundsvall is almost empty. The long building makes a desolate impression in the gloomy light. Dark brown bricks interspersed with white windows that look blind to the world. Joona walks straight through some low bushes towards the main entrance.

The reception counter in the foyer is unstaffed. He waits for a while at the darkened desk until a cleaner stops.

'Where's the pathology department?' Joona asks.

'Two hundred and fifty kilometres north of here,' the cleaner says good-naturedly. 'But if you want the pathologist, I can show you the way.'

They walk together through deserted corridors, then take a large lift down into the bowels of the hospital. It's cold, and the floor has cracked in several places.

The cleaner pulls open a pair of heavy metal doors, and at the far end of the corridor is a sign: Department of Clinical Pathology and Cytology.

'Good luck,' the man says, and gestures towards the door.

Joona thanks him and carries on along the corridor alone, following the tracks left on the linoleum floor by trolley wheels. He passes the laboratory, opens the door to the post-mortem room, and walks straight into the white-tiled space with a stainless-steel table at its centre. The light from the fluorescent lamps is overwhelming. A door hisses, and two people wheel a trolley in from the cold store.

'Excuse me,' Joona says.

A thin man in a white coat turns around. A pair of white-framed pilot's glasses glint in the light. Senior pathologist Nils 'the Needle' Åhlén from Stockholm, and a very old friend of Joona's. The man next to him is his young apprentice, his dyed dark hair hanging in clumps over the shoulders of his coat.

'What are you doing here?' Joona asks cheerfully.

'A woman from National Crime called and threatened me,' the Needle replies.

'Anja,' Joona says.

'I got really scared . . . she snapped at me and said that Joona Linna couldn't be expected to go all the way up to Umeå to talk to a pathologist.'

'But we're taking the opportunity to go to Nordfest seeing as we're here,' Frippe explains.

'The Haunted are playing at Club Destroyer,' Nils smiles.

'I can see why that would sway the balance,' Joona says.

Frippe laughs, and Joona notices the worn leather trousers beneath his coat, and the cowboy boots with bright blue shoe covers over them.

'We're done with the woman . . . Elisabet Grim,' Nils says. 'The only thing of any real note is probably the wounds to her hands.'

'Defence wounds?' Joona asks.

'Yes, but on the wrong side,' Frippe says.

'We can take a look in a while,' Nils says. 'But first it's time to give Miranda Ericsdotter a bit of attention.'

'When did they die – can you say?' Joona asks.

'As you know, body temperature sinks . . .'

'Algor mortis,' Joona says.

'Exactly, and that reduction follows a curve that levels out when it reaches room temperature . . .'

'He knows that,' Frippe says.

'So, taking that, together with the hypostasis and rigor mortis, we can say that the girl and the woman died at roughly the same time, late on Friday.'

Joona watches them roll the trolley over to the examination table, count to three, and then lift the light body in its sealed bag. When Frippe opens the bag, a rancid smell of wet bread and old blood spreads through the room.

The girl is lying on the table in the position she was found in, with her hands over her face and her ankles crossed.

Rigor mortis is caused by an increase in calcium in the motionless muscles, resulting in two different types of protein starting to combine. It almost always starts in the heart and diaphragm. After half an hour it can be detected in the jaw, and in the neck after two hours.

Joona knows it's going to take a lot of force to move Miranda's hands from her face.

Odd ideas suddenly start to float through his head. The possibility that it might not be Miranda behind those hands, that her face might have been altered, that her eyes might have been damaged or removed.

'We haven't received a formal request to examine her,' Nils Åhlén says. 'Why has she got her hands over her face?'

'I don't know,' Joona replies quietly.

Frippe is carefully photographing the body.

'I assume we're talking about a comprehensive post-mortem examination, and that you'll want a forensic statement?' Nils says.

'Yes,' Joona replies.

'We should really have a secretary when we're dealing with a homicide,' the pathologist mutters as he walks around the body.

'You're moaning again,' Frippe smiles.

'Yes, sorry,' Nils says, and stops for a moment behind Miranda's head before moving on.

Joona thinks of how the German-language poet Rilke wrote that the living were obsessed with drawing distinctions between the living and the dead. He claimed that there were other beings, angels, which didn't notice any difference.

'The hypostasis indicates that the victim has been left lying still,' Nils mutters.

'I believe Miranda was moved directly after the murder,' Joona says. 'The way I read the blood-spatter pattern, her body would have been limp when it was placed on the bed.'

Frippe nods.

'If it happened as soon as that, there wouldn't be any marks.'

Joona forces himself to look on while the two doctors conduct a thorough external examination of the body. He can't help thinking of his own daughter, who isn't much younger than this girl, lying still and inscrutable in front of him.

A network of yellow veins has started to show through the white skin. Around her neck and down her thighs the veins look like a pale river system. Her previously flat stomach has become rounder and darker.

Joona watches them work, registers the two doctors' actions, sees Nils Åhlén cut calmly through her white underpants and pack them for analysis, listens to their conversation and conclusions, but is at the same time back at the crime scene in his mind.

Nils states that there is a total absence of defensive injuries, and Joona hears him discuss the lack of soft tissue damage with Frippe.

There are no signs of a fight or other abuse.

Miranda waited for the blows to her head, she didn't try to run, didn't put up any resistance.

Joona thinks back to the bare room where she spent her last hours as he watches the two men pulling out strands of hair by the root for comparative tests, and filling EDTA tubes with blood.

Nils scrapes beneath her fingernails, then turns towards Joona and clears his throat sharply: 'No traces of skin . . . she didn't defend herself.'

'I know,' Joona says.

When they start to examine the injuries to her skull, Joona moves closer and stands where he can see everything.

'Repeated blows to the head with a blunt object is the probable cause of death,' Nils says when he sees how closely Joona is watching.

'From the front?' Joona asks.

'Yes, from the front, slightly off to one side,' Nils replies, pointing at the bloody hair. 'Compression fracture of the temporal bone . . . We'll do a digital tomography scan, but I assume that the large blood vessels on the inside of the skull have been detached and that we'll find fragments of bone in the brain.'

'Just like with Elisabet Grim, we're bound to find trauma to the cerebral cortex,' Frippe says.

'Myelin in the hair,' Nils says, pointing.

'Elisabet had broken blood vessels in her skull, and blood and cerebrospinal fluid had run into her nasal cavity,' Frippe says.

'So you think they were killed at roughly the same time?' Joona says.

'Close together,' Frippe nods.

'They were both attacked from the front, both have the same cause of death,' Joona says. 'The same murder weapon, and . . .'

'No,' Nils interrupts. 'They were killed with different implements.'

'But the hammer . . .' Joona says, almost inaudibly.

'Yes, Elisabet's skull was crushed with the hammer,' Nils says. 'But Miranda was killed with a rock.'

Joona stares at him.

'She was killed with a rock?'

43

Joona stayed in the pathology lab until he had seen Miranda's face behind her hands. The notion that she hadn't wanted to be seen after death is still lingering. He had felt a peculiar unease when they forced her hands away.

Now he's sitting at Gunnarsson's desk in Sundsvall police station reading the preliminary forensic report. Yellow light is streaming through the blinds. A woman is sitting a short distance away in the glow of a computer screen. The phone rings and she mutters irritably as she looks at the number on the display.

One wall is covered with maps and pictures of Dante Abrahamsson, the missing boy. The bookcases on the other walls are full of files and piles of paper. The photocopier rumbles almost nonstop. A radio is switched on in the staffroom, and when the pop music falls silent Joona hears the announcement for the third time.

'We have a public announcement,' the presenter says, before reading the description. 'The police are looking for a fifteen-year-old girl and a four-year-old boy. They might be together. The girl has long blonde hair, and the boy is wearing glasses, a dark blue top, and dark corduroy trousers. They were last seen in a red Toyota Auris on Highway 86, heading towards Sundsvall. Please contact the police on 114 14 if you have any information . . .'

Joona gets up and goes into the empty staffroom, changes the channel to P2, then goes back to the desk with a cup of coffee. An old recording of an icily clear soprano rings out: Birgit Nilsson singing the role of Brünnhilde in Wagner's *Ring of the Nibelung*.

Joona sits with the cup of coffee in his hand, thinking about the boy who has been abducted by a girl who might be psychotic.

He can see them in his mind's eye, hiding in a garage, the boy forced to lie under blankets on a cement floor, tied up and with tape over his mouth.

He must be extremely frightened, if he's still alive.

Joona goes on reading the forensic report.

It's been confirmed that the keys in the lock of the isolation room of the Birgitta Home belonged to Elisabet Grim, and the boots that left the bloody footprints at the crime scenes were found in Vicky Bennet's wardrobe.

Two murders, Joona thinks. One appears primary, the other secondary. Miranda was the primary victim, but in order to kill her, the perpetrator was forced to take the keys from Elisabet.

According to the forensics team's conjectured reconstruction of events, an argument earlier on Friday evening could have been the trigger, although there could be a longer period of rivalry in the background.

Vicky Bennet had taken the hammer from the store before bedtime, along with the large boots that they all used, and then waited in her room. Once the others had fallen asleep, she went to see Elisabet Grim and demanded the keys. Elisabet refused and fled down the corridor, out into the yard, and into the brew-house. Vicky Bennet followed her and beat her to death with the hammer, took the keys, and returned to the main building, where she unlocked the isolation room and beat Miranda to death. For some reason she laid her victim on the bed and arranged her hands to cover her face. Vicky then returned to her room, hid the hammer and boots, and escaped out of the window into the forest.

That's the crime scene investigation team's outline of events.

Joona thinks to himself that it will be several weeks before the National Forensics Laboratory produce their results, and that the CSI team have simply assumed that both Miranda and Elisabet were killed with the hammer.

But Miranda was killed with a rock.

Joona can see her before him, a thin girl lying on her bunk, her skin already as pale as porcelain, her legs crossed at the ankle, the bruises on her thigh, the cotton pants, the little stud in her navel, the hands covering her face.

Why was she killed with a rock, when Vicky had access to a hammer?

Joona stares hard at every single photograph from the crime scene, then imagines the chain of events the way he usually does. He puts himself in the murderer's place and forces himself to see each horrifying choice as unavoidable. Because to anyone who kills another person, murder is the only possible option. The simplest and best option at the time.

The murder doesn't seem unpleasant or bestial, but rational or attractive.

Sometimes the perpetrator can't see further than one blow at a time, merely needs to vent and then justify a single blow. The next blow is away in the distance, might feel decades away until it's suddenly upon him. For the murderer, death can be the conclusion to an epic saga that began with the first blow and concludes just thirteen seconds later with the last.

All the evidence is pointing at Vicky Bennet, everyone is assuming that she murdered Miranda and Elisabet, yet at the same time, no one really seems to consider Vicky capable of doing it, either physically or mentally.

But everyone has it in them, Joona thinks, putting the report back in Gunnarsson's tray. We see reflections of it in our dreams and fantasies. Everyone carries violence inside them, but most people manage to tame themselves.

Gunnarsson comes into the police station and hangs his crumpled coat up. He puts his hand to his mouth and belches, then walks into the staffroom. When he comes out with a cup of coffee and catches sight of Joona, he grins: 'Aren't they missing you in Stockholm?'

'No,' Joona replies.

Gunnarsson sniffs a pack of cigarettes, then turns to the woman sitting at the computer: 'All reports come straight to me.'

'OK,' she says, without looking up.

Gunnarsson mutters something.

'How did your conversation with Daniel Grim go?' Joona asks.

'Fine. Not that it's any of your business. I had to take it bloody carefully, though.'

'What did he have to say about Vicky?'

Gunnarsson makes a whistling sound with his lips and shakes his head: 'Nothing that's any use to the police.'

'You asked about Dennis?'

'That fucking doctor was on me like he was the guy's mother and put a stop to the whole thing.'

Gunnarsson scratches his neck hard, and seems unaware that he's holding a packet of cigarettes and a lighter in his hand.

'I want copies of Holger Jalmert's report when it arrives,' Joona says. 'And the test results from the National Forensics Lab, and—'

'OK, you need to fuck off out of my sandpit now,' Gunnarsson interrupts.

He smiles broadly towards his female colleague, but becomes less certain when he sees the serious look in Joona's grey eyes.

'You have no idea of how to find Vicky Bennet and the boy,' Joona says slowly, getting to his feet. 'And you have no idea how to make any progress with the murder investigation.'

'I'm counting on getting information from the public,' Gunnarsson replies. 'There's always someone who's seen something.'

44

This morning Flora woke up just before her alarm clock went off. Hans-Gunnar wanted his breakfast in bed at 8.15. Once he had got up, Flora had to air and make his bed. Ewa sat in a chair wearing yellow jogging bottoms and a flesh-coloured bra watching her. She stood up and checked that the bottom sheet was perfectly smooth, and properly tucked under the corners of the mattress. The crocheted bedspread had to be arranged with exactly the same amount of overhang on both sides, and Flora had to do it three times before it was good enough for Ewa.

Now it's lunchtime, and Flora has returned home from the Ica supermarket with the groceries and cigarettes for Hans-Gunnar. She hands over the change, then stands and waits as usual while he checks the receipt.

'Bloody hell, that cheese was expensive,' he says unhappily.

'You told me to buy cheddar,' Flora points out.

'Not if it's that damn expensive, surely you can understand that? If it's that much, you buy a different cheese.'

'Sorry, I thought—'

She doesn't have time to finish the sentence. Hans-Gunnar's signet ring suddenly flashes in front of her face as he gives her a hard slap. It happens very fast. Her ear starts to ring and her cheek stings.

'You did say you wanted cheddar,' Ewa says from the sofa. 'It's hardly her fault.'

Hans-Gunnar mutters something about idiots, then goes out onto the balcony to smoke. Flora puts the food away, then goes back to her room and sits on the bed. She touches her cheek gingerly and thinks about how tired she is of getting slapped about by Hans-Gunnar. Sometimes he hits her several times a day. She always knows when it's coming because he never looks at her otherwise. The worst thing isn't the pain, but how breathless he gets when he stares at her afterwards.

She can't remember him hitting her when she was little. He used to work, and wasn't at home much. Once he even pointed out different countries to her on the globe in his room.

Ewa and Hans-Gunnar go out to play boules with their friends. Flora sits in her room. As soon as she hears the front door close she looks over to the corner. On the old dresser she keeps an ornament her teacher gave her in high school. A horse and cart made of glass. In the top drawer she has one of the stuffed toys she had as a child, a Smurf with blonde hair and high heels. The middle drawer contains a stack of neatly ironed towels. Flora lifts the towels out and takes out her smart green dress. She bought it earlier in the summer from the Salvation Army, she's never worn it outside her room, but she often tries it on in there when Ewa and Hans-Gunnar aren't home.

She starts to unbutton her cardigan when she hears voices from the kitchen. It's the radio. She goes to turn it off and discovers that Ewa and Hans-Gunnar have been eating cake. The floor in front of the larder is covered with crumbs. They've left half a glass of strawberry juice on the worktop, and the bottle is still out.

Flora fetches a cloth and wipes the crumbs from the floor, then rinses the cloth and washes the glass.

On the radio there's a report about a murder in the north of Sweden.

A girl has been found murdered in a care home for girls with histories of self-harm.

Flora rinses the cloth and hangs it on the tap.

She listens as the report says that the police have no comment

to make about the ongoing investigation, but the reporter interviews some of the other girls live on air.

'You want to know what's happened, don't you, so I pushed
my way through,' one girl says in a broken voice. 'I didn't have
time to see much because they pulled me away from the door,
I screamed, but then I realised there was no point.'

Flora picks up the bottle of juice and starts to walk towards
the fridge.

'Can you tell us what you saw?'

'Yes, I saw Miranda, she was lying on her bed like this, just
like this, yeah?'

Flora stops and listens to the radio.

'She had her eyes closed?' the reporter says.

'No, like this, with both hands in front of her face, like she
was—'

'God, you're such a liar!' someone shouts behind her.

Flora suddenly hears something hit the floor and feels something splash her legs. She looks down and sees that she's dropped
the bottle. Suddenly her stomach churns, and she only just gets
to the bathroom in time before she throws up.

45

When Flora comes out from the bathroom the news has finished. A woman with a German accent is discussing autumn menus. Flora picks up the pieces of glass, wipes the spilled juice, and then stands there in the middle of the floor. She stares at her cold white hands, then walks to the phone in the hall and calls the police.

Flora waits, listening to the dry crackle on the line as the call goes through.

'Police,' a woman answers in a weary voice.

'Hello, my name is Flora Hansen, and I'd like to—'

'Hold on,' the woman says. 'I didn't catch that.'

'OK,' Flora says. 'My name is Flora Hansen, and I've got a tip-off about the murder of the girl up in Sundsvall.'

There's a moment's silence. Then the weary but calm voice speaks again.

'What did you want to tell us?'

'Do you pay for tip-offs?' Flora asks.

'No, I'm afraid not.'

'But I . . . I think I saw the dead girl.'

'You mean you were there when it happened?' the police officer says quickly.

'I'm a spiritual medium,' Flora says in a secretive voice. 'I'm in contact with the dead . . . and I saw it all, but I think . . . I think I'd remember better if I got paid.'

'You're in contact with the dead,' the police officer repeats tiredly. 'Is that your tip-off?'

'The girl was holding her hands in front of her face,' Flora says.

'For heaven's sake, that's been in all the newspapers!' the woman snaps impatiently.

Flora's heart shrinks with shame. She feels like being sick again. Cold sweat is running down her back. She hadn't planned what she was going to say, but realises now that she should have said something else. The papers had been on display at the supermarket when she was getting the food and Hans-Gunnar's cigarettes.

'I didn't know that,' she whispers. 'I'm just saying what I've seen . . . I saw lots more things, things you might be interested in paying for.'

'We don't pay for—'

'But I saw the murder weapon, you might think you've found the murder weapon, but that's wrong, because I saw—'

'You do know you can be fined for wasting police time?' the police officer interrupts. 'It's a genuine offence. I don't mean to sound angry, but surely you appreciate that while I'm talking to you someone who might have real information could be trying to get through.'

'Yes, but I—'

Flora is about to start talking about the murder weapon when the line clicks. She looks at the phone, then dials the number for the police again.

46

Pia Abrahamsson is staying in a flat owned by the Swedish Church in a large wooden house in one of the leafier parts of Sundsvall. The apartment is large and beautiful, furnished with classic pieces by Carl Malmsten and Bruno Mathsson. The deacons who have been bringing her food have encouraged her to talk to one of the priests, but Pia can't bring herself to do it.

She's spent the whole day driving her rental car along the same route, past the small villages, around Indal, up and down the logging tracks.

Several times she encountered police officers who told her to go home.

Now she's lying on the bed with her clothes on, staring out into the darkness. She hasn't slept since Dante went missing. Her phone rings. She reaches for it, stares at it, then hits the mute button. It's her parents. They keep calling. Pia gazes out into the darkness of the unfamiliar flat.

Inside her head she can hear Dante crying the whole time. He's frightened and asking for his mum, keeps saying he wants to go home to his mummy.

She can't lie there any longer, and gets up.

Pia grabs her jacket and opens the front door. She can taste blood in her mouth as she gets back in the rental car and starts driving. She has to find Dante. What if he's sitting in a ditch by the side of the road? He might have hidden under a piece of cardboard. Perhaps the girl has just dumped him somewhere?

The roads are dark and empty. Almost everyone seems to be asleep. She tries to see into the dense darkness beyond the headlights.

She pulls in at the spot where her car was taken, and sits there with her hands shaking on the steering wheel before she turns and starts to drive back. She heads into the small town of Indal, where the car – and Dante – probably disappeared. She drives slowly past a preschool, then turns at random into Solgårdsvägen and rolls past the dark villas.

A movement under a trampoline makes her stop abruptly and get out of the car. She stumbles into the garden through a low rose hedge, scratching her legs, and goes over to the trampoline, only to find a fat cat hiding in the darkness.

She turns towards the brick house and stares at the closed blinds with her heart thudding.

'Dante?' she calls. 'Dante? It's Mummy! Where are you?'

Her voice is hoarse and sad. Lights go on inside the house. Pia walks to the next house, rings on the door, then bangs on it before moving on to an outhouse.

'Dante!' she cries as loudly as she can.

She goes from house to house along Solgårdsvägen calling for her son, beating on locked garage doors with her hands, looking inside small playhouses. She scrambles through thorny undergrowth and crosses a ditch, only to find herself back on Indalsvägen again.

A car brakes with shrieking tyres, and she takes a step back and falls. She stares up at the uniformed police officer as she hurries over to her.

'Are you OK?'

The policewoman helps her to her feet, and Pia stares blankly at the woman's large nose and blonde plaits.

'Have you found him?' Pia asks.

The second officer comes over and says they'll drive her home.

'Dante's scared of the dark,' she says, and hears how weak her voice sounds. 'I'm his mum, but I used to lose my patience

135

with him, I'd force him to go back to his own bed when he came to mine. He'd stand there in his pyjamas and tell me he was scared, but I . . .'

'Where have you left the car?' the woman asks, taking hold of Pia's arm.

'Let go of me!' Pia shouts, and pulls free. 'I have to find him!'

She hits the policewoman in the face and screams as they overpower her and hold her down on the tarmac. She struggles to get free, but they lock her arms behind her back and hold her still. Pia feels her chin scrape the road hard, and weeps as helplessly as a child.

47

Joona Linna is thinking about the lack of witnesses: no one seems to know anything about Vicky Bennet, and no one has seen anything. He's driving along a stunningly beautiful stretch of road, past rolling fields and sparkling lakes, until he reaches a white stone house. There's a lemon tree in a huge pot on the veranda, covered with small yellow-green fruit.

He rings on the door, waits, then walks around the house.

On one of the white garden chairs beneath an apple tree sits Nathan Pollock, with a large plaster-cast around his leg.

'Nathan?'

The thin man stiffens as he turns towards Joona. He shades his eyes with one hand, then smiles in surprise: 'Joona Linna, is that really you?'

Nathan's silver-grey hair is gathered in a small ponytail over one shoulder, and he's wearing black trousers and a loose-knit sweater. Nathan Pollock is a member of the National Homicide Commission, a group of six experts who help out with complex murder cases throughout Sweden.

'Joona, I'm really sorry about the internal investigation, I shouldn't have taken you to visit the Brigade.'

'It was my choice,' Joona says, sitting down.

Nathan shakes his head slowly.

'I've fallen out badly with Carlos about the fact that you're being scapegoated like this.'

'Was that how you broke your leg?' Joona asks.

'No, there was an angry female bear that came rushing into the garden,' Nathan replies, and grins, showing his gold tooth.

'Either that or he fell off a ladder when he was picking apples,' a high voice says behind them.

'Matilda,' Joona says.

He gets up and hugs the woman with thick, red-brown hair and skin covered with freckles.

'Superintendent,' she smiles, and sits down. 'I hope you've brought some work for my dear husband before he has to start doing sudoku.'

'I might have,' Joona says tentatively.

'Really?' Nathan smiles, scratching his leg.

'I've seen the crime scene, and I've seen the bodies, but I haven't got access to any reports or test results . . .'

'Because of the internal investigation?'

'It isn't my preliminary investigation, but I'd like to hear your opinion.'

'That'll cheer him up,' Matilda smiles, and pats her husband's cheek.

'Nice of you to think of me,' Pollock says.

'You're the best detective I know,' Joona replies.

He sits back down and starts to give a thorough account of what he knows about the case, and after a while Matilda leaves the table and goes back to the house. Pollock listens intently, occasionally asking questions about some of the details, before nodding and asking Joona to go on.

A grey tabby cat comes over and rubs against Nathan's legs. Birds sing in the trees as Joona describes the rooms and the positions of the bodies, the blood-spatter patterns, the stains and puddles, dried blood and encrustation. Nathan closes his eyes and concentrates on Joona's description of the hammer under the pillow, the blood-stained duvet, and the open window.

'Let's see,' Pollock whispers. 'Extreme violence, but no bite marks, no attempt at dismemberment . . .'

Joona says nothing and lets Pollock think things through for himself.

Nathan Pollock has put together plenty of perpetrator profiles – and he hasn't been wrong yet.

Profiling is a way of closing in on a perpetrator by interpreting the crime as a metaphor for the perpetrator's psychological state. The logical basis for this is that the inner life of an individual is to some extent reflected in that person's actions and behaviour. If a crime is chaotic, the criminal's mental state is chaotic, and this chaos can only be concealed if the perpetrator is a loner.

Joona watches Nathan Pollock's lips move while he thinks. Every so often he whispers something to himself, or fiddles unconsciously with his ponytail.

'I think I can picture the bodies . . . and the spatter pattern,' he says. 'You know all this, of course . . . that most murders are committed in the heat of the moment. Then the blood and chaos leads to panic. That's when people reach for the angle-grinders and bin-bags . . . or slide about in the blood with a scrubbing brush and leave evidence everywhere.'

'But not this time.'

'This murderer really hasn't tried to hide anything at all.'

'That same thought occurred to me,' Joona agrees.

'The violence is extreme, and methodical. This isn't a punishment that's got out of hand, the intent in both cases was to kill . . . no more, no less. Both victims are shut in small rooms, they can't escape . . . The violence isn't frenzied, but more like an execution, slaughter, even.'

'We think the perpetrator is a girl,' Joona says.

'A girl?'

Joona meets Nathan's surprised gaze and shows him a photograph of Vicky Bennet.

Nathan lets out a laugh and shrugs his shoulders.

'I'm sorry, but I seriously doubt that.'

Matilda comes out with tea and jam doughnuts, and sits down at the table. Nathan pours out three cups.

'You don't think a girl could have done this?' Joona asks.

'I've never come across anything similar,' Nathan smiles.

'Not all girls are nice,' Matilda says.

Nathan points at the photograph.

'Is she known to be violent?'

'No. Quite the reverse.'

'Then you're chasing the wrong person.'

'We're sure she kidnapped a young boy yesterday.'

'But she hasn't killed him?'

'Not as far as we know,' Joona says, picking up a doughnut.

Nathan leans back in his chair and squints up at the sky.

'If the girl isn't considered violent, if she has no criminal record and hasn't been the subject of a similar investigation before, then I don't think it's her,' he says, looking at Joona intently.

'But if it is?' Joona persists.

Nathan shakes his head and blows on his tea.

'It doesn't make sense,' he replies. 'I've just been reading about one of David Canter's research projects . . . I'm sure you know that he focuses his profiles on the role the perpetrator allocates to the victim during the crime. I've thought something similar myself . . . that the perpetrator uses the victim as a sort of opposite number in the drama.'

'Yes . . . that's one way of putting it,' Joona says.

'And according to David Canter's model, covering the girl's face means that the murderer wants to deny her her face, turn her into nothing but an object . . . Men who belong to that group often use excessive violence . . .'

'What if they're just playing hide-and-seek?' Joona interjects.

'How do you mean?' Nathan says, looking into his grey eyes.

'The victim counts to a hundred and the perpetrator hides.'

Nathan smiles and then lets the idea sink in.

'In which case the search is the whole point . . .'

'Yes, but where?'

'The only advice I have is to look in old haunts,' Pollock says. 'The past reflects the future . . .'

48

The National Crime Unit is the only centralised operational police department tasked with combatting serious crime on both a national and an international level.

The head of the National Crime Unit, Carlos Eliasson, is standing at the low window of his eighth-floor office looking out at the steep slopes of Kronoberg Park.

He doesn't know that Joona Linna is currently walking along one of the paths across the park after a brief visit to the old Jewish cemetery at its far corner.

Carlos sits down at his desk again and doesn't notice the tousle-haired detective cross Polhemsgatan and walk into the glazed entrance hall of Police Headquarters.

Joona passes a banner about the role of the police in a changing world. Benny Rubin is sitting hunched in front of his computer, and he overhears part of a conversation from Magdalena Ronander's room about increased cooperation with Europol.

Joona has returned to Stockholm because he has been summoned to a meeting with the two officers from Internal Investigations later in the day. He fetches the post from his pigeonhole, sits down at his desk, and as he starts to look through the envelopes he can't help thinking that he agrees with Nathan Pollock.

It's hard to reconcile the image of Vicky Bennet with the two murders.

Even if the police don't have access to her psychiatric records, there's nothing to indicate that Vicky Bennet might be dangerous. She isn't in any police databases, and people who have met her seem to regard her as withdrawn and well-meaning.

Even so, all the forensic evidence so far points to her.

And everything indicates that she's abducted the little boy.

Perhaps he's lying in a ditch somewhere with his head smashed in.

But if he's still alive, there's no time to lose.

Perhaps he's sitting inside the car with Vicky, in some dark garage, perhaps she's shouting at him right now, working herself up into a state of violent rage.

Look backwards, that was Nathan's advice, as usual.

Simple and obvious, really – the past always reflects the future.

During her fifteen years Vicky has managed to move house plenty of times, from her homeless mother, to foster homes, emergency placements, and children's homes.

She's out there somewhere.

The answer could lie with any of the families she lived with, it could be buried in a conversation with social workers, counsellors, or foster parents.

There must be people she's trusted and confided in.

Joona is about to get up to go and ask Anja if she's managed to find any names and addresses, when she appears in the doorway. Her bulky frame is squeezed into a tight black skirt, and she's wearing an angora sweater as usual. Her blonde hair is artistically arranged, and her lipstick is bright red.

'Before I go on, I just want to say that over fifteen thousand children are rehomed each year,' Anja begins. 'The politicians said they were introducing choice into the system when they allowed private companies to take part. Now most children's homes are owned by venture capitalists. It's just like auctions of children in the past, the one that demands least money gets custody . . . they cut back on staffing, education, therapy, and dental care, all to make a profit . . .'

'I know,' Joona says. 'But Vicky Bennet . . .'

'I thought I might try to get hold of the latest placement supervisor.'

'Can you do that?' Joona asks.

She smiles indulgently and tilts her head.

'I've already done it, Joona Linna . . .'

'You're brilliant,' Joona says seriously.

'Anything for you.'

'I don't deserve that,' Joona smiles.

'No, you're right,' she says, and leaves the room.

He sits there for a few moments, then gets up, goes out into the corridor, and knocks on Anja's door.

'The addresses,' she says, pointing to a bundle of papers on top of the printer.

'Thanks.'

'When the placement supervisor heard my name, he said that Sweden used to have a brilliant butterfly swimmer with the same name,' she says, and blushes.

'I hope you told him that was you?'

'No, but he still told me that Vicky Bennet didn't appear in the population register until she was six years old. Her mother, Susie, was homeless, and seems to have given birth to her without the involvement of the health service. Her mother was eventually taken into psychiatric care, and Vicky was placed with two voluntary carers here in Stockholm.'

Joona holds the still-warm list, looks at the dates and placements, the rows of names and addresses, from the first – Jack and Elin Frank at Strandvägen 47 – to the last, Ljungbacken children's home in Uddevalla, and then the Birgitta Home outside Sundsvall. Several times there is a note indicating that the child had expressed a wish to return to the first foster family.

'The child has asked to be allowed to return to the Frank family, but the family has declined,' is the repeated rather dry comment.

Eventually Vicky Bennet ended up living in institutions rather than foster homes. Emergency placements, evaluation clinics, treatment centres, and care homes.

He thinks about the bloody hammer under her pillow and the blood on the windowsill.

The clenched, thin face in the photograph, and the tangled fair hair.

'Can you check to see if Jack and Elin Frank still live at the same address?'

A look of amusement crosses Anja's round face, and she pouts and says: 'You should try reading a few gossip magazines.'

'What do you mean?'

'Elin Frank and Jack are divorced, but she kept the apartment . . . it was her money, after all.'

'So they're famous?' Joona asks.

'She does a lot of charity stuff, more than most rich people . . . she and her ex-husband Jack put a lot of money into Children's Villages, aid funds, and so on.'

'So Vicky Bennet actually lived with them?'

'It doesn't seem to have gone very well,' Anja replies.

Joona starts to walk out with the printouts, but turns and looks back at Anja in the doorway.

'How can I thank you?'

'I've signed us up for a course,' she replies quickly. 'Promise you'll come with me.'

'What sort of course?'

'Relaxation . . . Kama Sutra something or other . . .'

49

Strandvägen 47 is located directly opposite the Djurgården Bridge. It's a smart building with an elaborate entrance and a dark, ornate stairwell.

Elin and Jack Frank were the only family Vicky wanted to go back to, even though she only lived there a short time. She kept asking to go back, but the Franks chose to reject her appeals.

When Joona Linna rings the door with the name Frank embossed on a shimmering black sign it opens almost at once. A relaxed man with short, straw-coloured hair and an even suntan looks curiously at the tall detective.

'I'm looking for Elin Frank.'

'Robert Bianchi, I'm Elin's *consigliere*,' the man says, and holds out his hand.

'Joona Linna, National Crime Unit.'

A slight smile plays across the man's lips.

'That sounds exciting, but—'

'I need to speak to her.'

'May I ask what this is regarding? I don't want to disturb her unnecessarily . . .'

The man tails off when he sees the cool look in Joona's grey eyes.

'Wait in the hall and I'll see if she's accepting visitors,' he says, and disappears through a door.

The hall is white and completely devoid of furniture. There are no cupboards, no objects, no shoes and coats. Just smooth white walls and a single large mirror with tinted white glass.

Joona tries to imagine a child like Vicky in this environment. An anxious, troubled little girl whose existence wasn't even known to the authorities until she was six years old. A child who had got used to home meaning the garage or pedestrian underpass where you just happened to spend the night.

Robert Bianchi returns with a calm smile and asks Joona to follow him. They pass through a large, airy sitting room containing several sofas and an ornamental tiled stove. Thick carpets muffle the sound of their steps as they walk through the various reception rooms until they reach a closed door.

'Go ahead and knock,' he tells Joona with a hesitant smile.

Joona knocks, and hears someone walk across a hard floor in heels. The door is opened by a slim, middle-aged woman with dark blonde hair and big blue eyes. She's wearing a thin red dress that stops just below her knees. She's beautiful, tastefully made-up, and has three rows of snow-white pearls around her neck.

'Come in, Joona,' she says in a low but clear voice.

He walks into a brightly lit room containing a desk, a pair of white leather sofas, and built-in bookcases.

'I was just thinking of having some chai – is it too early for you?' she asks.

'No, that sounds great.'

Robert leaves the room, and Elin gestures towards the sofas. 'Let's sit down.'

Without any hurry, she sits down opposite him and crosses her legs.

'What's this about, then?' she asks, looking at him seriously.

'Several years ago you and your husband Jack Andersson acted as foster parents to a young girl . . .'

'We helped a lot of children in different ways when—'

'Her name was Vicky Bennet,' Joona says softly.

Something flits across Elin's controlled face, but the tone of her voice doesn't change.

'I remember Vicky very well,' she replies with a brief smile.

146

'What do you remember?'

'She was sweet and kind, and she . . .'

Elin Frank falls silent and stares ahead of her. Her hands are lying perfectly still.

'We have reason to believe she may have murdered two people at a children's home outside Sundsvall,' Joona says.

The woman quickly turns her face away. Joona manages to see her eyes grow darker. She adjusts her dress over her knees with hands that are unable entirely to suppress a tremble.

'How does that concern me?' she asks.

Robert knocks and comes in with a tinkling tea-trolley. Elin Frank thanks him and asks him to leave the trolley.

'Vicky Bennet has been missing since Friday,' Joona explains once Robert has left the room. 'There's a chance that she may try to contact you.'

Elin doesn't look at him. She bows her head slightly and swallows hard.

'No,' she says in a cold voice.

'Why don't you think Vicky Bennet would contact you?'

'She'll never contact me,' she replies, and gets to her feet. 'It was a mistake to let you in without checking what you wanted first.'

Joona starts to lay the tea things out on the table, and looks up at her.

'Who do you think Vicky would turn to? Would she contact Jack?'

'If you have any more questions you're welcome to talk to my lawyer,' she says, and leaves the room.

After a while Robert comes back in.

'I'll see you to the door,' he says curtly.

'Thanks very much,' Joona replies, then pours tea into both cups, picks up one of them, blows on it, and takes a cautious sip.

He smiles and takes a lemon biscuit from a plate lined with a white napkin. Without any haste he eats the biscuit and drinks his tea, takes the napkin from his lap and dabs his mouth, folds the napkin and puts it down on the table, before finally getting to his feet.

Joona hears Robert's footsteps behind him as he walks through the huge apartment, through the drawing rooms and the reception room with the tiled stove. He walks across the stone floor of the white entrance hall and opens the door to the stairwell.

'Something I should mention before you leave is that it's very important that Elin isn't associated with any negative—'

'I understand what you're saying,' Joona interrupts. 'But this isn't primarily about Elin Frank, but rather—'

'It is to me, and it is to her,' Robert interrupts.

'Yes, but the past doesn't draw any distinctions when it comes back,' Joona says, then sets off down the stairs.

50

The apartment's gym is located close to the largest bathroom. Elin usually runs seven kilometres each day, and sees her personal trainer at the Mornington Health Club twice a week. In front of the treadmill there's a television, switched off at the moment, and to her left Elin can see the rooftops and the tower of Oscar's Church.

She's not listening to music today. The only sounds are the thud of her feet, the clanking echo of the weights, the whirr of the treadmill, and her own breathing.

Her ponytail bounces between her shoulder blades. She's dressed in just a pair of jogging bottoms and a white sports bra. After fifty minutes the sweat has soaked through the fabric between her buttocks, and her bra is drenched.

She thinks back to the time when Vicky Bennet came to her home. That was eight years ago. A small girl with fair, tangled hair.

Elin had had chlamydia when she was young, on a language trip to France. She didn't get it treated in time and was left infertile. At the time she wasn't bothered, because she was sure she would never want children anyway. For years she told herself that it was just nice not to have to think about contraceptives.

She and Jack had only been married two years when he started to talk about adopting, but every time he raised the subject she explained that she didn't want children, that they were too much of a responsibility.

Jack was still in love with her in those days, and he supported her when she suggested that they volunteer to help children who had problems with their own families and needed to get away for a while.

Elin called the Norrmalm branch of Stockholm Social Services, and Jack went with her to meet a social worker who asked about their home, work, marital status, and whether or not they had any children of their own.

A month later Elin and Jack were called in for separate in-depth interviews. They were asked an awful lot of questions and follow-up questions, in line with the Kälvesten method.

Elin can still remember the astonished reaction when the social worker realised who she was.

It only took three days after that before they got a phone call. The social worker explained that she was hoping to house a child who needed a lot of security and a period of calm.

'She's six years old and . . . I think it could work . . . I mean, it's a question of feeling your way forward a lot of the time, but as soon as she's settled in we can recommend a number of psychologists,' the woman explained.

'What's her background?'

'Her mother is homeless and mentally ill . . . The authorities intervened when the girl was found sleeping in an underground carriage.'

'But she's OK?'

'She's mildly dehydrated, but the doctor says she's healthy apart from that . . . I've tried to talk to her . . . she seems sweet, but withdrawn.'

'What's her name – do you know?'

'Yes . . . Vicky . . . her name's Vicky Bennet.'

Elin Frank starts to run faster as she gets close to the end, the treadmill whirrs faster, her breathing speeds up. She increases the resistance, keeps going, and then she slows down.

Afterwards she does some stretches at the ballet bar in front of the big mirror, without looking herself in the eye. She kicks off her shoes and leaves the room on heavy, tingling legs. Outside the bathroom she takes off the already cold bra, drops it on the floor, pulls down her jogging bottoms and underpants and pushes them off with her feet, then goes into the shower.

As the warm water washes over her neck and her muscles relax, her anxieties return. It's as if hysteria is only just below the surface, darting beneath her skin. Something inside her wants to cry and scream out loud and never stop. But instead she composes herself and changes the temperature of the water until it's ice-cold. She forces herself to stand underneath it. She turns her face towards the jet of water until her temples ache with cold, before turning the water off and drying herself.

51

Elin leaves her walk-in closet wearing a mid-length velvet skirt and a nylon fine-mesh body from Wolford's latest collection. The skin on her arms and shoulders shines through the black material with its tiny, shimmering gems. The garment is so thin that she has to wear a special pair of silk gloves when she's putting it on.

In the reading room Robert is sitting on a lambskin armchair going through papers, which he places in different leather folders.

'Who was that girl the policeman was asking about?'

'No one,' Elin replies.

'Anything we need to worry about?'

'No.'

Robert Bianchi has been her advisor and assistant for six years. He's homosexual, but has never had a long-term relationship. Elin can't help thinking he mostly just likes being seen in the company of handsome men. It was Jack's idea that she should have a gay assistant, to stop him getting jealous. She remembers saying that it didn't make any difference to her – as long as he didn't speak in an affected voice.

She sits down beside him in the other armchair and stretches out her legs to show him her high heels.

'Wonderful,' he smiles.

'I saw the schedule for the rest of the week,' she says.

'In an hour you've got the reception at the Clarion Hotel Sign.'

A heavy bus far below on Strandvägen makes the large sliding doors rattle. Elin feels him looking at her, but doesn't look back, and merely moves the little diamond cross she's wearing on a chain around her neck.

'Jack and I looked after a young girl called Vicky . . . once upon a time,' she says, and swallows hard.

'Was she adopted?'

'No, she had a mother, we were just temporary foster carers, but I . . .'

She coughs and pulls the diamond cross along the necklace.

'When was this?'

'Only a couple of years before you came,' she replies. 'But I wasn't helping to run the business then, and Jack had only just started working with Zentropa.'

'You don't have to tell me.'

'I honestly think that we were prepared, as well as we could be. We knew it wasn't going to be easy, but . . . Can you understand this country? I mean, to start with it took forever, we kept having meetings with social workers and counsellors, absolutely everything had to be examined, from our finances to our sex life . . . but as soon as we were accepted it only took three days before we suddenly had a child and were left to cope on our own. It all seemed a bit odd. You know, they didn't tell us anything about her, we basically got no help at all.'

'Sounds typical.'

'We really did want to do the right thing . . . and the girl lived here for nine months, on and off. They tried to get her back with her mother loads of times, but it always ended up with Vicky being found among some old boxes in some garage outside Stockholm.'

'Tragic,' he says.

'In the end Jack couldn't handle all the nights we had to go out and rescue her, take her to hospital, or just put her in the bath and give her some food . . . I'm sure we would have split up anyway, but . . . one night he told me I had to choose . . .'

Elin smiles blankly at Robert.

'I don't understand why he had to force me to choose.'

'Because he only ever thinks about himself,' Robert says.

'But we were only here as backup, I could hardly choose between him and a child who was only going to live here for a few months, it was crazy . . . And of course he knew that I was utterly dependent on him at the time.'

'No,' Robert says.

'But it's true, I was,' Elin says. 'So when Vicky's mother got a new home, I agreed to let him call Social Services . . . I mean, things looked pretty good for the mother by that time . . .'

Her voice breaks, and to her own surprise she feels tears start to fall.

'Why haven't you ever mentioned this before?'

Elin wipes her tears and doesn't know why she lies: 'It's not a big deal, nothing I spent a lot of time thinking about.'

'We all have to move on,' Robert says, as if he's making excuses for her.

'Yes,' she whispers, then covers her face.

'What is it?' he asks anxiously.

'Robert,' she sighs, and meets his gaze. 'This is nothing to do with me, but that policeman who was here, he told me that Vicky has killed two people.'

'Do you mean that thing that's only just happened, up in Norrland?'

'I don't know.'

'Do you have any connection to her?' he asks slowly.

'No.'

'Because you can't let yourself be associated with this.'

'I know . . . obviously I'd like to do something to help her, but . . .'

'Keep your distance.'

'Perhaps I should call Jack.'

'No, don't.'

'He needs to know.'

'Not from you,' Robert points out. 'It would only upset you, you know that, every time you talk to him . . .'

She tries to smile in agreement, and puts her hand on Robert's warm fingers.

'Come back tomorrow morning at eight o'clock and we'll go through next week's diary.'

'Good,' Robert says, and leaves the room.

Elin picks up her phone, but waits until Robert has closed the front door and locked it behind him before she calls Jack.

He sounds hoarse and sleepy when he answers.

'Elin? Do you know what time it is here? You can't just call whenever . . .'

'Were you asleep?'

'Yes.'

'Alone?'

'No.'

'Are you being honest to hurt me or to—'

'We're divorced, Elin,' he interrupts.

Elin walks into the bedroom, but stops when her eyes land on the large bed.

'Tell me you miss me,' she whispers.

'Goodnight, Elin.'

'You can have the Broome Street apartment if you like.'

'I don't want it, you're the one who likes New York.'

'The police seem to think Vicky has murdered two people.'

'Our Vicky?'

Her mouth starts to tremble, and tears well up in her eyes.

'Yes . . . they've been here asking about her.'

'That's a great shame,' he says quietly.

'Can't you just come back? I need you . . . you can bring Norah if you want, I'm not jealous.'

'Elin . . . I'm not going to come back to Stockholm.'

'Sorry I rang,' Elin says, and ends the call.

52

The Prosecution Authority's national department for complaints against the police, and the National Police Committee's Internal Investigations Unit are both based at the top of Kungsbron 21. Joona is sitting in a small office with Mikael Båge, who's in charge of the investigation, and senior secretary Helene Fiorine.

'At the aforementioned time, the Security Police conducted a raid against the Brigade, an extreme left-wing group,' Båge says, then clears his throat. 'The complaint alleges that Detective Superintendent Joona Linna of the National Crime Unit was at the aforementioned address either simultaneously or immediately prior to—'

'That's correct,' Joona replies, looking out of the window at the railway tracks and the water of Barnhusviken.

Helene Fiorine looks troubled as she puts her pen and notepad down and says with an almost beseeching gesture: 'Joona, I have to ask you to take this internal investigation seriously.'

'I am,' he replies distantly.

She stares into his silver-grey eyes a little too long before nodding quickly and picking up her pen again.

'Before we conclude,' Mikael Båge says, then picks at his ear for several seconds. 'I need to mention the primary suspicion raised against you in this internal investigation . . .'

'It could obviously be a misunderstanding,' Helene explains

quickly. 'That the different investigations unfortunately got in each other's way.'

'But in the complaint against you,' Båge goes on, looking at his finger, 'it is claimed that the Security Police operation failed because you had warned members of the Brigade.'

'Yes, I did,' Joona says.

Helene Fiorine gets up from her chair, unsure of what to say, and just stands there looking sadly at Joona.

'You warned the group about the raid?' Båge asks with a smile.

'They were immature youngsters,' he explains. 'They weren't dangerous, and they weren't—'

'The Security Police had formed a different opinion,' Båge interrupts.

'Yes,' Joona says calmly.

'Let's end this preliminary interview there,' Helene Fiorine says, and gathers her papers together.

53

It's already half past four by the time Joona is driving past Tumba, where he once investigated a triple murder in a terraced house.

On the seat beside him is the list of places where Vicky Bennet has lived over the years. The last entry is the Birgitta Home, and the first, Strandvägen 47.

She must have spoken to at least one of the people she stayed with. She must have confided in someone, must have mentioned if she had friends somewhere.

The only thing Elin Frank had said about Vicky was that she was sweet and kind.

Sweet and kind, Joona thinks.

To the Frank family Vicky was a troubled child, a child who needed help, someone to show kindness to.

It was about charity.

But to Vicky, Elin was her first mother after her biological mum.

Life on Strandvägen must have been utterly alien to her. She was warm, and received regular meals. She slept in a bed, and wore nice clothes. Her time with Elin and Jack must have remained shrouded in a special glow for years afterwards.

Joona indicates, and pulls out into the left-hand lane.

He's studied the list and decided to start from the end this time. Prior to the Birgitta Home she was at Ljungbacken children's home, and before that she spent two weeks with the Arnander-Johansson family in Katrineholm.

In his mind's eye he sees Nils 'The Needle' Åhlén and Frippe forcing Miranda's hands away from her face again. They had to make a real effort to move her rigid arms. The dead girl seemed to resist, as if she didn't want to do it, as if she was ashamed.

But her face was calm and white as mother-of-pearl.

She had been sitting with the duvet wrapped around her when she was beaten with a rock, according to Nils. Six or seven times, if Joona had read the blood-spatter pattern correctly.

Then she was laid out on the bed and her hands positioned in front of her face.

The last thing she saw in her life was the murderer.

Joona slows down and drives through an established residential area full of large detached houses, and parks in front of low hedge of flowering potentilla.

He gets out of the car and walks towards a large wooden mailbox with a brass nameplate: Arnander-Johansson. A woman walks around the side of the house carrying a bucket of red apples. She seems to have a problem with her hips, and grimaces occasionally with pain. She's stocky, with big breasts and thick upper-arms.

'You just missed him,' the woman says when she catches sight of Joona.

'Typical,' he jokes.

'He had to go to the warehouse . . . something about shipping dockets.'

'Who are we talking about?' Joona asks with a smile.

She puts the bucket down.

'I thought you'd come to look at the treadmill?'

'How much is it?'

'Seven thousand kronor, brand new,' she replies, then falls silent.

She rubs one hand on her trouser leg and looks at him.

'I'm from the National Crime Unit, I'd like to ask you a few questions.'

'About what?' she asks in a weak voice.

'About Vicky Bennet, she stayed here briefly almost a year ago.'

159

The woman nods sadly, gestures towards the door, then goes inside. Joona follows her into a kitchen containing a pine table with a crocheted cloth, and flowery curtains framing the windows looking out on the garden. The grass is freshly mown, and the boundary with the next property is marked by plum trees and gooseberry bushes. There's a small, pale-blue swimming pool surrounded by wooden decking. Some inflatable toys are floating on the water close to the overflow channel to the right.

'Vicky's run away,' Joona says bluntly.

'I read about it,' she whispers as she puts the bucket of apples on the counter.

'Where do you think she'd go and hide?'

'No idea.'

'Did she ever talk about any friends, boys . . . ?'

'Vicky never really lived here,' the woman says.

'Why not?'

'It just didn't work out,' she says, and turns away.

The woman fills the coffee pot with water, then pours the water into the top of the coffee machine before she suddenly stops.

'It's customary to offer coffee, isn't it?' she says listlessly.

Joona looks through the window at two blond boys playing karate in the garden. They're both slim and tanned, wearing long trunks. Their game is a little too vigorous, a little too rough, but they're still laughing the whole time.

'You take children and young people into your family?'

'Our daughter is nineteen, so it . . . we've done it for several years now.'

'How long do the children usually stay?'

'It varies . . . and sometimes they keep coming and going,' she replies, and turns towards Joona. 'A lot of them come from very troubled homes, of course.'

'Is it hard?'

'No, not really . . . obviously there are rows, but it's mostly a question of being very clear about the boundaries.'

One of the boys does a jump-kick over the swimming pool and lands with a big splash. The other strikes out at the air, then follows him into the pool with a somersault.

'But Vicky only stayed two weeks?' Joona says, and looks at the woman. She evades his gaze and idly scratches her lower arm.

'We've got two boys,' she says vaguely. 'They've been here for two years . . . they're brothers . . . we hoped it would work out with Vicky, but unfortunately we had to put a stop to it.'

'What happened?'

'Nothing . . . not really, anyway . . . It wasn't her fault, it wasn't anyone's fault . . . it just got too much, we're an ordinary family and we just couldn't deal with it.'

'So Vicky . . . was she difficult, hard to handle?'

'No,' she says weakly. 'It was . . .'

She tails off.

'What were you about to say? What happened?'

'Nothing.'

'You've had a lot of experience,' Joona says. 'What would make you give up after just two weeks?'

'It is what it is.'

'I think something happened,' Joona says seriously.

'No, it just got too much for us.'

'I think something happened,' he repeats, in the same calm voice.

'What do you want?' she asks awkwardly.

'Please, tell me what happened.'

Her cheeks turn red. The blush spreads down her neck to her chest.

'We received a visit,' she whispers, looking down at the floor.

'Who from?'

She shakes her head. Joona holds out a notepad and pen. Tears start to run down her cheeks. She looks at him, then takes the pad and writes something.

54

Joona's been driving for three hours when he pulls up outside Skrakegatan 35 in Bengtsfors. The woman had been in tears when she wrote the address on his notepad. He had had to pull the pad from her hand, and when he tried to get her to say more she merely shook her head, hurried out of the kitchen, and locked herself in the bathroom.

He drives slowly along the row of red-brick houses towards the turning circle and garages. Number 35 is the last house in the row. The white plastic garden furniture in the tall grass has been blown over by the wind. The mailbox is overflowing with advertising fliers from pizzerias and supermarkets.

Joona gets out of the car, walks through the weeds by the gate, and up the damp stone path towards the house.

There's a drenched mat in front of the door with the words 'keys, wallet, mobile' on it. Black bin-bags have been taped over the inside of the windows. Joona rings the doorbell. A dog barks, and after a while someone looks at him through the peephole. He hears two locks turn, then the door opens a fraction before the security bolt stops it. He is struck by a smell of spilled red wine. He can't see the person in the dark hallway.

'Can I come in for a moment?'

'She doesn't want to see you,' says a boy with a dark, hoarse voice.

The dog is panting, and Joona can hear the links on its choke-collar tightening.

'I need to talk to her.'

'We're not buying anything,' a woman calls from another room.

'I'm from the police,' Joona says.

He hears footsteps inside the house.

'Is he alone?' the woman asks.

'I think so,' the boy whispers.

'Can you hold Zombie?'

'Are you going to open the door? Mum?' he asks in a worried voice.

The woman comes over to the door.

'What do you want?'

'Do you know anything about a girl called Vicky Bennet?'

The dog's claws scrabble at the floor. The woman closes the door and locks it. Joona hears her shout something at the boy. After a while the door opens, ever so slightly. She's removed the security bolt. Joona pushes it open a little more and walks into the hall. The woman is standing with her back to him. She's wearing flesh-coloured leggings and a white T-shirt. Her long blonde hair is hanging over her shoulders. When Joona closes the door behind him it gets so dark that he has to stop. There are no lights on anywhere.

She walks ahead of him. The sun is shining directly at the windows covered by the bin-bags. Tiny holes and tears are lit up like stars. A faint grey light permeates the kitchen. There's a box of wine on the table, and a large puddle on the brown linoleum floor beneath it. When Joona walks into the darkened living room the woman is already sitting on a denim sofa. The dark purple curtains reach all the way to the floor, and behind them he can see more bin-bags. Even so, a weak strip of light enters the room from the balcony door, falling across the woman's hand. Joona notes that her nails are neatly manicured, and painted red.

'Sit down,' she says calmly.

'Thanks.'

Joona sits down opposite her on a large footstool. When his

163

eyes get used to the gloom he sees that there's something not quite right about her face.

'What do you want to know?'

'You paid a visit to the Arnander-Johansson family.'

'Yes.'

'Why did you go and see them?'

'I warned them.'

'What did you warn them about?'

'Tompa!' the woman calls. 'Tompa!'

A door opens, followed by slow steps. Joona can't see the boy in the darkness, but can still feel his presence, and can make out a silhouette over by the bookcase. The boy comes into the darkened living room.

'Turn the light on.'

'But Mum . . .'

'Just do it!'

He flicks the switch and a large rice-paper ball lights up the whole room. The tall, slim boy stands in the strong glare with his head lowered. Joona looks at him. The boy's face looks as if it's been bitten by an attack dog, and then healed completely wrongly. He has no bottom lip at all, his teeth are exposed, and his chin and right cheek are hollow and meat-coloured. A deep red groove runs from his hairline, across his forehead, and through his eyebrow. When Joona turns to the woman he sees that her face is even more badly damaged. Even so, she is smiling at him. Her right eye is missing, there are deep incisions in her face and neck, at least ten wounds. Her left eyebrow droops over her eye, and her mouth has been cut in several places.

'Vicky got angry with us,' the woman says, and her smile disappears.

'What happened?'

'She cut us with a broken bottle. I didn't think a person could get that angry, she wouldn't stop. I passed out, came around and just lay there feeling her stab me with the broken glass. I felt each jab, as pieces broke off inside me, and I realised I didn't have a face any more.'

164

55

Sundsvall Council negotiated with the Orre care company, and had to pay handsomely to resolve the situation that had arisen. The girls from the Birgitta Home were taken from the Hotel Ibis to temporary accommodation in the small town of Hårte.

Hårte is an old fishing village with no church. The school closed almost a century ago, the mine was abandoned, and the Ica supermarket shut when the owners got too old. But each summer the fishing village comes back to life again, with its sandy beaches along the Virgin Coast.

The six girls are going to spend a few months living in the former shop, a spacious building with a large glassed-in veranda, located where the road running through the village forks like a snake's tongue.

The girls have finished their dinner, and some of them are still in the dining room looking at the calm, misty blue sea. In the large sitting room alongside, Solveig Sundström from Sävstagården children's home is sitting with her knitting in front of the crackling fire in the open hearth.

From the living room a cold corridor leads to a small kitchen. A guard is sitting there, positioned where he can see both the hall and door as well as the window looking out onto the lawn and road.

Lu Chu and Nina are looking for crisps in the pantry, but have to make do with Frosties.

'What will you do when the murderer comes?' Lu Chu asks.

The guard's tattooed hand twitches on the table and he smiles stiffly at her.

'You can feel safe here.'

He's in his fifties, and has a shaved head and sharp little beard running from his lower lip to the end of his chin. His bulging muscles are visible beneath the dark blue top bearing the security company's logo.

Lu Chu doesn't reply, just looks back at him as she stuffs the breakfast cereal into her mouth and chews noisily. Nina is looking through the fridge, and takes out a pack of smoked ham and a jar of mustard.

At the other end of the house Caroline, Indie, Tuula, and Almira are sitting around the dining table on the veranda playing a card game.

'Can I have all your jacks?' Indie says.

'Go fish!' Almira giggles.

Indie draws a card and looks at it happily.

'Ted Bundy was just like a butcher,' Tuula says in a quiet voice.

'God, you really are banging on about it,' Caroline sighs.

'He went from room to room clubbing the girls to death, like baby seals. First Lisa and Margaret, then . . .'

'Shut up,' Almira laughs.

Tuula smiles down at the table, and Caroline can't help shuddering.

'What the fuck's that old bag doing here?' Indie asks loudly.

The woman by the fireplace looks up, then carries on with her knitting.

'Are we still playing, or what?' Tuula asks impatiently.

'Whose go is it?'

'Mine,' Indie says.

'You're such a cheat,' Caroline smiles.

'My phone's completely dead,' Almira says. 'I left it charging in my room, and now . . .'

'Do you want me to look at it?' Indie asks.

She removes the back of the phone, takes out the battery, and puts it back in, but nothing happens.

'Weird,' she mutters.

'Don't bother,' Almira says.

Indie takes the battery out again.

'There isn't even a bloody SIM card!'

'Tuula,' Almira says sternly. 'Have you taken my SIM card?'

'Don't know,' the girl replies sullenly.

'I need it – OK?'

The woman has put her knitting down and comes into the dining room.

'What's going on?' she asks.

'We can handle this ourselves,' Caroline says coolly.

Tuula purses her lips sadly.

'I haven't taken anything,' she whines.

'My SIM card is missing,' Almira says, raising her voice.

'That doesn't necessarily mean that she's taken it, does it?' the woman says indignantly.

'Almira says she's going to hit me,' Tuula says.

'I won't tolerate violence of any sort,' the woman explains, then goes and sits down with her knitting again.

'Tuula,' Almira says in a subdued voice. 'I really do need to be able to use my phone.'

'That's going to be hard, isn't it?' Tuula smiles back.

The forest on the other side of the inlet is getting blacker and blacker, and then the sky grows dark while the water is still glowing like molten lead.

'The police think it was Vicky who beat Miranda to death,' Caroline says.

'Fucking morons,' Almira mutters.

'I don't know her, none of us knows her,' Indie says.

'Don't be stupid.'

'What if she's on her way here to—'

'Shh . . .' Tuula interrupts.

She gets up and stands perfectly still as she stares out into the darkness.

'Did you hear that?' she says, turning to Caroline and Almira.

'No,' Indie sighs.

'We'll soon be dead,' Tuula whispers.

'You're so sick, you bitch,' Caroline says, but can't help smiling.

She grabs Tuula's hand and pulls her towards her, puts her on her lap and pats her gently.

'There's no need to be afraid, nothing's going to happen,' she says consolingly.

56

Caroline wakes up on the sofa. The last embers are glowing in the hearth. Gentle heat radiates towards her. She sits up and looks around the dark living and dining room. She realises that she must have fallen asleep on the sofa, and that everyone has gone off to bed and just left her there.

Caroline gets up, goes over to the large windows, and looks out. It's still just about possible to discern the water beyond the black fishermen's sheds. Everything is quiet. The moon is shining above the sea behind veils of cloud.

She opens the creaking pine door and feels the cool air from the corridor on her face. Behind her the wooden furniture ticks softly. The shadows in the corridor are deep, and the doors to the girls' rooms are only just visible. Caroline takes a step into the darkness. The floor is ice-cold. Suddenly she imagines she hears a sound, a sigh or moan.

It's coming from the toilet.

She approaches carefully, her heart thudding. The door is ajar. There's someone in there. She hears the peculiar sound again.

Caroline looks cautiously through the narrow crack.

Nina is sitting on the toilet with her legs wide apart and a look of indifference on her face. A man is on his knees in front of her with his face between her thighs. She's pulled up her pyjama top so he can squeeze one of her breasts as he licks her.

'That's enough, now,' Nina says heavily.

'OK,' he replies, and stands up quickly.

When he pulls off some toilet paper to wipe his mouth Caroline sees that it's the guard.

'Give me the money, then,' Nina says, holding out her hand.

The guard starts to search his pockets.

'Damn, I've only got eighty kronor,' he says.

'Five hundred, you said.'

'What the hell am I supposed to do? I've only got eighty.'

Nina sighs and takes the money.

Caroline hurries past the door and slips into the cold little room she's been allocated. She closes the door and switches the light on. She sees her own reflection in the black window, realises that she's completely visible to anyone outside, and hurries over and pulls the blind down. For the first time in ages she feels frightened of the dark.

Caroline shudders when she thinks about the glint in Tuula's eyes when she spoke about different serial killers. Little Tuula was upset, and wanted to frighten the others by saying Vicky had followed them to the little fishing village.

Caroline decides not to bother about brushing her teeth. Nothing could persuade her to go back out into the long, dark corridor.

She moves the chair to the door and tries to push its back-rest under the door handle. With her hands trembling she fetches some old magazines and puts them on the floor beneath the chair-legs, so that the back of the chair presses against the bottom of the handle.

She imagines she can sense someone creeping along the corridor right outside, stares at the keyhole and feels a shiver run down her spine.

Suddenly there's a sharp bang behind her. The roller-blind flies up and spins around with a clatter.

'God!' she gasps, and pulls it down again.

She stands motionless and listens. Then she turns out the main light and hurries into bed, wrapping the duvet tightly around her body and waiting for the sheets to warm up.

She lies there completely still, staring at the door handle

through the darkness, and thinking about Vicky Bennet again. She seemed so shy and cautious. Caroline can't believe she did those terrible things, the thought of it is incredible. Before she forces herself to think about something else, she remembers Miranda's crushed head and the blood dripping from the ceiling.

Suddenly she hears tentative footsteps out in the corridor. They pause, then carry on before stopping outside her door. Through the shimmering darkness Caroline sees someone try to push the door handle down. It stops when it hits the back of the chair. Caroline screws her eyes shut and covers her ears, and starts to say a prayer.

57

In the middle of the night a weary knocking sound rings out as a child's car seat repeatedly hits the large dam at the Bergeforsen hydroelectric plant.

With its grey plastic back uppermost, barely visible above the surface of the water, the seat has been carried all the way down Indalsälven.

Since the snow melted in the Jämtland mountains, the river has been running high. The hydroelectric plant downstream from the vast expanse of Storsjön has had to constantly monitor water levels so that the dams don't overflow.

After the heavy rain of the past two weeks they had to start opening the floodgates very gradually to prevent a flood. More than two million litres of water are gushing through every second.

For months now Indalsälven has resembled a sluggish lake, but now the current is unmistakeable, and strong.

The child's car seat hits the dam, drifts away slightly, then hits the edge again.

Joona jogs along the narrow road that runs across the top of the dam. To his right the river spreads out like a shimmering floor, but to his left a smooth concrete walls drops away some thirty metres, straight down. It's dizzyingly high. White water froths with a roar over the black rocks far below, and water jets out of the openings in the dam with immense force.

Ahead of him, by the edge of the dam, stand two uniformed police officers together with a guard from the power station, looking and pointing over the railing into the smooth surface of the water. One of the police officers is holding a boathook.

Rubbish that has been carried along on the current has started to gather around the floating child's car seat. An empty plastic bottle rolls towards the edge, knocking against some pine cones, some twigs, and some half-dissolved fast-food cartons.

Joona looks down into the black water. The current is tugging at the seat. The hard grey plastic back is the only part that's visible.

It's impossible to tell whether there's still a child strapped in the chair.

'Turn it over,' Joona says.

The other police officer gives him a curt nod and leans over the railing as far as he can. The boathook breaks the surface of the water and nudges a pine branch aside. He pushes the boathook deeper under the car seat, then raises it slowly until the hook gets a purchase. He pulls upwards, and there's a splash as the seat finally rolls over to reveal the drenched chequered cushion.

The seat is empty, its straps drifting slowly in the water.

Joona looks at the car seat, the black straps, and thinks that the child's body could have slid out of the straps and sunk to the bottom.

'Like I said on the phone, it looks like the right seat . . . it doesn't seem to be badly damaged, but of course it's hard to see in detail,' the police officer says.

'Make sure forensics use a watertight bag when they pull it out.'

The police officer lets go of the seat, and it rolls slowly over again.

'Meet me at the end of the bridge in Indal,' Joona says, and starts to walk back towards his car. 'There's a swimming spot there, isn't there?'

'What are we going to do?'

'Go swimming,' Joona says without a trace of a smile, and carries on walking.

58

Joona stops at the end of the bridge and leaves the car door open as he walks over and looks down the grass slope. A floating jetty stretches out from the small sandy beach into the rushing water.

His jacket blows open in the wind, and his muscles stand out against his dark grey shirt.

He carries on walking along the side of the road, sensing the moisture rising from the warm vegetation, the smell of the grass and the sweetness of the willowherb.

He stops and bends over, and picks up a tiny cube of glass from between the plants, holds it in his hand, then looks down at the water again.

'This is where they drove off the road,' he says, indicating the direction.

One of the police officers goes down to the water's edge, looks off to where Joona is pointing, and shakes his head.

'There's no sign of it, nothing,' he calls back.

'I think I'm right,' Joona says.

'We'll never know – there's been too much rain,' the other police officer says.

'But there hasn't been any rain underwater,' Joona says.

He leaves the side of the road and strides down towards the water. He walks past the police officer, all the way to the water, then follows the river upstream a few metres before he sees the tyre tracks under the water. The parallel lines across the sandy riverbed disappear into the black water.

'Can you see anything?' the policeman calls.

'Yes,' Joona replies, and walks straight out into the river.

The cool water streams around his legs, dragging him gently sideways. He marches out with long strides. It's hard to see anything through the shimmering, gliding surface of the water. Long strands of weed are swirling about. The current is full of bubbles and dirt.

The policeman follows him out into the river, swearing to himself.

Joona can make out a dark shape about ten metres out.

'I'll call for a diver,' the officer says.

Joona quickly takes off his jacket, hands it to the police officer and keeps walking.

'What are you doing?'

'I have to know if they're dead,' he replies, handing the officer his pistol.

The water is freezing and the current is tugging at his increasingly heavy trousers. A shiver of cold runs up his legs and the base of his spine.

'There are logs in the river,' the other police officer calls. 'You can't swim here.'

Joona wades out, the bottom slopes away sharply, and when the water reaches his waist he dives forward smoothly. His ears roar as they fill with water. His open eyes are stung by the cold. Rays of sunlight cut through the water. Mud that has been stirred up swirls on the various currents.

He kicks his legs and glides further out, and suddenly he sees the car. It's off ahead of him, to one side of the tyre tracks. The current has dragged the vehicle towards the middle of the river.

The red metal shimmers. The windscreen and two windows on the right-hand side are completely missing, and the water is gushing through the car.

Joona swims closer and tries not to think about what he might be about to see. He just has to remain alert and try to register as many details as possible in the few seconds he can stay down there, but his brain is still conjuring up images of the girl in the front seat with the safety belt diagonally across her body. Arms outstretched, mouth gaping, hair swirling in front of her face.

His heart is beating faster now. Visibility is poor down here. Twilight and thunderous silence.

He's approaching the rear door with the missing window, and grabs hold of the empty frame. The current of the river is tugging his body sideways. There's a metallic creaking sound, and he loses his grip when the car slides another metre away from him. Mud swirls up, and he's having trouble seeing. He takes a few strokes. The cloud of mud disperses and it gets easier to see again.

Above him, some three metres away, is the other, sun-drenched world.

A waterlogged tree trunk is gliding just below the surface like a slow, heavy torpedo.

His lungs are starting to ache now, contracting in empty cramps. The water is moving fairly fast down here.

Joona grabs the empty window frame again and sees blood spread out from his hand. He forces himself down to the same level as the car door, and tries to look inside. His vision is blocked by swirling dust and weeds.

The car is empty. There's no one there, no girl, no child.

The windscreen is gone, the wipers hanging loose. Their bodies could have been washed out and tumbled away across the riverbed.

He manages to register the area immediately around the car. There's nothing for the bodies to catch on. The rocks are smooth and the weeds too thin.

His lungs are screaming for oxygen, but he knows that there's actually always more time.

His body will have to learn to wait.

In the military, he had to swim twelve kilometres with the signal flag several times, he's made his way up from a submarine with an emergency balloon and no equipment, and he's swum under the ice in the Gulf of Finland.

He can manage without oxygen a few more seconds.

With powerful strokes he swims around the car and looks at the scene. The water is rushing past like a strong wind. The shadows of floating logs move quickly across the riverbed.

Vicky drove off the road here, down the beach in the pouring rain, and into the water. The windows had already been knocked out in the collision with the traffic light, and the car would have filled with water instantly as it rolled on and then came to a stop under the water.

But where are the bodies?

He has to try to find the children.

Five metres out he sees something shimmering on the riverbed, a pair of glasses rolling further and further from the car, towards deeper, faster water. He ought to return to the surface, but tells himself he can last a little longer. He eyes flare as he swims forward, reaches out his hand, and grabs the glasses just as the water lifts them from the riverbed. He turns, kicks off, and swims upward. His vision is flickering, he doesn't have time to check first, he needs to breathe or he's going to pass out. He breaks the surface, draws air into his lungs, and only just has time to see the log before it hits his shoulder. It hurts so badly that he roars with pain. His arm is wrenched from its socket by the heavy impact. Joona sinks below the surface again. His ears are ringing like church bells. Ahead of him the sun sparkles in fragmented reflections.

59

Joona's colleagues from the Västernorrland Police had got hold of a boat and were already on their way out to him when they saw him get hit by the log. They managed to grab hold of him, pull him over the railing, and onto the deck.

'Sorry,' Joona gasped. 'But I had to know . . .'

'Where did the log hit you?'

'There are no bodies in the car,' Joona went on, wincing with pain.

'Look at his arm,' one of the officers said.

'Shit,' the other whispered.

Blood was running down Joona's wet shirt, and his arm was unnaturally twisted, and seemed to be hanging by the muscle alone.

They carefully took the glasses from his hand and put them in a plastic bag.

One of the police officers drove him to Sundsvall Hospital. Joona sat still in the car with his eyes closed, holding his wounded arm close to his body. In spite of the great pain, he tried to come up with some explanation for the way that the car had slid across the riverbed, the water streaming through the broken windows.

'The children weren't there,' he said, almost in a whisper.

'The river can carry bodies a very long way,' the police officer said. 'There's no point sending divers into the water, because either the bodies get wedged somewhere and we never find them . . . or they end up down at the power station like the car seat.'

Two cheerful nurses looked after Joona at the hospital. They were both blonde, and looked like mother and daughter. Quickly and efficiently they got him out of his wet clothes, but when they started to dry him and caught sight of his arm they fell completely silent. They cleaned and dressed the wound before he was taken off for an X-ray.

Twenty minutes later a doctor came into the examination room to say that he'd looked at the X-rays. He quickly explained that nothing was broken, and that they were dealing with a luxation. The bad news was that Joona's shoulder was dislocated, but the good news was that his cartilage seemed to be intact. He had to lie face down on the bed with his arm hanging straight down. The doctor injected 20 milligrams of lidocaine directly into the joint in order to be able to put the arm back in its socket. He sat down on the floor while one nurse pushed Joona's shoulder blade towards his spine and the other pushed the ball-joint at the top of his arm back into place. There was a cracking sound, Joona clenched his teeth, then slowly breathed out.

The car with Vicky Bennet and Dante in it vanished from a stretch of road that had hardly any other roads leading off it. The police claimed to have checked all possible hiding places, and criticism in the media was getting louder.

When Joona saw the child's car seat in the water he realised what they had all missed. If the car had driven into the river and been swallowed up by the water, there was only one place where that could have happened without being discovered by the police and emergency services.

Just past Indal, Highway 86 turns sharp right onto the bridge across the river, but the car must have kept going straight on, down the grass slope, across the sand, and out into the water.

The broken windows meant that the car would have filled with water at once, and the heavy rain erased the evidence left by the wheels on the sand almost immediately. The car had vanished in a matter of seconds.

60

Joona makes his way down to one of the police's garages. The air is cool. His arm has been stabilised, and is protected by a dark blue sling.

A large plastic tent surrounds the car that Vicky Bennet stole. It has been raised by crane from the Indal River, packed in plastic, and moved here. All the seats have been removed and placed beside the car. A long bench is covered with an array of items wrapped in labelled plastic bags. Joona looks at the evidence that's been secured. Fingerprints from both Vicky and Dante. Bags full of broken glass, an empty water bottle, a trainer that probably belonged to Vicky, and the boy's small pair of glasses.

The door to a neighbouring office opens, and Holger Jalmert walks into the garage with a folder in his hand.

'You wanted to show me something?' Joona says.

'Yes, I suppose we should get it over with,' Holger sighs, and gestures towards the car. 'The whole of the windscreen was missing, you saw that for yourself when you dived down there, knocked out when the car hit the traffic light . . . but I'm afraid I've found strands of the boy's hair on the frame.'

'That's sad news,' Joona says, and feels a great emptiness fill him.

'Yes, even if it was what everyone suspected.'

Joona looks at a close-up photograph of the right-hand side

of the jagged windscreen, and an enlargement showing three strands of hair torn out by the root.

The car was probably driving fast, and would have hit the water hard. The evidence suggests that Vicky Bennet and Dante Abrahamsson were thrown through what remained of the windscreen.

Joona reads that splinters of glass have been found with the boy's blood on.

The bonnet of the car buckled on impact.

Joona finds it hard to imagine how the hairs could have been pulled from Dante's head if he wasn't propelled out of the car above the glove compartment and into the river.

The current would have been very strong, given that the dam gates at the power station were open.

Joona thinks to himself that Vicky Bennet's rage must have subsided, seeing as she hadn't killed the boy and still had him with her in the car.

'In your opinion, do you think the boy was alive when they hit the water?' Joona asks quietly.

'Yes. He was probably knocked unconscious when he hit the edge of the windscreen and drowned . . . but we'll have to wait until the bodies get caught in the dam.'

Holger holds up a plastic bag containing a red water pistol.

'I've got a young lad myself . . .'

He falls silent and sits down.

'I know,' Joona says, and puts his good hand on Holger's shoulder.

'We have to tell the mother that we're going to stop looking, and just wait now,' Holger says, and his mouth begins to twitch sadly.

It's unusually quiet in the little police station. A few men in uniform are talking in low voices by the coffee machine, a woman is typing slowly on her computer. The grey daylight outside is heavy and gloomy, reminiscent of miserable schooldays.

When the door opens and Pia Abrahamsson walks in, even the quiet talking stops. Pia is wearing jeans and a buttoned denim jacket that sits tightly across her chest. The nut-brown hair hanging lankly from her black beret is greasy and unwashed.

She's not wearing any make-up, and her eyes look tired and frightened.

Mirja Zlatnek quickly gets up and offers her a chair.

'I don't want to sit down,' Pia says weakly.

Mirja undoes the button on her shirt collar.

'We asked you to come because . . . I'm afraid we fear that . . .'

Pia puts her hand on the back of the chair.

'What I'm trying to say,' Mirja goes on, 'is that . . .'

'What?'

'I'm afraid we don't think they're still alive.'

Pia doesn't show much reaction. She doesn't collapse, she just nods slowly and moistens her lips.

'Why don't you think they're alive?' she asks in a low and strangely calm voice.

'We've found your car,' Mirja says. 'They drove off the road and ended up in the river. The car was found at a depth of four metres, badly damaged, and . . .'

She tails off.

'I want to see my son,' Pia says in the same horribly calm voice. 'Where's his body?'

'It's . . . We haven't found their bodies yet, but . . . It's difficult, but the decision has been taken to call off the divers.'

'But . . .'

Pia Abrahamsson's hand flies towards her throat to clasp the crucifix hanging inside her clothes, but stops at her heart.

'Dante's only four,' she says in a perplexed tone. 'He can't swim.'

'No,' Mirja says sadly.

'But he . . . he likes playing in the water,' Pia whispers.

Her cheeks start to tremble. She stands there in her denim outfit, her clerical collar visible under her jacket. Very slowly, like an old, broken person, she finally sits down on the chair.

61

Elin Frank is showering after her steam sauna, then walks across the smooth stone floor to the large mirror above the double basin where she dries herself with a warm bath towel. Her skin is still hot and damp as she puts on the black kimono Jack gave her the year they split up.

She leaves the bathroom and walks through the bright rooms, across the white parquet floor, and into the bedroom.

She has already laid out the shimmering copper dress by Karen Millen, and a pair of gold Dolce & Gabbana pants.

She takes the kimono off and perfumes herself with La Perla, waits for a few seconds, then gets dressed.

When she walks into the large sitting room she sees her advisor Robert hide his phone with a sudden movement. A nagging anxiety suddenly takes hold of her again, weighing heavily in the pit of her stomach.

'What is it?' she asks.

Robert's boyish striped T-shirt has slid up from his white jeans, revealing his rounded stomach.

'The photographer from *Vogue* is ten minutes late,' Robert says, without meeting her gaze.

'I haven't had time to watch the news,' she says, trying to sound bright. 'Do you know if the police have got hold of Vicky yet?'

She hasn't dared to listen to the news or read the papers for the past few days. She's having to take a pill to get to sleep at ten o'clock, then another at three o'clock.

'Have you heard anything?' she repeats weakly.

Robert scratches his short hair.

'Elin, I really don't want you to worry.'

'I'm not, but . . .'

'No one's going to drag you into this.'

'It doesn't do any harm to know what's going on,' she says nonchalantly.

She's composed her face again, and smiles directly and coolly at him.

'Am I going to have to get cross with you?'

He shakes his head and pulls his T-shirt down to cover his stomach.

'I caught the end of the news on the radio when I was on my way here,' he replies. 'They've evidently found the stolen car submerged in a river . . . I think they said divers were going to start looking.'

Elin quickly turns her face away again. Her lips are trembling and her heart is beating as if it were about to break.

'That doesn't sound good,' she says in an empty voice.

'Do you want me to turn the television on?'

'No, no need,' she whispers.

'Obviously it would be a great shame if it turns out that they've drowned.'

'Don't be like that,' Elin says.

She has to swallow. Her throat hurts, and she coughs quietly and looks down at her hands.

62

Elin never has any problem remembering the day Vicky came to her. The girl stood stony-faced outside the door, her arms covered with yellowing bruises. The moment Elin saw her, she realised that Vicky was the daughter she had been longing for. She didn't even know she had been fantasising about having a daughter, but when she saw Vicky she realised how much she had wanted a child.

Vicky was her own person right from the start, just as it should be.

At first the little girl would come running to her bed at night. She would stop, stare at her, and turn around. Perhaps she was expecting to find her biological mother, hoping to curl up with her, or perhaps she just changed her mind when she got there, didn't want to show that she was afraid, or risk being rejected.

Elin can still remember exactly how the little feet sounded as they padded away across the parquet floor.

Sometimes Vicky used to want to sit on Jack's lap to watch children's television, but never on hers.

Vicky didn't trust her, didn't dare to, but Elin noticed that she often used to look at her in secret.

Little Vicky, the silent girl who only used to play when she didn't think anyone was watching. Who didn't dare open her Christmas presents because she didn't believe those beautiful parcels were really for her. Vicky, who used to flinch from every hug.

Elin bought her a little white hamster in a big cage full of red plastic ladders and tunnels. Vicky looked after it over the Christmas holiday, but before she went back to school it had vanished without trace. It turned out that Vicky had let it go in a park near the school. When Jack explained that it might not survive in the cold, she ran into her room and slammed the door ten times. That night she drank a bottle of Bourgogne and was sick all over the sauna. That same week she stole two diamond rings Elin had inherited from her grandmother. She refused to say what she'd done with them, and Elin never got the rings back.

Elin could see that Jack had had enough. He started talking about their lives being too complicated to provide enough security to a child who needed so much help. He withdrew, and kept to himself, and stopped engaging with the troublesome little girl.

She realised that she was on the brink of losing him.

When Social Services made a fresh attempt to rehouse the girl back with her mother again, Elin felt that she and Jack needed the break to sort their relationship out. Vicky wouldn't even take the phone that Elin had bought her so they could keep in touch.

After Jack and Elin had eaten a late supper at Operakällaren, then made love and slept undisturbed all night for the first time in months, he explained the following morning that he didn't want to stay with her unless she ruled out further involvement with Vicky.

Elin got him to call the social worker to explain that they couldn't help any more, that they couldn't handle it.

Vicky and her mother ran away from sheltered accommodation in Västerås and took refuge in a small shed next to a playground. Her mum started leaving her alone at night, and when she didn't come back after two days Vicky made her way to Stockholm, all alone.

Jack wasn't home the evening Vicky showed up on the landing outside Elin's door.

Elin hadn't known what to do. She remembers standing pressed against the wall in the hallway listening as the little girl rang the doorbell and whispered her name.

In the end Vicky started to cry and opened the letterbox.

'Please, let me come back. I want to be with you. Please, Elin, open the door . . . I'll be good. Please, please . . .'

When Jack and Elin had pulled out of the programme, the social worker had warned them: 'You shouldn't tell Vicky why you can't carry on.'

'Why not?' Elin asked.

'Because then she'd blame herself,' the social worker explained. 'She'd feel it was her fault you can't go on.'

So Elin had stood there in silence, and after what felt like an eternity Vicky's footsteps disappeared down the stairs.

63

Elin stands in front of the large bathroom mirror and looks into her eyes. The indirect lighting casts sparkling reflections across her irises. She's taken two Valium and poured herself a glass of Riesling from Alsace.

In the large sitting room, Nassim Dubois, a young photographer from French *Vogue*, is unpacking his equipment and preparing the lighting. The actual interview was conducted last week when Elin was in Provence for a charity auction. She sold the whole of her collection of contemporary art and her Jean Nouvel-designed house in Nice in order to set up a microloans scheme for women in North Africa.

She moves away from the mirror, pulls out her phone, and dials Jack's number to tell him that the car Vicky stole has been found in the Indal River. She listens as the phone rings, even though Jack's lawyer has explained that any communication relating to Vicky should be conducted via his office.

She doesn't care if Jack sounds tired. She's not in love with him any more, but sometimes she just needs to hear his voice.

Perhaps she'll just tell him that she sold his Basquiat in the auction. But before he answers she regrets calling and hangs up.

Elin leaves the bathroom, one hand trailing along the wall for support as she walks through the sitting room to the glass doors.

When she emerges onto the large terrace with a languidness that could be interpreted as sensual Nassim lets out an impressed whistle.

'You look wonderful,' he says with a smile.

She knows the copper-coloured dress with the thin shoulder straps suits her. She's wearing a flat necklace of beaten white gold, which, like her earrings, casts reflections across her chin and long neck.

He asks her to stand with her back against the railing with an enormous white shawl from Ralph Lauren around her shoulders. She lets it blow in the wind, and watches as it fills like a sail and billows attractively behind her.

He doesn't use his light meter, but angles a silvery reflector screen so that her face is filled with light.

He takes a lot of photographs of her from a distance with a telephoto lens, then comes closer and kneels down in his tight jeans to take a sequence of pictures on an old-fashioned Polaroid camera.

She sees that beads of sweat have appeared on Nassim's forehead. He doesn't stop praising her, but always with his mind elsewhere, concentrating on the composition and lighting.

'Dangerous, sexy,' he mutters.

'You think?' she replies with a smile.

He stops, looks her in the eye, nods, then gives her a wide, embarrassed smile.

'Mostly sexy.'

'You're very sweet,' she says.

Elin isn't wearing a bra, and can feel her skin coming out in goosebumps. Her stiff nipples are visible through the dress. She realises she's hoping he notices, and concludes that she's starting to feel a bit drunk.

He lies down right in front of her with an old Hasselblad camera, and asks her to lean forward and pout her lips as if she wants to be kissed.

'*Une petite pomme,*' he says.

They smile at each other, and she feels suddenly happy, almost ecstatic at his flirting.

She can see his chest clearly through his thin, tight T-shirt.

It's slipped up from his trousers to expose his flat stomach.

She pouts and he takes photographs, mutters that she's the best, that she's a top model, then he lowers the camera to his chest and looks up at her.

'I could carry on like this forever,' he says frankly. 'But I can see that you're freezing.'

'Let's go inside and have a whisky,' she nods.

64

They get inside to find that Ingrid has already lit the large tiled stove. They sit on the sofa, drink malt whisky, talk about the interview, about the microloans that have become such an important tool in helping women to change their lives.

Elin can feel the Valium and alcohol making her perfectly relaxed, almost becalmed inside.

Nassim tells her that the French interviewer was very pleased with the interview. Then he tells her that his mother comes from Morocco.

'You're doing a very good thing,' he says with a smile. 'If my grandmother had been able to get a microloan, my mother's life would have been very different.'

'I'm trying to make a difference, but . . .'

She falls silent and looks into his serious eyes.

'Nobody's perfect,' he says, moving closer to her.

'I let a little girl down . . . someone I wasn't supposed to let down . . . someone . . .'

He pats her cheek consolingly and whispers something in French. She smiles at him, and feels intoxication tingle in her body.

'If you weren't so young I'd fall in love with you,' she says in Swedish.

'What did you just say?' he asks.

'I envy your girlfriend,' she explains.

She feels his breath, he smells of mint and whisky. Like herbs, she thinks, looking at his neatly-shaped mouth and suddenly feeling an urge to kiss him, before thinking that it would probably scare him.

She remembers how Jack stopped having sex with her just after Vicky disappeared from their lives. She didn't understand it was simply because he had stopped finding her attractive. She thought it was because of stress and tiredness, because they weren't spending enough time together. So she started to make an effort. She made herself look good, arranged romantic dinners, time together.

But he was no longer looking at her.

One night, when he came home and saw her lying there in her flesh-coloured negligee, he told her straight out that he no longer loved her.

He wanted a divorce, he'd met another woman.

'Watch out, you're spilling it,' Nassim says.

'Oh, God,' she whispers, just as she manages to spill some whisky on the dress.

'Don't worry.'

He picks up a napkin, kneels down, and carefully presses it against the stain, holding it against her as his other hand goes around her waist.

'I need to change,' she says, and stands up, trying hard not to fall sideways.

She can feel the Valium, wine, and whisky rushing through her brain.

He helps support her as they walk through the rooms side by side. She feels weak and tired, leans against him, and kisses him on the neck. The bedroom is cool, the lighting subdued. Only the cream-coloured lamp on the bedside table is lit.

'I need to lie down.'

She doesn't say anything else as he lays her on the bed and slowly pulls off her shoes.

'I'll help you,' he says in a low voice.

She pretends to be more drunk than she is, just lies there still, as if she doesn't notice him unfastening her dress with trembling hands.

She hears his heavy breathing and wonders if he's going to dare to touch her, exploit the fact that she's intoxicated.

She lies still on the bed in her gold-coloured pants looking at him through a swaying haze, then closes her eyes.

He murmurs something, and his fingers feel ice-cold with nerves as he pulls off her underwear.

She squints at him as he gets undressed. His body is tanned, as if he worked out in the fields. He's boyishly slim, and has a grey tattoo on one shoulder, an eye of Horus.

Her heart starts to beat faster when he mutters something and gets on the bed. Perhaps she should stop him, but she feels flattered by his desire. She tells herself she won't let him enter her, just let him look and masturbate like a teenager.

She tries to concentrate on what's going on and enjoy the moment. He's breathing fast as he gently parts her thighs, and she lets it happen.

She's wet, very slippery, but at the same time she can't quite lose herself in the situation. He lies on top of her, and she feels his penis against her, warm and hard. Very slowly she rolls away and puts her thighs together.

She opens her eyes, meets his frightened gaze, then closes them again.

Cautiously, as if anxious not to wake her, he parts her thighs again. She smiles to herself and lets him look, then feels him on top of her, and suddenly he just slides into her.

She lets out a quiet groan and feels his heart thudding as he lies on top of her.

He's inside her now, gasping as he thrusts harder.

She feels nausea rising inside her, she'd like to be able to want him now, but he's too eager, pushing too fast and far too hard. She starts to feel horribly lonely, and loses all desire. She lies there unmoving until he finishes and pulls out.

'Sorry, sorry,' Nassim whispers as he gathers his things. 'I thought you wanted . . .'

I thought so too, she thinks, but can't be bothered to explain. She hears him getting dressed quickly and quietly and hopes he's just going to leave. She wants to get up and have a wash, then pray to God that Vicky is still alive until she falls asleep.

65

Joona is standing by the railing looking along the high concrete wall. Water is gushing from three openings twenty metres below. Beneath them the wall curves like an immense waterslide. Vast quantities of water crash down the wall and foam across the rocky riverbed.

His arm is still held by the sling, and his jacket is draped around his shoulder. He leans out over the railing, looks down at the river, and thinks about the car with the two children in it in the heavy rain. The way the car hits the traffic light in Bjällsta, knocking the windscreen out. Vicky is wearing her seatbelt, but still hits her head on the window with the force of the impact. The car is suddenly full of pieces of glass, and cold rain pours in.

A few empty moments of silence follow.

The boy starts to scream in terror. Vicky gets shakily out of the car, glass falls from her clothes, she opens the back door, unfastens the seat and looks at the boy, checks to see if he's hurt, then tries to get him to be quiet before she drives on.

Perhaps she was planning to cross the bridge when she suddenly sees the flashing blue lights of the police car at the roadblock on the other side. She swings off the road in panic, can't stop the car in time, and drives into the water. The abrupt impact means that Vicky's face hits the steering wheel and she loses consciousness.

The two of them must have passed out before the car sank into the water. The current would have seized their limp bodies and gently pulled them out through the broken windows, sweeping them along the rocky riverbed.

He takes out his phone to call Carlos Eliasson. The diver from the rescue service is already standing by the power station's jetty. His blue wetsuit pulls taut across his back as he checks his breathing apparatus.

'Carlos,' Joona's boss says when he answers.

'Susanne Öst wants to shut down the investigation,' Joona says. 'But it's not finished.'

'That's always a shame, but the murderer is dead . . . which means that it's not financially justifiable to continue, unfortunately.'

'We haven't got any bodies.'

He hears Carlos mutter something, and then suffer an outburst of coughing. Joona waits as Carlos drinks some water. He thinks about how he was searching through Vicky's past when the child's car seat was found, and how he had been looking for someone she might have confided in, someone who knew where she might have gone.

'It could take several weeks for the bodies to show up,' Carlos whispers, and clears his throat again.

'But it's not finished,' Joona objects.

'Now you're being stubborn again,' Carlos sighs.

'I need—'

'It isn't even your case,' Carlos says, cutting him off.

Joona looks down at a black log floating in the current as it hits the edge of the dam with a dull thud.

'Yes, it is,' he says.

'Joona,' Carlos sighs.

'The forensic evidence may point to Vicky, but there are no witnesses, and she hasn't been convicted.'

'You can't convict the dead,' Carlos says wearily.

Joona thinks about the girl, and the lack of a motive, and the fact that she went back to bed after the brutal murders. He thinks about Nils Åhlén's claim that she killed Elisabet with a hammer, but Miranda with a rock.

'Give me a week, Carlos,' he says evenly. 'I need to get a few answers before I come home.'

Carlos mutters something away from the receiver.

'I can't hear,' Joona says.

'This is informal,' Carlos says more loudly. 'But as long as the internal investigation is still going on you can continue.'

'What resources have I got?'

'Resources? You're still only an observer, so you can't—'

'I've requested a diver,' Joona says with a smile.

'A diver?' Carlos says in an alarmed voice. 'Do you know what a—'

'And a dog-handler.'

Joona hears the sound of an engine, turns around, and sees a small grey car with a spluttering engine pull up beside his. It's a Messerschmitt Kabinenroller from the early 1960s, with two wheels at the front and one at the back. The door opens, and Gunnarsson clambers out with a cigarette in his mouth.

'I decide whether or not we use divers,' Gunnarsson calls, and hurries over to Joona. 'This is nothing to do with you.'

'I'm an observer,' Joona says calmly, and walks down towards the jetty where the diver is getting ready.

66

The diver is a man in his fifties, showing the first signs of putting on weight, but he still has broad shoulders and powerful biceps. His Neoprene wetsuit sits tightly around his belly and neck.

'Hasse,' he says by way of greeting.

'The dam-gates can't be closed, there's a risk of flooding,' Joona says.

'I understand,' Hasse replies curtly, gazing out across the choppy water.

'The current's going to be very strong,' Joona points out.

'Yes,' Hasse replies with a calm look in his eyes.

'Can you handle it?' Joona asks.

'I was a mine-clearer at KA1 . . . can't be any worse than that,' Hasse replies with a trace of a smile.

'Have you got nitrox in those tanks?' Joona asks.

'Yes.'

'What the hell is that?' Gunnarsson asks, having just reached them.

'Like air, but with a bit more oxygen,' Hasse says as he pulls his vest on.

'So how long can you be down there?'

'With these – maybe two hours . . . so no problem.'

'I'm grateful to you for volunteering,' Joona says.

The diver shrugs and explains honestly: 'My lad's at football camp in Denmark . . . place called Ishøj . . . I said I'd go with him, but you know, there's just me and him now, so a bit of extra money's always useful . . .'

He shakes his head and points at the diving mask and the digital camera attached to it, then at the cable attached to his lifeline and connected to a computer.

'I film all my dives. You'll be able to see what I see . . . and we can communicate while I'm down there.'

A log that's floated down the river bumps into the edge of the dam.

'Why are there logs in the water?' Joona asks.

Hasse pulls his equipment on and says nonchalantly: 'Who knows? Someone's probably been dumping wood that's been ruined by bark beetles.'

A woman with a worn face dressed in blue jeans, wellington boots, and an open padded jacket is leading an Alsatian dog from the car park towards the power plant.

'And here comes a damn bloodhound,' Gunnarsson says, and shivers.

The dog-handler, Sara Bengtsson, walks past the winch and says something in a low voice. The dog stops instantly and sits down. She doesn't even look at it, just keeps walking, taking for granted that it's doing what she's told it to.

'It's good that you're able to come,' Joona says, shaking her hand.

Sara Bengtsson looks at him very briefly, then pulls her hand away and seems to look for something in her pockets.

'I take the decisions here,' Gunnarsson says. 'And I don't much care for dogs – just so you know.'

'Well, I'm here now,' Sara says, glancing over at the dog.

'What's her name?' Joona asks.

'Jackie,' the woman smiles.

'We're about to send a diver down,' Joona explains. 'But it would be great if Jackie could identify areas we should check . . . do you think she can do that?'

'Yes,' Sara Bengtsson replies, kicking at a loose stone.

'There's a lot of water, and one hell of a current,' Gunnarsson warns.

'Back in the spring she found a body at a depth of sixty-five metres,' Sara replies, her cheeks flushing.

'So what the hell are we waiting for?' Gunnarsson says, taking out a cigarette.

Sara Bengtsson doesn't appear to hear him. She's looking out across the shimmering black water. She puts her hands in her pockets and stands there perfectly still before saying gently: 'Jackie.'

The dog immediately leaves its post and comes over to her. She crouches down and pats the dog on its neck and behind its ears. She talks encouragingly to it, explaining what they're looking for, then they start to walk along the edge of the dam.

The dog is specially trained to detect the smell of blood and the lungs of dead bodies. The dogs are supposed to associate the smell of corpses with something positive, but Sara knows that Jackie gets upset and needs comforting afterwards.

They pass the place where Dante's car seat was found floating. Sara gently directs Jackie's nose out across the high water.

'I don't think this is going to work,' Gunnarsson smiles. He lights the cigarette and strokes his stomach.

Sara stops and holds up her hand when Jackie smells something. The dog stretches its long nose over the edge of the dam.

'What can you smell?' she asks.

The dog sniffs and moves sideways, then loses the scent and moves on along the dam.

'Hocus pocus,' the diver mutters, adjusting his vest.

Joona watches the dog-handler and the unusually red-haired Alsatian. They're moving slowly along the railing and are now approaching the middle of the dam, directly above the open floodgates. Some curls of hair have come loose from the woman's ponytail and are blowing in front of her face. Suddenly the dog stops and whines, leans forward, licks its nose, then gets anxious and turns around on the spot.

'Is there someone down there?' Sara asks almost silently, and looks down into the black water.

The dog doesn't want to stop, it walks on and sniffs around an electricity junction-box, but returns to the same place and starts to whimper again.

'What is it?' Joona says, walking towards them.

'I don't actually know, she's not giving the usual signal, but she's behaving as if—'

The dog barks, and the woman crouches down beside her.

'What is it, Jackie?' she asks gently. 'What's the matter?'

The dog wags its tail when Sara hugs her and tells her she's a clever girl. Jackie whines and lies down, scratches behind her ear with her hind leg, and licks her nose again.

'What on earth are you doing?' Sara asks with a surprised smile.

67

The dam is rumbling and vibrating very slightly. There's a pile of neatly-folded watertight body-bags on top of the plastic container with flags sticking out of it that marks the search location.

'I'll start by the power plant and search according to a grid pattern,' Hasse says.

'No, we go straight down where the dog reacted,' Joona says.

'So the women are in charge now, are they?' Hasse asks in a hurt voice.

Far below the relatively calm surface of the water are the openings to the spillways, covered by huge mesh that catches everything swept along by the river.

The diver checks the supply of gas from the tanks of nitrox 36 on his back. He plugs the camera cable into the computer, then puts his diving mask on. Joona sees himself on the screen.

'Wave to the camera,' Hasse says, and slips into the water.

'If the current's too strong we'll stop,' Joona says.

'Be careful,' Gunnarsson calls.

'I'm used to diving in strong currents,' Hasse says. 'But if I don't come up again you can tell my boy that I should have gone with him instead.'

'We'll have a beer in the Laxen Hotel when we're done,' Gunnarsson says with a wave.

Hasse Boman disappears into the water, the surface rocks and then settles again. Gunnarsson smiles and flicks the stub of his cigarette over the edge. The diver's movements are just visible as a dark outline. Bubbles of air break the tight surface of the water. The only thing visible on the computer screen is the rough concrete wall passing by in the light of the camera. The diver's heavy breathing hisses from the speaker.

'How far down are you now?' Joona asks.

'Only nine metres,' Hasse Boman replies.

'How's the current?'

'Feels like someone's pulling my legs.'

Joona follows the diver's descent on the screen. The concrete wall glides upward. His breathing sounds heavier. Sometimes the diver's hands come into view on the wall. His blue gloves glow in the light from the lamp.

'There's nothing there,' Gunnarsson says impatiently, walking up and down anxiously a couple of times.

'The dog—'

'It didn't indicate that it had found anything,' Gunnarsson says, raising his voice.

'No, but something was bothering it,' Joona replies stubbornly.

He thinks of how the dead bodies could have been carried on the water, tumbling over the riverbed, closer and closer to the fast-moving current.

'Seventeen metres . . . the current's strong as hell now,' the diver says through the tinny speaker.

Gunnarsson is measuring out the lifeline as it runs over the metal railing and disappears into the water.

'It's going too fast,' Joona says. 'Inflate your vest.'

The diver starts to inflate his vest with air from the tanks. He usually only does that to maintain his level or rise to the surface, but he realises that Joona is right, he needs to slow his descent given the amount of debris in the water.

'No problem,' he reports a few moments later.

'If it's possible, I want you to go down and look at the mesh,' Joona explains.

Hasse moves slowly for a while before his speed starts to increase again. It feels as if the power plant has opened the gates even more. Rubbish, sticks, and leaves are drifting past his face, heading straight down.

Gunnarsson moves the camera cable and lifeline to one side as a log approaches fast and hits the edge of the dam with a thud.

68

Hasse Boman feels the strong current dragging him straight down. It's going far too fast again. The water is roaring in his ears. If there was a collision he could break both his legs. His heart is beating fast, and he tries to inflate his vest a bit more, but the valves are playing up.

He tries to slow his descent with his hands, and strands of weed come loose from the concrete wall and drift off on the current.

He doesn't mention anything to the police officers up above, but he's starting to get worried.

The suction is far stronger that he could have imagined. The water is moving faster and faster. Bubbles and grit float through his narrow field of vision and vanish. Everything outside the beam of his light is completely black.

'How deep are you now?' the superintendent from Stockholm asks.

He doesn't answer, he hasn't got time to check his depth meter, he has to stop his descent. He fumbles with his inhaler with one hand as he tries to keep himself upright with the other.

An old plastic bag swirls past.

He's hurtling down, tries to reach the vent on his back, but can't reach the valve and hits his elbow against the wall. He sways badly, can feel the adrenaline in his blood, and realises in something of a panic that he has to regain control of his descent.

'Twenty-six metres,' he gasps.

'Then you're almost at the mesh,' the superintendent says.

The water being sucked down the smooth concrete wall towards the mesh is making his legs shake uncontrollably.

Hasse is falling fast, and realises he could get skewered on a sharp branch or piece of broken wood. He's going to have to release his lead weights in order to stop, but knows he's going to need the weights to regulate his ascent when he heads back to the surface again.

The air-bubbles from his mask are being sucked downward in a sparkling stream. The suction seems to get even stronger, and a new current appears, hitting him from behind. The water gets colder very quickly. It feels like the whole river is pushing him towards the wall.

He sees a large branch, covered with leaves, heading towards him from above through the black water. The leaves brush against the concrete wall. He tries to move out of the way but it catches on the lifeline and hits him before brushing past and disappearing into the darkness.

'What was that?' the superintendent asks.

'There's a load of stuff in the water.'

With trembling hands, the diver loosens the weights from his vest, and finally slows his violent descent. Badly shaken, he floats beside the concrete wall. The visibility of the lamp is getting worse and worse as soil and grit cloud the water.

Suddenly he stops, his feet have hit something, and he looks down and realises he's reached the top edge of the mesh, a concrete shelf. There are loads of branches, leaves and rubbish, even a few tree trunks, in front of the mesh. The suction from the spillway is so strong that all movement feels impossible.

'I'm there,' he says quickly. 'But it's hard to see anything, there's a hell of a lot of crap down here . . .'

He climbs cautiously down through the branches, trying to keep his lifeline free. He makes his way past a quivering tree trunk. There's a soft dark shape moving behind a twisted pine branch. He sighs with effort as he gets closer.

'What's going on?'

'There's something here . . .'

69

The water is grey, and bubbles stream past in front of the diver's face. Clinging on with one hand, he reaches out with the other, trying to pull back the dense branches.

Suddenly it's right in front of his face. An open eye and a bare row of teeth. He gasps and almost slips, taken by surprise by how close it is. It's an optical illusion – everything feels much closer underwater. You get used to it, but when you're caught unawares it's hard to make allowances. The elk's bulky body is pressed against the mesh, but its neck is caught between a thick branch and a broken oar. The head is swinging from side to side in the strong current.

'I've found an elk,' he says, moving backwards, away from the dead animal.

'So that's what the dog was reacting to,' Gunnarsson says.

'Shall I come up?'

'Look around a bit more,' Joona replies.

'Further down or off to the side?'

'What's that? Right in front of you?' Joona asks.

'Looks like fabric,' Hasse says.

'Can you get to it?'

Hasse can feel the lactic acid in his arms and legs. He looks slowly across all the debris that has collected in front of the mesh, trying to see past black sprigs of pine and between the branches.

Everything is trembling. He tells himself that he's going to buy the new PlayStation with his earnings from this dive. He'll surprise his son with it when he comes back from football camp.

'A box, it's just a cardboard box . . .'

He tries to push the sodden cardboard aside. It disintegrates, and a large piece floats off on the current and catches against the mesh.

'I'm running out of energy, I'm coming up,' he says.

'What's that white thing?' Joona asks.

'Where?'

'Where you were looking just now, there was something there,' Joona says. 'I thought I saw something among the leaves, a bit further down by the mesh.'

'Could be a plastic bag,' the diver suggests.

'No,' Joona says.

'Come up now,' Gunnarsson calls. 'We found an elk, that's what the dog could smell.'

'A sniffer dog can be unsettled by dead bodies, but not like this one was,' Joona says. 'I think she was reacting to something else.'

Hasse Boman slowly climbs down and pulls the tangle of leaves and twigs aside. His muscles are shaking with the effort, as the strong current keeps pushing at him. He has to hold one arm out to brace against it. The lifeline is shaking the whole time.

'I can't find anything,' he gasps.

'Abort,' Gunnarsson calls.

'Shall I abort?' Hasse asks.

'If you have to,' Joona replies.

'We're not all like you,' Gunnarsson hisses at him.

'What should I do?' the diver asks. 'I need to know what to . . .'

'Keep going sideways,' Joona says.

A branch hits Hasse Boman in the neck, but he carries on looking. He pulls away some reeds and bulrushes that are covering the bottom corner of the mesh. More debris is arriving the whole time. He digs faster, and suddenly sees something unexpected. A shoulder bag, made of white, reflective fabric.

'Wait! Don't touch it!' Joona says. 'Move closer and shine the light on it.'

'Can you see now?'

'It could be Vicky's. Put it carefully in a bag.'

70

The smooth surface of the river runs inexorably towards the dam. A log is moving fast in the strong current, a protruding branch dragging across the water. Gunnarsson doesn't manage to move the lifeline out of the way in time, there's a dull thud followed by a splash, and suddenly the digital connection to the diver is gone.

'We've lost contact,' Joona says.

'He needs to come up.'

'Pull on the line three times.'

'He's not responding,' Gunnarsson says, pulling at the line.

'Pull harder,' Joona says.

Gunnarsson tugs the line three more times, and receives a response almost at once.

'He replied with two tugs,' Gunnarsson says.

'That means he's coming up.'

'It's gone slack – he's on his way. But there are more logs coming.'

'He needs to act fast,' Joona replies.

Another ten logs are heading towards the dam, moving quickly. Gunnarsson climbs over to the outside of the railing, and Joona hauls in the lifeline with his one good arm.

'I think I can see him,' Gunnarsson says, pointing.

The blue wetsuit comes into view like a flag in the wind beneath the rapidly moving water.

Joona pulls off his sling, grabs the boathook from the ground, and watches as the first log hits the dam two metres away and starts to spin around.

Joona holds the next log back, pushing it with the boathook, and it slides under the first, and they start to roll together.

Hasse Boman breaks the surface. Gunnarsson leans out and reaches his hand out towards him.

'Come on, get out!'

Hasse looks up at him in surprise and grabs hold of the edge of the dam. Still holding the boathook, Joona climbs over the railing so that he'll be able to push the logs away.

'Hurry up!' he shouts.

A log with wet black bark is approaching fast, almost hidden beneath the water.

'Look out!'

Joona drives the boathook into the log and holds the other end in line with the edge of the dam. The momentum of the log snaps the shaft of the boathook, but it changes direction and misses Hasse's head by the narrowest of margins before crashing into the dam with great force. The log swings around, hitting Hasse in the back with a wet branch so hard that he is knocked back beneath the water again.

'Try to reach him!' Joona calls.

The cable gets tangled on the log, and Hasse is dragged down with it. Bubbles break the surface. The line tenses over the metal railing with a clang. The log rolls against the concrete wall. Hasse pulls out his knife and cuts the lifeline, kicks out with his legs, and grabs Gunnarsson's hand.

Another log thuds into the previous ones, followed by three more just as Gunnarsson drags Hasse out of the water.

Gunnarsson helps him remove the heavy tanks, and Hasse slumps onto the ground. Joona takes the bag from him. With his hands shaking, the diver takes off his wetsuit. He's bruised and bleeding from scratches on his back that stain his sweaty T-shirt. He aches badly, and swears to himself when he stands up.

'This probably wasn't the smartest thing I've ever done in my life,' he pants.

'But I think you've recovered something important,' Joona says.

He looks at the handbag in the water-filled plastic bag and watches it move, almost weightless in the murky water. Some straws of yellow grass move about. He gently turns the heavy bag over and holds it up against the sun. His fingers sink into the pliant plastic and touch the bag.

'We're looking for dead bodies, and you're happy with a bloody handbag,' Gunnarsson sighs.

The sunlight passes through the plastic bag, and a shimmering yellow shadow crosses Joona's forehead. He can see dark brown marks on the bottom of the bag. Blood. He's sure it's blood.

'It's got blood on it,' Joona says. 'That's what the dog could detect, mixed with the smell of the elk . . . that's why she didn't know what signal to give.'

Joona turns the heavy, cool bag over again. The handbag moves gently as the murky water swirls around it.

71

Joona is standing outside the locked gates of the police garage in the large industrial estate on Bergsgatan in Sundsvall. He wants to talk to the forensics officers and take a look at the bag found at the dam, but no one's answering the telephone, or the intercom at the gate. The area behind the high fence looks abandoned: the car park is empty, and all the doors are closed.

Joona gets back in his car and drives to the police station on Storgatan where Gunnarsson is based. On the steps he meets Sonja Rask. She's not in uniform, her hair is wet from the shower, she's lightly made-up, and looks happy.

'Hi,' Joona says. 'Is Gunnarsson up there?'

'Ignore him,' she says, pulling a weary grimace. 'He feels so bloody threatened the whole time, he's convinced you're trying to take his job.'

'I'm just an observer.'

Sonja's dark eyes sparkle warmly at him.

'Yes, I heard you walked straight into the water and swam down to find the car.'

'Only to make observations,' Joona smiles back.

She laughs, pats him on his arm, then looks embarrassed and hurries down the steps.

Joona carries on up. Inside the police station the radio in the staffroom is switched on as usual. Someone is talking on the phone in a monotone, and through a pair of glass doors he sees about a dozen people gathered around a conference table.

Gunnarsson is sitting at one end of the table. Joona walks over to the door. A woman at the table meets Joona's gaze and shakes her head, but Joona still reaches for the handle and walks in.

'What the hell?' Gunnarsson mutters when he catches sight of him.

'I need to take a look at Vicky Bennet's handbag,' Joona says tersely.

'We're in a meeting,' Gunnarsson says in a tone that indicates that the matter is settled, then looks down at his papers.

'Everything's out at the forensic unit on Bergsgatan,' Rolf explains in an embarrassed voice.

'There's no one there,' Joona says.

'Just drop it, will you?' Gunnarsson snaps. 'The preliminary investigation has been closed, and the internal investigators can have you for breakfast as far as I'm concerned.'

Joona nods and walks out of the station, goes back to his car, and then sits there for a while before he sets off towards Sundsvall Hospital. He tries to identify what it is about the murders at the Birgitta Home that's really bothering him.

Vicky Bennet, he thinks. The nice girl who might not always be so nice. Vicky Bennet, who slashed a mother and son's faces with a broken bottle.

They've been left severely disfigured, but haven't sought medical help, and they never reported the incident to the police.

Before Vicky drowned she was the main suspect in two extremely violent murders.

The evidence suggests that she prepared in advance for events at the Birgitta Home, waited for night to fall, killed Elisabet with a hammer to get hold of her keys, returned to the house, unlocked the door to the isolation room, and killed Miranda.

The peculiar thing is that Nils Åhlén says Miranda was killed by a rock.

Why would Vicky leave the hammer in her room and use a rock instead?

Joona has thought several times that his old friend might be wrong. That's one of the reasons why he hasn't mentioned it to anyone. Nils Åhlén can present his theory himself when his report is finished.

The other odd thing is that Vicky went back to bed after the murders.

Holger Jalmert had said that Joona's observation was interesting, but impossible to prove.

But Joona knows that he saw the results of fresh blood being wiped or dried on the sheet, and how that blood left smeared marks an hour or so later when Vicky moved her arm.

Without witnesses, he's unlikely ever to get any definite answers.

Joona has read the Birgitta Home's logbook, and Elisabet Grim's last entry that Friday night, but nothing in her brief notes gives any hint of the violence that was to come.

The other girls hadn't seen anything.

None of them really knew Vicky Bennet.

Joona has already decided that he needs to try to talk to the counsellor, Daniel Grim.

It's worth a try, even though he's reluctant to intrude upon someone who's grieving. But Daniel Grim is the person the girls seemed to trust most, and if there's anyone who can understand what went on there, it's probably him.

Joona slowly pulls out his phone, feeling the pain in his shoulder, dials the number, and thinks back to the counsellor's behaviour when he arrived at the home. The way Daniel Grim tried to hold everything together in front of the girls, but when he realised that Elisabet had been murdered his face contorted with pain and confusion.

The doctor had described his state of acute shock as arousal, a condition of traumatic stress which could seriously influence his ability to remember what happened, at least for a while.

'Psychiatric clinic, Rebecka Stenbeck,' a woman answers after five rings.

'I'd like to talk to one of your patients . . . his name's Daniel Grim.'

'One moment.'

He hears the woman tap at the keyboard.

'I'm sorry, but that patient isn't taking any calls,' she says.

'Whose decision was that?'

'The doctor in charge of his care,' the woman replies coolly.

'Can you put me through to him instead?'

There's a click, and then the phone starts to ring again.

'Rimmer.'

'My name is Joona Linna, I'm a detective superintendent with the National Crime Unit,' he says. 'It's very important that I talk to a patient of yours, Daniel Grim.'

'That's as may be, but it's out of the question,' Rimmer replies at once.

'We're investigating a double murder, and—'

'No one is permitted to disregard my decision and jeopardise the patient's recovery.'

'I understand that Daniel Grim is going through an incredibly difficult time, but I promise—'

'In my estimation,' Carl Rimmer interrupts in a friendly tone, 'the patient will be well enough to be questioned by the police before too much longer.'

'When?'

'In a couple of months, I'd say.'

'I really do need to have just a very short conversation with him now,' Joona tries.

'As his doctor I have to say no,' Rimmer replies, in a tone of voice that doesn't invite discussion. 'He was extremely upset after your colleague spoke to him.'

72

Flora hurries home from the supermarket with the heavy bag of groceries. The sky is dark, but the streetlamps haven't come on yet. Her stomach clenches when she thinks about her call to the police, when her offer was rejected and she was left sitting there with her face burning with shame. The police had said it was a criminal offence to call and waste police time, but she still picked up the phone and called back to tell them about the murder weapon. Now she can't help thinking through the second conversation: 'Police,' said the same woman who had just given her a warning.

'My name is Flora Hansen,' she said, and swallowed hard. 'I called just now . . .'

'About the murders in Sundsvall,' the woman said steadily.

'I know where the murder weapon is,' she lied.

'Are you aware that I'm going to have to report this call, Flora Hansen?'

'I'm a medium, I've seen the blood-stained knife, it's lying in water . . . In dark, shimmering water – that was all I saw, but I . . . if I was paid, I could put myself in a trance and identify the exact location.'

'Flora,' the police officer said sternly. 'Within the next few days you will be informed that you are suspected of having committed an offence, and the police will . . .'

Flora had hung up at that point.

As she passes the little halal shop, she stops and looks in the rubbish bin for empty bottles, moves the bag of groceries to her left hand, and carries on towards the door. She notes that the lock has been smashed and walks straight into the stairwell.

The lift is stuck in the basement. She walks up the stairs to the second floor, unlocks the door of the flat, walks into the hall and turns the light on.

There's a click, but the light doesn't come on.

Flora puts the bag down, locks the door and takes her shoes off, but when she bends down to move them the hairs on her arms stand up.

The flat suddenly feels cold.

She takes the receipt and the change from her purse and walks into the dark living room.

She can see the sofa, the big, saggy armchair, the black screen of the television. There's a smell of electrical dust, overheated circuits.

Without walking in, she reaches out with her hand and feels across the wallpaper for the light switch.

Nothing happens when she turns it on.

'Is anyone home?' she whispers.

The floor creaks, and a teacup rattles on its saucer.

Someone moves in the darkness, and the door to the bathroom closes.

Flora follows the noise.

The linoleum floor is cold under her feet, like when you've aired rooms for too long on a winter's day. Just as Flora is reaching out to open the bathroom door she remembers that Ewa and Hans-Gunnar weren't going to be home this evening. They were going to the pizzeria to celebrate a friend's birthday. Even though she knows there can't be anyone in the bathroom, she still takes hold of the handle and opens the door.

In the grey light reflected in the bathroom mirror she sees something that makes her gasp for breath and take a step back.

A child is lying on the floor, between the bath and the toilet. It's a girl, and she's covering her eyes with her hands. There's a large dark pool of blood beside her head, and small red drops have sprayed across the white bath, and up the bathroom wall-paper and shower curtain.

Flora stumbles over the hose of the vacuum cleaner, throws her arm out, and pulls down Ewa's painted plaster picture from Copenhagen, falls backwards, and hits the back of her head on the floor in the corridor.

73

The floor is as cold as a frozen field beneath Flora's back when she raises her head and stares into the bathroom.

Her heart is thudding hard in her chest.

She can't see the girl any more.

There's no blood spattered on the edge of the bath or the shower curtain. A pair of Hans-Gunnar's jeans are lying on the floor next to the toilet.

She blinks and tells herself that she must have been mistaken.

She swallows and rests her head on the floor, and waits for her heart to calm down. An unmistakeable taste of blood spreads through her mouth.

Further along the corridor she sees that the door to her little room is open. She shivers, and goosebumps appear all over her body.

She knows she left the door closed, because she always does.

Icy air is suddenly being sucked towards her room. She sees dust-balls bouncing along the floor, and watches as they get carried along with the draught in the corridor, and past two bare feet.

Flora hears herself make a peculiar moaning sound.

The girl who was lying next to the bath is standing in the doorway to her room.

Flora tries to sit up, but her body is numb with fear. Now

she knows that she's seeing a ghost. For the first time in her life she's seeing a real ghost.

It looks like the girl's hair was once arranged smartly, but now it's tangled and bloody.

Flora is breathing fast, and can hear her pulse beating in her ears.

The girl is hiding something behind her back as she starts to walk towards Flora. She stops with her bare feet just one pace from Flora's face.

'What have I got behind my back?' the girl asks in a voice so low that her words are almost inaudible.

'You're not real,' Flora whispers.

'Do you want me to show you my hands?'

'No.'

'But I'm not holding anything . . .'

A rock falls to the floor behind the girl, making it shake and fragments of the broken plaster picture bounce.

With a smile, the child holds out her empty hands.

The rock lies behind her, between her feet, dark and heavy. It has sharp edges.

The girl tentatively puts one foot on it, making it sway, then pushes it heavily to the side.

'Just die, will you,' the girl mutters to herself. 'Just die, will you.'

The child crouches down, puts her pale grey hands on the rock and tries to take a firm grip of it, but her hands slip, and she wipes them on her dress and starts again, tipping the rock onto its side with a dull thud.

'What are you going to do?' Flora asks.

'Close your eyes and I'll be gone,' the girl replies, picking the sharp rock up and raising it above Flora's head.

The rock is heavy, but she holds it in her trembling arms immediately above Flora's face. The dark underside of the rock looks wet.

Suddenly the electricity comes back on. Lights go on all over the place. Flora rolls sideways and sits up. The girl is gone. She can hear loud voices from the television, and the fridge is rumbling.

She gets up and switches more lights on, goes to her room, opens the door, turns the light on, opens the wardrobes, and looks under the bed. Then she goes and sits down at the kitchen table. She only realises how badly her hands are shaking when she tries to call the police.

The automatic exchange offers her a number of options. She can report a crime, leave information, or she can ask a question. This last option offers her the chance to talk to an operator.

'Police,' a friendly voice says in her ear. 'How can I help you?'

'I'd like to talk to someone working on what happened up in Sundsvall,' Flora says in a shaky voice.

'What's this about?'

'I think . . . I think I've seen the murder weapon,' Flora whispers.

'I see,' the receptionist says. 'Then I suggest that you talk to our tip-off team. I'll put you through to them.'

Flora is about to protest when she hears the line click. After just a few seconds another woman answers.

'Police tip-off unit, how can I help?'

Flora doesn't know if it's the woman who got cross with her when she lied about the bloody knife.

'I'd like to talk to someone working on the murders up in Sundsvall,' she says.

'You can talk to me first,' the voice says.

'It was a rock,' Flora says.

'I can't hear what you're saying, can you speak a bit louder, please?'

'The murders up in Sundsvall . . . You need to look for a rock. The underside is covered in blood, and . . .'

Flora falls silent and feels sweat starting to run down her sides.

'How do you come to know anything about the murders in Sundsvall?'

'I . . . someone told me.'

'Someone told you about the murders in Sundsvall?'

'Yes,' Flora whispers.

She can hear her pulse thudding in her temples, and there's a rushing sound in her ears.

'Go on,' the woman says.

'The murderer used a rock . . . a rock with sharp edges, that's all I know.'

'What's your name?'

'That doesn't matter, I just wanted . . .'

'I recognise your voice,' the police officer says. 'It was you who called and talked about a large knife before. I've filed a report against you, Flora Hansen . . . but you ought to contact a doctor, because you probably need help.'

The policewoman ends the call, and Flora is left standing with the phone in her hand. She jumps and knocks over the kitchen-roll holder when the bag of groceries falls over out in the hall.

74

An hour ago Elin Frank returned home to her apartment from a long meeting with the board of Kingston, a large subsidiary, to discuss two holding companies in the United Kingdom.

She feels a surge of angst when she remembers that she mixed Valium and alcohol and had sex with the photographer from *Vogue*. She tells herself that she needed a distraction, it was a little adventure, she needed it, it had been a long time since she last had sex. But the thought of it still leaves her sweaty with embarrassment.

She grabs a bottle of Perrier from the fridge and walks through the rooms in her old pale red jogging bottoms and a washed-out T-shirt with a faded picture of Abba. In the sitting room she stops in front of the television just as a very tall woman leaps at the high-jump in a large arena. Elin puts the bottle of mineral water on the glass table, takes the scrunchie she's wearing around her wrist, and gathers her hair in a ponytail before carrying on into the bedroom.

Later that evening she has a conference call with her subdivision in Chicago while she gets a manicure and paraffin bath, and at eight o'clock she's due to go to a charity dinner, where she'll sit at one of the top tables with the head of Volvo as her partner. The Crown Princess is going to present an award from one of the big national funds, and Roxette will be providing the entertainment.

She walks among the tall wardrobes in her walk-in closet, still hearing the sound of the television but no longer listening actively, so she doesn't realise that the news has started. She opens a few of the wardrobes and glances at the outfits. Eventually she pulls out a metallic green dress that Alexander McQueen designed for her himself.

The name Vicky Bennet rings out from the television.

With anxiety thudding through her, she drops the dress on the floor and hurries back to the sitting room.

The large television has a thin white frame and looks like the sharp picture is being projected directly onto the white wall. A superintendent named Olle Gunnarsson is being interviewed in front of a nondescript police station. He's trying to smile patiently, but looks irritated. He rubs his moustache and nods.

'I can't comment on that while the investigation is still ongoing,' he replies, and clears his throat.

'But you've broken off the search using divers?'

'That's correct.'

'Does that mean you've found the bodies?'

'I'm not in a position to answer that.'

The light from the television flickers around the room, and Elin stares at the images of the damaged car being raised from the water. The crane lifts it straight up, it breaks the surface and starts to sway. Water cascades from it as a serious voice explains that the car stolen by Vicky Bennet was found in the Indal River earlier in the day, and that both Vicky Bennet, who is suspected of murder, and four-year-old Dante Abrahamsson are feared dead.

'The police haven't made an official statement about the discovery, but according to sources we've spoken to, the divers have been called off and the national alert withdrawn . . .'

Elin doesn't hear what the newsreader says as they show a picture of Vicky. She's older and thinner, but she hasn't really changed. It feels as if Elin's heart has stopped. She has a sudden memory of how it felt to carry the little girl when she was asleep.

'No,' Elin whispers. 'No . . .'

She stares at the girl's thin, pale face. At her messy, tangled hair, always so hard to sort out.

She's still a child, and now they're saying she's dead. The look in her eyes is obstinate, as if she's being made to look at the camera.

Elin moves away from the television, sways, and reaches out to the wall for support, and doesn't notice as an oil painting by Erland Cullberg comes loose and falls to the floor.

'No, no, no,' she whimpers. 'Not that, not that . . . no, no . . .'

The last thing she heard from Vicky was her sobbing out on the landing, and now she's dead.

'No! It can't be true!' she screams.

With her heart pounding she goes over to the illuminated display case containing the large Passover Seder plate she was given by her father, which has been passed down the family for generations. She grabs hold of the top of the case and pulls it over with all her strength. It falls to the floor with a loud crash. The glass sides shatter, scattering shards across the parquet floor, and the beautifully decorated dish smashes.

As if she has terrible cramp, she doubles over and curls up on the floor. She gasps for breath as she keeps thinking over and over that she once had a daughter.

I had a daughter, I had a daughter, I had a daughter.

She sits up, grabs a large piece of her father's Seder plate, and pulls the sharp edge hard across her wrist. Warm blood starts to flow, dripping into her lap. She pulls the sharp splinter across her wrist again and sighs with pain, then hears the lock on the front door rattle as someone opens the door and comes in.

75

Joona is browning two thick slices of fillet steak in a cast-iron pan. He's sealed the meat and spiced it with coarsely ground black and green pepper. When the surface of the tournedos has caramelised he transfers them to the oven, adds salt, and places them on top of the potato wedges. As the meat finishes cooking he makes a sauce from port, currants, veal stock, and truffle.

With detached calm he pours two glasses of Saint-Émilion.

The kitchen is full of the earthy scent of Merlot and Cabernet Franc by the time the doorbell rings.

Disa is standing there in a red and white spotted raincoat. Her eyes are wide, and her face wet with rain.

'Joona, I was thinking of testing you to see if you're as good a police officer as everyone says.'

'How do you test that?' he asks.

'It's just a test,' she says. 'Do you think I look the same as usual?'

'More beautiful,' he replies.

'No,' she smiles.

'You've had your hair cut and are using the hairgrip from Paris for the first time in a year.'

'Anything else?'

He looks at her thin, blushing face, her glossy bobbed hair, and slender body.

'Those are new,' he says, pointing at her high-heeled boots.

'Marc Jacobs . . . a bit too expensive for me.'

'Nice.'

'Nothing else?'

'I haven't finished,' he says, and takes her hands in his, turns them over and looks at her nails.

She can't help smiling when he mutters that she's wearing the same lipstick she had on when they went to the Södermalm Theatre. He gently touches her earrings, then meets her gaze, and holds it, then steps aside so the light from the floor lamp shines on her face.

'Your eyes,' he says. 'Your left pupil isn't contracting in the light.'

'Clever policeman,' she says. 'I've got some drops.'

'You've had your eyes looked at?' he asks.

'The vitreous body is slightly dented, but it's nothing to worry about,' Disa says, and walks into the kitchen.

'Food's nearly ready. The meat just needs to rest a bit longer.'

'You've made it look lovely,' Disa says.

'We haven't seen each other for a long time,' he says. 'I'm very glad you've come.'

They raise their glasses in a silent toast, and, as always when Joona looks at her, she feels hot, as if she's starting to shimmer. Disa forces herself to look away from his eyes, rolls the wine around the glass, inhales the bouquet, then tastes it again.

'Right temperature,' she says.

Joona lays the steak and potatoes on a bed of rocket, basil, and thyme.

He carefully drizzles the sauce over the plate while he thinks to himself that he should have had a serious talk with Disa a long time ago.

'How have you been?'

'Without you, you mean? Better than ever,' Disa says waspishly.

Neither of them speaks, and she gently places her hand over his.

'Sorry,' she says. 'But I get so angry with you sometimes. When I'm my worst self.'

'Who are you at the moment?'

'My worst self,' she says.

Joona takes a sip of the wine.

'I've been thinking a lot about the past recently,' he begins.

She smiles and raises her eyebrows: 'Recently? You're always thinking about the past.'

'Am I?'

'Yes, you think . . . but you don't talk about it.'

'No, I . . .'

He falls silent, and his pale grey eyes narrow. Disa feels a chill run down her spine.

'You asked me to dinner because we needed to talk,' she says. 'I'd made up my mind never to talk to you again, but then you call out of the blue . . . after a gap of several months . . .'

'Yes, because . . .'

'You don't give a damn about me, Joona.'

'Disa . . . think what you like about me,' he says seriously. 'But I want you to know that I care about you . . . I care about you, and I think about you all the time.'

'Yes,' she says slowly, and stands up without meeting his gaze. 'It's do with other things, about terrible things that . . .'

Joona stands there and watches as she puts her raincoat back on.

'Goodbye,' she whispers.

'Disa, I need you,' he hears himself say. 'I want you.'

She stares at him. Her dark, glossy fringe reaches her eyelashes.

'What did you say?' she asks after a pause.

'I want you, Disa.'

'Don't say that,' she mumbles, zipping up her boots.

'I need you, I've needed you all along,' he goes on. 'But I haven't been prepared to put you at risk, I couldn't bear the thought that anything might happen to you if we . . .'

'What would happen to me?' she interrupts.

'You could disappear,' he explains simply, cupping her face in his hands.

'You're the one who disappears,' she whispers.

'I don't frighten easily, I'm talking about real things that . . .'

She stretches up on tiptoe and kisses him on the lips, then

stays close enough to feel the warmth of his breath. He feels for her mouth and kisses her tentatively several times until she parts her lips.

They kiss slowly, and Joona unbuttons her raincoat and lets it fall to the floor.

'Disa,' he whispers, stroking her shoulders and back.

He presses himself against her, breathes in her silky scent, kisses her collarbone and slender neck, and ends up with her gold chain in his mouth, then kisses her chin and soft, moist mouth.

He feels for her warm skin inside her thin blouse. The small press-studs open with a click. Her nipples are stiff and her stomach fluttering with her rapid breathing.

She looks seriously into his eyes and pulls him with her towards the bedroom. Her blouse is open and her breasts glow white as porcelain.

They stop and feel for each other's mouths again. His hands slide over the base of her spine, her backside, and in under the slippery fabric of her pants.

Disa gently pulls away and she feels the heat in her crotch and knows that she's already wet. Her cheeks flush red and her hands tremble as she unbuttons his trousers.

76

After breakfast Disa stays in bed with her cup of coffee and reads the *Sunday Times* on her iPad while Joona showers and gets dressed.

Yesterday he decided not to go to the Nordic Museum to look at the Sami bridal crown made of woven roots.

He spent the time with Disa instead. It wasn't planned. But it was probably the result of Rosa Bergman's dementia finally severing all links to Summa and Lumi.

More than twelve years have passed.

He has to accept that there was nothing to be frightened about.

But he should have talked to Disa before, should have warned her and told her about what he's scared of, so that she can make the decision for herself.

He stands in the doorway looking at her for a long time before she notices, then goes out into the kitchen and calls Professor Holger Jalmert.

'This is Joona Linna.'

'I heard that Gunnarsson got unpleasant,' Holger says with amusement. 'I've promised him that I wouldn't send you any copies of the report.'

'But you're allowed to talk to me?' Joona asks, taking his sandwich and coffee and waving at Disa, who's frowning as she reads.

'Probably not,' Holger laughs, then turns serious again.

'Have you had a chance to look at the handbag we found at the dam?' Joona asks.

'Yes, I've finished. I'm in the car on my way home to Umeå now.'

'Was there anything with writing on inside the bag?'

'Nothing but a receipt from a newsagents.'

'Mobile phone?'

'Sadly not,' Holger says.

'So what have we got?' Joona says, as his eyes scan the grey sky above the rooftops.

Holger breathes in through his nose, and then says, as if he's reading out loud: 'In all likelihood the stains on the bag are blood. I cut off a fragment and sent it to the National Forensics Laboratory at once . . . A bit of make-up, two different lipsticks, a stub of black eyeliner, a pink plastic hairgrip, hairpins, a purse with a skull on it, a bit of money, a photograph of herself, some sort of cycling tool, a tub of pills with no label . . . also sent for analysis . . . a blister-pack of Stesolid, two pens . . . and hidden in the lining of the bag I found a cutlery knife that had been sharpened as keenly as a sushi-knife.'

'No writing, no names or addresses?'

'No, that was everything . . .'

Joona hears Disa's footsteps on the wooden floor behind him, but doesn't move. He feels the warmth of her body, shivers, then feels her soft lips against the back of his neck and her arms around his body.

While Disa is in the shower Joona sits at the kitchen table and calls Solveig Sundström, who is now responsible for the girls from the Birgitta Home.

She might know what medication Vicky was taking.

The phone rings eight times, then there's a click, and voice says: 'Caroline here . . . answering an ugly phone that was lying on the sofa.'

'Is Solveig there?'

'No, I don't know where she is right now – can I give her a message?'

Caroline is the older girl, a head taller than Tuula. She had the scars of old injections in the crook of her arm, but seemed sensible, intelligent, and serious about her attempt to change.

'Is everything OK with you all?' he asks.

'You're that detective – aren't you?'

'Yes.'

Silence, then Caroline asks tentatively: 'Is it true that Vicky's dead?'

'I'm afraid we believe it is,' Joona replies.

'It feels really weird,' Caroline says.

'Do you know what medication she was taking?'

'Vicky?'

'Yes.'

'She was incredibly thin and pretty for someone on Zyprexa.'

'That's an antidepressant, isn't it?'

'I used to be on it, but now I only take Imovane to help me sleep,' the girl says. 'It's a hell of a relief not to have to take Zyprexa.'

'Side effects?'

'It probably varies, but for me . . . I must have put on at least ten kilos.'

'Does it make you tired?' Joona asks, seeing in his mind's eye the blood-stained sheets that Vicky had slept in.

'At first it's the other way around . . . I only had to lick one of those pills and all the crap started . . . your skin starts to crawl and you get irritated about nothing and yell at everyone . . . I threw my phone at the wall once, and pulled the curtains down . . . but after a while it all changes and you feel like you've got a warm blanket wrapped around you . . . you feel all calm and just want to sleep.'

'Do you know if Vicky was on any other medication?'

'She probably did the same as most people, and kept a little stock of all the things that actually work . . . Stesolid, Lyrica, Ketogan . . .'

There's a voice in the background, and Joona understands

that the nurse has come into the room and has seen Caroline holding a phone to her ear.

'I'm going to report this as theft,' the woman says.

'It rang and I answered,' Caroline says. 'It's a detective who wants to talk to you . . . You're suspected of the murder of Miranda Ericsdotter.'

'Don't be stupid,' the woman snaps, then takes the phone and clears her throat before speaking: 'Solveig Sundström.'

'My name is Joona Linna, I'm a detective superintendent with the National Crime Unit, and I'm investigating . . .'

The woman ends the call without a word, and Joona doesn't bother to call back, given that he's already found out what he wanted to know.

77

A white Opel stops beneath the flat Statoil canopy, and a woman wearing a pale blue knitted top gets out, turns towards the card-payment pump, and searches in her bag.

Ari Määtilainen looks away from the woman and lays two chunky sausages on a bed of mashed potato with bacon mayo and fried onions. He looks at the fat biker waiting for the food and explains automatically that he can help himself to coffee and Coca-Cola from the dispenser.

The array of zips on the biker's leather jacket scrapes the glass counter as he leans forward to take the food.

'*Danke*,' he says, and walks off to the coffee machine.

Ari turns the radio up slightly and sees that the woman in the pale blue top has walked away a little as the petrol pours into the Opel's tank.

Ari listens as the newsreader gives the latest developments in the ongoing kidnapping case.

'The search for Vicky Bennet and Dante Abrahamsson has been called off. The Västernorrland Police haven't released a statement, but sources indicate that the two missing children are now believed to have died on Saturday morning. There has been some criticism of the fact that the police issued a national alert. We have tried to reach the head of the National Crime Unit, Carlos Eliasson, for a comment . . .'

'What the hell . . . ?' Ari whispers.

He finds the Post-it note next to the till, picks up his phone, and dials the number for the police again.

'Police, Sonja Rask here,' a woman's voice answers.

'Hello,' Ari says. 'I saw them . . . I saw the girl and the little boy.'

'Who am I talking to?'

'Ari Määtilainen . . . I work at the Statoil petrol station in Dingersjö . . . I was just listening to the radio, and they said they're supposed to have died on Saturday morning, but they can't have done, because I saw them late on Saturday night.'

'Do you mean Vicky Bennet and Dante Abrahamsson?' Sonja asks sceptically.

'Yes, I saw them here that night, it was actually early Sunday morning, so they can't have died on Saturday like they said on the radio, can they?'

'You saw Vicky Bennet and Dante Abrahamsson on—'

'Yes.'

'Why didn't you call and tell us straight away?'

'I did, I talked to a police officer.'

Ari remembers that he had been listening to Radio Gold on Saturday night and Sunday morning. The national alert hadn't yet been issued, but the local media were asking the public to keep an eye out for the girl and little boy.

At eleven o'clock an articulated lorry pulled into the car park on the far side of the pumps.

The driver slept for three hours.

It was the middle of the night, a quarter past two, when he saw them.

Ari looked at the screen showing the various security cameras. One of them showed the lorry from a different angle. The petrol station looked deserted as the large vehicle started up and drove off. Suddenly Ari saw a shape at the back of the building, fairly close to the exit from the car wash. Not one, but two people. He stared at the screen. The lorry turned and drove towards the exit. The headlights swept across the big window, and Ari left his place behind the counter and ran around the building. But they were already gone. The girl and the little boy were gone.

78

Joona parks in front of the Statoil petrol station in Dingersjö, 360 kilometres north of Stockholm. It's a sunny day, there's a brisk wind, and torn advertising banners are flapping noisily. Joona and Disa were sitting having lunch together at Villa Källhagen when he received a phone call from a nervous Constable Sonja Rask in Sundsvall.

Joona walks into the shop. A hollow-eyed man wearing a Statoil cap is arranging paperback books on a rack. Joona looks at the menu, then at the shiny sausages rotating on the mechanical grill.

'What would you like?' the man asks.

'*Makkarakeitto,*' Joona says in Finnish.

'*Suomalainen makkarakeitto,*' Ari Määtilainen says with a smile. 'My grandmother used to make sausage soup when I was little.'

'With rye bread?'

'Yes, but sadly I only get to sell Swedish food here,' he says, pointing at the hamburgers.

'I'm not actually here to eat – I'm from the police.'

'Yes, I gathered that . . . I spoke to one of your colleagues the night I saw them,' Ari says, gesturing towards the screen.

'What had you seen when you called?' Joona asks.

'A girl and a little boy out the back here.'

'You saw them on the screen?'

'Yes.'

'Clearly?'

'No, but . . . I'm used to keeping an eye on what goes on here.'

'Did the police come out here that night?'

'He came the next morning, Gunnarsson, his name was, he didn't think you could see anything, and told me I could wipe the tape.'

'But you haven't,' Joona says.

'What do you think?'

'I think you store recordings on an external hard drive.'

With a smile Ari Määtilainen shows Joona into a small office next to the stockroom. There's an unfolded sofa bed, some cans of Red Bull on the floor, and a carton of soured milk by the frost-covered window. On an old school desk there's a small laptop connected to an external hard drive. Ari Määtilainen sits down on the creaking office chair and quickly looks through the files, which are arranged by date and time.

'I'd heard on the radio that everyone was looking for a girl and a little boy, then I saw them here in the middle of the night,' he says, and clicks on one of the files.

Joona leans closer to the grubby screen, which shows four different views of the interior and exterior of the petrol station. A digital clock indicates the time. The grey images are completely static. Ari is visible behind the counter. Occasionally he turns the page of his newspaper and eats some fried onion rings.

'That articulated lorry had been here for three hours,' Ari says, pointing at one of the images. 'But it's about to set off . . .'

A dark shadow moves inside the cab.

'Can you enlarge the image?' Joona asks.

'Hang on . . .'

Suddenly a clump of trees lights up in a white glow as the lorry starts up and the headlamps come on.

Ari clicks on the other external image and switches to full-screen.

'This is where you see them,' he whispers.

The screen shows the lorry from a different angle. It starts to move, and rolls slowly forward. Ari points towards the bottom of the screen, at the back of the petrol station, with its bins and recycling containers. The area is in deep shade, and completely still. Then suddenly there's a sign of movement in the black glass of the door to the car wash, and then there's someone there, a thin figure right by the wall.

The image is grainy and flickering in various shades of grey. It's impossible to see a face or any other details. But it's definitely a person, and something else too.

'Can the picture be improved?' Joona asks.

'Hold on,' Ari whispers.

The lorry turns towards the exit. Suddenly the light from the headlamps hits the garage door beside the figure. The glass flares white for a few seconds, and the back of the petrol station is briefly bathed in light.

Joona sees that the figure is a thin girl and a younger child. They watch the lorry go, then everything goes dark again.

Ari points at the screen, which shows the two figures running along the dark grey wall and disappearing into grainy blackness and out of shot.

'You saw them?' Ari asks.

'Rewind,' Joona says.

He doesn't have to say which sequence he wants to look at again. Moments later Ari replays the brightly lit fragment very slowly.

The lorry barely seems to be moving now, but the light from the headlamps moves jerkily through the trees and across the façade of the petrol station, filling the panes of glass with white. The smaller child's face is looking down and in shadow. The thin girl is barefoot, and it looks like she's got plastic bags over both her hands. The light becomes jaggedly brighter as the girl slowly raises her hand.

Joona sees that they aren't plastic bags, but bandages that have unravelled. They swing wetly in the strong light, and he knows that Vicky Bennet and Dante Abrahamsson didn't drown in the river.

The digital clock shows fourteen minutes past two on Sunday morning.

Somehow they got out of the car and across the fast-flowing water to the other side of the river, and then made their way 150 kilometres south.

The girl's tangled hair is framing her face. Her dark eyes flare intensely before the screen turns almost black again.

They're alive, Joona thinks. They're both still alive.

79

The head of the National Crime Unit, Carlos Eliasson, is standing demonstratively with his back to the door when Joona walks into his office.

'Sit down,' he says in an oddly expectant tone of voice.

'I've just driven back from Sundsvall and—'

'Wait,' Carlos interrupts.

Joona looks at his back in bemusement, and sits down on the light brown leather chair. He looks at the shiny surface of the untouched desk, the reflections in the wood veneer from the aquariums.

Carlos takes a deep breath, then turns around. He looks different, unshaven. There are sparse patches of greying stubble on his top lip and chin.

'So what do you think?' he asks with a broad smile.

'You've got a beard,' Joona says slowly.

'A full beard,' Carlos says happily. 'Well . . . I'm expecting it to thicken up soon. I'm not going to shave again, I've thrown my razor away.'

'Great,' Joona says curtly.

'But my beard isn't what we were going to talk about,' Carlos declares. 'As I understand it, the diver didn't find any bodies.'

'No,' Joona says, and pulls out a printout from the security-camera footage at the petrol station. 'We didn't find the bodies . . .'

'Here we go,' Carlos mutters to himself.

'Because they weren't in the river,' Joona says.

'And you're sure about that?'

'Vicky Bennet and Dante Abrahamsson are still alive.'

'Gunnarsson called me about the recording from the petrol station, and . . .'

'Issue another national alert,' Joona interrupts.

'A national alert? You can't keep turning a national alert on and off.'

'I know it's Vicky Bennet and Dante Abrahamsson in this picture,' Joona says sternly, pointing at the printout. 'And it was taken hours after the car went into the river. They're alive, and we have to issue another national alert.'

Carlos stretches one leg out.

'You can put the Spanish boot on me if you like, but I'm not going to report them missing again.'

'Look at the photograph,' Joona says.

'The Västernorrland Police have been to the petrol station today,' Carlos says, folding the printout into a tiny, hard square. 'They've sent a copy of the hard drive to the National Forensics Laboratory, and two of their experts have examined the recording and have concluded that it's quite impossible to identify the people outside the petrol station with any degree of certainty.'

'But you know I'm right,' Joona says.

'OK,' Carlos nods. 'Let's say that, you could be right, we'll see . . . but I'm not going to make a fool of myself by issuing a missing person's report for someone the police regard as dead.'

'I'm not backing down until—'

'Hold on, hold on,' Carlos interrupts, and takes a deep breath. 'Joona, the senior prosecutor is currently looking at the internal investigation into your conduct.'

'But that's—'

'I'm your boss, and I have to take this complaint against you seriously, and I want to hear you admit that you're not actually in charge of the preliminary investigation up in Sundsvall.'

'I'm not in charge of the preliminary investigation.'

'And what does an observer do if the district prosecutor in Sundsvall decides to close the case?'

'Nothing.'

'Then we're agreed,' Carlos smiles.

'No,' Joona says, and walks out of the room.

80

Flora is lying on her bed staring up at the ceiling. Her heart is still racing. She was dreaming that she was in a small room with a girl who didn't want to show her face. The girl was hiding behind a wooden ladder. There was something wrong with her, something dangerous. All she was wearing was a pair of white cotton underpants, and Flora could see her girlish breasts. She waited for Flora to come closer, then turned away, giggled, and covered her eyes with her hands.

The previous evening Flora had read about the murders in Sundsvall, about Miranda Ericsdotter and Elisabet Grim. She can't stop thinking about the ghost that visited her. It already feels like a dream, even though she knows it was the dead girl that she saw in the corridor. The girl can't have been more than five years old, but now in her dream she was the same age as Miranda.

Flora lies completely still and listens. Every creak in the furniture and floors makes her heart beat faster.

Someone who's afraid of the dark isn't the master of their own house. They creep about, wary of their own movements.

Flora doesn't know what to do. It is a quarter to eight. She sits up, then goes over to the door, opens it, and listens for noises in the flat.

No one else is awake yet.

She creeps to the kitchen to prepare Hans-Gunnar's coffee. The morning sun reflects off the scratched worktop.

Flora takes an unbleached filter, folds the edges, places it in the holder, and gets so scared that she holds her breath when she hears sticky footsteps behind her.

She turns and sees Ewa standing in the doorway of her bedroom in a blue T-shirt and underpants.

'What is it?' she asks when she sees Flora's face. 'Have you been crying?'

'I . . . I have to ask . . . because I think I've seen a ghost,' Flora says. 'Have you seen her? Here in the flat. A little girl—'

'What's wrong with you, Flora?'

She turns to go into the living room, but Flora puts her hand on her chunky arm and stops her.

'But this is real, I swear . . . someone had hit her with a rock on the back of—'

'You swear,' Ewa interrupts sharply.

'I just . . . Can't there be ghosts for real?'

Ewa grabs her by one ear, holds it tight and pulls her forward.

'I don't understand why you like telling lies, but you do,' Ewa says. 'You always have done, and you—'

'But I saw—'

'Shut up,' Ewa hisses, and twists her ear.

'Ow—'

'But we're not going to tolerate this,' she says, and twists harder.

'Please, stop . . . Ow!'

Ewa gives Flora's ear a final twist, then lets go. Flora stands there with tears in her eyes, clutching her hand to her stinging ear as Ewa walks to the bathroom. After a while she starts the coffee machine and goes back to her room. She closes the door behind her, turns the light on, and lies down on the bed to cry.

She has always assumed that all spiritual mediums were only pretending to see spirits.

'I don't understand anything,' she mutters.

What if she really did summon the ghost with her seances? Maybe it didn't make any difference that she didn't believe in them herself. When she called them and formed a circle with the other participants, the portal to the other side opened, and those who were waiting beyond could suddenly just walk through.

Because I really did see a ghost, she thinks.

I saw the dead girl as a young child.

Miranda wanted to show me something.

It's not impossible, it must be able to happen. She's read about how the energy of people who die doesn't disappear. Plenty of people have claimed that ghosts exist without being regarded as mentally ill.

Flora tries to gather her thoughts and go through everything that's happened in the past few days.

The girl came to me in a dream, she thinks. I've dreamed about her, I know that, but when I saw her in the corridor I was awake, so it was real. I saw her standing there in front of me, I heard her speak, I felt her presence.

Flora lies back on the bed, closes her eyes, and thinks that she could actually have fainted when she fell and hit her head on the floor.

There was a pair of jeans lying on the floor between the toilet and the bath.

I got scared, stumbled backwards, and fell.

She is filled with a sudden sense of relief when she realises that she could actually have been dreaming the first time she saw the girl.

She must have passed out on the floor and dreamed about the ghost.

That was what happened.

She shuts her eyes again and smiles to herself when she suddenly notices the strange smell in the room, like burned hair.

She sits up and shivers when she sees that there's something lying under her pillow. She angles the bedside lamp and folds the pillow back. On her white under-sheet is the large, sharp rock.

'Why haven't you closed your eyes?' a high-pitched voice asks.

The girl is standing in the gloom behind the bedside lamp,

looking at her without breathing. Her hair is matted and dark with dried blood. The light from the lamp is dazzling Flora, but she can see that the girl's thin arms are grey, and her brown veins form a rusty network under her dead skin.

'You mustn't look at me,' the girl says harshly, and turns the light out.

The room goes dark, and Flora falls off her bed. Pale blue spots are dancing in front of her eyes. The lamp hits the floor, the bedclothes rustle, and she hears quick footsteps across the floor, walls, and ceiling. Flora crawls away and gets to her feet, fumbles with the door, and stumbles into the corridor. She manages to stop herself screaming. She just whimpers quietly, tries to stay calm, and walks towards the kitchen, leaning on the wall to stop herself falling. Gasping for breath, Flora grabs the phone from the hall table, but drops it on the floor. She kneels down and calls the police.

81

Robert had come in and found Elin on her knees beside the shattered display case.

'Elin, what on earth's going on?'

She got to her feet without looking at him. Blood was running down her left arm into her hand, and dripping steadily from three fingertips.

'You're bleeding from . . .'

Elin merely walked across the broken glass heading towards her bedroom, when he stopped her and said he'd call for her doctor.

'I don't want you to, I don't care . . .'

'Elin!' he cried anxiously. 'You're bleeding.'

She looked at her arm and said maybe it would be a good idea to get it seen to, then went into her office, leaving a trail of blood behind her.

She sat down at the computer and looked up the number for the National Crime Unit, called the main switchboard, and asked to talk to whoever was in charge of the investigation into the murders at the Birgitta Home. A woman connected her call and she repeated her question, then heard a slow intake of breath as someone tapped at a keyboard, sighed, then tapped some more.

'The preliminary investigation is being led by the district prosecutor in Sundsvall,' a man with a high voice explained.

'Aren't there any police officers I could talk to?'

'The prosecutor is working with the Västernorrland Police.'

'I received a visit from a superintendent from National Crime, a tall man with grey eyes and—'

'Joona Linna.'

'Yes.'

Elin picked up a pen and wrote the number on the front of a glossy fashion magazine, thanked him for his help, and hung up.

She quickly dialled the superintendent's number, only to be told that he was away on police business and expected back the following day.

Elin was just about to call the district prosecutor's office in Sundsvall when her doctor arrived. He didn't ask any questions, and Elin sat in silence while he washed and dressed her wounds. She looked at the phone, which was lying on the August issue of British *Vogue*. Joona Linna's number was written across Gwyneth Paltrow's breasts.

After she'd been patched up, she went back to the sitting room, where the cleaners had already removed all the glass and mopped the floor. The display cabinet had been taken away, and Robert had gathered the fragments of the Seder plate so that they could be taken to a conservator at the Museum of Mediterranean Culture.

82

Elin Frank doesn't smile at anyone as she walks slowly along the corridor leading to Joona Linna's room in Police Headquarters. She's wearing dark sunglasses to hide the fact that she's been crying. Her graphite-grey trench coat from Burberry is open, and she's wearing a silver-coloured silk shawl over her hair. The deep cuts in her wrist ache and throb constantly.

Her heels click on the shabby floor of the corridor. A poster with the words 'If you think you're worthless and that bruises are a normal part of everyday life, you should talk to us' flutters as she passes. A few men in dark blue police sweaters disappear towards the part of the building where the rapid-response unit is based. A stocky woman in a bright red angora jumper and a tight black skirt comes out of a room and waits for her with her hands by her sides.

'My name is Anja Larsson,' the woman says.

Elin tries to say that she wants to talk to Joona Linna, but her voice won't hold. The large woman smiles at her and says she'll show her to the superintendent's room.

'Sorry,' Elin whispers.

'Don't worry,' Anja says, leading her to Joona's room, then knocking and opening the door.

'Thanks for the tea,' Joona says, pulling up a chair for Elin.

She sits down heavily, and Anja and Joona exchange a brief glance.

'I'll fetch some water,' Anja says, and leaves them.

Silence settles on the room. Elin tries to calm down enough to be able to speak. She waits a little while, then says: 'I know it's too late for anything, and I know I didn't help you when you came to see me, and . . . and I can guess what you think of me, and . . .'

She loses her thread, the corners of her mouth turn down, and tears start to flow, running behind the sunglasses and down her cheeks. Anja comes back in with a glass of water and a bunch of damp grapes on a saucer, then leaves the room again.

'I'd like to talk about Vicky Bennet now,' Elin says in a steady voice.

'I'm listening,' he says warmly.

'She was six years old when she came to me, and I had . . . I had her for nine months . . .'

'So I understand,' he says.

'But what you don't know is that I . . . I let her down in a way that no one should ever let anyone else down.'

'Sometimes we have no choice,' Joona Linna says.

She takes her sunglasses off with trembling hands. She looks intently at the detective sitting opposite her, his fair, untidy hair, serious face, and those constantly-changing grey eyes.

'I really don't like myself any more,' she says. 'But I . . . I'd like to make a proposal . . . I'm happy to cover all the costs . . . so that you can find the bodies . . . and so that the investigation can carry on without being cut back.'

'Why would you do that?' Joona asks.

'Even if I can't put anything right, at least I can . . . I mean, what if she's innocent?'

'There's nothing to support that.'

'No, but I just can't believe . . .'

Elin falls silent, and her eyes fill with tears again.

'Because she was so sweet as a child?'

'Most of the time she wasn't even that,' Elin smiles.

'I was starting to get that impression.'

'Will you continue the investigation if I pay?'

'We can't accept money from you in order to—'

'I'm sure there's a legal way of arranging it.'

'Perhaps, but it wouldn't change anything,' Joona explains gently. 'The prosecutor is about to close the investigation . . .'

'What can I do?' Elin whispers desperately.

'I shouldn't be telling you this, but I'm going to carry on, because I'm certain that Vicky is still alive.'

'But they said on the news . . .' Elin whispers, then stands up with one hand over her mouth.

'The car was found at a depth of four metres, and there was blood and strands of hair on the frame of the shattered windscreen,' he says.

'But you don't believe they're dead?' she asks, quickly wiping the tears from her cheeks.

'I know they didn't drown in the river,' he replies.

'Dear God,' Elin whispers.

83

Elin sits back down in the chair and sobs with her face turned away. Joona gives her some space, and goes over to look out of the window. Thin rain is falling, and the trees in the park are swaying in the afternoon wind.

'Have you got any idea where she might be hiding?' he asks after a while.

'Her mother often sleeps in various garages . . . I met Susie when she was going to try looking after Vicky over a weekend . . . she had a flat in Hallonbergen at the time, but that didn't work out, they slept in the underground, and Vicky was found on her own in the tunnel between Slussen and Mariatorget.'

'It could be very hard to find her,' Joona says.

'I haven't seen Vicky for eight years, but the staff at the Birgitta Home . . . people who've spoken to her, they must know something,' Elin says.

'Yes,' Joona says, then falls silent.

'What?'

He meets her gaze.

'The only people Vicky spoke to were the nurse who was murdered . . . and her husband, who works as a counsellor. He ought to know a lot . . . or something, at least, but he's in a very bad way, and his doctor won't let the police talk to him. There's nothing I can do about that, the doctor believes being questioned by the police would harm his recovery.'

'But I'm not a police officer,' Elin says. 'I could talk to him.'

She looks up at Joona and realises that that was exactly what he was hoping she'd say.

In the lift down, she can feel the heavy, almost drugged tiredness that comes after a lot of crying. She thinks about the superintendent's voice, his soft Finnish accent. His eyes were a beautiful grey colour, yet simultaneously incredibly sharp.

The big woman who was his assistant called the hospital in Sundsvall and discovered that the counsellor, Daniel Grim, had been moved to the psychiatric ward, but that the doctor responsible for his care had issued a strict ban on the police visiting or contacting him for the duration of his recuperation.

Elin emerges from the large glass entrance to the National Police Committee, crosses the street, gets in her BMW, and dials the number for Sundsvall Hospital. She gets put through to ward 52B, and is told that no calls can be put through to Daniel Grim's room, but that visiting time lasts until six o'clock.

She taps the address into the satnav, which tells her that it's 375 kilometres away, and that she would reach the hospital at a quarter to seven if she sets off now. She does a U-turn on Polhemsgatan, driving up onto the kerb in front of the entrance, then drives off towards Fleminggatan.

At the first set of traffic lights Robert Bianchi calls to remind her about her meeting with Kinnevik and Sven Warg in twenty minutes, over at the Waterfront Expo.

'I'm not going to make it,' she says curtly.

'Shall I tell them to start without you?'

'Robert, I don't know when I'll be back, it won't be today.'

On the E4 motorway she sets a speed precisely twenty-nine kilometres an hour above the speed limit. Fines don't matter to her, but it wouldn't be a good idea to lose her driving licence.

84

Joona is certain that Vicky Bennet and the little boy are alive. He can't abandon them now.

A girl who has beaten two people to death, and has slashed two people's faces with a broken bottle, has now kidnapped a young boy from his mother and has gone into hiding somewhere with him.

Everyone else already thinks that they're dead.

No one is looking for them now.

Joona thinks back to where he was with his investigation when his colleague Sonja Rask in Sundsvall called to tell him about the security-camera footage at the petrol station. He had just spoken to one of the girls from the Birgitta Home, who told him that Vicky took Zyprexa.

Joona has checked the side effects with Nils Åhlén's wife, who works as a psychiatrist.

There are still too many pieces missing, he thinks. It's possible that Vicky Bennet had overdosed on Zyprexa, an antidepressant.

Caroline had said that just licking a pill could make your skin crawl, and described sudden attacks of restlessness and anger.

He closes his eyes and tries to imagine Vicky demanding the keys. She threatened Elisabet with the hammer, got angry, and just started hitting her with the hammer, again and again. Then

Vicky took the keys from the dead woman and unlocked the door to the isolation room. Miranda was sitting on the chair with the duvet wrapped around her shoulders when Vicky went in and smashed her head in with a rock.

She dragged her over to the bed and positioned her hands over her face.

And only then did her rage start to subside.

Vicky got confused, took the blood-soaked duvet with her, and hid it under her bed just as the tranquilising effect of the drug kicked in. She probably became incredibly tired, kicked off her boots in her wardrobe, hid the hammer under her pillow, and fell asleep. Then a few hours later she woke up, realised what she'd done, got scared, and escaped through the window, and ran off into the forest.

The medication could explain the rage and the fact that she fell asleep on those blood-stained sheets.

But what did she do with the rock? Was there even a rock?

Once again Joona feels very unsure. For only the second time in his life he finds himself wondering if Nils Åhlén might be mistaken.

85

At five minutes to six Elin enters the doors to ward 52B, stops a nurse, and says she's there to see Daniel Grim.

'Visiting time is over,' the woman replies, and carries on walking.

'In five minutes,' Elin says with a smile.

'We usually stop new people arriving at a quarter to six to keep things manageable.'

'I've driven here from Stockholm,' she pleads.

The nurse stops and looks at her with a hesitant expression on her face.

'If we start making exceptions for everyone we'll have people here all hours of the day and night,' she says sternly.

'Please, just let me—'

'You won't even have time for a cup of coffee.'

'That doesn't matter,' Elina assures her.

The nurse still looks dubious, but nods to Elin to follow her, goes off to the right, and knocks on the door to one of the patients' rooms.

'Thanks,' Elin says, then waits for the nurse to leave, before going in.

Over by the window stands an ashen-faced middle-aged man. He hasn't shaved today, maybe not the day before either. He's dressed in jeans and a creased shirt. He looks at her uncertainly as he runs one hand through his thin hair.

'My name is Elin Frank,' she says gently. 'I know I'm disturbing you, and I'm sorry about that.'

'No, it's . . . it's . . .'

She can't help thinking it looks as though he's been crying for days. In another context she would have found him very attractive. Friendly features, mature intelligence.

'I need to speak to you, but I'll understand if you don't feel up to it.'

'Don't worry,' he says in a voice that sounds as if it might break at any moment. 'The papers were all here the first few days, but I couldn't talk then, I couldn't bear to, there was nothing to say . . . I mean, I'd like to help the police, but that hasn't gone too well either . . . I can't seem to focus my thoughts.'

Elin tries to find a way to start talking about Vicky. She realises that the girl must be a monster to Daniel because she's ruined his life – it's not going to be easy to persuade him to help.

'Is it OK if I come in for a few minutes?'

'To be honest, I don't know,' he says, and rubs his face.

'Daniel, I'm so sorry about what's happened to you.'

He whispers his thanks and sits down, then looks up and comments on his own remark.

'I say thank you, but it hasn't really sunk in,' he says slowly. 'It's so unreal, because I was so worried about Elisabet's heart condition . . . and . . .'

His face goes blank, turning grey and introverted again.

'I can't imagine what you're going through,' she says quietly.

'I've got a psychologist of my own now,' he says with a broken smile. 'I'd never have believed that, that I'd ever need a psychologist . . . He listens to me, sits and waits while I cry, I feel . . . You know, he won't let the police question me . . . I'd probably have taken the same decision in his position . . . but at the same time I know myself, I'll be all right . . . maybe I should tell him that I think I could handle talking to them . . . not that I know if I could be of any use . . .'

'It probably makes sense to listen to your psychologist,' she says.

'Do I sound that confused?' he smiles.

'No, but . . .'

'Sometimes I think of something that I should maybe tell the police, but then I forget it again, because I . . . it's odd, but I can't quite gather my thoughts, it's like when you feel really exhausted.'

'I'm sure that will improve.'

He wipes his nose, then looks up at her again.

'Did I ask what paper you write for?'

She shakes her head and says: 'I'm here because Vicky Bennet lived with me when she was six years old.'

86

The hospital room is quiet. Footsteps can be heard out in the corridor. Daniel blinks behind his glasses and purses his mouth as if he's summoning all his strength to understand what she's just said.

'I heard about her on the news . . . about the car and the boy,' he whispers after a while.

'I know,' she replies in a subdued voice. 'But . . . if she was still alive – where do you think she'd hide?'

'Why are you wondering that?'

'I don't know . . . I'd like to know who she trusted.'

He looks at her for a few seconds before asking: 'You don't believe she's dead?'

'No,' she replies quietly.

'You don't believe it because you don't want to,' he says. 'But have you got any evidence to suggest that she didn't drown in the river?'

'Don't be alarmed,' she says, 'but we're fairly sure she got out of the water.'

'We?'

'Me and a detective superintendent.'

'I don't understand . . . why are they saying she's drowned if she . . . ?'

'They think she did, most people still believe she drowned, the police have stopped looking for her and the boy . . .'

'But not you?'

'I might be the only person who really cares about Vicky for her own sake,' Elin says.

She can't bring herself to smile at him, can't bring herself to make her voice soft and amenable.

'And now you want my help to find her?'

'She could harm the boy,' Elin says tentatively. 'Or other people.'

'Maybe, but I don't think so,' Daniel says, and looks at her with an unguarded expression. 'Right from the start I've doubted that she killed Miranda. I still can't believe it . . .'

Daniel falls silent, and his mouth moves slowly even though no sound is coming out.

'What are you saying?' she asks gently.

'What?'

'You were whispering something,' she says.

'I don't believe Vicky killed Elisabet.'

'You don't believe . . .'

'I've worked with seriously troubled girls for many years and I . . . it just doesn't make sense.'

'But . . .'

'In my time as a counsellor I've encountered a number of really dark patients who . . . who had killing in them . . . who . . .'

'But not Vicky?'

'No.'

Elin smiles, and feels her eyes fill with tears before she gets her feelings under control again.

'You have to tell that to the police,' she says.

'I already have, they know that I don't think Vicky is violent. Of course I could be wrong,' Daniel says, and rubs his eyes hard.

'Can you help me?'

'Did you say that Vicky lived with you for six years?'

'No, she was six years old when she lived with me,' she replies.

'What do you want me to do?'

'I have to find her, Daniel . . . You've spent hours talking to her, you must know something about her friends, boyfriends . . . anything at all.'

'Yes, maybe . . . We spent a lot of time talking about group dynamics, and . . . I'm sorry, I'm having trouble getting my thoughts straight.'

'Try.'

'I saw her most days, and I suppose we had . . . I don't know, something like twenty-five one-to-one sessions . . . Vicky, she's . . . the problem with her is that she often drifts off, in her mind, I mean . . . I'd be concerned that she might just leave the boy somewhere, in the middle of the road . . .'

'Where could she be hiding? Was there ever a particular family that she liked?'

87

The door opens and the nurse comes in with Daniel's medication for the evening. She stops abruptly, her neck stiffens as if she's seen something indecent, then she turns to face Elin.

'What's going on?' the nurse says. 'You were supposed to stay five minutes, no longer than that.'

'I know,' Elin replies, 'but it's really important that I—'

'It's almost half past six,' she interrupts.

'Sorry,' Elin says, turning quickly back to Daniel again. 'Where should I start looking for—'

'Get out,' the nurse shouts.

'Please,' Elin says quietly, putting her hands together beseechingly. 'I really do need to—'

'Are you a bit simple?' the nurse snaps. 'I told you to leave . . .'

The nurse curses and leaves the room. Elin grabs Daniel's arm.

'Vicky must have mentioned places, friends?'

'Yes, of course, but I can't think of anything, I'm having trouble . . .'

'Please, try—'

'I know I'm being completely useless, I ought to remember something, but—'

Daniel raps at his forehead.

'How about the other girls – they must know something about Vicky?'

'Yes, they should . . . Caroline, maybe . . .'

A man in a white uniform comes into the room with the nurse.

'I'm going to have to ask you to leave,' the man says.

'Just give me a minute,' Elin says.

'No, you're coming with me right now,' he says.

'Please,' Elin says, looking him in the eye. 'This is about my daughter . . .'

'Come on,' he says, slightly more gently.

Elin's mouth quivers with suppressed sobbing as she sinks to her knees in front of them.

'Just give me a few more minutes,' she begs.

'We'll drag you out if we—'

'No! That's enough!' Daniel says in a loud voice. He helps Elin up from the floor.

The nurse protests.

'She's not allowed to be on the ward after—'

'Shut up,' Daniel snaps, and leads Elin out of the room. 'We can talk down at the entrance or out in the car park.'

They walk together along the corridor. They can hear footsteps behind them, but just keep walking.

'I'm thinking of going to talk to the girls at the Birgitta Home,' Elin says.

'They're not there, they've been moved,' Daniel tells her.

'Where to?'

He holds a glass door open for her, then follows her through.

'To an old fishing village north of Hudiksvall.'

Elin presses the button for the lift.

'Will I be let in if I go?' she asks.

'No, but you will if I come with you,' he says as the lift doors open.

88

Daniel is sitting beside Elin in her BMW. When they pull out onto the E4 she takes out her phone and calls Joona Linna.

'Sorry to bother you,' she says in a voice that can't hide a hint of desperation.

'You can call whenever you want,' Joona replies amiably.

'I'm sitting here with Daniel, and he doesn't think Vicky did those terrible things,' Elin explains quickly.

'All the forensic evidence points to her, and all—'

'But it doesn't make sense, because Daniel says she isn't violent,' she interrupts agitatedly.

'She's probably capable of being violent,' Joona says.

'You don't know her,' Elin says, almost shouting.

Neither of them speaks for a moment, then Joona says calmly: 'Ask Daniel about the drug Zyprexa.'

'Zyprexa?'

Daniel looks at her.

'Ask him about the side effects,' Joona says, and ends the call.

She drives fast along the coast road, and into the vast forests.

'What are the side effects?' she asks in a quiet voice.

'Patients can become aggressive if they exceed the maximum dose,' Daniel says matter-of-factly.

'Was Vicky taking it?'

He nods, and Elin doesn't say anything.

'It's a good drug,' Daniel tries to explain, but falls silent again.

Almost all the light from the headlamps is absorbed by the trees at the edge of the forest, then the shadows overlap until in the end only darkness remains.

'Were you aware that you said Vicky was your daughter?' Daniel asks.

'I know,' she replies. 'Back at the hospital. It just slipped out . . .'

'She was your daughter for a while, though.'

'Yes, she was,' Elin says, keeping her eyes on the road.

They pass Armsjön, its expanse of water glistening like molten iron in the gloom. Daniel takes a deep breath.

'I was just thinking about something Vicky said right at the start . . . But now I can't remember,' he says, and thinks for a while. 'I've got it . . . she talked about some Chilean friends who had a house . . .'

He stops and looks out of the side window, wiping tears from his cheeks.

'Elisabet and I were planning to go to Chile, before the earthquake . . .'

He lets out a deep sigh and sits there with his hands in his lap.

'You were talking about Vicky,' Elin prompts.

'Oh, yes . . . what was I saying?'

'That she had Chilean friends.'

'Yes . . .'

'And that they had a house somewhere.'

'Did I say that?'

'Yes.'

'Bloody hell,' he mumbles. 'What's wrong with me? I mean . . . this is ridiculous – I should have stayed in the hospital.'

Elin smiles gently at him.

'I'm glad you didn't.'

89

The gritted road winds through the dark forest, past sunken barns and traditional farmsteads. The road comes to an end, opening up onto a landscape of rust-red houses, with the sea stretching out beyond. The Midsummer pole is still standing, decked with brown birch leaves and dead flowers. The nearest building is a large wooden house with a beautiful veranda overlooking the water. It was once a shop, but has been owned for the past few years by a private care company, Orre.

The car rolls gently in through the gates and when Elin unbuckles her seat belt Daniel says seriously: 'You need to be prepared for . . . these girls, they've had it really tough all their lives,' he says, nudging his glasses up his nose. 'They push at boundaries and will try to provoke a reaction from you.'

'I can handle that,' Elin says. 'I was a teenager myself.'

'This is different, I promise,' he says. 'It isn't easy . . . not even for me, because they really can be fucking awful at times.'

'So what's the best way to respond if they try being provocative?' she asks, looking him in the eye.

'The best response is to be honest, and unambiguous . . .'

'I'll remember that,' she says, and opens the car door.

'Wait, I just need . . . before we go in,' he says. 'They've got a security guard, and I think he should stick with you the whole time.'

Elin smiles briefly.

'Isn't that a bit over the top?'

'I don't know, maybe . . . I don't mean that you should be frightened, but . . . I just don't think you should be alone with two of the girls, not even for a moment.'

'Which ones?'

Daniel hesitates, then says: 'Almira, and a girl called Tuula.'

'Are they really that dangerous?'

He holds his hand up.

'I just want you to have the guard with you when you talk to them.'

'OK.'

'Don't worry,' he says reassuringly. 'They're all absolutely fine really.'

They get out of the car. The air is still mild, and carries the smell of the sea.

'One of the girls must know something about Vicky's friends,' Elin says.

'But it's by no means certain that they're going to feel like talking.'

A black slate path leads around the end of the house to a flight of steps leading up to the door and veranda.

Elin's red, high-heeled sandals stick in the wet grass between the stones. It's late evening, but one girl is smoking in the swing seat by a large lilac. Her bare face and tattooed arms shine white in the gloom.

'Hello, Almira,' Daniel says. 'This is Elin.'

'Hi,' Elin smiles.

Almira looks at her, but doesn't return the smile. Her thick black eyebrows meet above her large nose, and her cheeks are covered with dark spots.

'Vicky killed his wife,' Almira suddenly says, looking Elin in the eye. 'And once Elisabet was dead, she killed Miranda . . . I don't think she'll stop until we're all dead.'

Almira walks up the steps and goes in through the door.

90

Elin and Daniel follow Almira into an old-fashioned kitchen with copper pans, and rag-rugs on the scrubbed floor, and a pantry in the corner. Lu Chu and Indie are sitting at a pine table eating ice cream straight from the tub and looking through old comics.

'Good that you're here,' Indie says when she catches sight of Daniel. 'You need to talk to Tuula. She's really crazy now, I think she needs to go back on the medication.'

'Where's Solveig?' he asks.

'She went off somewhere,' Almira replies, taking a spoon from a drawer.

'When did she go?' Daniel asks sceptically.

'Just after we'd eaten,' Lu Chu mutters without taking her eyes off the comic.

'So there's only the security guard here?'

'Anders,' Almira says, sitting down on Lu Chu's lap. 'He was only here the first two nights.'

'What?' Daniel says, astonished. 'What are you saying? Are you all on your own?'

Almira shrugs and starts to eat ice cream again.

'I need to know,' Daniel says.

'Solveig said she'd be back,' Indie says.

'For heaven's sake, it's eight o'clock,' Daniel says, taking out his phone.

He calls the care company and gets hold of an out-of-hours number. When there's no answer on that number he leaves an irritated message telling them that they must always have qualified staff on duty, that they can't make cutbacks like this, that they have a responsibility.

While Daniel is on the phone Elin looks at the girls. Almira is eating ice cream and sitting on the lap of a pretty girl with East Asian features and acne all over her round face. She's reading an old copy of *Mad*, and keeps kissing the back of Almira's neck.

'Almira,' Elin says. 'Where do you think Vicky's hiding?'

'Don't know,' she replies, licking her spoon.

'Vicky's dead, for fuck's sake,' Indie says. 'Haven't you heard? She killed herself, and a little boy.'

'Shit,' Lu Chu exclaims, pointing at Elin with a smile. 'I recognise you . . . Aren't you, like, the richest person in Sweden?'

'Stop that,' Daniel says.

'Fuck, I swear,' Lu Chu goes on, drumming the table before yelling out loud: 'I want lots of money too!'

'Lower your voice a bit.'

'I just recognised her, that's all,' she says quickly. 'I've got to be able to say that I recognised her.'

'You can say what you like,' Daniel says calmly.

'We want to know if you have any idea where Vicky was planning to hide,' Elin says.

'She kept to herself most of the time, of course,' Daniel says. 'But you did talk to her sometimes, and you don't have to be best mates to know each other . . . I mean, I know what your ex's name is, Indie, for instance.'

'We're back together,' she says with a smile.

'When did that happen?' he asks.

'I called him yesterday and we talked it out,' she says.

'Well done,' Daniel smiles. 'I'm glad.'

'Towards the end Vicky really only hung out with Miranda,' Indie says.

'And Caroline,' Daniel says.

'Because they all did ADL together,' Indie adds.

'Who's Caroline?' Elin asks.

'One of the older girls,' Daniel says. 'She had Activities of Daily Life training with Vicky.'

'I don't see why anyone's bothered about Vicky,' Almira says loudly. 'I mean, she slaughtered Miranda like she was a little pig.'

'That's not certain,' Elin tries to say.

'Not certain?!' Almira repeats harshly. 'You should have seen her, she was fucking dead, I swear, there was so much fucking blood—'

'Don't shout,' Daniel says.

'So what? What the fuck are we supposed to say? Are we supposed to say nothing happened?' Indie goes on in a loud voice. 'Are we supposed to say that Miranda's alive, that Elisabet's alive . . .'

'I just mean—'

'You weren't fucking there!' Almira screams. 'Vicky smashed Elisabet's head in with a fucking hammer, but you think she's alive.'

'Let's try to talk one at a time,' Daniel says with hard-won calm.

Indie holds her hand up like a schoolgirl.

'Elisabet was a fucking junkie,' she says. 'I hate junkies, and I—'

Almira grins.

'Just because your mum was fucking one—'

'One at a time, Almira,' Daniel interrupts, quickly wiping the tears from his cheeks.

'I don't give a shit about Elisabet, she can burn in hell for all I care, I don't give a damn,' Indie concludes.

'How can you say that?' Elin asks.

'We heard her that night,' Lu Chu lies. 'She screamed for help for ages, but we just sat in bed and listened.'

'She screamed and screamed,' Almira grins.

Daniel has turned away towards the wall. Silence settles on the kitchen. Daniel sits motionless for a while, then wipes his face with his sleeve and turns around.

'You know you're being cruel, carrying on like that,' he says.

'Fun, though,' Almira says.

'You think?'

'Yes.'

'How about you, Lu Chu?'

She shrugs her shoulders.

'You don't know?'

'No.'

'We've talked about situations like this,' he says.

'OK . . . sorry, that was mean.'

He tries to smile reassuringly at her, but just looks incredibly upset.

'Where's Caroline?' Elin asks.

'In her room,' Lu Chu says.

'Can you show us the way?'

91

An ice-cold corridor leads from the kitchen to the living room with the open fireplace, and the dining room with the glazed veranda facing the sea. One side of the corridor is lined with doors leading to the girls' rooms. Lu Chu is walking ahead of Elin in baggy jogging bottoms and trodden-down trainers. She points out her own room and Tuula's, before stopping in front of a door with a colourful little porcelain bell tied to the handle.

'This is Carro's room.'

'Thanks,' Elin says.

'It's starting to get late,' Daniel says to Lu Chu. 'Go and brush your teeth and get ready for bed.'

She hesitates for a few moments, then walks off towards the bathroom. When Daniel knocks on the door, the porcelain bell tinkles gently. The door opens, and a young woman looks at Daniel wide-eyed, then gives him a tentative hug.

'Can we come in?' he asks gently.

'Of course,' she says, and holds out her hand. 'Caroline.'

Elin shakes the girl's hand, and holds the thin hand in hers for a moment. Caroline's pale face is freckled and carefully made-up, her sand-coloured eyebrows plucked, and her straight hair gathered in a thick ponytail.

The wallpaper in the room is brightly patterned, there's a

chest of drawers by the window, and on one wall is a picture of an old fisherman in a sou'wester smoking a pipe.

'We're here to talk about Vicky,' Daniel says, sitting down on the neatly made bed.

'I was Vicky's foster mother many years ago,' Elin says.

'When she was little?'

Elin nods, and Caroline bites her lip and looks of the window, which faces away from the sea.

'You know Vicky a little bit,' Elin says after a while.

'I don't think she really dared to trust people,' Caroline smiles. 'But I liked her . . . she was calm, and had a really sick sense of humour when she got tired.'

Elin clears her throat and asks straight out: 'Did she ever talk about people she met? Maybe she had a boyfriend somewhere, friends?'

'We hardly ever talk about old crap in here, because it only ends up as ammunition.'

'Good things, then – what were her dreams, what did she want to do when she got out?'

'Sometimes we used to talk about working abroad,' Caroline says. 'You know, the Red Cross, Save the Children – mind you, who'd employ us?'

'You were thinking of doing it together?'

'It was just talk,' Caroline says patiently.

'Something I was thinking about,' Daniel says, rubbing his forehead. 'I was off duty that Friday, but I understand that Miranda was in the isolation room – do you know why?'

'She'd hit Tuula,' Caroline says matter-of-factly.

'What for?'

The girl shrugs.

'Because she deserved it – she keeps stealing things the whole time. She took my earrings yesterday, said they wanted to be with her instead.'

'What did she take from Miranda?'

'When we went swimming, she took Vicky's bag, then later that evening she took one of Miranda's hairclips.'

'She took Vicky's bag?' Elin says in a tense voice.

'She gave it back, but she kept hold of something . . . I didn't really understand what, but it was something Vicky had been given by her mother.'

'Did Vicky get angry with Tuula?' Elin asks.

'No.'

'Vicky and Caroline never get involved in any arguments,' Daniel says, patting Caroline's thin arm.

'Daniel, we need you,' Caroline says, looking at him honestly. 'You have to take care of us.'

'I'll be back soon,' he replies. 'I want to, but I . . . I'm not quite well enough to . . .'

When Daniel starts to pull his hand away from her arm she tries to hold onto it.

'But you are going to come back? Aren't you?'

'Yes, I am.'

They walk out, leaving Caroline standing in the middle of her room looking utterly abandoned.

92

Daniel knocks on Tuula's door. They wait for a while, but when there's no answer they start to walk back towards the living room.

'Remember what I told you before,' Daniel says seriously.

The open fireplace is dark and cold. A few dirty plates have been left on the table. The harbour is dimly visible through the large windows of the veranda. The silvery, sun-bleached fishing sheds are arranged in rows and reflected in the water. It's a beautiful view, but the small, red-haired girl has turned her chair to face the white-painted wooden panelling.

'Hello, Tuula,' Daniel says brightly.

The girl turns her pale eyes towards them. A hunted expression disappears, to be replaced by something less easily defined.

'I've got a fever,' she mutters, and turns to face the wall again.

'Nice view.'

'Isn't it?' she replies, staring into the wall.

Elin sees her smile before she turns serious again.

'I need to talk to you,' Daniel says.

'Go on, then.'

'I want to see your face while we talk.'

'Shall I cut it off?'

'It's easier to turn your chair.'

She sighs deeply, turns the chair, and sits down again with an impassive expression.

'You took Vicky's bag on Friday,' Elin says.

'What?' she exclaims. 'What did you say? What the fuck did you say?'

Daniel tries to smooth things over.

'She was wondering—'

'Shut up!' Tuula screams.

They fall silent, and Tuula purses her lips and picks at one of her cuticles.

'You took Vicky's bag,' Elin repeats.

'You're such a fucking liar,' Tuula says in a low voice, and looks down at the floor.

She's sitting perfectly still with a sad look on her face and her body trembling. Elin leans forward to pat her on the cheek.

'I don't mean . . .'

Tuula grabs hold of Elin's hair, picks up a fork from the table, and tries to stab Elin in the face, but Daniel manages to catch her hand in time. He holds Tuula tightly as she struggles and kicks and screams: 'Fucking cunt, I'm going to beat all the fucking . . .'

Tuula starts sobbing hoarsely, and Daniel holds her still. He sits with her on his lap, and after a while she calms down. Elin has moved away, and her fingers feel the tender part of her scalp.

'You only borrowed the bag, I know,' Daniel says.

'There was only rubbish in it anyway,' Tuula replies. 'I should have set fire to it.'

'So there was nothing in the bag that wanted to be with you?' Daniel asks.

'Just the flower button,' the girl says, meeting his gaze.

'That sounds nice – can I see it?'

'A tiger's guarding it.'

'Wow.'

'You can nail me to the wall,' she mutters.

'Was there anything else that wanted to be with you?'

'I should have set fire to Vicky when we were in the forest . . .'

While Tuula talks to Daniel, Elin leaves the veranda, walks

through the living room and out into the cold corridor. It's dark and empty. She walks to Tuula's room, looks back towards the living room, makes sure that Daniel is still talking to the girl, then goes into her small room.

93

Elin is standing in a small room with a single window just below the eaves of a low roof with curved tiles. A table lamp is lying on its side on the floor, its weak glow illuminating the room from below.

On the wall is an embroidered sampler with the words 'We are the best of each other'.

Elin thinks about Tuula, and the way she licked her dry lips as she tried to stab her with the fork, her body shaking with the effort.

The still air in the room has a strangely cloying, rancid smell.

Elin hopes that Daniel has realised this is where she is, and that he can stop Tuula coming to her room.

On the narrow bed, which has no covers or mattress, there's a small red suitcase lying directly on the slats. Carefully she walks over and opens it. The case contains a photograph album, a few crumpled clothes, some bottles of perfume with Disney princesses on, and a sweet wrapper.

Elin closes the case again and looks around the room, and sees that the chest of drawers has been moved half a metre away from the wall. Behind it are the bedsheets, pillows, and duvet. Tuula has been sleeping there instead of on the bed.

Elin moves cautiously, stopping when a floorboard creaks, then stands and listens for a while before she carries on and pulls out the drawers, but all she finds are mangled sheets and small fabric bags of dried lavender. She lifts the sheets, but doesn't find anything. She carefully pushes the bottom drawer back and is just standing up again when she hears footsteps it the corridor. She stands still, trying to breathe silently, then hears the little porcelain bell on Caroline's door tinkle, and everything goes quiet again.

Elin waits a few moments, then walks around the chest of drawers and looks at the bedclothes and pillows in the gloom. The smell seems stronger now as she moves the duvet and starts to lift a grey blanket. As she lifts the mattress a smell of decay rises up. There are scraps of old food on a sheet of newspaper: mouldy bread, some chicken bones, brown apples, dried-up sausages, and fried potatoes.

94

Tuula mutters that she's tired, wriggles out of Daniel's grasp, and goes over to the big windows, where she licks the glass.

'Has Vicky ever said anything that you've overheard?' Daniel asks.

'Like what?'

'If she had any secret places, anywhere she—'

'No,' she replies, and turns towards him.

'But you do sometimes listen to the older girls?'

'So do you.'

'I know, but I'm having trouble remembering things right now, it's called arousal,' he explains.

'Is it dangerous?'

He shakes his head, but can't bring himself to smile.

'I'm seeing a psychologist, and I'm taking medication.'

'You shouldn't be sad,' she says, tilting her head to one side. 'It was probably a good thing that Miranda and Elisabet were murdered . . . because there are far too many people anyway.'

'But I loved Elisabet, I needed her, and—'

Tuula hits the back of her head against the window, making the glass rattle. A diagonal crack appears in one of the panes.

'I think it would be best if I went to my room and hid behind the chest of drawers,' she says.

'Wait a moment,' Daniel says.

95

Elin is kneeling down in front of a hand-painted trunk at the end of the bed in Tuula's room. The words 'Fritz Gustavsson 1861 Harmånger' are written on the lid in ornate writing. By the early years of the twentieth century more than a quarter of Sweden's population had emigrated to America, but perhaps Fritz never set off in the end. Elin tries to open the lid, loses her grip, and breaks a nail. She tries again, but the trunk is locked.

She hears what sounds like a window breaking out on the veranda, then a moment later hears Tuula scream, until her voice cracks.

Elin shivers and walks over to the window. There's an array of small containers on the windowsill, some tin, some porcelain. She opens two of them. One is empty, the other contains some old parcel string.

Through the small window she can see the other wing of the building. In the gloom she can't make out the grass at the back. It looks like a black chasm. But the light from another room is lighting up the outdoor privy and stinging nettles.

She opens another of the porcelain jars, finds some old copper coins, puts the jar back, and picks up a tin with a colourful harlequin on the side instead. She gets the lid off, tips the contents in her hand, and just has time to see some nails and a dead bumblebee when from the corner of her eye, she catches sight of movement outside. She looks out again and feels her racing pulse in her temples. Everything is quiet outside. The weak glow from the next room is still shining on the nettles. All she can hear is the sound of her own breathing. Suddenly a figure passes through the light, and Elin drops the tin on the floor and moves to one side.

The small window is dark, and she realises that someone could be standing right outside looking at her at that moment.

Elin decides to get out of Tuula's room when she happens to see a small sticker in the middle of the door of a cleaning cupboard. She walks over and sees that it's got a picture of the tiger from Winnie the Pooh on it.

Tuula said that a tiger was guarding the flower button.

Inside the cupboard an old oilskin is hanging from a hook in front of an old vacuum cleaner. With trembling hands she pulls the vacuum cleaner out onto the floor. Beneath it are some flattened trainers and a grubby cushion cover. She takes hold of one corner of the cushion cover and pulls at it, and immediately feels how heavy it is.

It rattles when she tips the sparkling contents onto the floor. Coins, buttons, hairgrips, glass marbles, the glinting SIM card of a mobile phone, a ballpoint pen, bottle tops, earrings, and a keyring attached to a small plate of metal with a pale blue flower on it. Elin looks at it, turns it over in her hand, and sees the name Dennis engraved on the metal.

This must be the object Caroline mentioned, the one Vicky had been given by her mother.

Elin puts the keyring in her pocket and quickly looks through the other things as she puts them back inside the cushion cover. She quickly puts everything back in the cupboard, presses the vacuum cleaner down on top of them, and adjusts the raincoat before closing the cupboard. She hurries over to the door of the room, listens for a moment, then opens it and walks out.

Tuula is standing outside.

The little red-haired girl is waiting in the gloomy corridor just a few steps away, looking at her without saying a word.

96

Tuula takes a step forward and shows Elin her bloody hand. Her face is completely pale. There's a staring, expectant look in her eyes. Her white eyebrows are invisible. Her red hair is hanging lankly around her face.

'Go back in the room,' Tuula says.

'I have to talk to Daniel.'

'We can go together and hide,' the girl says in a harsh voice.

'What's happened?'

'Go into the room,' she repeats, and licks her lips.

'Do you want to show me something?'

'Yes,' she replies quickly.

'What?'

'It's a game . . . Vicky and Miranda played it last week,' Tuula says, holding her hands in front of her face.

'I have to go,' Elin says.

'Come on, I'll show you how to do it,' Tuula whispers.

Elin hears steps in the corridor and sees Daniel with a first aid box in his hand. Lu Chu and Almira come out from the kitchen. Tuula feels the back of her head and gets more blood on her fingers.

'Tuula, you were going to sit and wait on the chair,' Daniel says, and starts to lead her towards the kitchen instead. 'We need to clean the wound and see if you need stitches . . .'

Elin just stands there, letting her heartbeat slow down. In her pocket she can feel the keyring that Vicky was given by her mother.

After a while the kitchen door opens again. Tuula walks out slowly with her hand trailing along the wooden panelling on the wall. Daniel is walking beside her, saying something in a serious, calm voice. She nods and disappears into her room. Elin waits until Daniel comes over to her before asking what happened.

'It's nothing serious . . . she banged her head against the window a few times until the glass broke.'

'Has Vicky even mentioned anyone called Dennis?' Elin says in a subdued voice, and shows him the keyring.

He looks at it, turns it over in his hand, and whispers the name to himself.

'It feels like I've heard the name before,' he says. 'But I . . . Elin, I feel so ashamed, I'm so useless because . . .'

'You're trying . . .'

'Yes, but it's not at all certain that Vicky ever told me anything that could help the police . . . she didn't really talk that much at all, and . . .'

He falls silent when they hear heavy steps outside, then the front door opens. A large woman in her fifties comes in and is about to lock the door with her key when she catches sight of them.

'You're not allowed to be here,' she says, walking towards them.

'My name is Daniel Grim, I'm—'

'Surely you understand that the girls can't have visitors at this time of night?' the woman interrupts.

'We're just leaving,' he says. 'But first we just want to ask Caroline about—'

'You're not asking anyone anything . . .'

97

Joona looks at the keyring in the lift on the way up to his room in Police Headquarters. It's in a small plastic bag, and looks like a large coin, a silver dollar, but with the name Dennis engraved on one side and a pale blue flower with seven petals on the other. A sturdy keyring is attached to it through a hole at the top of it.

Elin Frank called Joona late the previous evening. She was in the car, and was going to drive Daniel home and then book into a hotel in Sundsvall for the night.

Elin told her that Tuula had stolen the keyring from Vicky's bag early on Friday.

'It evidently meant a lot to Vicky. She got it from her mother,' Elin told him, and promised to courier it to him as soon as she got to the hotel.

Joona turns the bag over several times in the sharp light, before putting it in his jacket pocket and getting out on the fifth floor.

In his mind he's turning over different reasons why the girl was given a keyring with the name Dennis on it by her mother.

Vicky Bennet's father's name is unknown, her mother gave birth to her without medical help, and the child didn't appear in any official records until she was six years old. Perhaps her mother had always known who the father was? Perhaps this was a way of telling Vicky?

Joona goes in to see Anja, to check if she's found anything. He doesn't even have time to open his mouth before she says: 'There's no one called Dennis in Vicky Bennet's life at all. Not at the Birgitta Home, not at Ljungbacken, and not in any of the families she's stayed with.'

'Strange,' Joona says.

'I even called Saga Bauer,' Anja says with a smile. 'The Security Police have their own databases, of course.'

'Someone must know who this Dennis is,' he says, sitting down on the corner of her desk.

'Apparently not,' she sighs, drumming disconsolately at the desk with her long, bright red fingernails.

Joona looks out of the window. Hard-edged clouds are chasing across the sky.

'I'm stuck,' he says simply. 'I can't ask to see the report from the National Forensics Lab, I can't conduct any official interviews, and I've got nothing to go on.'

'Maybe you should accept the fact that it isn't actually your case,' Anja says quietly.

'I can't,' he whispers.

Anja smiles happily, and her round cheeks blush.

'In the absence of anything better, I want you to listen to something,' she says. 'And it's not Finnish tango this time.'

'I didn't think it would be.'

'You probably did, though, didn't you?' she mutters, and clicks at her computer. 'This is a phone call I received today.'

'You record your calls?'

'Yes,' she says in a neutral voice.

A thin female voice suddenly fills the room.

'Sorry I keep calling,' the woman says, almost breathlessly. 'I spoke to a police officer in Sundsvall, and he said that a superintendent called Joona Linna might be interested in—'

'You can talk to me,' Anja's voice says.

'As long as you just listen, because I . . . I need to say something important about the murders at the Birgitta Home.'

'The police have a dedicated line for tip-offs,' Anja explains.

'I know,' the woman says quickly.

A Japanese cat is waving repeatedly on Anja's desk. Joona can hear the ticking of the mechanism as he listens to the woman's voice.

'I saw the girl, she didn't want to show her face,' she says. 'And there was a blood-stained rock, you have to look for the rock . . .'

'Are you saying you saw the murder?' Anja says.

The woman's fast breathing is clearly audible before she goes on: 'I don't know why I've seen this,' she says. 'I'm frightened, and I'm really tired, but I'm not crazy.'

'Do you mean you saw the murder?'

'Maybe I am crazy,' the woman goes on in a shaky voice, without appearing to hear Anja's question.

The call ends abruptly.

'The woman's name is Flora Hansen, and she's had a report filed against her.'

'What for?'

Anja shrugs her round shoulders.

'Brittis who works on the tip-off line thought . . . Apparently Flora Hansen has called in with loads of fake information, trying to get paid for it.'

'Is she a regular caller?'

'No, she's only called about the Birgitta Home . . . I thought you ought to hear this before she calls you, because she will. She doesn't seem likely to back down, she's still calling even though she's been reported, and now she's found her way to my number.'

'What do you know about her?' Joona asks thoughtfully.

'Brittis said Flora has a cast-iron alibi for the night of the murders because she was holding a seance attended by nine people at Upplandsgatan 40 here in Stockholm,' Anja says with noticeable amusement. 'Flora calls herself a spiritual medium, and claims she can ask the dead questions if she gets paid.'

'I'll go and see her,' he says, and starts to walk towards the door.

'Joona, I just wanted to show you that people are aware of the case,' she says with a hesitant smile. 'And sooner or later we'll get a tip-off . . . if Vicky Bennet is alive, someone's bound to see her.'

'Yes,' he says, buttoning his jacket.

Anja is on the point of laughing, then she sees the look in Joona's grey eyes and realises what he's picked up on.

'The rock,' she says in a low voice. 'Is that accurate?'

'Yes,' he replies, looking her in the eye. 'But so far the only people who know that the killer used a rock are me and two pathologists.'

98

It's relatively unusual in Sweden, but the police have still sought the help of spiritual mediums on a number of occasions. Joona recalls the murder of Engla Höglund. That time the police used a medium who provided a detailed description of two murderers. The descriptions later turned out to be completely wrong.

The real perpetrator was eventually caught because someone who was trying out a new camera happened to take a photograph of both the girl and the murderer's car.

A while back Joona read that independent research had been conducted in the USA into the medium who had been used more times by the police than any other in the world. The report concluded that she hadn't contributed any information of value to any of the one hundred and fifteen cases she had participated in.

The chill afternoon sun has turned to evening shadows, and Joona shivers when he gets out of the car and walks over to a grey block of rental apartments with satellite dishes on the balconies. The lock on the main entrance is broken, and someone has tagged the entire entrance with pink spray paint. Joona takes the stairs up to the second floor and rings on the door with the name Hansen on it.

A thin woman in worn grey clothes opens the door and looks at him with bashful eyes.

'My name is Joona Linna,' Joona says, showing his ID. 'You've called the police several times . . .'

'Sorry,' she whispers, and looks down at the floor.

'You shouldn't call unless you have something to tell us.'

'But I . . . I called because I've seen the dead girl,' she says, meeting his gaze.

'Can I come in?'

She nods, and leads him through a dimly-lit hall with a faded linoleum floor into a small, clean kitchen. Flora sits down on one of the four chairs around the table and wraps her arms around herself. Joona goes over to the window and looks out. The façade of the building opposite is covered with builders' plastic. The thermometer that's been screwed to the outside of the window is swaying slightly in the wind.

'I think Miranda is coming to me because she knows I'm the one who let her through from the other side when I was holding a seance,' Flora begins. 'But I . . . I don't really know what she wants.'

'When was this seance?' Joona asks.

'Every week . . . I make my living talking to the dead,' she says, and a tiny muscle starts to twitch at the corner of her right eye.

'So do I, in a way,' Joona replies calmly.

He sits down opposite her.

'We've run out of coffee,' she whispers.

'That doesn't matter,' he says. 'You mentioned a rock when you called . . .'

'I didn't know what to do, but Miranda keeps showing me a blood-stained rock.'

She indicates its size with her hands.

'So you were holding a seance,' he says gently, 'and then a girl appeared and told you—'

'No, it wasn't then,' she interrupts. 'It was after the seance, when I got home.'

'And what did the girl say?'

Flora meets his gaze, and the look in her eyes is black with the memory.

'She shows me the rock, and tells me to close my eyes.'

Joona looks at her impassively.

'If Miranda shows up again, I'd like you to ask her where the murderer is hiding,' he says simply.

99

Joona takes out the little plastic bag containing Vicky's keyring from his pocket, opens it, and tips it onto the table in front of Flora.

'This belongs to the suspected murderer,' he says.

Flora looks at the object.

'Dennis?' she asks.

'We don't know who Dennis is, but I'm wondering . . . maybe you can get something from it,' he says.

'Maybe, but I . . . this is my job.'

She gives an embarrassed smile, covers her mouth with her hand and says something apologetic that he doesn't catch.

'Of course,' Joona says. 'How much does it cost?'

Keeping her eyes on the table, she tells him her fee for an individual half-hour sitting. Joona takes out his wallet and pays for an hour. Flora thanks him, fetches her bag, and turns the light out. It's still light outside, but the kitchen becomes gloomy. She takes out a tea-light and a black velvet cloth with gold embroidery. Then she lights the candle, puts it in front of Joona, and places the cloth over the keyring. She closes her eyes and gently runs her hand across the cloth.

Joona watches her dispassionately.

Flora slides her left hand under the cloth, sits still, then her body starts to shake and she takes a deep breath.

'Dennis, Dennis,' she mutters.

She fingers the metal disc beneath the black fabric. The neighbours' television is clearly audible through the wall, and outside a car alarm suddenly goes off.

'I'm getting odd images . . . nothing clear yet.'

'Keep going,' Joona says, looking at her intently.

Flora's fair, curly hair hangs down beside her cheeks. Her blotchy skin flushes, and her eyelids twitch with the movement of the eyes beneath.

'There's terrible power in this object. Loneliness and rage. I'm almost burning myself,' she whispers, and pulls out the keyring, holds it in her palm and stares at it. 'Miranda says . . . it's hanging on a thread from death . . . Because they were both in love with Dennis . . . yes, I can feel jealousy burning in the metal . . .'

Flora falls silent, holds the keyring in her hand for a while, mutters that contact has been broken, then shakes her head and hands it back to Joona.

Joona gets to his feet. He had been too eager. Coming here has been a waste of time. He had thought she really knew something, for reasons she didn't want to divulge. But it's obvious that Flora Hansen is just inventing things she thinks he wants to hear. Dennis belongs to a time long before the Birgitta Home, because Vicky was given the keyring by her mother several years ago.

'I'm sorry you're lying,' Joona says, and picks the keyring up from the table.

'Can I keep the money?' she asks weakly. 'I can't manage, I collect cans on the underground and from all the bins . . .'

Joona puts the keyring in his pocket and starts to walk back through the hall. Flora takes out a piece of paper and follows him.

'I think I saw a real ghost,' she says. 'I drew a picture of her . . .'

She shows him a childish drawing of a girl and a heart, and holds it up to his face, trying to make him look, but Joona brushes her hand aside. She drops it and it drifts to the floor, but he just steps over it, opens the door, and leaves the flat.

100

Joona is still feeling irritable when he gets out of the car and walks into Disa's building on Lützengatan near Karlaplan.

Vicky Bennet and Dante Abrahamsson are alive, they're hiding somewhere, and he wasted almost an hour going to speak to a mentally ill woman who lies for money.

Disa is sitting in bed with her thin laptop in her lap. She's wearing a white dressing-gown, and her brown hair is held back from her face by a broad white hairband.

He takes a shower in very hot water. Then he lies down beside her. When he leans his face against her he can smell her perfume.

'Have you been to Sundsvall again?' she asks distantly as he lets his hand run down her arm towards her narrow wrist.

'Not today,' Joona replies in a quiet voice, thinking about Flora's thin, pale face.

'I was up there last year,' Disa says. 'Helped excavate the Women's House at Högom.'

'Women's House?'

'In Selånger.'

She looks up from the screen and smiles at him.

'It's worth a look if you ever get a minute between murders,' she says.

Joona smiles and touches her hip, following her thighbone

towards her knee. He doesn't want Disa to stop talking, so he asks: 'Why is it called the Women's House?'

'It's a burial mound, but it was raised over the ruins of a house that burned down. We don't know the full story.'

'Were there people inside?'

'Two women,' she replies, putting the computer aside. 'I helped brush the soil from their combs and jewellery.'

Joona lays his head in her lap and asks: 'Where did the fire start?'

'I don't know, but there's at least one arrowhead embedded in the wall.'

'So the perpetrator was outside?' he murmurs.

'Maybe the whole village stood and let the house burn,' she says, running her fingers through his thick, damp hair.

'Tell me more about what you found,' Joona asks, and shuts his eyes.

'We don't really know much,' she says, twining a lock of his hair around her finger. 'But the women who lived in the house were weavers, weaving weights have been found in lots of places. It always seems funny that it's the little things, like combs and nails, that survive for thousands of years.'

Joona's mind conjures up an image of Summa's bridal crown of woven birch root, and the old Jewish cemetery in Kronoberg Park, where his colleague Samuel Mendel lies all alone in his family grave.

101

Joona is woken by a gentle kiss on his lips. Disa is already dressed. She's left a cup of coffee on the bedside table.

'I fell asleep,' he says.

'And slept for a hundred years,' she smiles, and walks out into the hall.

Joona hears her close the door behind her. He pulls on his trousers, then stands by the bed thinking about Flora Hansen the spiritualist medium. What lured him to go and see her was the fact that she had guessed right about the rock. Psychologists call this confirmation bias. Unconsciously we tend to favour results that confirm a theory rather than contradict it. Flora called the police several times to tell them about different murder weapons, but when she mentioned the rock he started to listen.

There were no other leads to follow, just the one leading to Flora.

Joona goes over to the large window and pulls back the white curtain. The grey morning light still carries some of the gloom of night. The fountain in the centre of Karlaplan is pulsing and foaming with ponderous monotony. Pigeons are moving about slowly in front of the closed entrance to the shopping centre.

A few people are on their way to work.

There was something desperate about Flora Hansen's eyes

and voice when she said she collected cans and bottles on the underground.

Joona closes his eyes for a while, then turns back towards the bedroom and picks his shirt up from the chair.

He pulls it on distractedly, staring blankly ahead of him as he buttons it up.

His mind had just nudged the edge of a logical connection, but he lost it at once. He tries to retrace his thoughts, but can feel it slipping further and further away.

It was something to do with Vicky, with the keyring and her mother.

He pulls on his jacket, and goes to stand by the window again.

Was it something he saw?

He looks over towards Karlaplan again. A bus is driving around the roundabout and stops to pick up passengers. Further away, an old man with a walking frame is smiling at a dog sniffing at a rubbish bin.

A red-cheeked woman in an unbuttoned leather jacket is running towards the underground station. She startles a flock of pigeons in the square. They take off and fly half a circuit in formation before landing again.

The underground.

It was something about the underground, Joona thinks, taking his phone out.

He's almost certain he's right, he just needs to check a few details.

He quickly scrolls through to find a number, and as the call goes through he walks into the hall and puts his shoes on.

'Yes, Holger—'

'Joona Linna here,' Joona says as he leaves the flat.

'Good morning, good morning, I've—'

'I just need to ask you something,' Joona says, locking the door. 'You examined the bag we found at the dam, didn't you?'

He runs down the stairs.

'I had time to take pictures and list the contents before the prosecutor called to say that the case had been deprioritised.'

'I'm not authorised to read your report,' Joona says.

'There wasn't anything special,' Holger says, rustling some paper. 'I mentioned the knife, didn't I—'

'You said something about a bicycle tool — did you look into that?'

Joona is out in the street now, hurrying along Valhallavägen towards his car.

'Yes,' Joona replies. 'You know what it's like with us Norrlanders, we take our time over things . . . It wasn't actually a tool, but a key to the driver's cab on underground trains—'

'Did it used to be attached to a keyring?'

'How the hell should I—'

Holger stops abruptly and looks at the photograph in his report.

'You're right, of course, it's been worn smooth on the inside of the hole.'

Joona thanks him and hangs up, then calls Anja. He runs the last bit of the way, thinking about what Elin Sand had said about Tuula stealing things she liked from everyone around her, earrings, pens, coins, lipstick holders. Tuula removed the ugly key from the nice keyring with the pale blue flower on it, and put the key back in the bag.

'Ghostbusters,' Anja answers in a bright, shrill voice.

'Anja, can you help me by talking to someone responsible for the underground system in Stockholm?' Joona says as he drives off.

'I can consult the spirits instead—'

'It's urgent,' Joona interrupts.

'Did you get out of bed the wrong side?' she mumbles in a hurt voice.

Joona drives towards the Olympic Stadium.

'Are you aware that all the carriages are given names?' he says.

'I was sitting in Rebecka today, she was lovely and—'

'Because I don't think Dennis is the name of a person, but an underground carriage, and I need to know precisely where it is right now.'

102

All the carriages on the underground system have numbers, just as they do throughout the world, but for years the carriages in Stockholm have also had names. It is said that the tradition started in 1887 with the name of the horses that used to pull tram carriages through the city.

Joona is pretty sure that the key Vicky was given by her mum, Susie, fits the electronic lock that opens all underground carriages, but that the keyring identified a specific carriage. Perhaps her mother stored personal belongings in one of the driver's cabs, or perhaps she slept there sometimes.

Vicky's mother had been homeless almost all her adult life, and sometimes slept in the underground, on benches in various stations, in trains, and in the forgotten spaces between the lines, deep inside the tunnels.

Somehow she had managed to get hold of this key, Joona thinks as he drives. It can't have been easy. It must have been incredibly valuable in the world she lived in.

Yet she still gave it to her daughter.

And she got hold of a keyring with the name Dennis on it so that the girl wouldn't forget which carriage was the important one.

Perhaps she knew Vicky was going to run away.

She's run away so many times, and managed not to be found

for a long time on two occasions. The first was when she was only eight years old, when she went missing for seven months and was found suffering from hypothermia with her mother in a multi-storey car park in the middle of December. The second occasion was when she was thirteen. Vicky was missing for eleven months that time, until she was picked up by the police for shoplifting in the shopping mall beside the Globe Arena.

It's possible to get into the drivers' cabs using other tools. An ordinary spanner of the right size would work.

Even if it's unlikely that Vicky would be inside the carriage if she didn't have the key, it may still contain clues from her periods on the run, clues that could lead to her current hiding place.

Joona has almost reached Police Headquarters when Anja calls to say that she's spoken to the Stockholm Transport Authority.

'There is a carriage called Dennis, but it's been taken out of circulation . . . serious fault, he said.'

'So where is it now?'

'They weren't sure,' she replies. 'It could be in their depot out in Rissne . . . but it's more likely to be out at the workshops in Johanneshov.'

'Put me through to them,' Joona says as he turns the car around.

The tyres thud over a speed-bump, and he drives through a red light and turns into Fleminggatan.

103

Joona is driving towards Johanneshov, just south of Stockholm, when a man finally answers the phone. It sounds as though he's got a mouthful of food.

'Underground Engineering . . . Kjell here.'

'Joona Linna, National Crime Unit. Can you confirm that you've got a carriage named Dennis with you in Johanneshov?'

'Dennis,' the man repeats. 'Have you got the carriage number?'

'No, I'm afraid not.'

'Hang on, I'll check the computer.'

Joona hears the man muttering to himself, then there's a clattering sound before he comes back on the line.

'There's a Denniz with a "z" at the end . . .'

'That doesn't matter.'

'OK,' Kjell says, Joona hears him swallow the mouthful of food. 'I can't see it in the register . . . it's a pretty old carriage, I don't know . . . but according to the records I've managed to bring up, it hasn't been in service for the past few years.'

'Where is it?'

'It should probably be here, but . . . Look, I'm going to pass you on to Dick. He knows everything that's not on the computer . . .'

Kjell's voice disappears and is replaced by an electronic buzzing. Then an older man answers, his voice echoing as if he were in a cathedral or a large metal room.

'Dick here.'

'I was just talking to Kjell,' Joona explains. 'And he seems to think you might have a carriage called Dennis somewhere there.'

'If Kjell says it's here, then it probably is – but I can go out and check if it's a matter of life and death and everything in between.'

'It is,' Joona says calmly.

'Are you in your car?' Dick asks.

'Yes.'

'Not on your way here?'

Joona hears the sound of the man going down some metal steps, followed by a large, heavy door squeaking, and the man sounds out of breath when he speaks again.

'I'm down in the tunnel know – you still there?'

'Yes.'

'We've got Mikaela and Maria down here. Denniz ought to be here as well.'

Joona hears echoing steps as the old man walks along, while he drives as fast as he can across the Central Bridge. He thinks about the periods of Vicky's life when she's been on the run. She slept somewhere, somewhere she felt safe.

'Can you see that carriage yet?' he asks.

'No, this one's Ellinor . . . and there's Silvia . . . even the lights don't work properly down here.'

Joona hears the crunch of the man's steps as he walks along the tunnel beneath the industrial estate.

'I haven't been down here for a while,' the old man says breathlessly. 'Just going to turn my torch on . . . Right at the back, naturally . . . Denniz, old and rusty as fuck—'

'Are you sure?'

'I can go and take a picture if you . . . What the hell? There are people here, there are people inside the—'

'Keep quiet!' Joona says quickly.

'There's someone in the carriage,' the old man whispers.

'Stay back,' Joona says.

'They've blocked the door with a ruddy gas cylinder.'

The line crackles as the man moves away, breathing hard.

'There . . . there were people inside the carriage,' the old man whispers into the phone.

Joona reasons that it's unlikely to be Vicky, seeing as she no longer has either her key or the card.

Suddenly Joona hears high-pitched shouting through the phone, distant but unmistakeable.

'There's a woman shouting in there.' the engineer whispers. 'She sounds completely mad.'

'Get out of there,' Joona says.

He hears the old man's footsteps and laboured breathing, then the screaming again, more distant now.

'OK, what did you see?' Joona asks.

'There was a ruddy great welding cylinder blocking the door.'

'Did you actually see anyone?'

'There's graffiti on the windows, but there was one large person, and one who was smaller. Maybe more, I don't know.'

'You're sure about that?' Joona Linna asks.

'We keep the tunnels locked, but if you're determined enough . . . well, of course there'll always be a way of getting in,' the old man pants.

'Listen to me carefully . . . I'm a detective superintendent, and all I want you to do right now is get away from there and wait outside for the police.'

104

A black van drives at speed through the gates of the Underground Engineering Depot in Johanneshov, throwing up grit and a cloud of dust. The van swings around and stops in front of a green metal door.

After his conversation with Dick, Joona called the Regional Chief of Police and explained that there was a possibility that a hostage situation might develop at the depot.

The National Rapid Response Team is a specially trained group within the National Crime Unit. Their prime responsibility is to combat acts of terrorism, but they can also be called in to carry out particularly challenging operations.

The five officers emerge from the van with a mixture of nervousness and anticipation. They're heavily equipped, in boots, dark blue overalls, ceramic protective vests, helmets, protective goggles, and gloves.

Joona walks towards the group and sees that they've been authorised to use enhanced weaponry – three of them are carrying green Heckler & Koch assault rifles with laser sights. They're not specialised weapons, but they're light, and can empty a magazine in less than three seconds.

The two other men in the group are carrying sniper rifles.

Joona quickly shakes hands with the operational leader, the

medical officer, and the three others before explaining that he considers the situation to be urgent.

'I want you to go in right away, as quickly as you can, but seeing as I don't know what briefing you've received, I want to stress that we haven't had positive identification of Vicky Bennet and Dante Abrahamsson.'

Before the Response Team arrived, Joona questioned Dick Jansson and got him to mark the positions of the various carriages on a map of the area.

A young man with a sniper rifle in a bag by his feet raises his hand: 'Can we assume that she's armed?' he asks.

'Almost certainly not with a projectile weapon,' Joona replies.

'So we're expecting to encounter two unarmed children?' the young man says, and shakes his head with a grin.

'We don't know what we're going to find. We never do,' Joona says, showing them a plan of a carriage the same model as Denniz.

'Where do we go in?' the operational leader asks.

'The door at the front is open, but blocked by one or more gas cylinders,' Joona says.

'Did you hear that?' the operational leader asks, turning to the others.

Joona lays the large map over the plan and points out the various sidings and the position of the carriages.

'I think we can get close without being seen. It's a bit hard to tell, but we can certainly get this far.'

'Yes, that looks reasonable.'

'The distance is short, but I still want a sniper on the roof of the nearest carriage.'

'That'll be me,' says one of the men.

'And I can take up position here,' the younger sniper says, pointing at the map.

They follow Joona to the steel door. One of the officers checks his reserve magazine one last time, and Joona pulls on a protective vest.

'Our primary objective is to get the boy out of the carriage, and our secondary objective is to arrest the suspect,' Joona explains, and opens the door. 'Live fire should be targeted at the girl's legs initially, followed by shoulders and arms.'

A long, pale grey staircase leads down to the sidings beneath the Johanneshov Engineering Depot, where faulty trains are left until they can be repaired.

The only sound Joona can hear behind him is the muffled noise of heavy boots and Kevlar vests.

105

When the team reaches the tunnel they move more cautiously, slower. The sound of their footsteps on the gravel and rusty rails bounces softly back off the metal-clad rock walls.

They approach a dented train giving off a peculiar smell. The carriages are like dark remnants of some long forgotten civilisation. The light from their torches darts across the tunnel walls.

They're moving in single file, quickly and almost silently. The tracks merge at a set of manually operated points. A red lamp with a broken cover is glowing dimly. There's a dirty work glove lying on the ground.

Joona gestures to the group to turn their torches off before they walk through the narrow gap between two carriages with broken windows.

There's a box of greased bolts by the wall, close to some loose cables, electrical sockets, and a grimy armature.

They're getting very close now, and moving even more carefully. Joona points out one carriage to the first sniper. The rest of the group attach the torches to their weapons and spread out, while the sniper makes his way up on top of the carriage without a sound, then unfolds the support of his rifle and starts to adjust the Hensoldt sights.

The rest of the group move closer to the carriage at the far end of the tunnel. One of the men keeps checking the strap of his helmet, like a nervous tic. The operational leader exchanges a glance with the younger sniper and indicates a line of fire.

Someone slips on the grit, and a loose stone clatters against the rail. A sleek rat runs along the wall and disappears into a hole.

Joona carries on alone by the side of the track. He can see the carriage named Denniz standing in a siding closest to the wall. Cables or ropes are hanging from the roof. He moves sideways and sees that there's dim light coming from inside the dirty, brown-streaked windows. The light is fluttering about like a yellow butterfly, making the shadows grow and shrink alternately.

The lead officer loosens a shock grenade from his belt.

Joona stands and listens for a moment before moving on, with a tingling awareness that he's in the line of fire, that the snipers' rifles are aimed at his back right now as they follow his movements.

A green metal gas cylinder has been wedged in the open doorway.

Joona approaches cautiously, going right up to the carriage and crouching in the darkness. He puts his ear to the metal and immediately hears someone shuffling across the floor.

The lead officer gestures to two of his men. Like shapeless demons they slip forward in the darkness. They're both big men, but they move almost silently. The only sounds are the muffled, watery echoes of holsters, protective vests, and heavy overalls, then suddenly they're by his side.

Joona hasn't even drawn his own pistol, but sees that the men from the response unit have already got their fingers on the triggers of their assault rifles.

It's hard to make anything out through the carriage's windows. There's a small lamp on the floor. Its glow lights up torn boxes, empty bottles, and plastic bags.

Between two of the seats there's a large bundle with rope around it.

The glow from the little lamp starts to quiver. The whole carriage vibrates weakly. Perhaps something's moving along the rails in the distance.

The tunnel walls and roof start to rumble.

Joona hears a faint whimpering sound.

He carefully draws his pistol.

At the far end of the carriage a shadow is moving, as a large man in jeans and dirty trainers crawls away.

Joona feeds the first bullet into the chamber, turns to the lead officer, indicates the man's position in the carriage, and gestures for them to move in immediately.

106

There's a sudden explosion when the middle door is blown off and falls on the ground, and the armed officers storm the underground carriage.

Windows shatter and broken glass showers the ripped seats and floor.

The man lets out a yell in a rattling voice.

The gas cylinder falls over with a heavy clang, and argon hisses out as it rolls into the carriage. All the internal doors in the carriage are forced open with heavy thuds.

Joona makes his way in across mouldy blankets and torn and trampled newspapers. The acrid smell of the gas fills the carriage.

'Lie still!' someone roars.

The beams from the torches mounted on two of the assault rifles scan the carriage section by section, between the seats and through filthy Plexiglas.

'Don't hit me!' a man yells from the other section.

'Don't move!'

The lead officer tapes the broken vent of the gas cylinder shut.

Joona hurries forward towards the driver's cab.

There's no sign of Vicky Bennet and Dante.

The carriage stinks of sweat and old food. The walls and windows are scratched and covered with graffiti.

Someone's been eating fried chicken from greasy paper on the floor, and there are beer cans and sweet wrappers between the seats.

The newspaper on the floor rustles beneath his feet.

The light from outside is uneven as it passes through the obscured windows.

Joona heads towards the driver's cab, accessed by the key with the name Dennis on it.

The response unit breaks the door open, and Joona goes inside. The cramped space is empty. The walls are scratched and covered in scrawl. On the instrument panel there's a syringe with no needle, some scorched foil, and an empty plastic capsule. On the narrow shelf in front of the two pedals is a packet of Alvedon, and a tube of toothpaste.

This was where Vicky's mother sometimes hid, this is the cab to which she gave her daughter a key many years ago.

Joona goes on searching and finds a rusty carpet knife tucked into the springs beneath the seat, sweet wrappers, and an empty jar of baby food – plum purée.

Through the side window he sees the armed officers drag out the man in jeans. His face is heavily furrowed and there's a frightened look in his eyes. He coughs some blood over his beard and lets out a cry. His arms are tied behind his back with plastic cuffs. He is forced to lie face down on the ground, and one of the officers holds the barrel of his rifle to the back of his head.

Joona stares around at the cramped space, his eyes darting across buttons and knobs, the microphone, and a lever with a polished wooden handle, but he isn't sure where he should be looking. He wonders about going back out into the carriage to search among the seats, but forces himself to stay in the cab and scan the instrument panel and driver's seat again.

Why did Vicky and her mother have keys to this cab?

There's nothing here.

He stands up and examines the screws holding the mesh over the vent, when his eyes slide sideways to a word that's been scribbled on the wall: *mum*.

He takes a step back and now notices that almost all the

writing and scratches on the walls are messages between Vicky and her mother. This must have been a place where they could meet without being disturbed, and when they missed each other they left messages.

Mum they were mean, I couldn't stay.

I'm freezing and need food. Have to go back now, I'll come again on Monday.

Dont be upset Vicky! they put me in secure housing thats why I missed you.

Thanks for the sweets.

Baby!! Im sleeping here for a while Uffe is a pig!! If you can leave some money that wd be grate.

Happy Christmas, Mum.

You must see that I cant keep ringing back now.

Mum are you angry with me for something?

107

When Joona comes back out, the response team have turned the bearded man over. He's sitting with his back against the wall, crying, and seems very confused.

'I'm trying to find a girl and a little boy,' Joona says, taking off his protective vest and squatting in front of the man.

'Don't hit me,' the man says.

'No one's going to hit you, but I need to know if you've seen a girl here, in this carriage.'

'I haven't touched her, I just followed her.'

'Where is she now?'

'I just followed her,' he repeats, licking some blood from his lips.

'Was she alone?'

'I don't know – she locked herself in the cab.'

'Did she have a little boy with her?'

'A boy? Yes, maybe . . . maybe—'

'Answer properly,' the lead officer snaps.

'You followed her here,' Joona goes on. 'But what did she do after that?'

'She left again,' he replies with a frightened look in his eyes.

'Where did she go? Do you know?'

'That way,' the man replies with a helpless gesture of his head towards the tunnel.

'Is she in there, in the tunnel – is that what you mean?'

'Maybe not . . . maybe—'

'Answer!' the officer roars.

'I can't,' the man sobs.

'Can you tell me when she was here?' Joona asks cautiously. 'Was it today?'

'Just now,' he says. 'She started shouting and—'

Joona sets off along the tunnel, and behind him hears the lead officer take over the questioning. In a hoarse, brusque voice he asks the man what he did with the girl, if he touched her.

Joona rushes along the rusty tracks. The darkness ahead of him seems to move in smoky formations.

Up ahead he can see a gate. Light is streaming in and reflecting off the damp concrete floor. The bottom of the gate is broken, and he manages to squeeze under it. He suddenly finds himself outside. He's standing in the middle of the rough crushed stones surrounding about fifteen rusty sets of rails. The tracks merge together like a ponytail up ahead and curve off gently into the distance.

A thin figure is walking along the embankment. She's got a dog with her. Joona starts to run after her. An underground train thunders past him at high speed. The ground shakes. He sees her between the wheels as he runs through the weeds at the side of the track. The ground is covered in broken glass, rubbish, and used condoms. There's an electrical hum, and another train approaches from Skärmarbrink. Joona has almost caught up with the slender figure, he jumps over the track, grabs hold of her thin arm and turns her around. Taken by surprise, she tries to hit him, but he moves his head away, loses his grip on her arm, grabs her jacket, and she hits again, then pulls away and wriggles out of the jacket, drops her bag, and falls backwards onto the stones.

108

Joona holds the woman down on the embankment among the thistles and remains of the cow parsley, grabs her hand to make her let go of the stone, and tries to calm her down.

'I just want to talk, I don't—'

'Get the fuck off me!' she screams, trying to pull free.

She kicks out, but he blocks her legs and holds her down. She's breathing like a frightened rabbit. Her small breasts heave in time with her panting. She's very thin, with a furrowed face and cracked lips. Forty years old, maybe, or possibly only thirty. When she finds she can't pull free she starts whispering apologies and trying to placate him.

'Now just take it easy,' he says, letting go of her.

She glances at him timidly as she gets to her feet and picks her handbag up from the ground. Her thin arms are full of needle tracks, and on the inside of one of her arms is a badly damaged tattoo. Her black T-shirt, bearing the words 'Kafka didn't have much fun either' is extremely dirty. She wipes the corners of her mouth, looks along the rails, and takes a few steps to the side, as if to test Joona.

'Don't be scared, I just need to talk to you.'

'I haven't got time,' she replies quickly.

'Did you see anyone else when you were back in that carriage?'

'I don't know what you're talking about.'

'You were inside an underground carriage.'

She doesn't answer, clenches her mouth shut, and scratches her neck. He picks up her jacket, turns it the right way around and passes it to her. She takes it without thanking him.

'I'm looking for a girl who—'

'Leave me the fuck alone, I haven't done anything.'

'I didn't say you had,' Joona replies amiably.

'So what do you want with me?'

'I'm looking for a girl called Vicky.'

'What's that got to do with me?'

Joona shows her the picture of Vicky the police have been using.

'Don't know her,' she says automatically.

'Take another look.'

'Have you got money?'

'No.'

'Can't you help me out with a bit of money?'

An underground train crosses the bridge, rattling and letting off showers of sparks.

'I know you hang out in the driver's cab,' Joona says.

'It was Susie who started that,' she says, trying to shift the blame.

Joona shows her the photograph of Vicky again.

'This is Susie's daughter,' he says.

'I didn't know she had kids,' the woman says, rubbing her nose.

The high tension wire running along the side of the track starts to hum.

'How do you know Susie?'

'We hung around the allotment cottages while that lasted . . . it was bloody rough at first, I had hepatitis, and Vadim was always having a go at me . . . I used to get knocked about a lot, but Susie helped me . . . Christ, she's one tough bitch, but I wouldn't have got through that winter without her, no chance . . . But when Susie died I took her stuff so that . . .'

The woman mutters something and digs in her handbag, then pulls up a key like the one Vicky had in her bag.

'Why did you take that?'

'Anyone would have done, no question . . . I actually took it before she was dead,' the woman admits.

'What's in the carriage?'

She wipes her mouth, mutters 'fucking hell' to herself, then takes a steps to one side.

Two trains are approaching along different tracks. One is coming from Blåsut, the other from Skärmarbrink station.

'I need to know,' Joona says.

'OK, what the hell,' she says, her eyes wavering. 'There was some whizz, and a phone.'

'Have you got the phone?'

The rumbling sound and metallic clatter are getting louder.

'You can't prove it isn't mine.'

The first underground train passes at speed. The ground shakes beneath their feet. A few loose stones roll down the embankment and the weeds sway as it passes. An empty McDonald's cup rolls between the other rails.

'I just want to look at it,' he calls.

'Sure,' she laughs.

Their clothes flap in the wind. The dog barks excitedly. The woman walks backwards, beside the carriages as they pass. She says something, then starts to run towards the depot. It happens so suddenly that Joona doesn't have time to react. She obviously hasn't seen the train coming from the other direction. The noise is already deafening. The train has already built up speed, but weirdly there's no sound when the front of it hits the woman.

She just disappears under the carriages.

In a screeching moment of slow motion Joona sees drops of blood spatter the cupped leaves of the lady's mantle growing on the embankment. The train lets out a long, eerie shriek as it brakes. The carriages groan and clank as they slow down and stop. Silence settles again, and the faint buzz of insects can be heard once more. The driver stays in his seat, as if he's frozen to ice. A long streak of blood is spread over the sleepers, leading to a dark red lump of fabric and flesh. The smell of the brakes spreads across the area. The dog whimpers as it walks up and down the tracks with its tail between its legs, unsure of what to do.

Joona walks over slowly and picks the woman's handbag from the ditch. The dog comes up to him and sniffs as he tips out its contents. Sweet papers blow off on the wind, along with a couple of banknotes. Joona picks up the black phone and ignores the rest, then goes and sits on a concrete plinth by the side of the tracks.

A westerly breeze is carrying a smell of rubbish and the city.

He clicks through to voicemail, calls, and hears that there are two new messages: 'Hi Mum,' a girl's voice says, and Joona realises at once that it's Vicky. 'Why don't you answer any more? If you're in detox I want to know in advance. The new place is OK, I'm happy here. Maybe I said that last time . . .'

'*Message received 1 August, at 23.10,*' the automated voice says.

'Hi Mum,' Vicky says in a tense, breathless voice. 'Some stuff's happened and I need to get hold of you, I can't talk long, I've borrowed a phone . . . Mum, I don't know what to do . . . I haven't got anywhere to go, I might have to ask Tobias for help.'

'*Message received yesterday at 14.05.*'

The sun suddenly breaks through the grey sky. Sharp shadows appear, and the top of the rails shimmers in the light.

109

Elin Frank wakes up in the large, strange bed. The clock on the television spreads a greenish glow across the bedroom of the executive suite. The colourful decorative drapes are visible against the blackout curtains.

She's been asleep for a long time.

The sweet scent of the flowers in the sitting room makes her feel slightly nauseous, and the hum of the air-conditioning is spreading an uneven chill, but she's too tired to try to turn it off or call reception.

She thinks about the girls in the house on the coast. One of them must know more. There must be a witness.

The little girl Tuula spoke and acted as if she was boiling with rage inside. Perhaps she saw something she daren't talk about.

Elin thinks about how the little girl grabbed hold of her hair and tried to stab her in the face with a fork.

That should have frightened her more than it does.

She slides her hand under the pillow, feeling a sting of pain from the wounds on her wrist. She thinks about how the girls ganged up on Daniel when they found a weak point.

Elin rolls over and thinks about Daniel's face, his neat mouth and sensitive eyes. Ridiculously, she had been faithful to Jack until the mistake with the French photographer. Not that it was something she'd planned. She knows they're divorced, and that he's never coming back.

Elin showers and moisturises using the anonymous lotion provided by the hotel, puts a fresh bandage around her wrist, and, for the first time in her life, gets dressed in the same clothes she was wearing the day before.

The previous day's events appear almost incomprehensible. The day had started with the nice detective from the National Crime Unit telling her that he was sure Vicky was still alive.

Without a moment's hesitation she had driven to Sundsvall Hospital and nagged her way to being allowed to see the counsellor, Daniel Grim.

Elin's face is flushed with emotion as she takes out her make-up bag and starts to apply it with slow, steady movements.

He went with her to Hårte, where Elin had found Vicky's keyring.

In the car on the way back, Daniel had tried to remember if Vicky had ever talked about someone called Dennis. Not being able to remember had made him feel frustrated and ashamed.

Her stomach tingles when she thinks about Daniel Grim. As if she's falling from a great height – and enjoying it.

It was late by the time she stopped outside his house in Sundsvall. A gravel path led into an old garden. Dark trees moved in the wind in front of a small red house with a white veranda.

If he had asked her if she wanted to go inside she probably would have done, and she would almost certainly have slept with him if she had. But he didn't ask, he was cautious and pleasant, and when she thanked him for his help he said the trip had been better than any therapy.

She felt horribly alone when she watched him walk through the low gate and go up to the house. She sat in the car for a while, then drove back to Sundsvall and booked into a room at the First Hotel.

Her phone purrs in her bag beside the fruit bowl in the sitting room. She hurries to answer it. It's Joona Linna.

'Are you still in Sundsvall?' the detective asks.

'I'm about to check out of the hotel,' Elin says, feeling a wave of anxiety rush through her. 'What's happened?'

'Nothing, don't worry,' he says quickly. 'I just need help with something if you've got time.'

'What with?'

'If it's not too much trouble, I'd be very grateful if you could ask Daniel Grim about something.'

'I can do that,' she says in a subdued voice, but can't help smiling to herself.

'Ask him if Vicky ever mentioned someone called Tobias.'

'Dennis and Tobias,' she says thoughtfully.

'Just Tobias . . . that's our only lead to Vicky right now.'

110

It's a quarter to nine in the morning, and Elin Frank is driving past the detached houses that line Bruksgatan in breezy sunshine. She parks outside the thick hedge, gets out of the car, and walks through the low gate.

The house is well-maintained, the black saddle roof looks new, and the ornate carpentry on the veranda is bright white. This is where Daniel and Elisabet Grim lived together until Friday night. Elin shivers as she rings the doorbell. She waits for a long time, listening to the wind rustling the leaves of the large birch tree. A lawnmower falls silent in one of the neighbouring gardens. She rings the bell again, waits a bit longer, then walks around to the back of the house.

Some small birds fly up from the lawn. There's a dark blue swing seat next to some tall lilac bushes. Daniel is lying asleep on it. His face is very pale, and he's curled up as if he's freezing.

Elin goes over to him, and he wakes with a start. He sits up and stares at her with a look of bewilderment.

'It's too cold to be sleeping out here,' Elin says gently, sitting down.

'I couldn't go into the house,' he says, moving to make room for her.

'The police called me this morning,' she says.

'What did they want?'

'Did Vicky ever mention someone called Tobias?'

Daniel frowns, and Elin is about to apologise for pressuring him, when he raises his hand.

'Hang on,' he says quickly. 'He's the guy with the attic flat in Stockholm, she lived there for a while . . .'

Daniel's weary face suddenly cracks into a large, warm smile.

'Wollmar Yxkullsgatan 9.'

Elin stammers something in surprise and pulls her mobile from her bag. Daniel shakes his head.

'How the hell could I know that?' he wonders. 'I can't remember anything. I can't even remember my parents' middle names these days.'

Elin gets up from the swing seat, walks a few steps across the sunlit grass, calls Joona, and tells him what she's found out. She hears the detective start to run while she's still talking, and by the time they end the call she hears a car door slam shut.

111

Elin's heart is beating fast when she sits back down beside Daniel on the swing seat, and feels the warmth of his body against her thigh. He's found an old wine cork between the cushions and is staring at it short-sightedly.

'We went on a wine-tasting course, and started to collect wine . . . nothing special, but some of them were OK, I got them as a Christmas present . . . Bordeaux . . . two bottles of Château Haut-Brion 1970. We were going to drink them when we retired, me and Elisabet . . . so many plans . . . We even saved a bit of marijuana. We often used to joke about it, how we were going to become kids again when we got old, lots of loud music and mornings in bed.'

'I ought to get back to Stockholm,' she says.

'Yes.'

They swing together on the seat for a while, and the rusty spring creaks.

'Nice house,' Elin says quietly.

She puts her hand on his, and he turns his over, and they lace their fingers together. They sit there in silence as the swing seat creaks slowly.

Her glossy hair has fallen across her face, and she brushes it aside and meets his gaze.

'Daniel,' she murmurs.

'Yes,' he replies in a whisper.

Elin looks at him, thinking that she's never needed another person's tenderness as much as she does right now. Something about the look in his eyes, his furrowed brow, is affecting her deeply. She kisses him lightly on the lips, smiles, and does it again, then takes his face in her hands and kisses him properly.

'Oh, God,' he says.

Elin kisses him again, scratching her lips on his stubble, then pulls her dress open and puts his hand on her breasts. He touches her tentatively, nudging one of her nipples.

Daniel looks incredibly vulnerable as she kisses him again, and she slips one hand under his shirt and feels his stomach tighten with the touch.

Waves of longing roll through her crotch. Her legs feel weak, and she wishes she could just lie on the grass with him and sit astride his hips.

She closes her eyes, presses herself against him, and he says something that she can't hear. Her blood is pulsing hard within her. She feels his warm hands on her body, then he suddenly stops and pulls away.

'Elin, I can't . . .'

'Sorry, I didn't mean to do that,' she says, trying to calm her breathing.

'I just need some time,' he explains, with tears in his eyes. 'It's too much right now, but I don't want to frighten you off . . .'

'You're not,' she replies, and tries to smile.

Elin simply walks out of the garden, adjusts her clothes, and gets in the car.

Her cheeks are flushed and her legs feel weak as she drives out of Sundsvall. After just five minutes, she turns into a forest track and stops, with her heart pounding and her crotch throbbing. She looks at her face in the rear-view mirror. Her eyes are glossy and her lips swollen.

Her pants are soaked. Blood is roaring through her body. She can't remember ever feeling sexual energy like this before.

Daniel seems so wonderfully unaware of her appearance. It's as if he can see straight into her heart.

She tries to breathe calmly, waits a little while, then looks around the narrow forest track, slips her dress open, and pulls her pants down over her thighs. She strokes herself quickly with both hands. Her orgasm comes fast and hard. Elin Frank sits there gasping and sweating, with two fingers inside herself as she looks out through the windscreen at the enchanted rays of sunlight through the branches of the fir trees.

112

It's started to get dark when Flora heads towards the recycling centre behind the Ica supermarket to look for bottles and cans she can claim the deposit back on. She keeps thinking about the murders up in Sundsvall, and has started to fantasise about Miranda and her life at the Birgitta Home.

The Miranda of her imagination dresses provocatively, smokes, and swears a lot. Her thoughts are interrupted as she passes the supermarket's loading bay and stops to check in the discarded boxes before moving on.

She starts to imagine Miranda playing hide-and-seek with some friends outside a church.

Flora's heart beats faster when she sees Miranda covering her eyes and counting to a hundred. A five-year-old girl runs off between the gravestones, laughing excitedly, already a little bit scared.

Flora stops in front of the recycling bins for old newspapers and cardboard boxes. She puts her bag of empty plastic bottles and cans down, goes over to the big container for clear glass and looks inside, using her torch. The light shimmers across the mixture of broken and intact bottles. It's almost dazzling. Off to one side Flora spots a bottle she can get money back on. She reaches in through the hole with her arm and carefully feels about, unable to look at the same time. The recycling centre is completely silent. Flora reaches a little further, and suddenly feels something touch her. It's like a gentle caress against the back of her hand, and a moment later she cuts her fingers on a piece of broken glass, snatches her arm back, and moves away.

A dog is barking in the distance, then she hears a slow crunching sound from amongst the glass in the large container.

Flora runs away from the recycling centre, then slows down and walks for a while, with her heart pounding as she gasps for breath. Her injured fingers are stinging. She looks around, thinking to herself that the ghost had been hiding in amongst the glass.

I see the dead girl as a young child, she thinks. Miranda is haunting me because she wants to show me something, she won't leave me in peace because I was the one who summoned her with my seances.

Flora sucks the blood from her fingertips and imagines the girl trying to grab and cling onto her hand.

'There was someone there, someone who saw everything,' is what she imagines the girl was trying to tell her. There weren't supposed to be any witnesses, but there were . . .

Flora speeds up again, looks back over her shoulder, and lets out a scream when she walks into a man who smiles and mutters 'Oops' as she hurries on.

113

Joona hurries in through the door of Wollmar Yxkullsgatan 9. He runs up the stairs to the top floor and rings on the only door. His heartbeat calms down as he waits. Screwed to the door is a brass sign with the name Horáčková engraved on it, and immediately above that a strip of tape bearing the name Lundhagen. He knocks hard, but there's no sound from inside the flat. He opens the letterbox and looks inside. It's dark, but he can see that the hall floor is covered with post and advertisements. He rings the bell again, waits for a while, then calls Anja.

'Can you look up a Tobias Horáčková?'

'No such person,' she replies after a few seconds.

'Horáčková, at Wollmar Yxkullsgatan 9.'

'Yes, Viktoriya Horáčková,' she replies, tapping at her keyboard.

'Is there a Tobias Lundhagen?' Joona asks.

'I was just going to say that Viktoriya Horáčková is the daughter of a Czech diplomat.'

'Is there a Tobias Lundhagen?'

'Yes, he lives there, either on a sublet or as a lodger.'

'Thanks.'

'Joona, wait,' Anja says quickly.

'Yes?'

'Three little things . . . we can't break into a flat owned by a diplomat without a court order . . .'

'That's one thing,' he says.

'You're due to see the Internal Investigations people in twenty-five minutes.'

'Haven't got time.'

'And you've got a meeting with Carlos at half four.'

Joona is sitting perfectly still and straight-backed in an armchair in the National Police Cases Department of the Public Prosecutors' Authority. The head of the internal investigation is monotonously reading out the transcript of the first interview with Joona, then hands it over for him to accept and sign.

Mikael Båge snorts noisily, passes the document to senior secretary Helene Fiorine, then goes on to read out the transcript of the witness statement given by Göran Stone from the Security Police.

Three hours later Joona crosses Kungsbron and walks the short distance to Police Headquarters. He takes the lift up to the eighth floor, knocks on the door of Carlos Eliasson's office, and sits down at the table where his colleagues Petter Näslund, Benny Rubin, and Magdalena Ronander are already waiting for him.

'Joona, I'm a fairly reasonable person, but enough is enough,' Carlos says as he feeds his paradise fish.

'The National Rapid Response Unit,' Petter says with a grin.

Magdalena sits quietly, staring down at the table.

'I think you should apologise,' Carlos says.

'Because I was trying to save a little boy's life?' Joona asks.

'No, because you know you were wrong.'

'Sorry,' Joona says.

Petter grunts. There are beads of sweat on his forehead.

'I'm going to suspend you,' Carlos goes on, 'from all active service until the internal investigation is over.'

'Who's taking over?' Joona asks.

'The preliminary investigation into the deaths at the Birgitta Home have been deprioritised and will in all likelihood be—'

'Vicky Bennet is alive,' Joona interrupts.

'And will in all likelihood be shut down tomorrow morning once the prosecutor has made her decision,' Carlos concludes.

'She's alive.'

'Pull yourself together, for God's sake,' Benny says. 'I've looked at the recording myself, and—'

Carlos raises his hand to stop him, then says: 'There's nothing to suggest that the people caught by the security camera at the petrol station are Vicky and the boy.'

'She left a message on her mother's voicemail the day before yesterday,' Joona says.

'Vicky hasn't got a phone, and her mother is dead,' Magdalena says seriously.

'Joona, you're getting careless,' Petter says sadly.

Carlos clears his throat, hesitates, then takes a deep breath: 'I don't take any pleasure from this,' he says slowly.

Petter is looking expectantly at Carlos, Magdalena is staring down at the table again with flushed cheeks, and Benny is doodling on a sheet of paper.

'I'll go on leave for a month,' Joona says.

'Good,' Carlos says quickly. 'That solves—'

'If I can have access to a particular apartment first,' Joona concludes.

'An apartment?'

Carlos's face darkens, and he sits down behind his desk as if all the energy has drained out of him.

'It was bought seventeen years ago by the Czech ambassador to Sweden . . . he passed it on to his twenty-year-old daughter.'

'Forget it,' Carlos sighs.

'But the daughter hasn't used the flat in the past twelve years.'

'That doesn't make any difference . . . as long as it's owned by someone with diplomatic immunity, paragraph 21 doesn't apply.'

Anja Larsson enters the room without knocking. Her blonde hair is arranged in an elaborate bun on top of her head, and she's wearing glittery lipstick. She walks over to Carlos, looks at him, then gestures towards his cheek.

'Your face is dirty,' she says.

'Beard?' Carlos says weakly.

'What?'

'I might have forgotten to shave,' Carlos says.

'It doesn't look very nice.'

'No,' he replies, looking down.

'I need to talk to Joona,' she says. 'Are you finished?'

'No,' Carlos says in an unsteady voice. 'We . . .'

Anja leans across the desk. The red plastic beads on her necklace swing in front of her cleavage. Carlos stifles an impulse to tell her he's married, when he finds himself staring at her breasts.

'Are you having some sort of breakdown?' Anja asks with genuine interest.

'Yes,' he says quietly.

The others just watch as Joona gets up from his chair and follows Anja out of the room.

They walk off towards the lift, and Joona presses the button.

'What did you want, Anja?' he asks

'Now you're all stressed again,' she says, offering him a toffee in a striped wrapper. 'I just wanted to let you know that Flora Hansen called me and—'

'I need a search warrant.'

Anja shakes her head, unwraps the toffee, and feeds it to him.

'Flora wanted to return the money that you—'

'She lied to me,' Joona interrupts.

'Now she just wants us to listen,' she says. 'Flora says there's a witness . . . She really did sound frightened this time, and kept repeating that you have to believe her, that she doesn't want any money, that she just wants us to listen.'

'I have to get into that flat on Wollmar Yxkullsgatan.'

'Joona,' Anja sighs.

She unwraps another toffee, holds it up to his mouth and pouts her lips. He takes the sweet. Anja giggles delightedly and quickly unwraps another one, then holds it up to his lips, but it's too late, he's already walked into the lift.

114

On the ground floor of the building on Wollmar Yxkullsgatan 9 there are now balloons hanging from one of the doors. High-pitched children's voices are singing something in the courtyard. Joona opens the back door, and the glass window rattles as he glances out at the little garden with a patch of grass and an apple tree. A table has been laid in the last of the evening sun, with colourful plates and cups, balloons and streamers. A pregnant woman is sitting on a white plastic chair. She's been made up to look like a cat, and is calling to the playing children. Joona feels a pang of longing in his chest. Suddenly one of the little girls breaks away from the others and runs over to him.

'Hello,' she says, then pushes past and runs over to the door with the balloons.

Her bare feet leave prints on the white marble floor in the hallway. She opens the door, and Joona hears her call into the flat that she needs the toilet. One of the balloons comes loose and sinks to the floor, meeting its reflection as it falls. Joona sees that there are bare footprints all over the hallway and stair-well: to and from the front door, up and down the stairs, past the rubbish chute, and over to the cellar door.

Joona walks up to the attic flat for a second time and rings on the door. He stares at the brass sign with the name Horáčková and the yellowing tape with Lundhagen written on it.

The children's voices can still be heard from out in the courtyard. He rings the bell again and has just pulled out the case containing his lock-picks when the door is opened by a man in his thirties with spiky hair. The security chain isn't on, just swings noisily against the frame. The floor of the narrow entrance hall is covered with envelopes and advertisements. A flight of white brick steps leads up to the apartment.

'Tobias?'

'Who's asking?' the man wonders.

He's wearing a short-sleeved shirt and black jeans. His hair is stiff with gel, and his face has a yellowish tint.

'National Crime Unit,' Joona says.

'No shit,' the man smiles in surprise.

'Can I come in?'

'Now's not a good time, I'm just on my way out, but if—'

'You know Vicky Bennet,' Joona interrupts.

'Perhaps you'd better come in for a few minutes,' Tobias says seriously.

Joona suddenly becomes aware of the weight of his new pistol in his shoulder holster as he goes up the short flight of steps and finds himself in an attic flat with a sloping ceiling and dormer windows. There's a ceramic bowl full of sweets on a low table. On one wall is a framed poster of a Gothic-looking woman with angel's wings and large breasts.

Tobias sits down on the sofa and tries to close a grubby holdall on the floor between his legs, but gives up and leans back.

'You wanted to talk about Vicky?' Tobias says, reaching forward and helping himself to a handful of sweets from the bowl.

'When did you last hear from her?' Joona asks, leafing through the unopened envelopes on a sideboard.

'Now you're asking,' Tobias sighs. 'It must be almost a year ago now, she called from . . . damn,' he says, interrupting himself when he drops some sweets on the floor.

'What were you going to say?'

'Just that she called from . . . Uddevalla, I think it was? She talked a lot, but I don't actually know what she wanted.'

'No calls in the past month or so?'

Joona opens a small wooden door leading to a wardrobe. It contains four ice-hockey games, still in their boxes, and there's an old computer on a shelf.

'I really do need to get going,' Tobias says.

'When did she live here?'

Tobias tries to close the large holdall again. One window looking out onto the courtyard is open slightly, and the children are now singing 'Happy Birthday'.

'Almost three years ago now.'

'How long was she here?'

'She wasn't here the whole time, but seven months in all, I'd say,' Tobias replies.

'Where else was she living?'

'Who knows?'

'You don't know?'

'I threw her out a few times . . . look . . . you wouldn't understand, she's only a kid, but that girl can be a real nightmare to have around the house.'

'In what way?'

'The usual . . . drugs, stealing, suicide attempts,' he says, scratching his scalp. 'But I'd never have believed she could kill anyone. I've been following the story in *Expressen* . . . I mean, it's turned into quite a story.'

Tobias looks at his watch, then meets the detective's calm grey gaze.

'Why?' Joona asks after a while.

'Why what?' Tobias asks awkwardly.

'Why did you let her live here?'

'I had a hard time when I was a kid,' he replies with a smile, trying once more to close the zip on the holdall.

The large bag is full of e-readers in their original packaging.

'Can I help you with that?'

Joona holds the sides of the holdall together while Tobias pulls the zip shut.

'Sorry about that,' he says, patting the bag. 'I swear, it's not my stuff, I've just been looking after it for a friend.'

'Oh well, in that case,' Joona says.

Tobias laughs, and manages to spit a piece of sweet on the

floor. He stands up and hauls the holdall down the steps to the hall. Joona follows him slowly towards the door.

'How does Vicky think? Where would she hide?' he asks.

'I don't know – she could be anywhere.'

'Who does she trust?' Joona asks.

'No one,' he replies, opening the front door and going out into the stairwell.

'Does she trust you?'

'I don't think so.'

'So there's no likelihood she'd come here?'

Joona lingers in the small hallway, and surreptitiously opens the key cabinet on the wall.

'No, but she might . . . no, forget it,' Tobias says, pressing the lift button.

'What were you going to say?' Joona asks, looking at the different keys.

'I really am in a hell of a rush now.'

Joona carefully slips a set of spare keys to the flat off their hook and slides them into his pocket before he leaves the flat, closes the door, and gets in the lift next to Tobias.

115

They get out of the lift and hear happy cries from the garden as they leave the building. The balloons on the door bounce softly against each other in the draught. They walk out onto the sunlit pavement. Tobias stops and looks at Joona, scratches one eyebrow, and then looks off down the street.

'You almost said something about where she might try to go,' Joona says.

'I don't even remember the guy's name,' Tobias says, shading his eyes with one hand. 'But he's kind of an extra dad to Mickan, a girl I know . . . and I know that before Vicky moved to mine she was sleeping on a sofa bed around at his, up on Mosebacke torg . . . sorry, I don't know why I'm saying this.'

'Which address?'

Tobias shakes his head and adjusts the heavy holdall.

'It's the little white building opposite the theatre.'

Joona watches as he disappears around the corner with the heavy bag full of stolen goods, and is just thinking about driving up to Mosebacke to knock on doors, but an unsettling feeling leaves him rooted to the spot. He's suddenly freezing. It's evening already, and it's been a long time since he last had anything to eat or got any sleep. A nagging headache is making it hard to keep his thoughts straight. Joona starts to walk towards the car, but stops when he suddenly realises what was wrong.

He can't help smiling to himself.

It's astonishing that he didn't see it before: he must be really tired if he's only just noticed.

Maybe it was a bit too straightforward, like the missing link in a classic detective story.

Tobias said he'd been following the case in one of the evening papers, but the whole time he was talking to Joona he referred to Vicky as if she was still alive.

Joona is pretty much on his own when it comes to believing that Vicky isn't dead.

The newspapers were printing articles saying that Vicky and Dante had drowned in the Indal River on Wednesday. They kept going on about all the suffering the slow police response had caused Dante's mother, and were trying to prompt her to file an official complaint.

But Tobias knows that Vicky's alive.

This realisation brings with it another observation.

Joona is certain of what he saw, and instead of following Tobias, he stops abruptly and hurries back towards Wollmar Yxkullsgatan 9.

His brain has suddenly summoned up the memory of the red balloon coming loose from the door. It rolled across the marble floor of the hallway, almost weightless.

The floor had been criss-crossed by children's footprints. They had been playing on the stairs and chasing each other in and out of the garden.

Joona reminds himself that Vicky could still be barefoot since she lost her trainers in the river. He yanks the door open and rushes into the hallway, and sees that his memory was correct.

Some of the larger footprints lead straight towards the cellar door, but there are none heading the other way.

116

Joona follows the footsteps towards the metal door, takes out the keys he stole from Tobias, and unlocks it. With one hand he finds the light switch. The heavy door swings shut behind him, and everything goes dark before the lights come on with a flicker. The walls radiate cold, and the acrid stench of the rubbish room reaches him through a vent. He stands perfectly still for a few seconds, just listening, before he goes down the steep steps.

He finds himself in an overfull cycle-store, and pushes past sledges, bicycles, and prams, and carries on into a low corridor. Insulated pipes run beneath the ceiling. The walls consist of the mesh-lined doors of the storage compartments belonging to the various apartments.

Joona turns the lights in the corridor on and walks in. There's a sudden whirring sound beside him, and he spins around to see that it's the lift motor.

There's a strong smell of urine in the stagnant air.

Suddenly he hears someone move further inside the cellar.

Joona thinks about the photograph of Vicky that has been circulated since her disappearance. It's hard to imagine that shy, blushing face transforming into something very different, full of uncontrolled rage. The only way for her to have wielded the heavy hammer would have been to hold it in both hands. He tries to imagine the scene, her striking, and blood spraying up at her face, then her hitting again and again, brushing the blood from one eye against her shoulder.

Joona tries to breathe quietly as he unbuttons his jacket with his left hand and draws his pistol. He still hasn't quite got used to the weight and balance of the new gun.

In one compartment the nose of a brown rocking horse is pressed against the mesh. Behind it, Joona can see steel-edged skis, poles, and a brass curtain rail.

It sounds as if someone is shuffling across the concrete floor, but he can't see anything.

He shudders at the thought that Vicky Bennet could have been hiding among the old sledges that he passed a few moments ago, and could now be sneaking up on him from behind.

There's a rustling sound, and Joona turns around.

The corridor is empty.

The drainage pipes running along the ceiling are gurgling.

Just as he turns back, the timed lights go out, and everything turns black. He can't see anything, and reaches out one hand towards the mesh on one of the compartments. A little further away he can see the glow of a light switch.

A tiny yellow light so you can find the switch.

Joona waits for his eyes to get more used to the darkness before he moves on.

Suddenly the light in the switch vanishes.

Joona stops dead in the corridor and listens hard.

It takes him a moment to realise that someone is standing in front of the switch.

He crouches down carefully so as to present less of a target for a blind attack.

The lift machinery rumbles behind him, then suddenly the light switch is visible again.

Joona moves backwards, and hears someone slide gently across the floor.

There's someone there, no doubt about it. There's someone inside one of the storage compartments in front of him.

'Vicky,' he says into the darkness.

Suddenly the door to the cellar opens and he hears voices

from up in the hallway as someone starts to walk down the steps to the cycle-store as the lights flicker into life.

Joona seizes his chance, and takes several quick steps forward, sees movement inside one of the compartments, and raises his pistol towards a hunched figure.

The sluggish fluorescent lights cut through the darkness. The door to the cycle-store closes again, and the voices fade away.

Joona holsters his pistol, kicks the small padlock off the door to the compartment, and hurries in. The figure is much smaller than he imagined. Its hunched back is moving quickly in time with its breathing.

There's no doubt that it's Vicky Bennet.

She has tape over her mouth, and her narrow arms are pulled behind her back and tied to the mesh.

Joona hurries over to loosen the rope. She's just standing there panting for breath with her head bowed. Her tangled hair is hanging down in front of her dirty face.

'Vicky, I'm going to get you—'

Without any warning she kicks him hard in the forehead just as he's bending down. The kick is so powerful that he stumbles back. Hanging from her bound arms, she kicks him in the chest, almost dislocating her shoulders in the process. She kicks again, but Joona blocks her foot with his hand. She screams behind the tape, kicks out again, and throws herself forward so hard that an entire section of mesh comes loose. Tugging hard with both hands, Vicky tries to grab hold of a metal bar, but Joona is quicker and stronger, and he knocks her to the concrete floor. Holding her down with one knee, he cuffs her wrists before loosening the rope and removing the tape.

'I'll kill you!' Vicky shrieks.

'I'm a superintendent at the—'

'Rape me then, go on, I don't care, I'll come after you and kill you and—'

'Vicky,' Joona repeats, raising his voice. 'I'm a detective superintendent, and I need to know where Dante is.'

117

Vicky Bennet is breathing rapidly through her half-open mouth, staring at him with dark eyes. Her face is streaked with blood and dirt, and she looks unbelievably tired.

'If you're a police officer, you have to stop Tobias,' she says hoarsely.

'I've just spoken to Tobias,' Joona explains. 'He went off to sell some e-readers that he—'

'The bastard!' she gasps.

'Vicky, you know I have to take you to Police Headquarters.'

'Yeah, what the hell, do what you like, I don't care—'

'But first . . . first you have to tell me where Dante is.'

'Tobias took him. And I believed him,' Vicky says, turning her face away.

Her body starts to shake.

'I believed him again, I—'

'What are you trying to say?'

'You won't listen anyway,' she says, looking at Joona with wet eyes.

'I'm listening now.'

'Tobias promised to get Dante back to his mother.'

'He hasn't done that yet,' Joona says.

'I know, and I believed him . . . I'm so fucking stupid, I—'

Her voice breaks, and panic shines in her eyes.

'Don't you get it? He's going to sell him, he's going to sell Dante.'

'What do you—'

'Don't you understand what I'm saying? And you let him go!' she yells.

'What do you mean by sell?'

'There isn't time! Tobbe, he . . . he's going to sell Dante to people who will sell him on, you'll never be able to trace him after that.'

They hurry through the cycle-store and up the steep steps. Joona holds Vicky's thin arm as he pulls out his phone and calls the Regional Communication Centre.

'I need a car to Wollmar Yxkullsgatan 9 to pick up a murder suspect,' he says quickly. 'And I need assistance finding someone who's suspected of kidnap . . .'

They rush out through the door, down the steps, and onto the sunlit pavement. Joona points to his car and explains to the duty officer: 'His name is Tobias Lundhagen, and . . . Hang on,' Joona says, and turns to Vicky. 'What sort of vehicle has he got?'

'A big black one.' She holds her hands up. 'I'd recognise it if I saw it.'

'What make?'

'No idea.'

'What does it look like? An SUV, a minibus, a van?'

'I don't know.'

'You don't know if it's—'

'What the fuck? Sorry!' Vicky shouts.

Joona ends the call and puts his hands on her shoulders and looks her in the eye.

'Who's he going to sell Dante to?' he asks.

'I don't know! God, I don't know . . .'

'So how do you know he's going to sell him? Did he say that? Did you hear him say it?' Joona asks, looking into her anguished eyes.

'I know him . . . I—'

'What is it?'

Her voice is thin and breaking with stress when she replies:

'The slaughterhouse district, we need to go to the slaughterhouse district.'

'Get in the car,' Joona says tersely.

They run the rest of the way. Joona yells at her to hurry up, and she gets in with her hands still cuffed behind her back. He hurries around, gets in, and starts the car, then pulls away hard. Loose grit flies up behind the tyres. Vicky falls sideways as Joona turns sharply into Timmermansgatan.

With a nimble movement Vicky slips her cuffed hands under her backside and legs so that they're in front of her instead.

'Put your belt on,' Joona says.

They speed up to ninety kilometres an hour, brake sharply, and slide into Hornsgatan.

A woman stops in the middle of a pedestrian crossing, looking at something on her phone.

'Moron!' Vicky shouts.

Joona passes the woman on the wrong side of the central reservation, and is heading straight for a bus before he swerves back into the right lane. He accelerates even more as they drive past Mariatorget. By the church, a can-collector stops poking through a bin and walks straight out into the road with his crumpled bag over his shoulder.

Vicky gasps and huddles up. Joona swerves sharply into the cycle lane as a car heading the other way blows its horn loudly. Joona speeds up again, ignores the traffic lights, turns right, and puts his foot down as they head into the Södermalm Tunnel.

The light from the lamps on the walls pulses monotonously inside the car. Vicky's face is still, almost stony. Her lips are cracked, and she has a thin layer of dried mud on her skin.

'Why the slaughterhouse district?' Joona asks.

'That's where Tobias sold me,' she replies.

118

The slaughterhouse district was established just south of Stockholm as a consequence of new legislation governing abattoirs and butchery in 1897, and is still the largest area in northern Europe dedicated to the slaughter and processing of meat.

There's not much traffic in Södermalm Tunnel, and Joona is driving very fast. Dry sheets of newspaper swirl in the air in front of the large ventilation units.

Vicky Bennet is sitting beside him, and from the corner of his eye he can see that she's biting her nails.

The comms unit crackles oddly when Joona requests police and ambulance backup, he tells them it's likely to be at the slaughterhouse district in Johanneshov, but that he doesn't have a precise address yet.

'I'll get back to you,' he says as the car thunders over the shredded remnants of an old tyre.

They head through the long, curved tunnel as yellow bands of light flash past.

'Drive faster,' she says, putting her hands against the dashboard as if to protect herself in case they crash.

The light pulses across her pale, dirty face.

'I said I'd pay double if he could sort out money and a passport . . . he promised to get Dante back to his mother . . . and I trusted him, can you believe it? After everything he did to me . . .'

She hits herself on the head with both hands.

'How the fuck can anybody be so fucking stupid?' she says quietly. 'All he wanted was Dante . . . he beat me with a length of pipe and locked me up. I'm so fucking stupid . . .'

They cross the Skanstull Bridge, pass beneath Nynäsvägen, and skirt around the Globe Arena, which sits like an off-white moon beside the football stadium.

Beyond the shopping mall the architecture quickly becomes squat and functional. They drive into a large fenced area full of industrial buildings and parked trailers. In the distance a neon sign is lit up above the two lanes of the road, white lettering on a red background: SLAUGHTERHOUSE DISTRICT.

The barriers are open, and they drive into the complex on thundering tyres.

'Where now?' Joona says as they drive along the side of the grey warehouse.

Vicky bites her lip as she looks around frantically.

'I don't know.'

119

The sky is dark, but the labyrinthine industrial estate is lit up illuminated by signs and streetlamps. Almost all activity has stopped for the day, but at the end of one of the side streets a crane is loading a blue container onto a truck with a lot of squealing and creaking.

Joona drives quickly past a dirty building with a buckled sign advertising pork chops, and is approaching some green metal buildings behind closed steel gates beside a turning circle.

They pass a yellow brick building with a loading bay and some rusting containers, and swing behind the central abattoir.

There's no one in sight.

They carry on into a darker street lined with large ventilation drums, rubbish containers, and old trolleys.

A van with a pornographic motif painted on its side is standing in the parking spaces beneath a sign saying 'Meaty sausages for you'.

There's a rumbling sound as they drive over an uneven drain cover. Joona turns left, skirting a crooked fence. Some seagulls fly up from a stack of pallets.

'There! That's it!' Vicky shouts. 'That's his . . . I recognise the building too, they're in there!'

A black van with the Confederate flag across its rear window is parked in front of a large liver-brown building with dirty windows and metal shutters. On the other side of the road, four cars are parked in a row beside the pavement. Joona drives past the building, swings left and stops in front of another brick building. Advertising banners are fluttering in the wind from three flagpoles.

Without saying anything, Joona takes out his key, removes the cuff from one of Vicky's hands, and fastens it to the steering wheel before he leaves the car. She looks at him darkly but doesn't protest.

Through the windscreen she watches the detective run, lit up by a street lamp. There's a strong wind, and sand and rubbish is flying through the air.

Between the closed-up buildings there's a narrow alleyway with loading bays, metal staircases, and containers for waste meat.

Joona is approaching the door she pointed out, glances back, and looks around at the deserted industrial estate. In the distance a forklift is driving around inside a hangar-like building.

He walks up a metal staircase, opens the door, and finds himself in a corridor with a creaking linoleum floor, and walks past three thin-walled offices. A dusty plastic lemon tree is sticking up from a white pot full of small clay balls. There's still some tinsel left over from Christmas draped through its branches. A framed butchers' licence from 1943 is hanging on the wall, issued by the Emergency Wartime Committee in Stockholm.

There's a laminated sign about hygiene and recycling rules fixed to the steel door at the end of the corridor. Someone has scrawled 'handling of cocks' across the regulations. Joona opens the door a couple of centimetres, listens, and hears voices some distance away.

Very carefully he peers into a large processing room full of belt-driven machinery where the sides of pork are butchered. The light reflects dimly off the yellow tiled floor and stainless steel benches. A blood-stained plastic apron is hanging out from below the lid of a rubbish bin.

He silently draws his pistol and his heart starts to beat a little faster at the smell of gun grease.

120

With his pistol in his hand Joona creeps in, crouching behind the large machines. The cloying smell of the drains and scrubbed rubber mats hits his nose as he realises he never gave the Regional Communications Centre an address. He assumed they've probably already reached the slaughterhouse district, but it will take them a while to find Vicky.

The memory flares up with merciless abruptness. The moments when our lives change are constantly in motion, as one time bleeds into another. Joona was eleven years old when his head teacher came to fetch him from his classroom, took him out into the corridor, and told him what had happened with tears in her eyes.

His father was a beat officer, and had been killed on duty when he went into a flat and got shot in the back. Even though it was against regulations, his father had gone into the flat alone.

Now Joona doesn't have time to wait for backup.

From the struts and conveyor belts beneath the ceiling hang pneumatic shoulder-blade extractors.

He moves silently forward, and can now hear the voices more clearly.

'No, he has to wake up first,' a man says in a low, gruff voice.

'Give it a bit longer.'

Joona recognises the innocent boyish tone of Tobias's voice.

'What the fuck were you thinking?' another man asks.

'I just wanted him to stay nice and calm,' Tobias says softly.

'He's almost dead,' the gruff man says. 'I'm not paying until I know he's OK.'

'We'll wait another two minutes,' a third man says.

Joona keeps moving, and when he reaches the end of the row of machinery he suddenly catches sight of the boy. He's lying on the floor on a grey blanket. He's wearing a crumpled blue top, dark blue trousers, and a small pair of trainers. His slack face has been washed, but his hair and hands are dirty.

Beside the boy stands a large man with a leather waistcoat and a huge beer-gut. His face is running with sweat, and he's walking up and down, tugging at his white beard and sighing irritably.

Something drips on Joona. The clamp on the end of a hose hasn't been fixed properly. The dripping water trickles across the tiled floor to a drain a short distance away.

The fat man walks about restlessly, looks at the time, and a drop of sweat falls from the end of his nose. He crouches down beside the boy with a sigh.

'We can take some pictures,' says a man, whose voice Joona hasn't heard before.

Joona doesn't know what to do, he thinks there are four men in the room, but he doesn't know if they're armed.

He could do with the Rapid Response Unit right now.

The light reflects off the fat man's face as he pulls the trainers from Dante's feet.

His small striped socks come off as well, and fall to the floor. His rounded heels bounce on the blanket.

When the man's huge hands start to unbutton the boy's jeans Joona can't hold back any longer. He stands up from his hiding place.

Without even trying to conceal his presence, he walks out between the butchers' benches, which are covered with a wide variety of freshly-sharpened knives.

He keeps his pistol pointing at the floor.

His heart is thudding with anxiety.

Joona knows he isn't following the rules, but he can't wait any longer, he just strides out into the open.

'What the hell . . . ?' the fat man says, looking up.

He lets go of the boy, but stays on his knees.

'You're all under suspicion of involvement in the kidnap of another person,' Joona says, and kicks the fat man hard in the chest.

Sweat flies off the man's face as he is thrown backwards. He tumbles helplessly into the cleaning buckets, rolls backwards over the drainage gulley, and manages to pull down a box of ear defenders before crashing into the bulky skinning machine.

Joona hears the safety catch of a gun being released, and a moment later feels the end of the barrel against his back, just below his shoulder blades. He stands perfectly still, because he knows that the bullet would go straight through his heart if the pistol were fired now.

A man in his fifties with a blond ponytail and a pale brown leather jacket approaches from one side. He moves smoothly, like a bodyguard, and is aiming a sawn-off shotgun at Joona.

'Shoot him!' someone cries.

The fat man is lying on his back, gasping for breath. He rolls over and tries to get up, loses his footing, and reaches out one hand to right himself, gets unsteadily to his feet and disappears from Joona's field of vision.

'We can't stay here,' Tobias whispers.

Joona tries to look at the reflections in the metal of the butchers' benches and machinery, but it's impossible to see how many men are standing behind him.

'Put your gun down,' a calm voice says.

Joona lets Tobias take his pistol, reasoning that the reinforcements must get here soon, and that this isn't the right moment to take any risks.

121

Vicky Bennet is still sitting in the passenger seat of Joona's car. She bites her dry lips as she stares at the reddish-brown building.

She's holding the steering wheel with her hand to stop the cuff digging into her wrist.

Whenever she's been angry or frightened before, she has trouble remembering anything afterwards. It's like trying to catch a flash of reflected light. It darts about and sometimes seem to settle on some detail before vanishing again.

Vicky shakes her head, screws her eyes shut for a few moments, then looks again.

She doesn't how much time has passed since the detective superintendent with the nice voice went off with his jacket flapping behind him.

Maybe Dante's already lost, maybe he's already disappeared into the black hole that swallows children.

She tries to stay calm, but realises she can't just wait in the car.

A rat scampers along the damp wall and disappears down a drain.

The man driving the forklift at the end of the road has finished work. He closed two huge doors of the hangar and locked up before he left.

Vicky looks at her hand, and the smooth metal holding her captive, the rattling chain.

He promised to take Dante back to his mother.

She lets out an anguished moan.

How could she trust Tobias again? If Dante disappears, it will all be her fault.

She turns to check if she can see anything through the rear window. All the doors are closed, there's no one in sight, the yellow fabric of a torn awning flaps in the wind.

She tugs at the steering wheel with both hands, trying to break it off, but it's no good.

'Shit . . .'

Breathing hard, she bangs her head against the headrest.

Someone has drawn an unhappy face on a poster advertising Swedish meat and groceries.

The detective should have been back by now.

Suddenly there's a loud bang, like an explosion.

A clattering echo fades away, then everything is quiet again. She looks around, but can't see anything: the area is deserted.

What are they doing?

Her heart is thudding hard in her chest.

Anything could be happening in there.

She starts to breathe faster, and in her mind's eye sees a lone child sobbing with fear in a room full of strange men.

The image appeared out of nowhere – she has no idea what it's about.

Vicky stretches and tries to look in through the windows, feeling the panic growing inside her as she tries to pull her hand free. It's impossible. She pulls harder, and winces with pain. The metal slides a short way over the back of her hand, then stops. Breathing through her nose, she leans back, puts one foot on the wheel and the other on the edge of the handcuff, then kicks out as hard as she can.

Vicky Bennet screams out loud when the metal tears the skin on her hand and her thumb breaks as her hand comes free.

122

The pressure of the pistol barrel disappears from Joona's back, rapid footsteps move away and he turns around slowly.

A short man in a grey suit and glasses backs away a little further. He's aiming a black Glock at Joona, while his left hand hangs pale and oddly inert by his hip. At first Joona wonders if it's injured, then realises that it's a prosthetic.

Tobias is standing behind a dirty bench holding Joona's Smith & Wesson, but doesn't seem to know what to do with it.

To his right, the blond man is pointing the sawn-off shotgun at Joona.

'Roger,' the short man says to the one with the shotgun, 'you and Micke take care of the policeman once I've gone.'

Tobias is standing over by the wall, staring at him with eyes that are dark with stress.

A young man with cropped hair and camouflage trousers walks up in front of Joona, aiming at him with a 'Carlo', a homemade submachine gun made up from parts from different weapons. Joona isn't wearing a protective vest, but if he had to choose which of the weapons in the room to be shot with, it would be this one. A Carlo can sometimes have the same fire-power as a normal automatic weapon, but they're often very badly made.

A red dot is hovering on Joona's chest.

The Carlo is fitted with laser sights of the sort some police officers used a few years ago.

'Lie down on the ground with your hands behind your head,' Joona says.

The man with cropped hair grins. The red dot slips down to Joona's crotch, then moves back up to the top of his chest.

'Micke, shoot him,' Roger says, still aiming at Joona with the sawn-off shotgun.

'We can't leave any witnesses,' Tobias agrees, wiping his mouth nervously.

'Put the kid in the car,' the man with the prosthetic hand tells Tobias in a low voice, then walks out of the processing room.

Without taking his eyes off Joona, Tobias goes over to Dante and drags him unceremoniously across the tiled floor by the hood of his top.

'I'll be along shortly,' Joona calls after him.

There are maybe six metres between him and the young man called Micke who's holding the Carlo.

Joona takes a very small step closer to him.

'Stand still!' the young man shouts.

'Micke,' Joona says calmly. 'If you lie down on the floor with your hands behind your head you'll get out of this OK.'

'Just shoot the cop!' the man called Roger calls out.

'Do it yourself,' Micke whispers.

'What?' Roger says, lowering the shotgun. 'What did you say?'

123

The young man with the Carlo is breathing quickly and shallowly. The red dot of the laser sight is quivering on Joona's chest, disappears for an instant, then comes back, even more unsteadily.

'I can see you're scared,' Joona says, moving towards him.

'Shut up, just shut up,' Micke says, backing away.

'The red dot's shaking.'

'Shoot him, for fuck's sake!' Roger roars.

'Put the gun down,' Joona says.

'Shoot!'

'He daren't shoot,' Joona tells him.

'No? Well, I do,' Roger says, raising the shotgun. 'I'm happy to shoot you.'

'I don't think so,' Joona says with a smile.

'You want me to? OK, I'll do it!' he yells, coming closer. 'You want me to do it?'

Roger strides towards Joona. He has a Thor's hammer dangling from a chain around his neck. He holds the sawn-off shotgun out in front of him, puts his finger on the trigger, and aims at Joona.

'I'm going to blow your head off,' he snarls.

Joona lowers his eyes and waits until the man is right in front of him before he thrusts his hand out, grabs the short barrel, pulls the gun towards him, swings it around, and hits Roger in the cheek with the butt. His head snaps sideways with the impact. The man stumbles into the Carlo's line of fire. Joona stands behind him, aims between his legs, and fires the shotgun. The blast is deafening, the gun jolts from the weight of the charge, and the shot passes between the man's legs and hits Micke's left ankle with immense force. The cluster of 258 pellets passes straight through his shinbone and calf muscle. His foot is torn from his leg and rolls in under the conveyor belt.

Blood squirts across the floor from the shattered stump, and Micke fires the homemade submachine gun. Six bullets slam into Roger's chest and shoulder. Micke collapses to the floor, screaming. The rest of the bullets hit the ceiling and ricochet off the pipes and struts.

The metallic clatter continues until the magazine is empty, and then Micke's howls of pain are the only sound.

The short man with the false hand comes running in and is just in time to see Roger sink to his knees and lean forward, his ponytail hanging across one cheek. He rests his hands on the floor in front of him as a steady stream of blood pours from his chest, through the grille on the floor, and into the gulley for draining away pigs' blood.

Joona quickly darts behind some machinery used to inflate the carcasses to make them easier to cut. He hears the man with the Glock come after him, kicking a rattling trolley away and breathing hard through his nose.

Joona moves backwards, opens the shotgun, and sees that it was only loaded with one cartridge.

The young man is crying for help, panting and screaming.

Just ten steps away Joona can see a doorway leading to a cold store. Behind the yellowing strips of clear plastic he can see sides of pork hanging in tightly-packed rows.

He reasons that there ought to be a door leading to the street and the loading bay at the other end of the cold store.

124

At the end of the red-brown building is a black metal door that's been wedged open with a rolled-up newspaper.

A white sign reads: Larsson's Charcuterie and Butchers' Products.

Vicky moves closer, stumbles slightly on the metal grille in front of the door, and opens it. Blood drips from her wounded hand into the newspaper as she goes inside.

She has to find Dante. That's her only plan.

Without making any effort to stay hidden, she walks into a changing room with a row of wooden benches in front of some dented red metal lockers. There's a poster of a smiling Zlatan Ibrahimović taped to the wall. On the windowsill there are some plastic cup-holders on top of a brochure from the Grocery Workers' Association.

She hears a scream through the walls. A man crying for help.

Vicky looks around the changing room, opens a locker, and pulls out some dusty plastic bags, opens the next one, then moves on and looks in the rubbish bin. Among the discarded chewing tobacco and sweet wrappers, she sees an empty glass soda bottle.

The man screams again, sounding more tired this time.

'Shit,' Vicky whispers, picking the bottle up and clutching

it tightly in her right hand as she makes her way through the other door into a cool storeroom full of pallets and packaging machines.

She runs as quietly as she can towards a large garage door. While she's running past the pallets of shrink-wrapped boxes she glimpses movement from the corner of her eye and stops.

She looks around, and sees a shadow moving behind a bright yellow forklift truck. Breathing as silently as she can she creeps forward, rests one hand on the forklift, moves around behind it, and sees a man leaning over a bundle lying on a blanket.

'I feel sick,' a high-pitched child's voice says.

'Can you stand up, little guy?' the man asks.

She takes a step towards them. The man turns around, and Vicky sees that it's Tobias.

'Vicky? What are you doing here?' he asks with a surprised smile.

She moves warily closer.

'Dante?' she asks softly.

The boy looks at her as if he can't quite see her face.

'Vicky, take him out to the van,' Tobias says. 'I'll follow you out in a minute . . .'

'But I'm—'

'Just do as I say and everything will be fine,' he snaps.

'OK,' she says tonelessly.

'Now hurry up – get him out to the van.'

The boy's face is grey, and he just lies down on the blanket again. His heavy eyelids sink lower and close.

'You'll have to carry him,' Tobias sighs.

'Yeah,' Vicky says, and walks over and smashes the glass bottle over Tobias's head.

At first he just looks surprised as he staggers and falls to one knee. He puts his hands to his head in amazement, then looks at the blood and broken glass on his fingers.

'What the fuck are you—'

She lunges at him with the jagged remains of the bottle and hits the side of his neck, twists, and feels his warm blood on her fingers. The rage that fills her is so powerful that she feels intoxicated. Fury burns like madness inside her. She jabs at him again, and hits his right cheek.

'You should have left the boy alone!' she yells.

Aiming for his eyes, she thrusts the bottle forward. He fumbles with his hands and grabs hold of her jacket, pulls her towards him, and punches her hard in the face. She falls backwards, her field of vision shrinks, and everything goes black for a fraction of a second.

As she falls she remembers the man who paid Tobias. She remembers waking up with a terrible pain in her crotch, and with damaged ovaries.

She lands on her back with a gasp, but manages to stop her head hitting the floor. She blinks, and her sight comes back, she gets to her feet, wobbles, but keeps her balance. Blood is trickling from her mouth. Tobias has found a plank with nails sticking out of it on the floor and is trying to stand up.

Vicky's left hand is burning with pain from her broken thumb, but she's still clutching the remains of the broken bottle in her right hand.

She walks forward and stabs Tobias hard in his outstretched hand, as her own blood drips into her eyes. She starts to stab randomly, hitting him in the chest and forehead. The remnants of the bottle shatter, and she cuts her hand, but goes on swiping at him until he falls to the floor and doesn't move.

125

Vicky can't run any more, but she keeps walking with Dante in her arms. It feels as though she's going to throw up. She's lost the feeling in both arms, and is worried about dropping the boy. She stops and tries to change her grip, but loses her footing and falls to her knees hard. Vicky lets out a sigh and gently puts Dante down on the floor. He's fallen asleep again. His face is extremely pale, and she can hardly hear his breathing.

They're either going to have to get out, or find somewhere to hide.

She tries to gather her strength, clenches her teeth, grabs hold of Dante's jacket, and drags him towards a large rubbish bin. It might be possible to squeeze in behind it. Dante whimpers, and his breathing suddenly becomes unsettled. She pats him and sees his eyes open for a moment before closing again.

They're only ten metres away from a glass door next to a large garage entrance, but she hasn't got the strength to carry him any more. Her legs are still shaking from the exertion. All she really wants to do is lie down behind Dante and go to sleep, but she knows she can't do that.

Her hands are bleeding, but she can't feel anything, her arms are still numb.

She can see the empty street through the door.

She sinks onto one hip, breathing heavily, and tries to gather

her thoughts. She looks at her hands, then at Dante, then brushes his hair from his face and leans forward.

'Time to wake up now,' she says.

He blinks, looks up at her blood-streaked face, and is instantly frightened.

'Don't worry,' she says. 'It doesn't hurt. Have you ever had a nosebleed?'

He nods and moistens his mouth.

'Dante, I can't carry you any more, you're going to have to walk the last little bit,' Vicky says, feeling a stifled sob lurking in her throat.

'I just want to sleep,' he says with a yawn.

'You're going home now, it's over—'

'What?'

'You're going home to your mum,' she says, and her exhausted face breaks into a wide smile. 'You just need to manage to walk a little way.'

He nods, rubs his head with his hands, and sits up.

At the far end of the large storeroom something falls to the ground with a clatter. It sounds like metal pipes falling over and rolling across the floor.

'Try to stand up now,' Vicky whispers.

The two of them get to their feet and start walking towards the glass door. Every step is unbearable, and Vicky realises she's not going to make it. Suddenly she sees the flashing blue lights of the first police car. It's followed by others, and Vicky thinks to herself that they're safe.

'Hello?' a man calls in a gruff voice. 'Hello?'

His voice echoes off the walls and high ceiling. Vicky feels dizzy and has to stop, but Dante keeps walking.

She leans her shoulder against the cold metal of the container.

'Go out through the door,' she says in a muted voice.

Dante looks at her, and is about to walk back to her.

'No, go outside,' she tells him. 'I'll follow you in a moment.'

She sees three uniformed police officers run in the wrong direction, towards a building on the other side of the road. Dante keeps walking towards the door. He takes hold of the handle and pulls, but nothing happens.

'Hello?' the man calls, closer now.

Vicky spits some bloody saliva on the floor, clenches her teeth, tries to calm her breathing, and starts to move again.

'Stuck,' Dante says, tugging at the handle.

Vicky's legs are shaking beneath her, and she feels as if her knees are going to buckle, but she forces herself to walk the last steps. Her hand stings with pain as she grabs the handle and pulls. The door doesn't move. She shoves it, but it's locked. She tries to bang on the glass, but makes almost no sound. There are four police cars parked outside. Their blue lights sweep across the buildings, glinting off the various windows. She tries waving, but none of the officers sees her.

Heavy steps thud across the storeroom floor behind them, rapidly coming closer. Vicky turns around and sees a fat man in a leather waistcoat walking towards them with a smile on his face.

126

Pig carcasses are hanging close together from an electrical belt mounted just below the ceiling. The smell of the meat is muffled by the low temperature in the cold store.

Crouching over, Joona moves between the sides of pork, further and further in, as he looks around for something to use as a weapon. He can hear muffled screams from the processing room, followed by some rapid thuds. He tries to see his pursuer through the thick strips of plastic covering the doorway. He can make out a blurred figure in front of the benches, as wide as four men, then thin again.

He's coming closer, fast.

And he's clearly holding a pistol in his right hand.

Joona backs away, ducks down, and looks around the floor beneath the pig carcasses. Over by the far wall there's a white bucket, and beside it a pipe of some sort and some dirty cloths.

A pipe that he can make use of.

He starts to move cautiously in that direction, but has to stop and pull back when the short man pushes the strips of plastic aside with his prosthetic hand.

Joona stands still, catching glimpses of the man reflected in the narrow chrome lintels. He sees the man enter the cold store, holding the pistol out in front of him as he looks around.

Joona takes a few silent steps towards the wall and tucks in behind one of the carcasses, which means he can no longer observe his pursuer – but he can still hear his footsteps and breathing.

Fifteen metres away is a door, which probably leads to a loading bay. Joona could run down the passageway between the hanging carcasses, but just before he reaches the door he would be presenting an open target to the man with the gun, for several seconds.

Several seconds too many, Joona thinks.

He hears slow, shuffling steps, then a heavy thud. One of the pigs starts to sway, and the hook connecting it to the belt in the ceiling creaks.

Joona takes the last few steps to the wall and crouches down beside one of the chiller units. His pursuer's shadow is gliding across the concrete floor ten metres away.

Time is starting to run out.

The man with the false hand will find him soon. Joona sidles along the wall and sees that the pipe is made of plastic, and is therefore useless as a weapon. He's about to move back when he sees that there are several tools in the old bucket. Three screwdrivers, a pair of pliers, and a knife with a short, sturdy blade.

Joona cautiously picks the knife out of the bucket, and there's a slight scraping sound as the blade slips against one handle of the pliers.

He tries to read his pursuer's movements from the sound of his steps, and realises that he has to get away from there.

A shot goes off and thuds into a side of pork with a dull thump, half a metre from Joona's head.

The man's footsteps speed up, he's running now. Joona lies flat on the floor and rolls away, into the next aisle of meat.

127

The policeman is unarmed and scared, the man thinks as he brushes his fringe aside with his prosthetic hand.

He stops, raises the pistol, and tries to see past the animal carcasses.

He must be scared, he repeats to himself.

He might be hiding now, but the man knows that the police officer will soon try to make a run for the door leading to the street.

His own breathing is faster than normal. The air feels cold and dry in his lungs. He coughs weakly, turns around, glances at the pistol, then looks up again. He blinks hard. Did he just see something over by the wall, behind that chiller unit? He starts to run along the row of carcasses.

It must be possible to bring this to a rapid conclusion. All he has to do is catch up with the policeman and shoot him from close range. First shot at his body, second through his temple.

He stops when he sees that the aisle by the wall is empty, just a white bucket and some rags on the floor.

He turns abruptly and starts to retrace his steps, then stops and listens.

All he can hear is the nasal sound of his own breathing.

He pushes at a side of pork with his false hand, but it's heavier than he expected. He has to give it a good shove to get it to swing. His arm starts to ache again when the prosthetic presses against the stump.

The hooks up at the ceiling creak.

The pig swings to the right, and he can see into the next aisle.

There's nowhere he can go, the man thinks. He's got him trapped in a cage. All he has to do is keep an open line of fire to the door in case the policeman tries to get out, but also keep an eye on the plastic-covered opening to the processing room to stop him going back that way.

His shoulder is starting to tire and he lowers the pistol for a few moments. He knows he risks losing vital seconds, but the gun will start to shake if his arm gets too tired.

He moves slowly forward, catches a glimpse of what he thinks is the man's back, raises the pistol, and fires. The recoil kicks back, and the percussive powder burns his knuckles. Adrenaline pumps through his blood, making his face feel cold.

He moves sideways, feels his heart beat faster, but realises that he was wrong, it was just a side of pork hanging crookedly.

This is starting to go seriously wrong, he thinks. He has to stop the policeman, he can't let him get away, not now.

So where the hell is he? Where is he?

The ceiling creaks and he looks up at the beams and struts. Nothing. He backs away, takes a misstep, and leans one shoulder against a side of pork, feeling the cold dampness of the meat through his shirt. The carcass is sparkling with tiny drops of condensation. He feels sick. There's something not right about this. The stress is starting to catch up with him, and he's not going to be able to stay in the cold store much longer.

The man keeps moving backwards, sees a fleeting shadow on the wall, and raises the pistol.

Suddenly the carcasses start to sway, all of them at once. As they begin to quiver, their outlines blur. There's an electronic whirring sound from the ceiling, the machinery rattles, and the heavy sides of pork start to move as one along the belt, causing a cold draught.

The man with the pistol turns around, his eyes scanning the

room, trying to cover all angles at the same time, and thinking to himself that it really wasn't worth this.

It should have been a simple matter, buying a Swedish boy whom the police already thought was dead. He wouldn't have had to go further than Germany or Holland to get a good price for him.

But it's not worth the effort now.

The pigs stop abruptly, and sway slowly. A red lamp is glowing on the wall. The policeman has pressed the emergency stop button.

The room falls silent again, and an unnerving atmosphere spreads like blood in water.

What the hell am I doing here? the man asks himself.

He tries to calm his breathing as he moves slowly closer to the red light, crouching in an attempt to see between the carcasses.

The door to the street is still closed.

He turns to look at the other exit, and suddenly the tall policeman is standing right in front of him.

The man feels a cold shiver run down his spine.

128

Joona watches as the short man tries to aim the pistol at him. He mirrors the man's movement, takes a step forward, and deflects the gun so it ends up pointing at the ceiling. He grabs the man's wrist and slams it against one of the carcasses, twists the pistol from his grasp, then drives the knife straight through the man's hand as hard as he can.

Joona lets go of the knife and takes a step back.

The man is panting hard, fumbling for the handle of the knife with the lifeless fingers of his prosthetic hand, but gives up. He's stuck, and realises that he needs to stand perfectly still to reduce the pain. His hand is skewered high above his head. Blood is running down his wrist and under the sleeve of his shirt.

Without giving him another glance, Joona picks the pistol up and walks out of the cold store.

The air in the large processing room suddenly feels very warm as he hurries along one wall towards the door where Tobias vanished with Dante. He quickly checks the pistol, sees that there's a bullet in the chamber, and probably more in the magazine. He opens the green metal door and finds himself in a large storeroom full of loaded pallets and motionless fork-lift trucks.

Light is coming in through the dirty windows close to the roof.

He can hear a rattling, groaning sound.

Joona works out where it's coming from, and runs over to a large rubbish bin. Blue light is playing across the floor from a glass door. He raises the pistol and moves around the container. The fat man in the leather waistcoat is kneeling on the floor with his back to Joona. He lets out a load groan as he beats Vicky's head on the floor. A short distance away Dante has curled up and is crying in a high, desolate voice.

Before the fat man has time to get up, Joona is on him. He grabs hold of the man's throat under his beard with one hand, pulls him to his feet, away from Vicky, gives him a shove, and breaks his collarbone with the pistol, then pushes him back again, letting go of his throat, and kicking him hard in the chest so that he lurches back, straight through the glass door.

The fat man falls backwards into the street in a shower of broken glass, and ends up lying there bathed in blue light.

Three uniformed policemen run over, weapons drawn, aiming at the man on the ground, who clutches his chest with one hand as he tries to sit up.

'Joona Linna?' one of the officers asks.

They stare at the tall superintendent as he stands in the remains of the shattered glass door with splinters still falling from the top of the frame.

'I'm just an observer,' Joona says.

He tosses the Glock on the ground and goes over and kneels down beside Vicky. She's lying on her back, gasping for breath. Her arm is lying at an unnatural angle. Dante has stopped crying and looks at Joona in astonishment as he gently strokes Vicky's cheek and whispers that it's over now. A steady trickle of blood is running from her nose. Joona crouches down and holds her head completely still. She doesn't open her eyes, and doesn't react when spoken to, although her feet are twitching.

129

The man who crashed through the glass door lay on his back for a while, then sat up and tried to crawl away, but was overpowered by two police officers and forced to lie on his front while his hands were cuffed.

The first paramedics on the scene took care to immobilise Vicky's head with a neck-brace before they lifted her onto a stretcher.

Joona informed the lead officer about the situation, while two police patrols made their way into the building from different directions.

In the cold store they discovered a silent, pale man with his right hand pinned to a hanging side of pork. The police officer who found him called in the paramedics, then had to get a colleague to help him pull the knife out. The blade squeaked against the animal's ribs before coming loose with a sigh. The man lowered his hand, pressed it to his stomach with the prosthetic, then staggered and slumped down onto the floor.

The man who was shot in the chest by the homemade gun was dead. The young man who had pulled the trigger when Joona shot his foot off was still alive. He had saved himself from bleeding to death by tying his belt around his shin immediately below the knee. When the police patrol reached him with their pistols raised, he simply gestured weakly towards the amputated foot that was lying in a pool of blood under one of the benches.

The last to be found was Tobias Lundhagen, who had hidden among the rubbish in the darkness of the storeroom with his badly cut face. He was bleeding profusely, but his injuries weren't life-threatening, although he would be left badly disfigured. He tried to crawl further in amongst the rubbish, and when the police pulled him out by his legs he was shaking with terror.

The head of the National Crime Unit, Carlos Eliasson, has already been informed of developments out in the slaughter-house district when Joona calls him from the ambulance.

'One dead, two seriously injured, and three more requiring hospital treatment,' Carlos reads.

'But the children are alive, they made it—'

'Joona,' he sighs.

'Everyone said they'd drowned, but I—'

'I know. You were right, you were definitely right,' Carlos interrupts. 'But you're under internal investigation and had been given other orders.'

'So I shouldn't have bothered?' Joona asks.

'Exactly.'

'I couldn't do that.'

The siren falls silent and the ambulance turns sharply as it heads towards the emergency room at Södermalm Hospital.

'The prosecutor and her people are in charge of the interviews, and you are now formally on sick leave and removed from all duties.'

Joona assumes that the internal investigation is going to get worse, and that they may even decide to press charges against him, but all he can feel right now is an immense relief that he managed to rescue the little boy from a terrible fate.

When they reach the hospital he climbs out of the ambulance himself, but is made to lie on a trolley. They fold the sides up and wheel him off to an examination room.

While he's being checked over and patched up he tries to find out about Vicky Bennet's condition, and instead of waiting his turn to be X-rayed, he goes to find the doctor responsible for her care.

Dr Lindgren is a very short woman, who is staring at a coffee machine with a frown on her face.

Joona explains that he needs to know if Vicky can be questioned today.

The short woman listens without meeting his gaze. She presses the button for mocha, waits for her cup to fill, then says that they have taken an emergency CT scan of Vicky's brain to check for possible intracranial bleeding. She's suffered a serious concussion, but fortunately her bridging veins are intact.

'Vicky needs to stay in hospital for observation, but there's no reason why she can't be questioned first thing tomorrow morning if it's important,' the woman explains, then walks away with her cup.

District Prosecutor Susanne Öst is driving down to Stockholm. She's decided to arrest the girl. At eight o'clock the following morning she's planning to conduct the first interview with Vicky Bennet, the fifteen-year-old girl suspected of two counts of murder and one of kidnap.

130

Joona Linna walks along the corridor, shows his ID, and says hello to the young police officer standing watch outside the door to room 703 in Södermalm Hospital in Stockholm.

Vicky is sitting up in bed. The curtains are open, and her face is covered with dark cuts and bruises. Her head has been bandaged, and the hand with the broken thumb is now in plaster. Over by the window stands Susanne Öst, the prosecutor from Sundsvall, with a second woman. Without bothering to acknowledge their presence, Joona walks straight over to Vicky and sits down in the chair by the bed.

'How are you feeling?' he asks.

She looks at him groggily and asks: 'Has Dante gone home to his mum?'

'He's still in hospital, but his mum's with him, she hasn't left his side.'

'Is he hurt?'

'No.'

Vicky nods, then stares in front of her.

'How are you feeling?' Joona asks again.

She looks at him, but doesn't get a chance to answer before the prosecutor clears her throat.

'I must ask Joona Linna to leave the room now,' she says.

'And now you've done that,' Joona replies, without taking his eyes off Vicky.

'You have no involvement in this preliminary investigation at all,' Susanne says, raising her voice.

'They're going to ask you an awful lot of questions,' Joona explains to Vicky.

'I want you to be here,' she says quietly.

'I can't stay,' Joona replies simply.

Vicky whispers to herself, then looks at Susanne Öst.

'I'm not talking to anyone unless Joona's here,' she says stubbornly.

'He can stay if he keeps quiet,' the prosecutor replies.

Joona looks at Vicky and tries to figure out a way of getting through to her.

Two murders is an immense burden to carry around inside.

Anyone else her age would already have crumbled, would be crying and confessing everything, but this girl seems to have a crystalline shell. She never really lets anyone in. She forms alliances quickly, but remains hidden, and is always in control of the situation.

'Vicky Bennet,' the prosecutor begins with a smile. 'Like I said, my name is Susanne, and I'm the person who's going to be talking to you, but before we start I want to let you know that I'm going to record everything we say so that we can remember it afterwards . . . and so I don't have to do so much writing, which is handy because I'm actually quite lazy . . .'

Vicky isn't looking at her, and is showing no reaction to her words. Susanne waits a few moments, still smiling, then runs through the time, date, and names of those present in the room.

'I have to do that before we start,' she explains.

'Do you understand who we are?' the other woman asks. 'My name is Signe Ridelman, and I'm your legal representative.'

'Signe's here to help you,' the prosecutor says.

'Do you know what a legal representative is?' she asks.

Vicky nods almost imperceptibly.

'I need an answer,' Signe says patiently.

'I understand,' Vicky says quietly, then suddenly smiles.

'What's so funny?' the prosecutor asks.

'This,' Vicky says, slowly pulling the narrow tube out from her vein, then watching as the dark blood trickles down her pale arm.

131

The sound of a small bird landing on the window ledge is clearly audible in the silence. The light fitting in the ceiling of the hospital room hums quietly.

'I'm going to ask you to tell me about various situations,' Susanne Öst says. 'And I want you to tell me the truth.'

'And nothing but the truth,' Vicky whispers with her head bowed.

'Nine days ago . . . you left your room at the Birgitta Home in the middle of the night,' the prosecutor begins. 'Do you remember that?'

'I haven't counted the days,' the girl says in a toneless voice.

'But you remember leaving the Birgitta Home in the middle of the night?'

'Yes.'

'Why?' Susanne Öst asks. 'Why did you leave the Birgitta Home in the middle of the night?'

Vicky pulls at a loose thread on the bandage around her hand.

'Had you done it before?' Susanne asks.

'What?'

'Left the Birgitta Home in the middle of the night?'

'No,' Vicky says in a bored voice.

'Why did you do it on this occasion?'

When the prosecutor doesn't get an answer she just smiles tolerantly and asks in a gentler tone of voice: 'Why were you awake in the middle of the night?'

'Don't remember.'

'If we go back a few more hours – do you remember what happened then? Everyone went to bed, but you were awake – what were you doing?'

'Nothing.'

'You did nothing until you suddenly left the Birgitta Home in the middle of the night – don't you think that sounds a bit strange?'

'No.'

Vicky stares out through the window. Wind is blowing across the rooftops, and the sun is covered by clouds drifting across the sky.

'Now I want you to tell me why you left the Birgitta Home,' Susanne says in a more serious tone of voice. 'Because I'm not going to give up until you tell me what happened. Do you understand?'

'I don't know what you want me to say,' Vicky replies quietly.

'It might feel difficult, but you still need to tell me.'

The girl looks up at the ceiling and her mouth moves, as if she were searching for words, before she says, in a dreamy voice: 'I killed . . .'

She falls silent and fiddles with the tube in her arm.

'Go on,' Susanne says, sounding tense.

Vicky moistens her mouth and shakes her head.

'It would make sense to tell me,' Susanne says. 'You said you killed . . .'

'Yeah, right . . . there was an annoying fly in my room, and I killed it and—'

'Oh, for God's sake . . . Sorry, I didn't mean that . . . but isn't it odd that you remember killing a fly, but can't remember why you left the Birgitta Home in the middle of the night?'

132

The prosecutor and Signe Ridelman have requested a short break, and have left the room. The grey morning light falls through the streaked glass of the window, and the white sky is reflected off the chrome of the bed frame and drip-stand. Vicky Bennet is sitting up in the high hospital bed, swearing quietly to herself.

'Couldn't agree more,' Joona says, and sits down on the chair beside the bed.

She looks up and gives him a brief smile.

'I keep thinking about Dante,' she says weakly.

'He's going to be OK.'

She's about to say something else, but stops herself when the prosecutor and lawyer come back in.

'You've admitted to running away from the Birgitta Home in the middle of the night,' the prosecutor says with renewed vigour. 'In the middle of the night. Straight out into the forest. That's not the sort of thing anyone would do. You had a reason for running away, didn't you?'

Vicky lowers her gaze, moistens her lips, but says nothing.

'Answer me,' she says, raising her voice. 'You might as well.'

'Yeah . . .'

'Why did you run away?'

The girl shrugs.

'You did something that's hard to talk about, didn't you?'

Vicky rubs her face hard.

'I have to ask you these questions,' Susanne says. 'You might think it's unpleasant, but I know everything will feel much better if you just confess.'

'Will it?'

'Yes.'

She shrugs her shoulders again, looks up, and meets the prosecutor's gaze, and asks: 'What do you want me to confess?'

'What you did that night.'

'I killed a fly.'

The prosecutor stands up abruptly and leaves the room without another word.

133

It's a quarter past eight in the morning when Saga Bauer opens the door to the senior prosecutor's room at the National Department for Complaints Against the Police. Mikael Båge, who's in charge of this investigation, gets up politely from his chair.

Saga's hair is still damp after her shower, and her long blonde locks with the colourful ribbons woven into them curl across her back and slender shoulders. She has a plaster across the bridge of her nose, but is still strikingly beautiful.

Saga has already run ten kilometres this morning, and is dressed as usual in a hooded jacket from Narva Boxing Club, faded jeans, and trainers.

'Saga Bauer?' the internal investigator asks with a broad and slightly odd smile.

'Yes,' she replies.

He walks over, rubs his hands on his jacket, and shakes hands with her.

'Forgive me,' he says. 'But I . . . what the hell, you've heard it before . . . but if I were twenty years younger.'

Mikael Båge is blushing as he sits down on a chair and loosens his tie slightly before looking up at Saga again.

The door opens, and Senior Prosecutor Sven Wiklund walks in. He shakes hands with them both, then stops in front of Saga as if he's about to say something, but just nods and sets out a carafe of water and three glasses on the table before he sits down.

'Saga Bauer, Detective Superintendent at the Security Police,' Mikael Båge begins, and then breaks into an irrepressible smile.

'Perhaps it would be just as well to get this out of the way,' the senior prosecutor says to Saga. 'But you really do look like one of John Bauer's fairy-tale princesses.'

He pauses and pours water into the glasses.

'You've been asked to come here to provide a witness statement,' the internal investigator goes on, tapping a folder. 'Seeing as you were present at the incident in question.'

'What do you want to know?' she asks levelly.

'The complaint against Joona Linna concerns . . . He's suspected of having warned—'

'Göran Stone is really fucking stupid,' she interrupts.

'There's no need to get upset,' Mikael Båge says.

Saga remembers very well how both she and Joona made their way inside the headquarters of a clandestine group of left-wing extremists. Daniel Marklund, the Brigade's expert at hacking and surveillance, gave them information that helped save the life of Penelope Fernandez.

'So you don't consider the Security Police operation a failure?'

'I do, because it was, but I was the one who warned the Brigade.'

'Well, this complaint has been filed against—'

'Joona's the best police officer in the country.'

'Loyalty is all very well, but we're going to press charges against—'

'Go to hell!' Saga snaps.

She gets up, overturning the whole table. The glasses and carafe hit the floor, spreading water and broken glass across the room. She snatches Mikael Båge's folder from his hand, empties its contents on the floor, tramples on the pages, then leaves the room, slamming the door so hard that one of the windows flies open.

Saga Bauer really does look like a fairy-tale princess, but the only thing she feels like right now is the superintendent at the Security Police that she actually is. She's one of the best snipers outside of the specialist units, and a champion-level boxer.

134

Saga is still swearing to herself when she emerges onto Kungsbron. She forces herself to walk more slowly as she struggles to calm down. Her phone rings in the pocket of her hooded jacket. She stops and looks at the screen, then answers when she sees it's her boss at the Security Police.

'We've received a request from National Crime,' Verner says in his deep bass voice. 'I've had a word with Jimmy and Jan Pettersson, but neither of them can take it . . . I don't know if Göran Stone is suitable, but—'

'What's it about?' she asks.

'Questioning an underage girl . . . she's mentally unstable, and the head of the preliminary investigation needs someone trained in interview techniques with experience of—'

'I can understand you asking Jimmy,' Saga says, aware of a jagged note of irritation in her voice. 'But why Jan Pettersson? Why would you ask Jan Pettersson before talking to me? And as for Göran . . . how can you begin to think that . . .'

Saga forces herself to stop. She can still feel the after-effects of her outburst a few minutes ago.

'Are you going to start arguing now?' Verner sighs.

'Look, I'm the one who went down to Pullach and did the BND's training course, and that—'

'Please—'

'I haven't finished,' she interrupts. 'You know perfectly well that I sat in when Muhammed al-Abdaly was cross-examined.'

'But you weren't lead interviewer.'

'No, but I was the one who . . . oh, what's the point?'

She ends the call and contemplates handing in her notice tomorrow morning. Her phone rings again.

'OK, Saga,' Verner says slowly. 'You can have a go.'

'Shut up,' she yells, and switches her phone off.

Carlos spills fish food on his desk when Anja suddenly throws the door open. He starts to sweep the dry flakes into his hand just as his landline rings.

'Please, put it on speaker,' he asks her.

'It's Verner,' Anja says, and presses the button.

'Hi there,' Carlos says brightly, brushing his hands above one of the aquariums.

'Verner here . . . sorry it took such a long time.'

'No problem.'

'Look, Carlos, I've done my best, but I'm afraid all my best guys are on loan to Alex Allan at the Joint Intelligence Committee,' the head of the Security Police says, and clears his throat. 'But there's one female . . . I think you've met her, Saga Bauer . . . she could at least sit in and—'

Anja leans towards the phone and snaps: 'She could sit in and look pretty, couldn't she?'

'Hello?' Verner says. 'Who am I talking—'

'Oh, just shut up!' Anja snarls. 'I know Saga Bauer, and I can tell you that the Security Police don't deserve to have such a good—'

'Anja,' Carlos says, quickly brushing his hands on his trousers and trying to insert himself between her and the phone.

'Sit down!' Anja roars.

Carlos sits down as Verner explains in a weak voice: 'I'm already sitting down—'

'Now call Saga and tell her you're sorry,' Anja says authoritatively into the phone.

135

The police officer posted in the corridor looks at Saga Bauer's ID and blushes badly. He tells her that the patient will soon be back, and holds the door to room 703 open for her.

Saga takes a few steps inside and stops in front of the two people waiting in the empty room. The bed is gone, but the drip-stand is still there.

'Excuse me,' the woman in the grey suit says.

'Yes?' Saga says.

'Are you a friend of Vicky's?'

Before Saga can say anything, the door opens and Joona Linna walks in.

'Joona,' she says in surprise, smiling broadly as she shakes his hand. 'I thought you'd been suspended from everything.'

'I have,' he confirms.

'Good to know,' she says.

'The internal investigators are doing a great job,' he says, grinning so hard that dimples appear in his cheeks.

Prosecutor Susanne Öst walks up to Saga with a confused expression on her face.

'Security Police?' she asks. 'I thought perhaps . . . I mean, I asked for—'

'Where's Vicky Bennet?' Saga asks.

'Her doctor wanted to perform another tomography,' Joona

says, then goes over to look out of the window with his back to the room.

'This morning I took the decision to charge Vicky Bennet,' the prosecutor says. 'Obviously it would be good to have a confession before the custody proceedings.'

'You're planning to press charges?' Saga asks in surprise.

'Look,' Susanne says drily. 'I was there, I saw the bodies. Vicky Bennet is fifteen years old, and she's in a league way beyond secure children's homes.'

Saga smiles sceptically.

'But a prison sentence—'

'Don't take this the wrong way,' the prosecutor interrupts. 'But I was actually expecting to get an experienced interviewer.'

'I can understand that,' Saga says.

'You can have a chance, though. You should definitely have a chance.'

'Thanks,' Saga says through clenched teeth.

'I've been here half a day already, and I can tell you that this isn't a normal interview,' Susanne Öst says, taking a deep breath.

'In what way?'

'Vicky Bennet isn't scared – she seems to enjoy power games.'

'How about you?' Saga asks. 'Do you enjoy power games?'

'I haven't got time for her games, or yours either,' the prosecutor says sternly. 'Tomorrow I shall be initiating custody proceedings in court.'

'I've listened to the first session, and I don't get the impression that Vicky Bennet is playing,' Saga says.

'It's just a game,' the prosecutor insists.

'I don't think so, but murder can be traumatic even for the murderer, meaning that their memories can be like separate islands with fluid boundaries.'

'So what do you get taught to do about that at the Security Police?'

'The lead interviewer should presume that all perpetrators want to confess and be understood,' Saga replies, choosing to ignore Susanne Öst's provocative tone.

'Is that all?' the prosecutor asks.

'I tend to think that a confession is linked to a feeling of power, seeing as the person confessing has power over the truth,' Saga goes on amiably. 'That's why threats don't work, whereas friendliness, respect and—'

'Just don't forget that she's suspected of committing two extremely brutal murders.'

The sound of footsteps and the squeak of the bed's wheels get louder out in the corridor.

136

Vicky Bennet is wheeled into the room by two auxiliary nurses. Her face has swollen up badly now, and her cheeks and forehead are covered with dark scabs. Her hands are still bandaged, apart from the plaster cast around her broken thumb. The bed is put back into position, and the drip reattached to the stand. Vicky is lying on her back with her eyes open, ignoring the nurses' attempts to make small talk. The look on her face is still sad and serious.

The sides of the bed are pulled up, but the straps are hanging loose.

When the nurses leave the room, Saga notices that there are now two police officers standing guard in the corridor.

Saga waits until the girl looks at her, before walking over to the bed.

'My name is Saga Bauer, and I'm here to help you remember the past few days.'

'Are you some sort of counsellor then, or what?'

'Superintendent.'

'Police?'

'Yes, Security Police,' Saga replies.

'You're the most beautiful person I've ever seen in real life.'

'That's a kind thing to say.'

'I've cut beautiful faces before now,' Vicky smiles.

'I know,' Saga replies calmly.

She takes out her phone and switches on the recording function. She quickly says the date, time, and location, then the names of the people in the room, before turning towards Vicky and looking at her for a while before speaking: 'You've been through some terrible things,' she says, without any artifice.

'I've seen the papers,' Vicky replies, and swallows a couple of times. 'I've seen my picture, and Dante's . . . and I've read things about myself.'

'Do you recognise the things they wrote?'

'No.'

'Tell me what happened instead, in your own words.'

'I've been running and walking and freezing . . . frozen.'

Vicky looks at Saga curiously, moistens her mouth, and then appears to search inside herself for memories that match what she's said, or lies that might explain it.

'I don't know anything about why you ran, but I'll listen if you decide you want to tell me,' Saga says slowly.

'I don't want to,' Vicky mumbles.

'How about we start with the previous day?' Saga goes on. 'I know a bit about that, I know you had lessons in the morning, but apart from that . . .'

Vicky closes her eyes, then after a short while says: 'It was normal, just routines and boring chores.'

'Don't you usually have activities in the afternoons?'

'Elisabet took everyone down to the lake . . . Lu Chu and Almira went skinny-dipping even though we're not allowed to, but that's just what they're like,' Vicky says, with a sudden smile. 'Elisabet got annoyed with them, so everyone else started to take all their clothes off.'

'But not you?'

'No . . . and not Miranda or Tuula either,' Vicky says.

'So what did you do instead?'

'I paddled at the edge of the water and watched the others playing.'

'What did Elisabet do?'

'She took all her clothes off and went swimming,' Vicky smiles.

'What about Tuula and Miranda?'

'They sat and threw pine cones at each other.'

'And Elisabet went swimming with the others?'

'She swam the way old ladies normally do.'

'How about you? What did you do?'

'I went back to the house,' Vicky says.

'How did you feel that evening?'

'Fine.'

'You felt fine? But if that was the case, why did you hurt yourself? You cut yourself on your arms and stomach.'

137

The prosecutor has been sitting on a chair following the conversation with intense concentration. Saga is looking at Vicky's face, and sees it become darker, harder for a few seconds. The corners of her mouth turn down, and there's a cold look in her eyes.

'It says in the notes that you cut your arms,' Saga explains.

'Yeah, but it was nothing . . . We were watching TV, and I felt a bit sorry for myself, and cut myself with a bit of a broken plate . . . I had to go to the office to get patched up. I like it when that happens. Because Elisabet is calm and she knows I need soft gauze bandages around my hands, or rather my wrists . . . Because it always feel disgusting afterwards, when I think about the open veins and everything . . .'

'Why did you feel sorry for yourself?'

'I was supposed to have a talk with Elisabet, but she said she didn't have time.'

'What did you want to talk about?'

'I don't know, nothing, really, it was just my turn to have a separate talk with her, but all my time got used up because Miranda and Tuula were fighting.'

'That doesn't sound very fair,' Saga says.

'Anyway, I felt sorry for myself and cut myself and got patched up.'

'So you got a bit of time alone with Elisabet after all.'

'Yeah,' Vicky smiles.

'Are you Elisabet's favourite?'

'No.'

'Who is her favourite?' Saga asks.

Vicky quickly lunges out with the back of her hand, but Saga merely rolls her head back without moving her body. Vicky can't understand what happened, how she managed to miss, or how the police officer has managed to press her hand very gently against Vicky's cheek.

'Are you feeling tired?' Saga asks, letting her hand rest soothingly against the girl's cheek.

Vicky looks at her, and holds the hand in place for a moment before suddenly turning her face away.

'You usually get thirty milligrams of Zyprexa before you go to bed,' Saga continues after a while.

'Yes.'

The girl's voice is now monotonous and dismissive.

'What time?'

'Ten.'

'Did you manage to get to sleep then?'

'No.'

'If I've understood correctly, you weren't able to sleep all night.'

'I don't want to talk any more,' Vicky says, resting her head heavily on the pillow and closing her eyes.

'That's enough for today,' her lawyer says, getting up from her chair.

'We've got twenty minutes left,' the prosecutor objects.

'My client needs to rest,' Signe Ridelman says, going over to Vicky. 'You're tired, aren't you? Would you like me to get you something to eat?'

The lawyer talks to her client, and the prosecutor stands by the window listening to her voicemail with a blank expression on her face.

Saga is about to stop the recording when she happens to catch Joona's eye and hesitates.

His eyes look remarkably grey – like ice melting in the spring

– before he walks out of the room. Saga asks the lawyer to wait, then follows Joona past the police officers outside the door and a little way down the corridor. He's waiting for her by the door to the fire escape.

'Have I missed something?' she asks.

'Vicky slept in her bed with blood-stained clothes on,' Joona tells her quietly.

'What?'

'It's not in the crime-scene report.'

'But you spotted it?'

'Yes.'

'So she did sleep, after the murders?'

'I haven't got access to the lab results, but one thought I had is that she gave herself an overdose of her medication because she was feeling bad. It's easy to think that would help, but it doesn't, it just makes you more and more restless, until you end up in a rage. We don't know anything yet, but maybe she wanted to get revenge on Miranda for using up all her conversation time, maybe she was angry with Elisabet for letting Miranda get away with it. Or maybe it's about something else entirely . . .'

'So you're thinking that one possible scenario is that she killed Elisabet, took the key, opened the door to the isolation room, killed Miranda, and then fell asleep?'

'Yes, because there are two distinct aspects to the evidence in the isolation room – uncontrollable rage and an almost melancholic concern.'

Joona looks directly at Saga, his eyes heavy and thoughtful.

'Once Miranda was dead, the rage faded away,' he says. 'She tried to arrange Miranda's body, laid her on the bed and put her hands over her eyes. Then she went back to her own room just as the tranquilising effect of the medication kicked in – it's pretty serious stuff, and would have left her feeling wiped out.'

138

When Saga returns to the patient's room, the prosecutor tries to explain that the remaining quarter of an hour is too little time to accomplish anything useful. Saga just nods as if she agrees, then goes over to the foot of the bed. The lawyer looks at her curiously. Saga waits with her hands on the smooth metal bedframe until Vicky raises her wounded face and meets her gaze.

'I thought you were awake all night,' Saga begins, very slowly. 'But Joona says you slept in your bed for a while before you left the Birgitta Home.'

Vicky shakes her head, and the lawyer tries to intervene: 'Today's session is over, and . . .'

Vicky whispers something and scratches one of the scabs on her cheek. Saga knows she has to get her to talk about what happened next. It doesn't have to be much, just a few honest words about her flight through the forest and the boy's abduction.

She knows that the more the lead interviewer can get the subject to talk about events surrounding the crime, the more likely they are to tell everything.

'Joona isn't usually wrong,' Saga says with a smile.

'It was dark, and I was lying in bed when everyone was shouting and slamming doors,' Vicky whispers.

'You're lying in bed and everyone's shouting,' Saga says, nodding. 'What are you thinking? What do you do next?'

'I'm frightened, that's the first thing, my heart is beating really hard and fast, and I lie there completely still under the covers,' Vicky says, without looking at anyone in the room. 'It's really dark . . . but then I realise that I'm wet . . . I think I've wet myself or got my period or something . . . Buster is barking, and Nina is screaming something about Miranda, and I switch the light on and see that I've got blood all over me.'

Saga forces herself not to ask about the blood and the murders, not to try to force a confession and just go with the flow.

'Do you start screaming as well?' she asks in a neutral voice.

'I don't think so. I don't know, I couldn't think,' Vicky goes on. 'I just wanted to get away from it all, disappear . . . I sleep with my clothes on, I always have . . . so I just grab my bag, put my shoes on, climb out through the window, and walk off into the forest . . . I'm frightened, and I go as fast as I can and the sky gets lighter and after a few hours it's easier to see through the trees. I just keep going, and suddenly I see a car . . . it's almost new, it's just sitting there abandoned, the door's open and the keys are in it . . . I know how to drive, I spent a whole summer doing it . . . so I just get in the car and start driving . . . And then I feel how knackered I am, my legs are shaking . . . I'm thinking of driving to Stockholm and getting hold of some money so I can go and stay with my friend in Chile . . . Then suddenly there's a bang and the car spins around and the side hits something . . . bang, then silence . . . I come around, my ear's bleeding and I look up, there are bits of glass everywhere, I've driven into a bloody traffic light, I don't know how, but the windows are gone and the rain's coming straight into the car . . . the engine's still running, and I'm alive . . . I put my hand on the gear stick, reverse, then carry on driving . . . the rain's blowing into my face, and then I hear someone crying, and I turn around and see that there's a kid sitting in a child's seat in the back, a little boy. It's mad, I've got no idea how he got there . . . I shout at him to shut up. The rain just keeps pouring down. I can hardly see at all, but just as I'm about to turn the corner and drive across the bridge I see flashing blue lights on the far side of the river . . . I panic and spin the steering wheel and we go off the road. It all happens too fast, we're rushing down the riverbank, and I try to brake, but

395

the car just keeps going, into the water, and I hit my head on the wheel. Water crashes over the bonnet into the car and we just keep going, further out into the river . . . Everything goes dark when we start to sink, but I find some air up by the roof and crawl back towards the boy, I manage to get his belt off and pull the whole child's seat out through the windscreen. We're already a long way down, but the car seat floats and pulls us up to the surface, and we float down the river and manage to get out on the opposite bank . . . we're soaked through, my bag and shoes have gone, but we start walking . . .'

Vicky pauses to catch her breath. Saga detects movement from the prosecutor, but doesn't take her eyes off Vicky.

'I told Dante we were going to find his mum,' Vicky goes on in a shaky voice. 'I held his hand and we walked and walked, and sang a song from his preschool about an old man who wore his shoes out. We were walking along a road with lamp posts by the side . . . a car stopped and we got in the back seat . . . the man looked at us in the mirror and turned the heater up and asked if we wanted to go to his house and get some food and new clothes . . . We would have gone if he'd hadn't checked us out in the mirror and said we could earn a bit of pocket-money too . . . When he stopped for petrol we sneaked out and started walking again instead . . . I don't know how far we got, but in a layby near a lake there was an Ikea lorry parked, and on one of the picnic tables we found a flask and a plastic bag full of hamburger rolls, but before we could grab the bag a guy came around the truck and asked if we were hungry . . . He's from Poland, and he gives us a lift all the way to Uppsala . . . I borrow his phone and call my mum . . . Several times I tell myself that I'll kill him if he touches Dante, but he just lets us sit there quietly and sleep . . . he doesn't want anything. He just drops us off and we catch the train the last bit of the way to Stockholm, hiding among the luggage . . . I haven't got my key for the underground any more, and I don't know anyone there now, it's been such a long time . . . I spent a few weeks with a couple who lived at Midsommarkransen, but I can't remember their name. I do remember Tobias, though, of course I remember him, and I remember that he lived on Wollmar Yxkullsgatan, and that I used to get off at Mariatorget station and . . . I'm so fucking stupid, I really am.'

She falls silent and rolls over, buries her face in the pillow, and just lies there motionless.

139

Saga stays where she is at the end of the bed, looking at Vicky, who's lying very still on her front, running one finger along the side of the bed.

'I'm thinking about the man in the car,' Saga says. 'The one who wanted you to go back to his house with him . . . I'm almost certain your instincts were right, and that he was dangerous.'

Vicky sits up and looks into Saga's pale blue eyes.

'Do you think you could help me track him down when we're done with all this?'

Vicky nods and swallows hard, then lowers her gaze and sits there quietly with her arms wrapped tightly around herself, covered in goosebumps. It isn't easy to see how this thin, fragile girl could have smashed two people's heads in.

'Before we go any further, I just want to say that it does usually feel better when you tell the truth,' Saga says.

She feels full of a tingling sense of calm, the way she usually does in the boxing ring. She knows she's very close to getting a full, honest confession. She can feel the change in the room, it's there in their voices, in the warmth, in the moistness of Vicky's eyes. Saga pretends to write something in her notepad before looking at the girl as if she's already confessed to the murders.

'You went to sleep in those blood-stained sheets,' Saga says softly.

'I killed Miranda,' Vicky whispers. 'Didn't I?'

'You tell me.'

Vicky's mouth trembles, and the wounds on her face flare darker as she blushes.

'I can get so horribly angry,' she says, then puts her hands over her face.

'Did you get angry with Miranda?'

'Yes.'

'What did you do?'

'I don't want to talk about it.'

The lawyer can't help going up to Vicky.

'You know you don't have to say, don't you?' she says.

'I don't have to,' Vicky repeats to Saga.

'This interview is over,' Susanne Öst says in a decisive voice.

'Thanks,' Vicky says.

'She needs time to remember,' Saga says.

'But we've got a confession,' Susanne says.

'I don't know,' Vicky mumbles.

'You've admitted that you killed Miranda Ericsdotter,' Susanne says, raising her voice.

'Don't shout at me,' Vicky says.

'Did you hit her?' Susanne persists. 'You hit her, didn't you?'

'I don't want to talk any more.'

'The interview is over,' the lawyer says sharply.

'How did you hit Miranda?' the prosecutor demands sternly.

'It doesn't matter,' Vicky replies with a sob catching in her throat.

'Your fingerprints were found on a bloody hammer that . . .'

'I can't fucking talk about it – can't you understand that?'

'You don't have to,' Saga says. 'You have the right to remain silent.'

'Why did you get angry with Miranda?' the prosecutor asks loudly. 'So terribly angry that you—'

'I shall be reporting this,' the lawyer says.

'How did you get into Miranda's room?' the prosecutor asks.

'I unlocked the door,' Vicky replies, trying to get out of the bed. 'But I can't answer any more questions about—'

'How did you get hold of the keys?' the prosecutor snaps.

'I don't know, I—'

'Did Elisabet have them?'

'I borrowed them,' she replies, standing up.

'Did she want to lend them to you?'

'I smashed her head in!' Vicky screams, throwing the break-fast tray at the prosecutor.

The plastic dish of cereal and yoghurt hits the floor, and orange juice splashes the wall.

'Go to hell!' she yells, shoving her lawyer so hard that she stumbles backwards onto one of the chairs.

Before Saga and Joona can reach her, Vicky grabs the drip-stand and hits the prosecutor in the shoulder with it as hard as she can, and the bag of fluid comes loose, hits the wall, and bursts.

140

Joona and Saga managed to get between Vicky and the others, and tried to calm her down. The liquid from the burst drip-bag ran down the wall. Vicky was breathing hard, looking at them with frightened eyes. She had cut herself on something, and was bleeding profusely from one eyebrow. Nurses and the two police officers rushed in and forced her down onto the floor. There were four of them, and she started to panic and struggled frantically to pull loose, screaming and kicking a trolley over.

Vicky was forced onto her front and placed in the recovery position, and was given an injection in one buttock. She screamed hoarsely but soon grew calm.

A couple of minutes later they lifted Vicky Bennet into the bed. She was crying and trying to say something, but was slurring her words too badly for anyone to understand her. One of the nurses supervised the process of strapping her down. First her wrists and ankles were tied to the guard rails on the sides of the bed, then her thighs, and finally a thick strap was placed across her chest in a star-pattern. The sheets and the nursing staff's white clothes were stained with Vicky's blood, and the room was a complete mess, with food and water on the floor.

Half an hour later, Vicky was lying perfectly still, her face grey and impassive, her lips cracked. Her eyebrow has stopped bleeding, and a new cannula has been inserted in the crook of her arm. One of the policemen waited by the door as the cleaner mopped the floor.

Joona knows the prosecutor is watching him, and that he mustn't get involved, but he doesn't like the way things are going. Now there won't be any more interview sessions before the custody negotiations. It would have been better to hold off the legal proceedings until the interview process was complete and the results from the National Forensics Laboratory were ready. But Susanne Öst has decided to press formal charges against the girl and request that she be remanded in custody the next day.

If Saga Bauer had been given a little more time, Vicky Bennet would have told her the truth. Now they've got a confession which can be regarded as forced.

But as long as the forensic evidence supports it, that may not matter too much, he thinks as he leaves the room containing the sleeping girl.

He walks along the corridor, where there's a strong smell of disinfectant coming from an open door.

Something about this case is still troubling him. If he disregards the rock, he really hasn't had too much difficulty imagining the scenario. It holds together, even if it's far from perfect. The sequence of events is still developing, as if in some pulsating shadow-world, still transparent and fluid.

He really needs to see all the material, the post-mortem reports, the forensics results, and all the test results from the lab.

Why were Miranda's hands covering her face?

He recalls how the blood-spattered room had looked, but he'd like to be able to see the crime-scene reports in order to dig deeper into the sequence of events.

Susanne Öst walks towards the lifts and stops beside Joona. They nod to each other. The prosecutor looks happy.

'Now everyone hates me for pushing too hard,' she says as they walk into the lift and she presses the button. 'But a confession carries a hell of a lot of weight, even if there might be a bit of fuss.'

'What's your impression of the forensic evidence?' Joona asks.

'So compelling that I've opted for the second-highest level of legal suspicion.'

The lift reaches the ground floor and they get out together.

'Could I see the report?' Joona asks, stopping.

Susanne looks surprised, then says, after a moment's hesitation: 'There's no need.'

'OK,' Joona says, and starts to walk off.

'Do you think there are holes?' the prosecutor asks, trying to keep up with him.

'No,' Joona replies curtly.

'I should have the crime-scene report here,' she says, opening her briefcase.

Joona walks out through the glass doors, and behind him he can hear the prosecutor rooting through her papers, then start to run. He's already reached his car by the time Susanne Öst catches up with him.

'It would be great if you could take a look at it today,' she says breathlessly, holding a thin leather folder out to Joona. 'I'll let you have some preliminary results from the lab, and the post-mortem reports.'

Joona looks her in the eye, nods, and tosses the folder onto the passenger seat before he gets in.

141

Joona is sitting alone in the back room of Il Caffè reading the material from Susanne Öst's folder. Her provocative behaviour during the interview had been a big mistake.

He can't believe that Vicky took Dante on purpose, it doesn't fit the picture he's got of her, but for some reason she killed Miranda and Elisabet.

Why?

Joona opens the folder, thinking that there's a chance that it might contain the answer.

Why does Vicky sometimes get so incredibly angry and violent?

It can't just depend on her medication.

She didn't start taking it until she arrived at the Birgitta Home.

He leafs through the papers.

Crime scenes are mirrors that reflect the perpetrator. There are small fragments of the motive hidden in the spatter-pattern of blood across the walls and floor, in the overturned furniture, footprints, and the positions of the bodies. Nathan Pollock would probably say that an open approach to a crime scene can be much more important than securing evidence. Because the perpetrator always assigns particular functions to the victim and the scene. The victim plays a role in the perpetrator's internal drama, and the scene can be regarded as a stage, with scenery and props. A lot of things can still be down to chance, but there's always some connection to that inner drama, something that can be linked to the motive.

Joona reads the report of the crime-scene investigation for the first time. He spends a long time studying the evidence and analysis.

The police had done a very good job, far more thorough than might have been required.

A waiter with a knitted hat comes in with a large mug of coffee on a tray, but Joona is so deep in thought that he doesn't notice him. In the next room a young woman with a pierced lip smiles as she tells the waiter that she saw Joona order the coffee.

Although the final results from the National Forensics Laboratory aren't included in the file, Joona can see that the evidence is unanimous: the fingerprints are Vicky Bennet's. In the conclusion, the level of probability is judged to be the highest possible, +4.

Nothing in the crime-scene analysis contradicts what he saw for himself at the scene of the murders, even if a lot of his own observations aren't included – such as the way the increasingly coagulated blood had been smeared across the sheets over a period of at least an hour. Nor does the report say anything about the way the backward spatter-pattern on the walls changes angle after three blows.

Joona reaches out for the coffee, drinks, and studies the photographs again. He looks slowly through the bundle, concentrating hard on each one in turn. Then he picks out two photographs of Vicky Bennet's room, two of the isolation room where Miranda Ericsdotter was found, and two of the old brewhouse where Elisabet Grim was found. He moves the coffee cup and everything else off the table and lays out the six pictures. He stands up and tries to see them all at the same time, looking out for new, unexpected patterns.

After a while Joona turns all the photographs over except one. He looks carefully at the last picture, and tries to return to the room in his memory, dredging up the smells, the atmosphere. The photograph shows Miranda Ericsdotter's slender body. She's lying on the bed in a pair of white cotton pants, with both hands over her face. The flash from the camera makes her body and the sheets dazzlingly white. The blood from her shattered head forms a dark pattern on the pillow.

Suddenly Joona sees something he wasn't expecting.

He takes a step back, and the empty coffee cup falls to the floor.

The girl with the pierced lip looks down at her table.

Joona leans over the photograph of Miranda. He's thinking about his visit to see Flora Hansen. He had been annoyed about wasting his time on her. When he was leaving she had followed him into the hall, repeating that she really had seen Miranda, and saying that she'd done a drawing of the ghost. She had shown him the drawing, but dropped it when he brushed her hand aside. The paper had drifted to the floor. Joona had taken a quick look at the childish sketch as he stepped over it and left the flat.

Now that he's studying the photograph of Miranda's arranged body, he tries to remember Flora Hansen's drawing. It had been done in two stages, first just a stick-figure, then the limbs had been filled in. Some of the outline of the girl's body was shaky, and some parts of the drawing were very vague. The head was too large, out of proportion. The straight mouth was only visible because the girl was holding her unfinished skeletal hands in front of her face. The picture was a reasonable match with the descriptions that had appeared in the tabloids.

But what the papers hadn't said was that Miranda had been hit in the head, and that her blood had seeped onto the bed around her head. No pictures from the crime scene had been circulated. The press had written about the hands in front of the face, they had speculated, but they didn't know anything about the injuries to her head. The whole of the preliminary investigation has been kept strictly confidential in advance of the custody proceedings.

'You've just realised something important, haven't you?' the girl in the next room says.

Joona looks into her sparkling eyes and nods, before looking back at the colour photograph on the table again.

What he realised when he was looking at Miranda's body in the photograph was that Flora had drawn a dark heart beside the girl's head, exactly like the dark pool of blood had looked in reality.

Same size, same place.

As if she really had seen Miranda lying on the bed.

It could still be a coincidence, but if he really is remembering Flora's drawing accurately, the resemblance is striking.

142

The bells of Gustav Vasa Church are ringing when Joona meets Flora outside Carlén Antiques on Upplandsgatan. She looks terrible, tired and pasty. The remains of a large bruise are clearly visible on one cheek. Her eyes are dull and heavy. On a narrow door next to the antiques shop a small sign announces that there's going to be an evening of spiritualism.

'Have you got the drawing with you?' Joona asks.

'Yes,' she replies as she unlocks the door.

They go down a flight of steps to the basement. Flora turns the lights on and goes into the room on the right, which has a small window close to the ceiling facing the street.

'I'm sorry I lied,' Flora says, looking in her bag. 'I didn't feel anything from the keyring, but I . . .'

'Can I just see the drawing?'

'I saw Miranda,' she says, handing him the sheet of paper. 'I don't believe in ghosts, but . . . she was there.'

Joona unfolds the paper and looks at the childish drawing. It looks as if the girl is lying on her back. She's holding her hands in front of her face, and her hair is loose. There's no bed or other furniture in the drawing. His memory was correct. Beside the girl's head is a dark heart, positioned right where Miranda's blood had seeped out and soaked into the sheet and mattress.

'Why did you draw a heart?'

He sees Flora lower her eyes and go red.

'I don't know, I don't even remember doing it . . . I was just frightened, I was shaking all over.'

'Have you seen the ghost again?'

She nods, and blushes even harder.

Joona tries to figure out how this all fits together. Could Flora have guessed everything? If the rock was a guess on her part, she must have realised that her guess was correct.

It wasn't that hard to read people's reactions.

And if the rock was right, then it was really only logical to assume that Miranda had been hit in the head with it, and that there would be blood on the bed.

But she didn't just draw blood, she drew a heart, he thinks. And that would make no sense at all if she was trying to deceive him.

It doesn't make sense.

She must have seen something.

It looks as though she saw Miranda on the bed very hazily, or very briefly, and then she drew what she saw without really thinking about it.

The image of Miranda with the bloodstain by her head just stuck.

She sat down and drew what she saw. She remembered the prone body and the hands in front of the face, and the fact that there was something dark beside the girl's head.

A dark shape.

When she drew the picture she interpreted the shape as a heart. Without thinking about the logic.

Joona knows that Flora was a long way from the Birgitta Home when the murders were committed, and that she has no connection to anyone involved or anything that's happened.

He looks at the drawing again and tests a different theory: what if Flora was told something by someone who was there?

Perhaps a witness to the murders told her what to write.

A childish witness who interpreted the blood as a heart.

In which case all this talk about ghosts is just Flora's way of protecting the witness's identity.

'I want you to try to contact the ghost,' Joona says.

'No, I can't . . .'

'How does it usually work?'

'I'm sorry, but I can't do this,' she says, in a very composed voice.

'You need to ask the ghost if she saw what happened.'

'I don't want to,' she whispers. 'I can't do any more.'

'I'll pay you,' he says.

'I don't want payment, I just want you to listen to what I've seen.'

'I am listening,' Joona says.

'I honestly don't know any more, but I don't think I'm mad.'

'I don't think you're mad either,' he replies seriously.

She looks at him and wipes tears from her cheeks. Then she stares ahead of her and swallows hard.

'I'll give it a try,' she says quietly. 'But I don't actually believe in—'

'Just try.'

'You'll have to wait in there,' she says, pointing to the smaller room alongside. 'Miranda usually only comes when I'm completely alone.'

'I understand,' Joona says, and gets up and walks out.

143

Flora sits absolutely still and watches the superintendent close the door behind him. The chair beside the pantry creaks when he sits down, then everything is quiet. She can't hear a sound, no cars, no dogs barking, and nothing from the room where the superintendent is waiting.

Only now does she realise how tired she is.

Flora doesn't know what to do. She isn't sure if she should light the candles and incense. So she just sits there, closes her eyes for a few moments, then looks at the picture.

She remembers how her hands were shaking when she drew what she'd seen, and how she had had trouble concentrating. She kept looking around the room to see if the ghost had come back.

Now she looks at the picture. She's no good at drawing, but it's clear that the girl is lying on the floor. She sees the small crosses, and remembers that they were supposed to represent the fringe of the bath mat.

Flora's hand had slipped, making one of the girl's thighs as thin as a bone.

The fingers in front of her face are no more than lines. The straight mouth is visible behind them.

The chair in the next room creaks again.

Flora blinks hard and stares at the drawing.

It looks like the fingers have slid apart slightly so that Flora can see one of the girl's eyes.

Flora looks at her.

She jumps when the pipes rumble. She looks around the little room. The couch is black with shadows, the table tucked away in a dark corner.

When she looks at the drawing again, the eye isn't visible. A fold in the thin paper runs right across the girl's face.

Flora's hands shake as she tries to smooth the paper. The girl's thin fingers are covering her eyes. Only part of the mouth is visible on the squared paper.

The floor suddenly creaks behind her, and Flora looks around quickly.

There's no one there.

She looks at the drawing again until she has tears in her eyes. The heart hanging over the girl's head has fluid edges now. She looks at the tangled hair, and then goes back to the fingers in front of the face again. Flora instinctively snatches her hands away from the paper when she sees that the mouth is no longer a straight line.

It looks as if it's screaming.

Flora leaps up from her chair, panting hard, and stares at the drawing, at the screaming mouth behind the fingers, and is about to call for the superintendent when she sees the girl for real.

She's hiding in the cupboard by the wall. It looks as if she's trying to stay as well hidden as possible. But the door won't close when she's there. The girl is standing completely still with her hands in front of her face. Then her fingers slip apart and she looks at Flora with one eye.

Flora stares at the girl.

She's saying something behind her hands, but it's impossible to make out the words.

Flora walks closer.

'I can't hear,' she says.

'I'm pregnant,' the girl says, and takes her hands from her face. She reaches to the back of her head, then pulls her hand back, looks at the blood and staggers. A steady stream of blood is pouring from the back of her head, running down her back and onto the floor.

Her mouth opens, but before she has time to say anything her head shakes and her thin legs give way.

Joona hears the crash from the next room and rushes in. Flora is lying on the floor in front of a half-open cupboard. She sits up and looks at him in confusion.

'I saw her . . . she's pregnant . . .'

Joona helps Flora up.

'Did you ask what happened?'

Flora shakes her head and looks at the empty cupboard.

'No one must see anything,' she whispers.

'What did you say?'

'Miranda said she was pregnant,' Flora sobs, moving backwards.

She wipes her tears, looks at the cupboard again, then leaves the room. Joona picks her coat off the chair and follows her. She's already halfway up the steps leading to the street.

144

Flora is sitting on the step outside Carlén Antiques buttoning her coat. She's got some colour back in her cheeks, but says nothing. Joona is standing on the pavement with his phone pressed to his ear. He's calling senior pathologist Nils Åhlén at the Pathology Department at the Karolinska Hospital.

'Hang on,' he hears Nils say. 'I've got myself a smartphone.'

There's a loud crackle in Joona's ear.

'Yes?'

'I've got a quick question,' Joona says.

'Frippe's fallen in love,' Nils Åhlén says in his tight, nasal voice.

'Great,' Joona says calmly.

'I'm just worried he'll be hurt when it ends,' Nils says. 'Do you know what I mean?'

'Yes, but—'

'What did you want to ask?'

'Was Miranda Ericsdotter pregnant?'

'Definitely not.'

'You remember, the girl who—'

'I remember them all,' he replies sharply.

'Do you? You've never said.'

'You've never asked.'

Flora has got to her feet and is smiling anxiously to herself.

'Are you sure she—'

'I'm absolutely sure,' Nils Åhlén interrupts. 'She wasn't even capable of getting pregnant.'

'She wasn't?'

'Miranda had a large cyst on her ovaries.'

'Well, now I know, thanks very much . . . Say hi to Frippe.'

'Will do.'

Joona ends the call and looks at Flora. Her smile slowly fades.

'Why do you do this?' Joona asks seriously. 'You said the murdered girl was pregnant, but she couldn't even get pregnant.'

Flora gestures vaguely towards the door to the basement.

'I remember that she—'

'But it wasn't true,' Joona interrupts. 'She wasn't pregnant.'

'What I meant,' Flora whispers. 'What I meant is that she said she was pregnant. But it wasn't true, she wasn't. She just thought she was, she thought she was pregnant.'

'*Jumala*,' Holger sighs in Finnish, and starts walking up Upplandsgatan towards his car.

145

The food is a little too expensive, and Daniel feels embarrassed when he looks at the wine list. He asks Elin if she'd like to choose, but she just smiles and shakes her head. He clears his throat slightly, asks the waiter about the house wine, but changes his mind before he has time to answer, and asks instead if he could recommend a red to go with the food. The young man looks at the wine list and suggests three wines in different price brackets. Daniel picks the cheapest, and says that a South African Pinot Noir will do fine.

The waiter thanks him and takes the list and menus away with him. A family is having a meal further inside the restaurant.

'You didn't have to invite me out to a restaurant,' she says.

'I wanted to,' he smiles.

'It's very kind of you,' she says, drinking a sip of water.

A waitress comes over to swap the cutlery and glasses, but Elin goes on talking as if she wasn't there.

'Vicky's legal representative has pulled out,' she says quietly. 'But my family lawyer, Johannes Grünewald . . . he's already on the case.'

'That sounds good,' Daniel says reassuringly.

'There won't be any more interviews for a while, they say she's confessed,' Elin says, and clears her throat carefully. 'I can see that Vicky looks the part. Foster homes, running away, institutions, violent mood swings . . . everything points to her. But I still think she's innocent.'

'I know,' Daniel says.

She lowers her head when the tears start to flow. Daniel gets up, goes around the table, and puts his arms around her.

'I'm sorry to talk so much about Vicky,' she says, shaking her head. 'It's just that you said you didn't think it was her. I mean, if you hadn't, I wouldn't . . . but it feels like we're the only people who don't think it was her . . .'

'Elin,' he says seriously. 'I don't really think anything. But I mean, the Vicky I got to know could never do something like this.'

'Can I ask you . . . Tuula seems to have seen Vicky and Miranda together,' Elin says.

'That night?'

'No, earlier . . .'

Elin falls silent, and Daniel holds her shoulders and tries to look her in the eye simultaneously.

'What is it?' he asks.

'Vicky and Miranda were playing something . . . and holding their hands in front of their faces,' Elin says. 'I haven't told the police because it would just make them suspect Vicky even more.'

'But Elin . . .'

'It doesn't necessarily mean anything,' Elin says quickly. 'I'll ask Vicky when I get the chance . . . I'm sure she'll be able to explain what they were doing.'

'But if she can't?'

He tails off when he sees the waiter approach with the bottle of wine. She wipes her eyes and Daniel goes back to his chair, puts his napkin on his lap, and tastes the wine with a trembling hand.

'Good,' he says, a little too quickly.

They sit in silence as the waiter pours the wine, thank him quietly, and then glance tentatively at each other once they're alone again.

'I want to help Vicky again, officially,' Elin says seriously.

'You've made your mind up?' he asks.

'Don't you think I can do it?' she smiles.

'Elin, it's not about that,' he says. 'Vicky has suicidal tendencies . . . She's better than she was, but she still demonstrates a serious tendency to self-harm.'

'She cuts herself? Is that what she does?'

'She's better, but she still cuts herself, and she's on medication . . . and in my opinion she needs someone with her twenty-four hours a day.'

'So you wouldn't recommend me as an official source of support?'

'She needs professional help,' Daniel says gently. 'I mean, I don't think she got enough help even at the Birgitta Home, there wasn't the money, but . . .'

'What does she need?'

'Twenty-four-hour care,' he replies simply.

'And therapy?'

'I've only had an hour a week with the girls, two with some of them, but that's nowhere near enough if you—'

Elin's phone rings and she apologises, looks at the screen, sees that it's Johannes Grünewald, and takes the call at once.

'What's happening?' she asks quickly.

'I've checked, and it's true that the prosecutor has decided to push for a custody hearing without any further interviews,' the lawyer says. 'I'm going to talk to the court about the timing, but we need a few more hours.'

'Is Vicky going to accept our help?'

'I talked to her, and she said she was prepared to accept me as her representative.'

'Did you mention me?'

'Yes.'

'Did she say anything?'

'She's . . . they've got her on a lot of medication and—'

'What exactly did she say when you mentioned my name?' Elin persists.

'Nothing,' Johannes replies bluntly.

Daniel sees a sudden flash of pain cross Elin Frank's beautiful smooth face.

'Meet me at the hospital,' she says into the phone. 'It makes sense to talk about it directly with her before we go any further.'

'Yes.'

'When can you be at Södermalm Hospital, Johannes?'

'Twenty minutes should be enough—'

'See you there,' she says, ends the call, and then looks at Daniel's quizzical face.

'OK . . . Vicky has accepted Johannes as her lawyer. I need to go over there now.'

'Now? You haven't got time to eat first?'

'It sounded really good,' she says, getting to her feet. 'We'll have to have dessert afterwards instead.'

'Sure,' he says quietly.

'Can't you come with me to the hospital?' she asks.

'I don't know if I'm up to that,' he replies.

'I don't mean that you should see her,' she says quickly. 'I was just thinking of myself, that I'd feel calmer if I knew you were waiting outside.'

'Elin, it's just . . . I haven't reached a point where I can think about Vicky . . . It's going to take a bit of time. Elisabet is dead . . . and even if I can't believe it was Vicky, I . . .'

'I understand,' Elin says. 'Perhaps it wouldn't be such a good idea for you to see her.'

'Unless perhaps it would be,' he says hesitantly. 'Maybe it would help me start to remember. It's just that I have no idea at all of how I might react.'

146

Vicky turns her face away when Saga enters the room. The girl has white straps across her ankles, wrists, and chest, like a snowflake.

'Remove the straps,' Saga says.

'I can't do that,' the nurse says.

'It's good that they're scared of me,' Vicky whispers.

'Have you had to lie like this all night?' Saga asks, sitting down on the chair.

'Mm . . .'

Vicky lies completely still, with her face turned away, her body almost inert.

'I'm going to meet your new lawyer,' Saga says. 'The custody hearing is going to take place this evening, and he needs the transcript of the interview.'

'I just get so angry sometimes.'

'The official interviews are over for now, Vicky.'

'Aren't I allowed to say anything?' she asks, looking into Saga's eyes.

'It's probably best if you ask your lawyer for advice before you—'

'What if I want to?' she interrupts.

'Of course you can speak, but we won't record the conversation,' Saga says calmly.

'It's like when there's a really strong wind,' Vicky says.

'Everything just . . . I get a roaring sound in my ears, and you have to go along with it or you'll fall.'

Saga looks at the girl's shredded fingernails, then repeats in a calm, almost indifferent tone: 'Like when the wind's blowing.'

'I can't explain . . . it's like, once, when they hurt Simon, a little boy who . . . we'd been placed in the same foster home,' Vicky says, her mouth trembling. 'The eldest boy in the family, he was their real son . . . he was really mean to Simon, he used to torment him. Everyone knew about it, I'd told the social worker, but no one cared . . .'

'What happened?' Saga asks.

'I went into the kitchen . . . the older boy had forced Simon's hands into boiling water, and the mother was there, she was just watching with a scared look in her eyes. I saw it all and just went really weird and suddenly I was hitting them, and I cut their faces with a bottle . . .'

Vicky suddenly pulls hard at the straps, her body tenses, then she relaxes with a gasp when there's a knock at the door.

A man with grey hair and a dark blue suit walks into the room.

'I'm Johannes Grünewald,' he says, and shakes Saga's hand.

'Here's the transcript,' Saga says.

'Thanks,' Johannes says, without looking at the document. 'There's no urgent rush to read it immediately now, because I've just reached agreement with the district court to postpone the custody hearing until tomorrow morning.'

'I don't want to wait,' Vicky says.

'I can understand that, but I've got a bit more work to do,' he smiles. 'And then there's someone here who I want you to meet before we go through all the questions.'

Vicky stares wide-eyed at the woman who's walking straight towards her without talking to the detective. Elin Frank looks nervous. Her lips tremble as she looks at the girl strapped to the bed.

'Hi,' she says.

Vicky slowly turns her face away, and lies like that while Elin removes the straps. With tender gestures she slowly releases the girl from her twenty-hour captivity.

421

'Is it OK if I sit down?' she asks, in a voice thick with emotion.

Vicky's eyes become bright and hard. But she still doesn't speak.

'Do you remember me?' Elin whispers.

Her throat hurts from all the words stuck halfway out, and from the tears that are welling up, making her veins swell and the blood beneath her skin heat up.

A church bell rings somewhere out in the city.

Vicky touches Elin's wrist, then pulls her finger back.

'We've got the same bandage, you and me,' Elin smiles, and her eyes instantly fill with tears.

Vicky still doesn't say anything, just closes her mouth and turns her face away again.

'I don't know if you remember me,' Elin goes on. 'But you lived with me when you were little, I was just there to support you for a while, but I've never stopped thinking about you . . .' She takes a deep breath, and her voice breaks again: 'And I know that I let you down, Vicky . . . I let you down, and . . .'

Elin Frank looks at the child in the bed, at her tangled hair, frowning forehead, the dark rings under her eyes, the wounds on her face.

'I know I'm nothing to you,' she goes on in a weak voice. 'Just one of all the people who passed through your life, who let you down . . .'

Elin falls silent and swallows hard before she continues: 'The prosecutor wants you to be remanded in custody, but I don't think that would be good for you, I don't think it's good for anyone to be shut up.'

Vicky shakes her head almost imperceptibly. Elin notices, and there's fresh eagerness in her voice when she says: 'So it's important that you listen to what Johannes and I tell you.'

147

Stockholm District Court has the use of a room on the ground floor of Police Headquarters for custody hearings. It's a simple meeting room with varnished pine tables and chairs. About twenty journalists have already gathered in the glass atrium of the National Police Committee, and large television vans are parked on Polhemsgatan outside.

The night's heavy rain has streaked the triple-glazed windows, and there are wet leaves stuck to the white sills.

Prosecutor Susanne Öst looks pale and tense in her new outfit from Marella, and low black pumps. A thickset uniformed police officer is standing by the wall beside the door. Behind the desk sits the judge, an older man with big, bushy eyebrows.

Vicky is leaning forward on her chair as if she has a stomach ache, sitting between Elin Frank and her lawyer Johannes Grünewald. She looks exhausted, and extremely small.

'Where's Joona?' she whispers.

'He wasn't sure he'd be able to come,' Johannes says calmly.

The prosecutor looks exclusively at the judge, and says with a sombre expression, 'I should like to request that Vicky Bennet be remanded in custody, suspected on reasonable grounds of the murders of Elisabet Grim and Miranda Ericsdotter, and also suspected on reasonable grounds of the abduction and kidnap of Dante Abrahamsson.'

The judge notes something down, and the prosecutor presents a spiral-bound bundle of papers, then starts to go through the findings of the preliminary investigation thus far.

'All of the forensic evidence points directly at Vicky Bennet, and at her alone.'

Susanne Öst pauses for a moment, then presents the findings of the crime-scene investigation. With barely concealed enthusiasm she gives an account of the biological evidence and prints: 'The boots that were found in Vicky Bennet's wardrobe match the prints found at the scenes of both murders, blood from both victims has been found in the suspect's room and on her clothes, and Vicky Bennet's bloody handprints were found on the windowsill.'

'Why do they have to say everything out loud?' Vicky whispers.

'I don't know,' Elin says.

'If you'd care to turn to the appendix of the report from the National Forensic Laboratory,' Susanne Öst says to the judge. 'Illustration 9 shows the murder weapon . . . Vicky Bennet's fingerprints were found on the handle, shown in detail in illustrations 113 and 114. Comparative analysis confirms that Vicky Bennet used the murder weapon.'

The prosecutor clears her throat and waits while the judge looks at the pages in question, then goes on to cite the conclusion of the full post-mortem report: 'Miranda Ericsdotter died as a result of being struck on the head by a blunt instrument, that's beyond any doubt . . . compression fracture of the temporal bone and—'

'Susanne,' the judge interrupts, not unkindly: 'This is a custody hearing, not the actual trial.'

'I know,' she nods, 'but bearing in mind the age of the suspect, I believe that a slightly more comprehensive presentation is justified.'

'As long it doesn't exceed reasonable boundaries,' the judge says.

'Thank you,' the prosecutor smiles, then continues to describe the injuries suffered by the two victims, the positions in which they lay according to the hypostasis seen on the bodies, and Elisabet Grim's attempts to defend herself.

'Where's Joona?' Vicky asks again.

Johannes puts a reassuring hand on her arm and whispers that he'll try calling him if he doesn't arrive before the break.

148

When they gather again to resume the custody proceedings after the break Joona still hasn't appeared. Johannes shakes his head when Vicky gives him a quizzical look. She's very pale, and just sits there quiet and hunched. With reference to the Västernorrland Police's reconstruction of events, the prosecutor describes how Vicky Bennet followed Elisabet Grim to the brew-house and murdered her in order to get hold of the keys to the isolation room.

Vicky sits with her face bowed, tears dropping on her lap.

The prosecutor describes the second murder, then Vicky's flight through the forest, the theft of the car, the impulsive kidnap, and then her arrest in Stockholm, her violent outburst during the interview, and having to be restrained.

The penalty for kidnap is between four years and life, and for murder a minimum of ten years.

Susanne Öst stands up as she makes Vicky Bennet out to be prone to extreme violence and very dangerous, but not a monster. In an effort to forestall the defence, she mentions Vicky's more positive sides several times. The prosecutor's argument is skilfully presented, and she concludes by reading from the transcript of the interview: 'During the third session the detainee confessed to both murders,' the prosecutor says slowly, leafing through the transcript. 'I quote: "I killed Miranda", then, in response to my question about . . . about whether Elisabet Grim was willing to lend her her keys, the detainee replied: "I smashed her head in".'

149

With a weary expression on his face, the judge turns to Vicky Bennet and Johannes Grünewald, and asks formally if they have any objections to the prosecutor's proposal. Vicky looks very upset as she stares at him. She shakes her head, but Johannes forces the smile from his face as he explains that he'd like to go through everything one last time to make sure that the court doesn't miss anything.

'I didn't think we'd get off that lightly with you in the room,' the judge replies calmly.

In his response, Johannes opts not to address the forensic evidence or the question of Vicky's guilt. He repeats the positive things Susanne Öst said about her, and emphasises Vicky's low age several times.

'Even if Vicky Bennet and her previous representative were prepared to accept the interview, the prosecutor ought not to have done so,' Johannes says.

'The prosecutor?'

The judge looks extremely curious until Johannes walks over to him and points out Vicky Bennet's response in the transcript of the recorded interview. The prosecutor has highlighted the words 'I killed Miranda' with a yellow marker pen.

'Please, read out her reply,' Johannes asks.

'"I killed Miranda",' the judge reads.

'The whole reply, not just the highlighted words.'

The judge puts his glasses on and reads: '"I killed Miranda – didn't I?"'

'Does that look to you like a confession?' Johannes asks.

'No,' the judge says.

Susanne Öst stands up.

'But the next answer,' she tries to say. 'The next confession—'

'Quiet,' the judge interrupts.

'Perhaps we should let the prosecutor read it out herself?' Johannes suggests.

The judge nods, and Susanne Öst's face starts to perspire as she reads in a trembling voice: '"I smashed her head in".'

'That sounds like a confession,' the judge says, turning to Johannes.

'Look a little earlier in the transcript,' Johannes says, pointing at the document.

'"This interview is over",' the judge reads.

'Who says that the interview is over?' Johannes asks.

The judge runs his finger across the transcript, then looks at the prosecutor.

'It was me,' the prosecutor replies quietly.

'And what does that mean?' the judge asks.

'That the interview is over,' Susanne replies. 'But I just wanted to—'

'Shame on you,' the judge interrupts sharply.

'Using this in custody proceedings is a breach of Swedish law, article 40 of the UN Convention on the Rights of the Child, and the Council of Europe's declaration on children's rights.'

150

Susanne Öst sits down heavily, pours water into her glass, but spills some on the table, wipes it away with her sleeve, then drinks with a shaky hand. Only when she hears Johannes call in Daniel Grim does she realise that she's going to have to reduce the strength of the suspicions filed against Vicky if she's to stand any chance of having her remanded in custody.

Elin tries to catch Vicky's eye, but the girl just sits there with her face lowered.

Johannes gives Daniel Grim a glowing introduction, emphasising the many years he has spent working at the Birgitta Home and other institutions. Vicky looks up for the first time and tries to look him in the eye, but he's just staring in front of him with his mouth clenched.

'Daniel,' Johannes says. 'I'd like to ask you how well you think you know Vicky Bennet.'

'Know . . .,' Daniel repeats thoughtfully. 'Well, it's . . .'

He falls silent, and Vicky starts to scratch one of the wounds on her arm.

'Is there any psychologist or counsellor who knows her better than you do?'

'No,' Daniel whispers.

'No?'

'No, well . . . it's hard to judge, of course, but I think I've had more sessions with her than anyone else.'

'Has it been long since your last session?'

'No.'

'You had an hour of cognitive behavioural therapy with her every week until she ran away, didn't you?' Johannes asks.

'Yes . . . and I've also been involved in her All Day Lifestyle training.'

'To help prepare her for a return to normal life,' Johannes explains to the judge.

'It's a big step,' Daniel adds.

Johannes becomes pensive, looks at Daniel for a few moments, then says in a serious voice: 'I have to ask a difficult question now.'

'OK.'

'It's been said that much of the forensic evidence suggests that Vicky Bennet was involved in the murder of your wife.'

Daniel nods almost imperceptibly, and a sombre atmosphere settles on the characterless meeting room.

Elin tries to read the look in Daniel's eyes, but he's not looking in her direction. Vicky's eyes are red, as if she's trying not to cry.

Johannes stands still, with the same calm expression on his face, and doesn't take his eyes off Daniel.

'You were Vicky Bennet's counsellor,' he says. 'Do you believe she's the person who murdered your wife?'

Daniel Grim looks up, his lips are very pale, and his hand is shaking so badly that he knocks his glasses askew when he tries to wipe the tears from his eyes.

'I haven't spoken to any of my colleagues. I haven't felt up to it,' he says weakly. 'But in my opinion . . . I simply can't believe that Vicky Bennet could have done this.'

'How have you reached that opinion?'

'Vicky responded well to both therapy and medication,' he goes on. 'But more than anything, you get to know people when . . . She doesn't fantasise about violence, and she isn't violent, not in that way.'

'Thank you,' Johannes says gently.

151

Everyone takes their seats in the meeting room after the break for lunch. Johannes is last in. He's holding his phone in his hand. The judge waits until the room is quiet, then sums up the first part of proceedings: 'The prosecutor has lowered the strength of the suspicions for both murders to the second lowest, but is still requesting that the suspect be remanded in custody on probable grounds for the charge of kidnapping.'

'Yes, it's impossible to disregard the fact that Vicky Bennet kidnapped Dante Abrahamsson and held the little boy captive for just over a week,' Susanne Öst says determinedly.

'Just one thing,' Johannes Grünewald says.

'Yes?' the judge asks.

The door opens and Joona Linna walks into the room. His face is serious and his blond hair is sticking up. A woman and a small boy in glasses follow him in, but stop just inside the door.

'Joona Linna,' Johannes says.

'I'm aware of that,' the judge says, leaning forward with interest.

'These are the old men I was telling you about,' Joona says to the boy, who's hiding behind the woman's legs.

'They don't look like trolls,' the boy whispers with a smile.

'Don't you think so? Look at that one?' Joona says, pointing at the judge.

The boy laughs and shakes his head.

'Say hello to Dante and his mum,' Joona says.

Everyone says hello, and when Dante catches sight of Vicky he gives her a cautious wave. She waves back, and her face lights up with a heart-breaking smile. The prosecutor closes her eyes for a few moments and tries to breathe calmly.

'You waved at Vicky – but isn't she mean?' Joona asks.

'Mean?'

'I thought she was really mean?' Joona says.

'She gave me piggybacks and I got all her Hubba Bubba.'

'But surely you just wanted to go back to your mum?'

'That wasn't possible,' he replies slowly.

'Why wasn't it possible?'

The boy shrugs his shoulders.

'Tell them what you said at home,' Pia says to her son.

'What?' he whispers.

'That she phoned,' she reminds him.

'She phoned,' Dante says.

'Tell Joona,' Pia nods.

'Vicky called, but wasn't allowed to go back,' the boy says, looking at Joona.

'Where did she call from?' Joona asks.

'From the lorry.'

'Did she borrow a phone in the lorry?'

'I don't know,' Dante says, with another shrug.

'What did she say on the phone?' Joona asks.

'That she wanted to go back.'

Dante's mother picks him up and whispers something to him, then puts him down again when he starts to wriggle.

'What does that mean?' the judge asks.

'Vicky Bennet borrowed the phone belonging to a driver working for Ikea. His name is Radek Skorża,' Johannes Grünewald explains. 'Joona Linna has traced the call. It was made to the Birgitta Home, and was forwarded automatically to the care provider's switchboard. Vicky spoke to a woman called Eva Morander. Vicky asked for help, and repeated that she wanted to return to the home. Eva Morander remembers the call, and says she told the girl, without being aware of who she was talking to, that they were unable to deal with individual cases at head office.'

'Do you remember this, Vicky?' the judge asks.

'Yes,' Vicky says in an unaffected voice. 'I just wanted to go back, I wanted them to take Dante home to his mum, but they said I wasn't welcome any more.'

Joona walks over to stand next to Johannes.

'It might seem unusual for a detective superintendent to support the defence,' he says. 'But I'm confident that Vicky Bennet was telling the truth about her flight when she was questioned by Saga Bauer. I don't believe this was kidnap . . . just a terrible accident. That's why I went to talk to Dante and his mother, and that's why I'm here . . .'

He turns to look at the girl's unmade-up face, her bruises and cuts, with his sharp grey eyes.

'But the murders are a different matter, Vicky,' he says seriously. 'You might think you can stay silent, but I'm not going to give up until I know what happened.'

152

The custody hearing is concluded just twenty minutes later. Looking very red in the face, Prosecutor Susanne Öst has to withdraw her request for Vicky to be remanded in custody pending the charge of kidnap.

The judge leans back in his chair and declares that Vicky Bennet will not be remanded in custody for the murders of Elisabet Grim and Miranda Ericsdotter, and that she is therefore free to go until such time as the prosecutor presses charges.

Elin sits very straight in her chair as she listens with a neutral expression on her face. Vicky is staring at the table, shaking her head very gently.

Responsibility for Vicky Bennet until the start of her trial would have reverted to the care company, Orre, if Social Services hadn't already accepted Elin Frank as her guardian.

When the judge turns to Vicky and tells her that she's free to go, Elin can't help breaking into a broad, grateful smile, but after the hearing Johannes takes Elin aside and warns her: 'Even if Vicky hasn't been remanded in custody, she's still suspected of having committed two murders, and—'

'I know she—'

'And if the prosecutor does decide to press charges, we'll probably win the court case, but that would only mean that there isn't enough evidence to convict her under the law,' he goes on. 'Vicky could still have committed those murders.'

'I know she's innocent,' Elin replies, and a shiver runs down her spine when she realises how naïve she must sound to him.

'It's my job to warn you,' Johannes says carefully.

'Even if Vicky was involved . . . I still think she's too young to go to prison,' Elin tries to explain. 'Johannes, I can give her the best care in the world, I've already employed carers, and I've asked Daniel to help, seeing as she feels comfortable with him . . .'

'That's good,' he says gently.

'We'll have to work out exactly what would best for her. That's the only thing I care about,' she says, taking his hands. 'Maybe Daniel will carry on with the CBT, maybe we'll bring in other people, I don't know. But what I do know is that I'm not going to let her down again. I can't do that.'

153

While Johannes Grünewald talks to the journalists in the press room of the National Police Committee, Elin and Vicky leave Stockholm in a four-wheel-drive SUV.

The spacious coupé is full of the smell of exclusive Italian leather. Elin's left hand rests on the wheel, and the amber glow from the instrument panel lights up her fingers.

Bach's first cello suite is playing through the speakers, like a gentle autumnal story.

The eight lanes of the motorway pass between the Haga Park, where the crown princess lives in her palace, and the huge cemetery when the socialist August Palm is buried.

Elin looks at Vicky's calm face and smiles to herself.

In order to evade the attentions of the media they have decided to spend the time leading up to the trial in Elin's home in the mountains, a house four hundred square metres in size on the slopes of Tegefjället, just outside Duved.

Elin has arranged for Vicky to have carers on hand twenty-four hours a day. Bella is already in the house, Daniel is coming in his own car, and the nurse will be arriving tomorrow.

Vicky had a shower at the hospital, and her hair smells of cheap shampoo. Elin has bought several pairs of jeans and plenty of tops, underwear, socks, trainers, and a waterproof jacket. Vicky chose a pair of black Armani jeans and a chunky grey sweater from Gant. The rest of the clothes are still in their bags on the back seat.

'What are you thinking about?' Elin asks.

Vicky doesn't answer. She just stares out at the road, through the windscreen. Elin turns the music down slightly.

'You're going to be found not guilty,' Elin says. 'I know you will, I'm sure of it.'

The suburbs disappear behind them, and fields and forest take over.

Elin offers Vicky some chocolate, but gets only a brief shake of the head in response.

'I'm so pleased Daniel is coming with us,' Elin says.

'He's good,' Vicky whispers.

Daniel is driving his own car, and is somewhere ahead of them. Elin saw his yellow estate car at Norrtull, but has lost ground since.

'Is he better than the counsellors you've seen before?' she asks.

'Yes.'

Elin turns the volume down a little further.

'So you'd like him to carry on?'

'If I have to.'

'I think it would probably be a good idea to carry on with the treatment for a while.'

'Then I want Daniel.'

The further north they drive, the further advanced autumn is. It's as if the seasons are changing at an accelerated rate. The green leaves become yellow and red. They fall like shimmering lakes around the trunks of the trees and swirl across the carriageway.

'I need my things,' Vicky suddenly says.

'Your things?'

'My things, everything . . .'

'I think they moved anything the police didn't want to that house the other girls are living in,' Elin says. 'I can get someone to collect them . . .'

She looks at the girl and thinks that it might be important for her.

'Or we could drive up there now, if that would make you feel better?'

Vicky nods.

'Would you like that? OK, I'll have a word with Daniel,' Elin says. 'It's pretty much on the way anyway.'

154

It's already starting to get dark among the trees in the forest when Elin turns right towards Jättendal and pulls in behind Daniel's car. He's just taken out a pink cool bag, and waves them over. They get out and stretch their legs, each eat a cheese sandwich, and have a drink, looking out across the railway tracks and fields.

'I called the carer on duty in the home,' Daniel says. 'She didn't think it was such a great idea for you to go in and see the others.'

'But what harm would it do?' Elin asks.

'I don't want to see them anyway,' Vicky mutters. 'I just want my stuff.'

They get back in their cars. A winding road leads them past lakes and traditional red-painted farms, through forests to the coastal plain.

They park in front of the building where the girls from the Birgitta Home are currently living. A black naval mine stands beside an old petrol pump, and there are seagulls perched on the telephone poles.

Vicky unbuckles her seat belt, but stays in the car. She watches Elin and Daniel walk across the road and up to a large red building, where they disappear from sight behind the black lilac bushes.

Where the road divides stands a faded Midsummer pole.

Vicky gazes out at the tranquil sea, then picks up the box containing the new mobile phone Elin has given her. She breaks the seal, lifts the lid, takes the phone out, and carefully peels the plastic from the screen.

The girls are standing at the windows as Daniel and Elin walk up the steps to the large veranda. Their temporary carer, Solveig Sundström, from Sävstagården children's home, is already standing at the front door. It's immediately apparent that she isn't happy about the visit. She makes it very clear that unfortunately they can't stay for dinner.

'Can we come in and say hello?' Daniel asks.

'Preferably not,' Solveig says. 'It would be better if you just told me what you've come to get, and I'll go in and look for it.'

'There are a lot of things,' Elin tries to explain.

'I can't promise anything . . .'

'Ask Caroline,' Daniel says. 'She's usually on top of things.'

While Daniel asks how the other girls are, and if any of their medication has been changed, Elin stands and looks at the girls through the window. They're jostling each other, and she can hear their voices through the glass. They sound enclosed, as if they're underwater. Lu Chu pushes to the front and waves. Elin waves back, then sees Indie and Nina standing next to each other. They keep pushing each other, taking turns to look and wave. The only one who isn't visible at all is Tuula, the little red-haired girl.

Vicky inserts the SIM card in the phone, then looks up. A shiver runs down her spine. She can't help thinking she just saw something from the corner of her eye, outside the car. Perhaps it was just the wind blowing the lilac leaves.

It's got darker now.

Vicky looks at Daniel's car, at the Midsummer pole, the hedge, the fence, and the grass in front of the dark red house.

A solitary lamp is shining from a mast at the end of the pier, glinting off the black water.

In a meadow closer to the harbour stand old frames for

cleaning fishing nets. They look like rows of linked football goals, with hundreds of iron hooks hanging from the crossbars.

Suddenly Vicky sees a red balloon rolling across the grass in front of the house where the girls are staying.

She puts the phone back in the box and opens the car door. The air is mild, and carries the smell of the sea. A lone gull cries in the distance.

The balloon rolls away across the grass.

Vicky walks cautiously towards the house, then stops to listen. Light from one of the windows is falling across the yellow leaves of a birch tree.

She can hear a vague mumbling sound a little further away. Vicky wonders if someone is out in the darkness. She continues walking quietly along the path. There's a row of dead sunflowers at the end of the building.

The balloon rolls under a volleyball net and catches on the conifer hedge.

'Vicky?' a voice whispers.

She turns around quickly, but can't see anyone.

Her pulse speeds up, and the sudden surge of adrenaline in her blood sharpens all her senses.

The swing seat creaks on its springs, swinging slowly. The old weathervane on the roof is spinning around.

'Vicky!' a sharp voice hisses, very close by.

She turns to her right and stares into the darkness with her heart pounding. It takes her a few seconds to see the thin face. It's Tuula. She's practically invisible, standing among the lilac bushes. She's clutching a baseball bat in her right hand. It's heavy, and so long that it's resting on the ground. Tuula moistens her mouth and stares at Vicky with bloodshot eyes.

Elin leans on the railing of the veranda, trying to see if Vicky is still in the car, but it's too dark. Solveig has come back from asking Caroline to help. Daniel is standing talking to her. Elin hears him try to explain that Almira needs counselling, and tends to react badly to stronger antidepressant medication. He asks if he can go inside again, but Solveig says the girls are now her responsibility. The front door opens, and Caroline comes out onto the veranda. She gives Daniel a hug and says hello to Elin.

'I've packed Vicky's things,' she says.

'Is Tuula in there?' Elin asks in a tense voice.

'Yes, I think so,' Caroline replies, somewhat surprised. 'Shall I get her?'

'Please, if you wouldn't mind,' Elin says, trying to appear calm.

Caroline goes back inside and calls for Tuula. Solveig looks at Elin and Daniel with barely concealed hostility.

'If you're hungry I can ask one of the girls to fetch you some apples,' she says.

Elin doesn't answer. She just walks down the steps and out into the garden. Behind her she hears voices calling for Tuula.

The garden seems darker when the sea is no longer in sight. The trees and shrubs cut out almost all the light.

The swing seat is creaking.

She's trying to breathe quietly, but her heels click on the garden path as she hurries around the corner.

The leaves in the big lilac bush rustle. It sounds like a hare darting away. The branches move, then suddenly Vicky is standing in front of Elin.

'God!' Elin gasps.

They look at each other. The girl's face is very pale in the weak light. Elin's pulse is throbbing in her ears.

'Let's get back to the car,' she says, and leads Vicky away from the house.

She looks over her shoulder, keeping her distance from the dark trees as she hears quick footsteps behind them. She carries on walking with Vicky, out of the garden. She doesn't look back again until she reaches the road, and sees Caroline hurrying after them with a large plastic bag in one hand.

'I couldn't find Tuula,' she says.

'Thanks anyway,' Elin says.

Vicky takes the bag and looks inside.

'I think most of it's there, even if Lu Chu and Almira wanted to play poker for your earrings,' Caroline says.

When Elin and Vicky drive off in the big black car, Caroline stands and watches them go with a sad expression on her face.

155

Elin sees the lights of Daniel's car in the rear-view mirror the whole way along the E14 motorway. There's hardly any traffic, just the occasional truck, but it still takes them three hours to reach the ski resorts. In the darkness along the sides of the mountains they see the static ski lifts and the tall pillars of the cable car at Åre. Six kilometres before Duved they turn off onto a road that leads up into the mountains. Leaves and dust swirl in the beam of the headlamps. The narrow gravel road leads diagonally up Tegefjället.

They slow down and pull off the road to Tegefors between two gateposts, and continue the last bit of the way to a large, modernist house. It's made of cast concrete, with straight terraces and huge windows hidden behind closed aluminium shutters.

They drive into a garage with space for five cars. A small blue Mazda is already parked there. Daniel helps Elin to carry the bags in. Several lights are already on inside the house, and Elin goes straight in and presses a button. There's a whirring sound, and the shutters covering all the windows begin to creak as the metal slats start to separate. Light from the car park suddenly filters in through hundreds of small holes, then the metal shutters start to rise up.

'It's like being in a safe,' Elin says.

A short while later everything falls silent again, and the dark mountain scenery is now visible through the vast windows. Tiny pricks of light from other buildings look like shimmering dots in the darkness.

'Wow,' Vicky says as she gazes out.

'Do you remember Jack, the man I was married to?' Elin asks, going over to stand beside her. 'He built this. Well, maybe not built . . . he didn't exactly do it himself, but . . . he said he wanted a bunker with a view.'

An older woman in a green apron appears from the floor above.

'Hello, Bella, I'm sorry we're so late,' Elin says, giving her a hug.

'Better late than never,' the woman smiles, then says she's made up the beds in all the rooms.

'Thanks.'

'I didn't know if you were going to buy any food on the way, so I bought a bit of everything. Enough to manage for a few days, anyway.'

Bella lights a fire in the large hearth, then Elin walks her to the garage and says goodnight. The doors close once the blue car has left, and she comes back inside. Daniel has started to prepare some food, and Vicky is sitting on the sofa crying. Elin hurries over and kneels down in front of her.

'Vicky, what is it? Why are you so upset?'

The girl just gets up and goes and locks herself in one of the bathrooms. Elin hurries back to Daniel.

'Vicky's shut herself in the bathroom,' she says.

'Do you want me to talk to her?'

'Yes, quickly, please!'

Daniel goes with her to the bathroom door, knocks, and tells Vicky to open the door.

'No locked doors,' he says. 'Remember that?'

Just a few seconds later Vicky comes out with moist eyes and returns to the sofa. Daniel exchanges a glance with Elin, and then goes and sits down beside her.

'You were upset when you first arrived at the Birgitta Home too,' he says after a short pause.

'I know . . . I really ought to be happy,' she replies without looking at him.

'Arriving in a new place . . . it's also the first step towards leaving it,' he says.

Vicky swallows hard, her eyes start to well up again, and she lowers her voice so that Elin can't hear what she says: 'I'm a murderer.'

'I don't want you to say anything like that unless you're absolutely sure that it's true,' he says calmly. 'And I can hear in your voice that you're not sure.'

156

Flora pours steaming hot water into the bucket, and, even though she hates the smell of rubber, pulls on the rubber gloves. The detergent clouds the water a greenish-grey colour, and a clean smell spreads through the little flat. Cool air is coming in through the windows, the sun is shining, and the birds are singing.

After the detective left her outside the antiques shop, Flora had just stood there. She should have been getting ready for the seance, but didn't dare go back down on her own, and waited for the first participants. As usual, Dina and Asker Sibelius were a quarter of an hour early. Flora pretended that she was a bit late, and they went downstairs with her and helped arrange the chairs. By five minutes past seven nineteen participants had arrived.

Flora went on for longer than usual, giving them time, pretending to see kindly old ghosts, happy children, and forgiving parents.

Very carefully, she had managed to find out from Dina and Asker why they came to the seances.

Their adult son had been left in a coma after a bad car accident, and they had had no choice but to accept medical advice to switch his life-support machines off and sign the forms for organ donation.

'Imagine if he doesn't find the Lord,' Dina whispered.

But Flora talked to the son and assured them that he was bathed in light, and that it had been his dearest wish to let his heart, lungs, corneas, and other organs live on.

Afterwards Dina kissed her hands, cried, and kept repeating that she was the happiest person on the planet.

Flora energetically mops the linoleum floor, and feels herself break into a sweat from the physical exertion.

Ewa is at her sewing circle with some of the neighbours, and Hans-Gunnar is watching an Italian football match with the sound turned up loud.

She rinses the mop, squeezes the water out of it, then stretches her aching back before she goes on.

Flora knows that Ewa will open the envelope in her bureau on Monday morning to pay that month's bills.

'Pass the fucking ball, Zlatan!' Hans-Gunnar yells in the living room.

Her shoulders ache when she carries the heavy bucket to Ewa's bedroom. She closes the door, blocks it with the bucket, goes over to the wedding photograph to get the brass key, then hurries over to the bureau and unlocks it.

A loud bang makes Flora start.

It was just the mop falling over, its long handle hitting the floor.

Flora listens for a moment, then opens the bureau. Her hands are shaking as she tries to pull out the little drawer, but it's stuck. She looks through the pens and paperclips and finds a small penknife. She carefully slips the blade into the gap above the drawers and tries very gently to prise it open.

Very slowly the drawer slides out a few centimetres.

She hears a scraping sound very close to her. A pigeon outside the window, its claws slipping on the metal sill.

Flora inserts her fingers into the drawer and pulls it out. The postcard from Copenhagen is badly crumpled. She takes out the envelope, opens it, and puts exactly the right amount of money back inside.

She puts everything back in place, tries to smooth out the postcard, slips the drawer back in, adjusts the pens and knife, closes the bureau, and locks it.

She walks quickly over to the bedside table and has just picked up the wedding photograph when the door to Ewa's bedroom flies open. The bucket tips over, and the water gushes out across the floor. Flora feels her feet become wet and warm.

'You fucking little thief!' Hans-Gunnar shouts as he marches in, bare-chested.

She turns towards him. His eyes are open wide and he's so angry that he's just lashing out blindly. The first blow hits her shoulder and she doesn't really feel it. But then he grabs hold of her hair and hits her with his other hand, a hard slap on the side of her neck and chin. The next blow hits her on the cheek. She falls, and feels some of her hair being pulled out. The wedding photograph hits the floor and the glass shatters. She lies on her side as the water from the bucket soaks into her clothes. The pain in her cheek and eye is so intense that she can hardly breathe.

Flora feels sick and rolls over onto her stomach, but tries not to throw up. Her vision flares. She notices that the photograph has slid out of the frame and is lying face-down on the wet floor. On the back are the words 'Ewa and Hans-Gunnar, Delsbo Church'.

Flora suddenly remembers what the ghost whispered to her. Not the most recent time in the basement, but before, here at home. Perhaps she'd dreamed it? She can't remember. Miranda had whispered about a tower ringing like a church bell. The little girl had shown her the wedding photograph and pointed at the black bell tower in the background, and whispered: 'She's hiding there, she saw everything, she's hiding in the tower.'

Hans-Gunnar is looming over her, panting for breath when Ewa comes into the bedroom with her outdoor clothes on.

'What's going on here?' she asks in an anxious voice.

'She stole our money,' he says. 'I knew it!'

He spits at Flora, picks the brass key off the floor and goes over to the bureau.

157

Joona is sitting in his office with all the material from the custody hearing laid out in front of him.

It will probably be enough to secure a guilty verdict.

His phone rings, and Joona probably wouldn't have answered if he'd looked at the screen first.

'I know you think I'm lying,' Flora says breathlessly. 'Please, don't hang up. You have to listen to me, I'm begging you, I'll do anything you want if you'll just listen to me . . .'

'Calm down and tell me.'

'There's a witness to the murders,' she says. 'A real witness, not a ghost. I'm talking about a real witness who's hiding . . .'

Joona can hear the hysteria lurking just beneath her voice, and tries to calm her down: 'That's good,' he says gently. 'But the preliminary investigation—'

'You have to go there,' she interrupts.

He doesn't know why he's listening to this person. Possibly because she sounds so desperate.

'Where exactly is the witness?' he asks.

'There's a bell tower, a black bell tower next to Delsbo Church.'

'Who told you—'

'Please, she's there, she's scared, and she's hiding there.'

'Flora, you have to let the prosecutor do—'

'No one's listening to me.'

Joona hears a man's voice in the background shouting at her to get off his phone, then there's a clattering sound.

'This little chat's over,' the man says, and hangs up.

Joona sighs and puts his phone down on the desk. He can't figure out why Flora is continuing to lie.

After the decision to charge Vicky, the preliminary investigation was deprioritised, and all that remains is for the prosecutor to compile the evidence in advance of the trial.

I missed out on this case, Joona thinks, feeling an odd sense of desolation.

It was already over by the time he got access to all the reports and expert statements.

Joona knows he was never in charge of the preliminary investigation, and that he was never really let into the investigation at all.

An overdose of antidepressant medication could be the cause of Vicky's violent behaviour and sudden need to sleep.

But he can't let go of the thought of the rock.

Nils Åhlén says in his report that the murder weapon is a rock, but no one has tried to follow that line of inquiry because it doesn't fit the other facts.

Joona remembers leaving Nils Åhlén and Frippe in Sundsvall just as they were about to start their internal examination.

He decides not to let go of the case just yet. A wave of stubbornness makes him look through the test results from the National Forensics Laboratory again, and read the pathologist's report.

He stops when he reaches the external examination of Elisabet Grim's body and reads the paragraph about the injuries to her hands before he goes on.

The light wanders slowly across Joona's noticeboard, with the notification of the internal investigation, and Disa's latest postcard: a picture of a chimpanzee wearing lipstick and heart-shaped glasses.

While Joona reads, the shadow of the plant in the window moves slowly off towards the bookcase.

There was nothing unusual in Miranda's abdominal cavity,

and her organs were in good condition. Same thing with her lungs and heart.

> 84. The heart is normal and weighs 198 grams. The surface
> is glossy and smooth. The valves and cavities are normal.
> There are no deposits in the coronary arteries. The heart
> muscles are greyish red and uniform.

Joona holds one finger on the post-mortem report and leafs through the test results from the National Forensics Laboratory, and reads that Miranda's blood group was type A, and showed traces of Venlafaxine, a component of many antidepressants, but was otherwise normal.

Joona returns to the post-mortem report and reads that her thyroid gland was greyish red and contained normal levels of colloid, and that her adrenal glands were yellow and of normal size.

> 104. The urinary ducts are of normal appearance.
> 105. The bladder contains approximately 100 ml of clear,
> pale yellow urine. The mucous membrane is pale.

Joona leafs through the lab results to find the urine sample. There were traces of the sedative Nitrazepam in Miranda's urine, and the hCG level was unusually high.

Joona jumps to his feet, grabs his phone, and calls Nils Åhlén.

'I'm sitting here looking at the results from the National Forensics Laboratory, and Miranda had a high level of hCG in her urine,' he says.

'Yes, obviously,' Nils Åhlén replies. 'The cyst on her ovaries was so—'

'Hang on a moment,' Joona interrupts. 'Don't pregnant women have high hCG levels?'

'Yes, but like I said—'

'So if Miranda took an ordinary pregnancy test, she'd think she was pregnant?'

'Yes,' Nils says. 'She'd definitely get a positive result.'

'So Miranda might have believed she was pregnant?'

Joona leaves his office and walks quickly along the corridor, looking up Flora's home number on his phone. He hears Anja call out behind him, but carries on down the stairs. There's no answer. Joona repeats to himself that Flora had changed her mind, and said that the girl who had appeared to her had only believed that she was pregnant.

'What I meant is that she said she was pregnant,' Flora had said. 'But it wasn't true, she wasn't. She just thought she was, she thought she was pregnant.'

Joona calls the number again, and the phone rings as he runs through the glass atrium, past the sofas, and he has just got through the revolving door when a voice answers breathlessly: 'Hans-Gunnar Hansen.'

'My name is Joona Linna, I work with National Crime Unit, and—'

'Have you found my car?'

'I need to talk to Flora.'

'What the fuck?' the man exclaims. 'If Flora was here then I wouldn't be asking about my fucking car, would I? She's the one who stole it, and if the police can't—'

Joona ends the call and runs the rest of the way to his black Volvo.

158

Elin has slept in the room next to Vicky with the doors open. She kept waking up at the slightest sound, listening, and getting up to check. When morning comes she stands in the doorway for a while watching the girl sleep deeply before she heads to the kitchen.

Daniel is standing at the stove making creamy scrambled eggs. The room smells of coffee and freshly-baked bread. The view through the huge picture windows is almost scarily immense. Round-topped mountains, shimmering tarns, and valleys of red and yellow trees.

'The view is almost too much,' he says with a smile. 'It kind of hurts my heart.'

They embrace, and he kisses her head gently several times. She just stands there, breathing in his scent, and feeling her stomach start to glow with sudden happiness.

A timer bleeps on the worktop, and Daniel pulls away to take the bread out of the oven.

They sit down to eat at the big dining table, every now and then reaching for each other's hands across the table.

The immense views take their words away. They drink their coffee in silence just looking out of the windows.

'I'm so worried about Vicky,' Elin eventually says in a low voice.

'It'll be OK.'

She puts her cup down.

'You promise?'

'I just need to get her to talk about what happened,' he says. 'Because I'm a bit worried that her feelings of guilt are making her more and more self-destructive . . . We really do need to keep a close eye on her.'

'The nurse will be arriving in Åre by bus in an hour's time, I'll drive down and pick her up,' Elin says. 'Shall I ask Vicky if she'd like to come – what do you think?'

'I don't know, I think it would be best if she stayed here,' he says.

'Yes, we've only just got here, after all,' Elin agrees. 'I can't help feeling worried . . . You'll have to stay with her the whole time.'

'She knows she's not even allowed to close the door when she isn't going to the toilet,' Daniel says seriously.

At that moment Elin sees Vicky though the glass. She's walking by herself out on the grass, kicking the red leaves. Her long hair is hanging down her back, and her thin body looks as though it's freezing. Elin grabs her cardigan from the back of the chair and goes out to give it to Vicky.

'Thanks,' the girl whispers.

'I'm never going to let you down again,' Elin says.

Without a word, Vicky takes her hand and squeezes it. Elin's heart beats hard with joy, and the lump in her throat stops her speaking.

159

The sky is strangely dark when Joona pulls off the E4 and sets off along Highway 84 to Delsbo. He's assuming that Flora took the car to drive to Delsbo Church in Hälsingland.

He can still hear her agitated voice when she told him that a witness was hiding in the bell tower.

Joona can't make any sense of her. It's as if she's getting the truth mixed up with lies, without being aware of it herself.

Despite the many lies Flora has told, he can't quite shake the feeling that she knows more about the murders at the Birgitta Home than everyone else.

Perhaps this witness is another one of her lies, but if there's a chance it could be true he can't afford to miss it – a witness would be crucial.

The low rain clouds make the fields grey and the pine trees almost blue. He turns off onto a narrow road. Autumn leaves swirl across the carriageway, and the road is so uneven and winding that it's difficult to maintain any speed at all.

He turns into a straight avenue leading to Delsbo Church. He can see a large field through the trees. A solitary combine harvester is making its way across the field in the distance. Its blades cut across the ground like a scythe. The air is full of chaff. Birds rise and fall behind it.

When he's almost at the church he sees a car that's driven

into one of the trees. The bonnet is crumpled, and one of the windows is broken.

The engine is still running, the driver's door is open, and the rear lights are glinting off the grass.

Joona slows down, but when he sees that the car is empty he just drives past. Flora must have rushed out, he thinks, and carries on towards the church.

Joona gets out of his car and hurries up the raked gravel path. The pitch-covered bell tower stands on a small mound a short distance from the church.

The sky is dark, and it looks as if it could start raining at any moment.

The huge, matt bell hangs beneath the tower's black onion-dome cupola. Beyond the tower he can see the fast-flowing river, black and foaming.

The door to the tower is open.

As Joona gets close to the tower he notices the unmistakeable smell of the pitch.

The wide bottom section is clad in dark wooden shingles. Inside, a steep wooden ladder leads up to the bell.

'Flora?' Joona calls out.

160

Flora walks over and stops in the dark doorway of the bell tower. Her face is sad, and her big eyes are tired and wet.

'There's no one here,' she says, and bites her lip.

'Are you sure?'

She starts to cry and her voice breaks: 'Sorry, but I thought . . . I was so sure . . .'

She steps down and whispers 'Sorry' again without looking at him, then holds one hand over her mouth as she starts to walk slowly back to the car.

'How did you find your way here?' Joona asks, following her. 'Why did you think the witness would be here?'

'My adoptive parents' wedding photograph . . . the tower is in the background.'

'But what does that have to do with Miranda?'

'It was the ghost that said . . .'

Flora falls silent and stops.

'What is it?' Joona asks.

He thinks back to Flora's drawing of Miranda, with her hands over her face and the dark blood beside her head. She hadn't drawn the blood like someone trying to stage a deception, but like someone who really had seen something but no longer remembered the exact circumstances.

Outside Carlén Antiques, Flora had talked about the ghost

like a memory. She tried to explain how she remembered what the ghost had said.

Narrow streaks of light shine down from between the heavy banks of rain clouds.

Like a memory, he repeats to himself, and looks at Flora's pale face.

Yellow autumn leaves are drifting through the air, and suddenly Joona realises how everything fits together. It's like a curtain being opened and light let into a large room. He knows he's found the key to unlocking the whole mystery.

'It's you,' he whispers, and his own words send a shiver through him.

Now he realises that Flora is the witness who could be found at the bell tower.

She's the witness, but it wasn't Miranda she saw being murdered.

It was another girl.

Someone who was killed in exactly the same way.

Another girl, but the same murderer.

The realisation is startling, and is followed by the stab of a migraine. For a long moment it feels like a bullet is passing through his head. He reaches out for support and hears Flora's anxious voice through the darkness before the pain vanishes again.

'You saw everything,' he says.

'You're bleeding,' she says.

Some blood is running from his nose, and he finds a paper napkin in his pocket.

'Flora,' he says. 'You're the witness in the tower . . .'

'But I haven't seen anything.'

He presses the napkin to his nose.

'You've just forgotten it.'

'But I wasn't there, you know that, I've never been to the Birgitta Home.'

'You saw something else . . .'

'No,' Flora whispers, shaking her head.

'How old is the ghost?' Joona asks.

'Miranda is maybe fifteen when I dream about her . . . but

when she comes to me when I'm awake, when it's like she's actually in the room, she's younger.'

'How much younger?'

'About five years old.'

'How old are you now, Flora?'

She starts to feel frightened when she looks into his strangely grey eyes.

'Forty,' she replies quietly.

Joona tells himself that Flora has been describing a murder she witnessed as a child, but that she has consistently believed she was talking about the murders at the Birgitta Home.

Joona knows he's right as he takes out his phone and calls Anja. Through a tunnel of years Flora suddenly saw what she had forgotten or suppressed. That's why the memories have been so confusing and powerful.

'Anja,' he says, the moment she picks up the phone, 'are you in front of your computer?'

'Are you sitting somewhere better?' she asks, sounding amused.

'Can you check to see if anything happened in Delsbo around thirty-five years ago?'

'Anything particular?'

'Involving a five-year-old girl.'

While Anja taps at her keyboard Joona watches Flora go over to the church, run her hand across the wall, and walk around the porch. He sets off after her so he doesn't lose sight of her. A hedgehog scurries off between the gravestones.

Beyond the avenue, the combine harvester is still moving across the field, surrounded by a cloud of dust.

'Yes,' Anja says, breathing through her nose. 'There was a death . . . Thirty-six years ago a five-year-old girl was found at Delsbo Church. That's all it says. The police concluded that it was an accident.'

Joona sees Flora turn and look at him with a heavy, curious expression.

'What was the name of the police officer in charge of the investigation?'

'Torkel Ekholm,' Anja replies.

'Can you try to find an address?'

161

Twenty minutes later Joona parks the car beside a narrow gravel road. He and Flora open an iron gate and walk through a leafy garden to a red wooden house with white eaves and asbestos cement tiles on the roof. The autumn vegetation is full of buzzing insects. The sky is an unsettled yellow with pent-up rain and thunder. Joona rings the doorbell and an ear-splitting ringing sound echoes across the garden.

There's a shuffling sound, then the door is opened by an old man wearing a knitted tank top, braces, and slippers.

'Torkel Ekholm?' Joona asks.

The man leans on a walking frame and looks at them through watery eyes. They can see a hearing aid tucked behind his big, wrinkled right ear.

'Who's asking?' he says in a barely audible voice.

'Joona Linna, detective superintendent with the National Crime Unit.'

The man squints at Joona's ID, and can't hold back a strange little smile.

'National Crime Unit,' he whispers, and gestures vaguely for Joona and Flora to go inside. 'Come in, we can have coffee.'

They sit down at the kitchen table while Torkel goes over to the stove, after telling Flora apologetically that he can't offer any biscuits. He speaks very quietly, and seems to be almost completely deaf.

A clock on the wall is ticking loudly, and above the kitchen sofa hangs a well-maintained elk rifle, a Remington. An embroidered sampler with the text 'contentment is a happy home' has partly come loose from its hanger, and its corners are drooping, like some faded postcard from a bygone Sweden.

The man scratches his chin and looks at Joona through the gloom of the kitchen.

When the water has come to the boil, Torkel Ekholm gets out three cups and a jar of freeze-dried instant coffee.

'You get lazy with old age,' he says with a shrug, and hands Flora the teaspoon.

'I'm here to ask about a very old case,' Joona says. 'Thirty-six years ago a girl was found dead at Delsbo Church.'

'Yes,' the old man says without meeting Joona's gaze.

'An accident?'

'Yes,' he replies tersely.

'That's not what I think,' Joona says.

'That's good to hear,' the old man says.

His mouth starts to shake, and he pushes the bowl of sugar lumps towards the detective.

'You remember the case?' Joona asks.

The spoon tinkles as the old man tips coffee powder into his cup and stirs it. His eyes are bloodshot when he looks at Joona: 'I wish I could forget it, but some cases . . .'

Torkel Ekholm stands up, goes over to a dark bureau by the wall, and unlocks the top drawer. He explains in an unsteady voice that he has kept his notes from the case for all these years.

'I knew you'd have to come and find me one day,' he says, so quietly that he's almost impossible to hear.

162

A drowsy autumn fly is buzzing against the window in the little kitchen. Torkel nods towards the papers lying on the table in front of them: 'The dead girl's name was Ylva, she was the daughter of the foreman at Rånne . . . By the time I got there they'd already laid her on a sheet . . . I was told that she'd fallen from the bell tower . . .'

The old policeman leans back in his chair, making the wood creak.

'There was blood on the base of the tower . . . They pointed, and I looked, but I could see it didn't make sense.'

'Why did you drop the preliminary investigation?'

'There were no witnesses, I didn't have a thing. I kept asking, but I wasn't getting anywhere. In the end they didn't want me to upset the gentry over at Rånne any more. They discharged the foreman and . . . that was . . . I've got a picture Janne took, he worked for *Arbetarbladet*, we used to use him as our crime-scene photographer.'

The old policeman shows them a black-and-white photograph. A small girl is lying on a sheet on the grass with her hair loose. Beside her head is a black bloodstain exactly the same as the one in Miranda's bed, in the same place.

The stain looks almost like a heart.

The little girl's face is relaxed, her cheeks childishly chubby, her mouth looks as if she's asleep.

Flora stares at the picture, feels for her hair with one hand, and all the colour drains from her face.

'I didn't see anything,' she whimpers, then starts to cry with her mouth open.

Joona moves the photograph away and tries to calm Flora, but she gets up and takes the picture from Torkel. Wiping the tears from her cheeks she stares at the photograph, leaning against the draining board and not noticing when she knocks an empty beer bottle into the sink.

'We were playing the close-your-eyes game,' she says in a subdued voice.

'The close-your-eyes game?'

'We had to close our eyes and cover our faces.'

'But you looked, Flora,' Joona says. 'You saw who hit the little girl with the rock.'

'No, I had my eyes closed . . . I . . .'

'Who hit her?'

'What did you see?' Torkel asks.

'Little Ylva . . . she looked so happy, covering her eyes with her hands, and then he hit her . . .'

'Who?' Joona asks.

'My brother,' she whispers.

'You haven't got a brother,' Joona says.

Torkel starts to shake, making his cup topple over on his saucer.

'The boy,' he mutters. 'Surely it wasn't the boy?'

'What boy?' Joona asks.

Flora's face is white, and tears are streaming down her cheeks. The former policeman tears off some kitchen roll and gets up heavily from his chair. Joona sees her shake her head, but her mouth is still moving.

'What did you see?' Joona asks. 'Flora?'

Torkel walks over to her and hands her the sheets of kitchen roll.

'Are you little Flora? The younger sister who wouldn't speak?' he asks gently.

163

Flora's childhood memory comes back to her as she stands in the former policeman's kitchen leaning against the draining board. It feels as though her legs are going to give way when she remembers what she saw.

The sun was shining on the grass beside the church. She was covering her face with her hands. The light was shining through her fingers, giving the two others shiny yellow edges.

'Oh God,' she whimpers, sinking to the floor. 'God . . .'

In flaring light she remembers seeing her brother hit the little girl with a rock.

The memory is so vivid that it feels as if the children are standing there in the kitchen.

She hears the thud, and sees Ylva's head shake.

Flora remembers how the girl fell to the grass. Her mouth opened and closed, her eyelids trembled, she muttered confused words, and he hit her again.

He hit her as hard as he could. And screamed that they all had to close their eyes. Ylva stopped moving, and he moved her hands to her face and repeated that she had to keep her eyes closed.

'But I didn't have my eyes closed . . .'

'Are you Flora?' the old policeman asks again.

Between her fingers Flora saw her brother stand up with the

rock in his hands. Very calmly he told Flora to keep her eyes closed, because they were playing the close-your-eyes game. He came closer with the bloody rock, and held it up in the air. She pulled back just as he went to hit her. The rock cut her on the cheek and hit her shoulder hard, she fell to her knees, but got up and started to run.

'Are you little Flora who lived at Rånne?'

'I can hardly remember anything,' she replies.

'Who's her brother?' Joona asks.

'People called them the kids from the children's home even though they'd been adopted by the people in the big house,' the former policeman says.

'And their name was Rånne?'

'Rånne, the timber baron . . . we just called them the gentry,' Torkel replies. 'It was even in the paper when they adopted two children, a noble act of charity, they wrote . . . but after the accident the girl moved away . . . The boy stayed behind on his own.'

'Daniel,' Flora says. 'His name is Daniel.'

Joona's chair scrapes the floor as he gets up from the table and leaves the house without a word. With his phone clutched to his ear he runs through the garden, past the windfalls and yellowing leaves under the trees, out through the gate to his car.

'Anja, listen to me, I need your help, it's urgent,' Joona says, getting in the driver's seat. 'See if Daniel Grim has any connection to a family called Rånne in Delsbo.'

Joona barely has time to switch the car's comms unit on to alert the National Communication Centre before Anja comes back with the answer.

'Yes, they're his parents.'

'Find out everything you can about him,' Joona says.

'What's this about?'

'Girls,' Joona replies.

He ends the call, and before he alerts the police, he quickly calls Elin Frank's number.

164

Elin is driving carefully down the steep gravel road towards Åre to fetch Vicky's nurse. One of the side windows is open, and fresh air fills the car. The long, thin lake gleams darkly below. The mountains are lined up like gigantic Viking burial mounds, gently rounded and covered in vegetation.

She thinks of how Vicky took her hand and squeezed it. Everything is taking a turn for the better again.

Just as the narrow road leads her below a rock face, her phone buzzes in her bag. She slowly drives a little further, pulls into a passing place, and stops. She pulls out her phone with an uneasy feeling. It carries on ringing in her hand. The call is from Joona Linna. She doesn't really want to hear whatever he has to say, but still unlocks the phone with trembling fingers.

'Hello?' she says.

'Where's Vicky?' the detective superintendent asks.

'She's up here, with me,' she replies. 'I've got a house in Duved which—'

'I know, but can you see her right now?'

'No, I—'

'I want you to go and get Vicky right now, put her in the car, and drive to Stockholm. Just you and Vicky. Do it right away, don't pack anything, just walk straight out to the car and—'

'I'm already in the car,' Elin shouts, feeling panic growing in her chest. 'Vicky's back at the house with Daniel.'

'That's not good,' Joona says, and she can hear the tone in his voice, a tone that makes her feel sick with worry.

'What's happened?'

'Listen to me . . . It was Daniel who murdered Miranda and Elisabet.'

'That can't be right,' she whispers. 'He's looking after Vicky while I drive to the bus station.'

'Then she's probably no longer alive,' Joona says. 'Just get yourself away from there. That's my advice to you as a police officer.'

Elin stares out at the sky through the windscreen. It's no longer white. The clouds are low, skimming the mountaintops, black and heavy with rain and autumn.

'I can't just abandon her,' she hears herself say.

'The police are on their way, but it will take a while for them to get there.'

'I'm going back,' she says.

'I can understand that,' Joona says. 'But be careful . . . because Daniel Grim is very, very dangerous, and you'll be completely alone with him until the police arrive . . .'

But Elin is no longer thinking. She just turns the car around and starts to drive back, up the steep road with the gravel rattling beneath the car.

165

Vicky is sitting on her bed downloading apps onto her phone when Daniel comes in and sits down on the white leather armchair beside the bed.

Outside the mountain landscape is laid out before them, with Ullådalen and the peaks of Åreskutan etched against the sky, grey and ancient.

'Did it feel wrong yesterday?' Daniel asks. 'I mean . . . just sitting and waiting in the car while we fetched your things?'

'No . . . I get that no one wants to see me,' she replies, still fiddling with her phone.

'When I went into the house I could see that Almira and Lu Chu were playing that game where you have to close your eyes,' Daniel lies. 'I know Miranda taught you that game . . .'

'Yes,' she replies.

'Do you know how Miranda learned it?' Daniel asks.

Vicky nods, and takes out the phone's charger.

'I sometimes use the game in therapy sessions,' Daniel says. 'It's a trust exercise.'

'Miranda fed me chocolate,' Vicky smiles. 'And then she drew a heart on my stomach and—'

Vicky suddenly stops herself. She thinks about what Tuula told her in Hårte, when she was outside in the lilac bushes.

'Have you told anyone about the game?' Daniel asks, looking at her.

'No,' she replies.

'I just wondered . . .'

Vicky looks down and thinks about Tuula, standing there in the darkness with the baseball bat in her hand, saying that the murderer only kills whores. Only whores needed to worry about getting their skulls smashed in, she had whispered. It was typical of Tuula to say weird, horrible things. Vicky had tried to smile, but Tuula said she'd found a pregnancy test in Miranda's bag when she took her necklace. Vicky's immediate reaction when she heard this was to assume that Miranda had had sex with one of the guys they met at ADL.

But now she realises it must have been Daniel.

Vicky had felt that something was wrong when Miranda showed her what to do. Because Miranda was only pretending that it was fun. She giggled and broke off pieces of chocolate, but all she wanted to do was find out if Vicky had experienced the same things as her without revealing what had happened.

Vicky remembers Miranda's attempts to sound nonchalant when she asked if Daniel had ever come into her room to play.

'Miranda didn't say,' Vicky tries to say, glancing up at Daniel's eyes for a moment. 'She never said anything about what you used to do in therapy sessions . . .'

Vicky's cheeks turn red when she suddenly realises how everything fits together. Daniel must be the person who killed Miranda and Elisabet. The murders had nothing to do with whores. Daniel killed Miranda because she was pregnant.

Maybe Miranda had already told Elisabet everything.

Vicky tries to breathe calmly, doesn't know what to say, and picks at her plaster cast, pulling at some of the crumbly mesh.

'It was . . .'

Daniel leans forward, picks up the phone from her lap, and puts it in his pocket.

'Therapy . . . it's really all about trusting each other,' Vicky goes on, even though she knows that Daniel has already realised.

He knows she has figured out that he killed Miranda and Elisabet with a hammer, and pinned the blame on her.

'Yes, that's an important step in therapy,' Daniel says, watching her carefully.

'I know,' she whispers.

'We could try it now, you and me. Just for fun,' he says.

She nods, thinking with growing panic that he's decided to kill her. Her heartbeat is thudding in her ears, and sweat is trickling from her armpits. He helped get her released, and has come with them to Elin's house to find out how much she knows, to make sure he wasn't going to be exposed.

'Close your eyes,' he says with a smile.

'Now?'

'It's fun.'

'But I—'

'Just do it,' he says sternly.

She closes her eyes and covers her face with her hands. Her heart is pounding with fear. He's doing something in the room. It sounds like he's pulling the sheet from the bed.

'I need to go to the toilet,' she says.

'Soon.'

She sits there with her hands over her face, and starts when he pulls a chair across the floor. She hears a scraping sound, but keeps her hands in front of her face.

166

Elin is driving as fast as she possibly can up the steep slope. A keyring is rattling in the tray beside the gear stick. The branches of a tree whip against the windows and roof. She brakes at a sharp bend and almost skids. The tyres slip across the loose stones, but she pushes the clutch down, gets around the bend and accelerates again.

The car jolts and rumbles uncomfortably. The meltwater has carved deep grooves in the road leading to Tegefors.

She keeps climbing the road, a little too fast, and tries to slow her speed slightly as she approaches the turning to the house. She turns sharply right, the left wing mirror flies off as the side of the car scrapes the gatepost. She puts her foot down again and it feels as though the car leaves the ground when she reaches the top of the slope. The crate of mineral water in the boot falls over with a crash.

She drives the last straight stretch of road towards the house and brakes hard, kicking up a cloud of dust. Elin leaps out of the car, leaving the engine running, and rushes into the house. The blinds are down. It's completely dark, and she stumbles over shoes and ski boots in the gloom as she hurries into the large living room.

'Vicky!' she calls.

Elin turns the lights on, runs up the stairs, slips, and hits her knee on one of the steps, gets up and rushes to Vicky's room. She pushes the handle down, but the door is locked. Elin bangs on the door, and hears the hysteria in her own voice when she screams: 'Open the door!'

There's no sound from inside the room, and Elin leans over to look through the keyhole. A chair is lying on the floor, and shadows are moving jerkily across the walls.

'Vicky?'

She takes a step back and kicks at the door. Nothing happens, apart from a dull thud. She kicks again, then runs to the next room, but the key isn't in the lock. She moves on to the next door, fumbles with her hand, and manages to pull the key out. She rushes back, knocking over a glass sculpture that falls to the floor with a loud crash. Her hands are shaking so badly that she has trouble inserting the key in the lock. She uses both hands, manages to turn it on her second attempt, and throw the door open.

'Oh, God!' she whispers.

Vicky is hanging from a twined bed sheet tied to the white, lime-wood beam. Her mouth is gaping open and her face is drained of colour. Her feet are moving gently in the air. She's still alive. Her toes are reaching for the floor, half a metre below, and she's clutching at the noose with her fingers.

Elin doesn't think. She just rushes over to Vicky and lifts her up as high as she can.

'Try to pull loose,' she sobs, holding Vicky's thin legs.

The girl struggles with the wound cotton, her body jerks as if it's cramping, she needs oxygen and is starting to panic as she fights to loosen the noose.

Suddenly Elin hears Vicky inhale some air and cough. Gasping deeply, she tenses her body.

'I can't get it off,' Vicky coughs.

Elin stands on tiptoe and tries to lift her up higher.

'Try to pull yourself up!'

'I can't . . .'

The noose tightens again. Vicky can't get enough air, and her body starts to convulse in panic. Elin's arms are starting to shake from the effort of holding her up. She can't give up. She tries to reach the overturned chair with her foot so she can

473

climb up on it, but it's impossible. Vicky is wet with sweat, and her body is twitching spasmodically. Elin tries to change her grip, but Vicky is just too heavy. Numbing weakness is creeping up on her, but even so she manages to lower one hand slightly, gets a better grip and is able to lift Vicky a little higher. Vicky exerts the last of her strength and eventually manages to pull the noose over her head. She coughs hard, and they sink to the floor together.

Vicky's neck looks blue and she's breathing very shallowly, but she's breathing, she's alive. Elin kisses her cheeks and strokes the hair from her sweaty face with a trembling hand, and whispers to her not to try to speak.

'It was Daniel . . .'

'I know, the police are on their way,' Elin whispers. 'You need to stay here. I'll lock the door, but you have to stay absolutely quiet.'

167

Elin locks the door behind Vicky and feels her body shaking as she goes down the stairs. Her arms and legs feel numb from the exertion. Her phone buzzes, and she sees that she's received a new text from Vicky's phone:

Sorry, but I can't lie any more. Don't be sad. Love, V

Elin feels sick, and her heart starts to beat hard with anxiety. Thoughts are spinning through her head far too quickly. It's impossible to understand what's happening. Daniel must have just texted her from Vicky's phone. She walks cautiously into the dark living room. The blinds have been lowered throughout the house.

Suddenly a shadow falls across the floor. It's Daniel. He's standing on the staircase to the lower floor. He must have come up from the garage. She knows she has to try to delay him until the police arrive.

'She's done it,' Elin says. 'Vicky had locked the door to her room, it took too long, I don't understand . . .'

'What are you saying?' he asks slowly, looking at her blankly.

'She's not breathing . . . can we go outside? We have to call someone,' she whispers.

'Yes,' he replies, coming closer.

'Daniel . . . I don't understand.'

'Don't you?'

'No, I . . .'

'After she killed you, Vicky went to her room and hanged herself,' he says.

'Why are you saying . . .'

'You shouldn't have come back so soon,' Daniel says.

Elin suddenly sees that he's hiding an axe behind his back. She starts to run towards the front door, but there's no time, he's right behind her, and she turns right abruptly instead, toppling a chair behind her. He trips, and she gains a slight advantage as she runs past the kitchen and into the corridor. His footsteps come closer. There's nowhere to hide. She hurries into Jack's old bedroom, locks the door behind her, and presses the button to activate the blinds.

I'm not going to get outside, she thinks. It would take too long.

The motor whirrs, and there's a creaking sound as the aluminium slats start to separate and light filters through the small holes.

Elin lets out a shriek when the first swing of the axe hits the door. The blade penetrates the wood next to the lock, then pulls sideways and back.

Slowly the blind starts to rise. A narrow strip of window is visible when the axe strikes a second time.

She can't wait, she has to move on, and hurries across the floor and into Jack's bathroom as Daniel kicks at the bedroom door. The wood creaks and cracks as long splinters splay out around the lock and the door flies open.

Elin catches sight of herself in the large mirror as she rushes through the bathroom, past the bath, shower, and sauna, and out through the other door into Jack's office. It's dark, and she trips over the low document cabinet. Old files fall to the floor. Her hands fumble across the desk, and she pulls out a drawer, tips the pens out, and grabs the letter opener.

The blinds in the bedroom falls silent once they've finished opening. She hears something fall into the large bathtub. Daniel is coming after her. Elin kicks off her shoes, creeps barefoot into the corridor, and closes the door behind her.

She's thinking she might be able to sneak around behind Daniel and go through the shattered door into Jack's bedroom again, and try to open the window.

She takes a few steps, but changes her mind and rushes further along the corridor instead.

'Elin!' he roars behind her.

The door to the larger guest room is locked. She turns the key, but the lock sticks. She glances backwards and sees Daniel approaching. He's not running, but his strides are long. She yanks at the handle and smells his sweat. A shadow passes quickly across the door. She throws herself sideways and hits her cheek against a picture.

The axe misses her head. The blade hits the concrete wall behind her. There's a sharp clanging sound, and the axe deflects so sharply that Daniel loses his grip on it. It hits the floor with a crash.

168

The locks clicks and Elin shoves the door open with her shoulder. She stumbles into the room. Daniel follows, trying to grab hold of her. She turns around and stabs him with the letter opener. It hits him in the chest, but only superficially. He grabs her by the hair and drags her down onto the floor with such force that she falls onto the television console and knocks a table lamp over.

He pushes his glasses further up his nose, then goes and retrieves the axe. Elin crawls beneath the wide bed.

Elin hopes that Vicky is staying hidden, because she's starting to think that she might just be able to hold out until the police arrive.

She can see Daniel's legs and feet as he walks around the bed. She shrinks back and feels him climb up onto the bed. The mattress and struts creak. She doesn't know which way she should go, and tries to stay close to the middle.

Suddenly he grabs hold of her foot and she screams, but he's off the bed now and dragging her out. She tries to hold on, but stands no chance. Still holding her ankle, he raises the axe. She kicks him in the face with her other foot. He loses his glasses and lets go, staggers backwards into the bookcase, pressing a hand to one of his eyes and staring at her with the other.

She crawls out and rushes towards the door. From the corner

of her eye she sees him bend over and pick up his glasses. She runs past Jack's old rooms and out into the kitchen. She hears Daniel's heavy steps behind her in the corridor.

Thoughts are flying through her head. The police ought to be here by now – Joona said they were on their way.

Elin snatches up a saucepan from the draining board as she runs through the kitchen, then dashes through the living room, opens the door to the garage, and throws the saucepan down the steps.

She hears it clatter down the staircase as she heads upstairs instead.

Daniel reaches the door to the garage, but isn't fooled. He can hear her steps going upstairs. She's running out of options. Elin is out of breath, but keeps going up, past the floor where Vicky is hiding, making sure to climb the stairs more slowly, trying to lure Daniel away from the girl and up to the top floor.

Elin knows she only has to hold out until the police arrive, she has to manage this somehow, she has to keep Daniel occupied so that he doesn't go back to Vicky's room.

The staircase creaks behind her under Daniel's feet.

She reaches the top floor. It's almost completely dark. She hurries over and grabs the poker from the fireplace. The other tools rattle on the stand. Elin walks to the middle of the floor and smashes the ceiling lamp with one blow. The large frosted glass chandelier falls to the floor and shatters with a loud crash. The shards of glass scatter across the floor, then the room falls silent.

The only sound is the heavy footsteps on the stairs.

Elin hides in the darkness beside a bookcase, just to the right of the doorway.

Daniel is panting as he climbs the last steps. He's in no hurry, he knows she can't escape from the top floor.

Elin tries to breathe more quietly.

Daniel stands still with the axe in his hand, staring into the dark room, then flicks the light switch.

There's a click but nothing happens. The room remains dark.

169

Elin is standing hidden in the darkness, clutching the poker with both hands. The adrenaline in her blood is making her tremble, but she feels peculiarly strong.

Daniel is breathing softly, moving very cautiously further into the room.

She can't see him, but can hear the crunch of glass beneath his feet.

Suddenly there's a click, followed by an electrical whirring sound. Light starts to filter through the tiny holes between the slats of the shutters. Daniel is standing just inside the door, waiting as the blinds slowly rise up and light fills the room.

There's nowhere to hide.

He stares at her, and she backs away, holding the poker out towards him.

Daniel is clutching the axe in his right hand. He glances at it, then starts to walk towards her.

She strikes at him with the poker, but he moves out of the way. Breathing hard, she aims the poker at him again. Her foot stings when she stands on a piece of broken glass, but she doesn't take her eyes off Daniel.

The axe swings in his hand.

She lunges again, but he moves aside.

His eyes stare at her impassively.

Suddenly he makes a rapid, unexpected move with the axe. The side of the blade hits the poker. There's a dull clang as metal strikes metal. The poker quivers so hard that it falls from her hand and clatters to the floor.

She has nothing to defend herself with now, and backs away with a bewildering realisation that she's not going to get out of this alive. Mortal dread courses through her body, making her feel strangely detached and apathetic.

Daniel follows her.

She looks into his eyes, he meets her gaze, but there doesn't seem to be any depth to him now.

She backs away until she hits the large window. Behind her the smooth concrete façade drops three and a half floors to the terrace containing the outdoor furniture and barbecue.

Elin's feet are bleeding, and her shuffling red footprints stand out on the pale wooden floor.

She's run out of fight, just stands still, and thinks to herself that she ought to be trying to bargain with him, promise him something, get him to talk.

Daniel is breathing harder now, and he looks at her for a few moments, moistens his lips, then quickly walks the last steps towards her. He raises the axe and strikes. Instinctively she moves her head aside. The axe crashes into the window. She feels the thick glass shake behind her back, and hears a splintering sound as it starts to crack. Daniel raises the axe again, but before he has time to swing it, Elin leans backwards. She presses her whole weight against the large window and feels it give way. Her stomach lurches. She falls back through the air, surrounded by glass and sparkling fragments. Elin Frank closes her eyes and doesn't even notice when she hits the ground.

Daniel leans one hand against the window frame and looks down. Pieces of glass are still falling from the sill. Elin is lying far below. There's glass everywhere. A steady stream of dark blood is spreading across the terrace from her head.

Daniel's breathing calms down. The back of his shirt is wet with sweat.

The view from the top floor is immense. The peak of

Tyskhuvudet feels incredibly close, and the chalet at the top of Åreskutan is draped in autumn mist. The flashing blue lights of a number of emergency vehicles are clearly visible heading up the road from Åre, but the road towards Tegefors is empty.

170

Joona understood everything the moment Flora mentioned her brother's name. He called Anja's number as he walked through Torkel's porch, and she answered as he was running through the garden. By the time he was sitting in the car, she had confirmed that Daniel Grim was the boy who had been adopted by the logging baron at Rånne Manor.

He was the Daniel that Flora was talking about.

Daniel Grim was the boy who had killed a little girl in front of Flora in Delsbo thirty-six years ago.

Joona sat in his car and called Elin Frank's number – Daniel had gone to Duved with her and Vicky.

While he waited for Elin to answer, he realised why Elisabet had defensive injuries on the wrong sides of her hands.

They had been covering her face.

Daniel doesn't leave any witnesses – no one is allowed to see what he does.

After warning Elin, he called the National Communications Centre and asked for police and an ambulance to be despatched to Duved. The helicopters were already busy up in Kiruna, and it would take the emergency vehicles at least half an hour to reach the house.

There was no way Joona could get there in time, it was more than three hundred kilometres from Delsbo to Duved.

He shut the car door, and had just switched the engine on when his boss, Carlos Eliasson, called and asked what reasons he had to suddenly suspect Daniel Grim.

'Thirty-six years ago he killed a child in exactly the same way as the girl at the Birgitta Home,' Joona replies as he began to drive slowly down the gravel road.

'Anja's shown me photographs of the accident at Delsbo,' Carlos sighed.

'It was no accident,' Joona said stubbornly.

'And what leads you to connect the two cases?'

'Both victims were covering their faces when they—'

'I know Miranda was,' Carlos interrupted. 'But I'm sitting here with the pictures from Delsbo in front of me, for God's sake. The victim is lying on a sheet and her hands are—'

'The body was moved before the police arrived at the scene,' Joona said.

'How do you know that?'

'I just know,' he said.

'Is this your usual stubbornness, or has your fortune-teller told you all this?'

'She's an eyewitness,' Joona replied in his dark Finnish accent.

Carlos laughed wearily and then said seriously: 'It's passed the statute of limitations. We've got a prosecutor leading the preliminary investigation against Vicky Bennet, and you're under internal investigation.'

Once Joona was back on Highway 84 and heading towards Sundsvall, he contacted the Västernorrland Police and asked for a patrol car and forensics team to be sent to Daniel Grim's home. Via the comms unit he heard that the Jämtland Police expected to be at Elin Frank's house in ten minutes.

171

The first patrol car stops in front of Elin Frank's house on the slopes of Tegefjället. One of the officers goes over to the large SUV and switches the engine off, while the other draws his pistol and walks towards the front door. Another police car pulls into the turning circle, followed by an ambulance.

The lights from the second ambulance are already visible on the steep drive.

The large house looks oddly shut up. The windows are covered by metal blinds.

Everything is disconcertingly quiet.

With their pistols drawn, two police officers go through the front door. A third officer stays by the cars while the fourth moves around the house, heading slowly up a broad flight of white concrete steps.

The house doesn't seem to be inhabited: it's shut up like a sealed box.

The police officer walks out onto a terrace, past a set of outdoor furniture, and then he sees the blood, the broken glass, and the two figures.

He stops.

A pale-faced girl with cracked lips and tangled hair is looking up at him. The look in her eyes is almost black. She's kneeling down beside the apparently lifeless body of a woman. A pool of blood has spread out around the pair of them. The girl is holding the woman's hand in both of hers. Her mouth is moving, but the police officer can't hear what she's saying until he gets closer.

'She's still warm,' Vicky whispers. 'She's still warm . . .'

The police officer lowers his gun, takes out his radio, and calls the paramedics.

The clouds are grey and cold as the paramedics silently bring two stretchers around. They immediately conclude that the woman has a fractured skull, and lift her carefully onto the stretcher even though the girl won't let go of her.

Vicky holds the woman's hand tightly between hers as heavy tears roll down her cheeks.

The girl herself is seriously injured, she's bleeding badly from her knees and legs from where she was sitting amongst the broken glass. Her neck is swollen and bruised, and her vertebrae are probably damaged, but she refuses to lie on a stretcher, and it's obvious that she has no intention of leaving Elin's side.

They need to get going, and take the quick decision to let the girl sit and hold Elin Frank's hand while they drive to Östersund for onward transportation by helicopter ambulance to the Karolinska Hospital in Stockholm.

172

Joona is driving across some rusting railway lines when the coordinator of the operation in Duved finally answers his phone. His voice sounds shaken, and he is simultaneously talking to someone else in the police van with him.

'It's a bit chaotic right now . . . but we're on the scene,' he says, and coughs.

'I need to know if—'

'No, for God's sake . . . it needs to be before Trångsviken and Strömsund!' the coordinator shouts at someone.

'Are they alive?'

'Sorry, I need to get the roadblocks set up.'

'I'll wait,' Joona says, and overtakes a truck.

He hears the coordinator put the phone down, talk to the lead officer, confirm the locations, then get back to the Regional Communications Centre and direct patrol cars to set up the roadblocks.

'OK, I'm back,' he says eventually.

'Are they alive?' Joona asks again.

'The girl's condition isn't serious, but the woman is . . . her condition is critical, they're preparing for an emergency operation at Östersund Hospital before she's transferred to the Karolinska.'

'And Daniel Grim?'

'There's no one else in the house . . . we're setting up road-blocks now, but if he goes for one of the smaller roads, we haven't got the resources to—'

'Helicopters?' Joona asks.

'We're liaising with the rangers up in Kiruna, but it's all taking too long,' the coordinator says in a voice that's rough with tired-ness.

Joona drives into Sundsvall, thinking to himself that Elin Frank went back to her house despite his warning. It's impossible to imagine what she did when she got there, but she evidently got back in time.

Elin is seriously injured, but Vicky is still alive.

Now there's a possibility that Daniel Grim will get caught in one of the roadblocks. Especially if he doesn't realise they're looking for him. But if he manages to slip through, the earliest he could get back to his house is in two hours, and by then the police need to have laid a trap for him.

And before that, a preliminary forensics search of the house needs to be completed, Joona thinks.

He slows down and stops behind a patrol car in Bruksgatan. The front door of Daniel Grim's house is open, and two uniformed officers are waiting for him in the hall.

'The house is empty,' one of them says. 'Nothing unusual so far.'

'Is the forensics officer on the way?'

'Give him ten minutes.'

'I'll take a look around,' Joona says, and walks in.

Joona walks quickly around the house without knowing what he's looking for. He opens cupboards, pulls out drawers, glances inside a wine cellar, moves on to the kitchen, looks in the cupboards, fridge and freezer, then runs upstairs and pulls off the tiger-striped bedspread, turns the mattress upside down, opens the wardrobe, pushes Elisabet's dresses aside, and taps the wall, kicks some old shoes out of the way, and pulls out a box of Christmas decorations, goes into the bathroom, looks in the cabinet full of aftershave, medicine, and make-up, then goes all the way down to the basement, looks at the tools on the wall, tries the locked door to the boiler room, pulls the lawnmower aside, lifts the drain, looks inside the bags of compost, then goes back upstairs.

He stops in the middle of the house and looks out through the window at the swing seat in the garden. In the other direction the front door is still open, and Joona can see the two police officers waiting by their car.

Joona closes his eyes and thinks about the hatch in the bedroom leading to the attic, the locked door to the boiler room in the basement, and the fact that the wine cellar under the stairs ought to have been bigger.

There's an old-fashioned sign on the narrow door under the stairs with the words 'Sobriety and Humour' on it. He opens it and looks inside the wine cellar once more. There are around a hundred bottles in racks on a high wooden shelf. There's obviously a space behind there, at least thirty centimetres between the back of the shelf and the outside wall. He pulls at it, removes the bottles at either end, and finds a sliding latch right at the top. Very carefully, he swings the whole shelf back on its hinges. A smell of dust and wood hits him. The space inside is almost empty, but on the floor is a shoebox with a heart painted on its lid.

Joona takes out his phone, photographs the box, then pulls on a clean pair of latex gloves.

173

The first thing Joona sees when he carefully lifts the lid of the box is a photograph of a girl with strawberry blonde hair. It isn't Miranda. It's another girl, perhaps twelve years old.

She's holding her hands over her face in the picture.

It's just a game. Her mouth is smiling and her sparkling eyes are visible through her fingers.

Joona gently lifts the photograph out and finds a dried wild rose.

The next photograph shows a girl curled up on a brown sofa eating crisps. She is looking questioningly at the camera.

Joona turns over a bookmark in the shape of an angel and sees that someone's written 'Linda S' with a gold pen on the back.

On top of a bundle of photographs held together by an elastic band lies a lock of light brown hair, a pink silk bow, and a cheap ring with a plastic heart on it.

He looks through the pictures of different girls. Somehow they all remind him of Miranda, but most of them are considerably younger. Some of them have their eyes closed, or are covering their faces with their hands.

A young girl in a pink ballet dress and legwarmers is covering her face.

Joona turns the picture over and reads 'Dear Sandy'. The

words are surrounded by a load of hearts drawn with red and blue pens.

A girl with short hair is pulling a face at the camera. Someone has scratched a heart into the glossy surface of the photograph, and the name Euterpe.

At the bottom of the box is a polished amethyst, some dried tulip petals, some sweets, and a piece of paper with childish writing on it: Daniel + Emilia.

Joona picks up his phone, holds it in his hand for a moment, looks at the photographs, and then calls Anja.

'I haven't got anything,' she says, 'I don't even know what I'm looking for.'

'Deaths,' Joona says, looking at a photograph of a girl with her hands over her face.

'Yes, but I'm afraid . . . Daniel Grim has worked as a counsellor at seven different institutions for vulnerable girls in Västernorrland, Gävleborg, and Jämtland. He has no convictions, and has never been a suspect in any crime. There are no internal reports against him . . . not even any notes.'

'I see,' Joona says.

'Are you sure you've got the right person? I've done a few comparisons . . . during the periods he's been there, the homes have actually seen lower mortality rates than the average.'

Joona looks at the pictures again, at all the flowers and hearts. It would almost have been rather sweet if it had been a small boy who had hidden the box.

'Isn't there anything unusual or unexpected?'

'Over the years just over two hundred and fifty girls have passed through the institutions where he's worked.'

Joona takes a deep breath.

'I've got seven first names,' he says. 'The most unusual name is Euterpe. Is there a Euterpe anywhere?'

'Euterpe Papadias,' Anja says. 'Suicide at an acute care home in Norrköping. But Daniel Grim has no connection there . . .'

'Are you sure?'

'Before she was moved to Fyrbylund Care Home there are just a few brief notes about her bipolar disorder, self-harming, and two serious suicide attempts.'

'Was she moved there from the Birgitta Home?' Joona asks.

'Yes, she was moved in June 2009 . . . then on 2 July the same year, just two weeks later, she was found in the shower with her wrists slashed.'

'But Daniel wasn't working there then?'

'No,' Anja replies.

'Any girls by the name of Sandy?'

'Yes, two . . . one of them is dead, an overdose of pills at an institution in Uppsala . . .'

'He's written Linda S on the back of a bookmark.'

'Yes, Linda Svensson . . . reported missing seven years ago, after returning to a regular school in Sollefteå . . .'

'They all die somewhere else,' Joona says heavily.

'But . . . is he the one doing all this?' Anja whispers.

'Yes, I think so,' Joona replies.

'Dear God . . .'

'Have you got a girl called Emilia?'

'Yes . . . I've got an Emilia Larsson, who left the Birgitta Home . . . There's a photograph . . . her arms are sliced open, from her wrists up to her elbows . . . he must have cut her arms and stopped her from calling for help, then blocked the door and watched her bleed to death.'

Joona goes out and sits in the car. The world is showing its darker side again, and he feels immense sorrow draw in like an icy wind.

He looks at the beautiful trees outside, takes a deep breath, and thinks to himself that the police are going to hunt Daniel Grim down until he's caught.

Out on the E4 motorway Joona talks to the coordinator of the operation in Duved, and finds out that the roadblocks will remain in place for another two hours, but that the lead officer no longer believes that Daniel Grim is going to be caught by any of them.

Joona thinks about the box containing pictures of the girls Daniel Grim picked out. He seems to have felt a childish infatuation for them. Among the pictures were hearts, flowers, sweets, short messages.

His little collection was pink and bright, whereas the reality was a nightmare.

The girls in the institutions and children's homes were locked in, some of them may have been strapped down and heavily medicated when he forced himself upon them.

And they had no one but him to talk to.

No one would listen to them, and no one would miss them.

He's picked girls with a history of self-harming behaviour and so many suicide attempts behind them that their relatives have given up on them and already begun to think of them as dead.

Miranda was an exception. He killed her before she was moved, out of panic. Perhaps the murder was triggered by the fact that she believed she was pregnant?

Joona thinks about the girls that Anja has traced. Now that the link has been identified, the police will be able to charge him with a number of murders. It will finally be possible to clear up these deaths and give the girls some form of restitution.

174

Memories of Torkel Ekholm's wife are visible in the fabrics, in the hand-sewn embroidery on the faded tablecloths. But the crocheted hems of the curtains are now grey with dust, and the knees of Torkel's trousers are worn thin.

The former policeman has taken his pills from a container with compartments for seven days, before slowly shuffling over to the kitchen sofa with his walking frame.

The clock on the wall ticks laboriously on. On the table in front of Flora are all of Torkel's notes, the newspaper cutting about the accident, and the little death notice.

The old man tells Flora all he can remember about logging baron Rånne, and the family's manor house, their forests and fields, how they couldn't have children, then the decision to adopt Flora and her brother Daniel. He tells her about the foreman's daughter, Ylva, who was found dead beneath the bell tower, and about the silence that spread across Delsbo.

'I was so little,' Flora says. 'It never occurred to me that they might be memories, I thought I'd just imagined those children . . .'

Flora thinks back to all the times she thought she was going mad after she heard about the murders at the Birgitta Home. She couldn't stop thinking about what had happened, the girl with her hands over her face. She dreamed about her, saw her everywhere.

'But you were there,' he says.

'I tried to explain what Daniel had done, but everyone just got angry . . . When I said what had happened, Daddy took me into his office and said that all liars end up burning in a sea of fire.'

'At least I've got my witness,' the old policeman says quietly.

Flora remembers being terrified of burning up, of her hair and clothes catching fire. She thought her whole body would turn as dry and black as the wood in the stove if she told anyone what Daniel had done.

Torkel slowly sweeps the crumbs from the table.

'So what happened with the girl?' he asks.

'I knew Daniel liked Ylva . . . he always wanted to hold her hand, gave her raspberries . . .'

She falls silent and once again sees the strange, yellow fragments of memory flicker, as if they were about to catch fire.

'We were playing the close-your-eyes game,' she goes on. 'When Ylva closed her eyes he kissed her on the mouth . . . she opened her eyes, laughed, and said that now she was going to have a baby. I laughed, but Daniel got . . . he told us we weren't allowed to look . . . and I could hear that his voice sounded funny. I peeped between my fingers, the way I always did. Ylva looked happy as she closed her eyes, and I saw Daniel pick up a rock from the ground and hit her and hit her . . .'

Torkel lets out a deep sigh, and then lies down on the narrow kitchen sofa: 'I see Daniel sometimes when he comes to visit at Rånne . . .'

When the old policeman has fallen asleep, Flora walks over and very carefully takes the hunting rifle down from the wall and leaves the cottage.

495

175

Flora walks down the narrow avenue leading to Rånne Manor with the heavy rifle in her arms. Black birds are perched in the yellowing treetops.

It feels as if Ylva is walking beside her. She remembers how they used to run about here on the estate with Daniel.

Flora has always thought it was a dream. The fine house they were brought to, with bedrooms of their own, and flowery wallpaper. She remembers now. The memories have risen from the depths. They were buried deep in the black soil, but now they're standing right in front of her.

The old cobbled courtyard looks just like it used to. There are several shiny cars parked over by the garage. She walks up the wide flight of steps, opens the door, and goes inside.

It feels strange to walk through the familiar house with a loaded weapon in her hands.

Just walking beneath the huge chandeliers, across the dark Persian carpets.

No one has seen her yet, but she can hear subdued voices from the dining room.

She walks through the succession of four drawing rooms, and can already see them sitting at the table in the distance.

She changes her grip, resting the barrel in the crook of her arm, clutching the butt, and putting her finger on the trigger.

Her former family are eating, talking, not looking in her direction.

There are fresh cut flowers in the tall vases in the window alcoves. She detects movement from the corner of her eye, and spins around with the gun raised. It's her own reflection in a huge, uneven mirror that stretches from floor to ceiling, aiming the rifle at herself. Her face is close to grey, and the look in her eyes is raw and wild.

With the rifle aimed in front of her, she carries on through the last drawing room and walks straight into the dining room.

The table is laid with the fruits of the harvest: small sheaves of wheat, bunches of grapes, plums, and cherries.

Flora remembers that it's Thanksgiving Day in Sweden.

The woman who was once her mother looks thin and frail. She's eating slowly, with trembling hands, a napkin laid out across her lap.

A man of her own age is sitting between the parents. She doesn't recognise him, but understands who he is.

Flora stops in front of the table, and the floor creaks beneath her feet.

The father is the first to notice her.

When the old man sees her a strange calmness settles over him. He puts his knife and fork down, and sits up, as if he wants to take a proper look at her.

The mother turns to look at what he's staring it, and blinks several times when the middle-aged woman with the shiny rifle steps forward out of the gloom.

'Flora,' the old woman says, dropping her knife. 'Is that you, Flora?'

She stands there with the rifle in front of their laid table, and can't bring herself to answer, she just swallows hard, looks the mother briefly in the eye, then turns towards the father.

'Why have you come here with a gun?' he asks.

'You made me into a liar,' she replies.

The father smiles briefly and joylessly. The wrinkles on his face are bitter and lonely.

'Anyone who lies shall be cast into the lake of fire,' he says wearily.

She nods, and hesitates for several seconds before asking her question: 'You knew it was Daniel who killed Ylva, didn't you?'

The father slowly wipes his mouth on the white linen napkin.

'We had to send you away because you told such terrible lies,' he says. 'And now you've come back and are telling lies again.'

'I'm not lying.'

'You admitted it, Flora . . . you admitted to me that you had just made it all up,' he says quietly.

'I was four years old, and you were shouting that my hair would burn if I didn't admit I was lying, you screamed that my face would melt and my blood boil . . . so I said I'd been telling lies, and then you sent me away.'

176

Flora squints at her brother, who is sitting at the dining table with the light behind him. She can't tell if he's meeting her gaze, his eyes look like frozen wells.

'Go now,' the father says, and carries on eating.

'Not without Daniel,' she replies, pointing at him with the rifle.

'It wasn't his fault,' the mother says weakly. 'I was the one who . . .'

'Daniel is a good son,' the father interrupts.

'I'm not saying otherwise,' the mother says. 'But he . . . You don't remember, but we were sitting and watching a play on television the evening before it happened. It was Strindberg's *Miss Julie*, and of course she feels such lust for the servant . . . and I said it would be better . . .'

'What's this nonsense?' the father interrupts.

'I think about it every day,' the old woman goes on. 'It was my fault, because I said it would be better for the girl to die than get pregnant.'

'That's enough.'

'And just as I said that . . . I saw that little Daniel had got up and was staring at me,' she says, with tears in her eyes. 'Of course I was only talking about Strindberg's play . . .'

Her hands are shaking badly when she picks her napkin up.

'After that business with Ylva . . . a week had passed since the accident, it was evening, and I was about to say Daniel's bedtime prayers with him . . . He told me that Ylva had been going to have a baby. He was only six years old, he didn't understand.'

Flora looks at her brother. He pushes his glasses further up his nose, and looks at his mother. It's impossible to work out what he's thinking.

'You need to come with me to the police and tell the truth,' Flora says to Daniel, aiming the rifle at his chest.

'What good would that do?' the mother says. 'It was an accident.'

'We may have been playing,' Flora says without looking at her, 'but it was no accident.'

'He was only a child,' the father bellows.

'Yes, but he's killed again . . . he's killed two people at the Birgitta Home. One was a girl of fourteen, and she was found with her hands covering her face, and . . .'

'You're lying!' the father screams, slamming his fist on the table.

'No. You're all lying,' Flora whispers.

Daniel stands up. Something happens to his face. Perhaps it's cruelty, but it looks like disgust and fear. A mixture of emotions. A knife has two sides, but only one cutting edge.

His mother pleads, tries to hold Daniel back, but he removes her hands and says something Flora can't hear.

It sounds as if he's swearing at her.

'Let's go,' Flora says to Daniel.

The father and mother stare at her. There's nothing more to say. She walks out of the dining room with her brother.

177

Flora and Daniel leave the manor house, walk down the broad flight of steps, across the yard and along the gravel drive, past a free-standing wing, and down towards some office buildings.

'Keep moving,' she mutters when he slows down.

They follow the drive around the big red barn to get to the field. Flora keeps the rifle trained on Daniel's back the whole time. She's starting to remember fragments of her two years at the manor house, but she's also aware that there was a time before that, when she lived in a children's home with Daniel, but that time is completely black.

But, before everything else, there must have been a time when she was with her mother.

'Are you going to shoot me?' Daniel asks softly.

'I could do,' she replies. 'But I want us to go to the police.'

The sun comes out from behind the heavy rain clouds and dazzles her for a moment. Once her eyes have got used to the glare, she realises that her hands are sweating. She wishes she could wipe them on her trousers, but daren't let go of the rifle.

A crow calls in the distance.

They pass two tractor tyres and an old bathtub in the grass, and carry on along the gravel track as it makes a wide curve around the big, empty barn. They walk silently past tall nettles and faded willowherb, around a wall and a stack of big sacks of hydro grains.

It's a long detour to the large field.

The sun is shaded by the barn when they reach the far side of it.

'Flora,' he mumbles, sounding bewildered.

Her arms are starting to tire, and her muscles ache.

The road to Delsbo is visible in the distance as a pencil line across the yellow fields.

Flora prods Daniel between the shoulders, and they walk on across the dry yard next to the barn.

She quickly wipes the sweat from her hand and then puts her finger back on the trigger again.

Daniel stops, waits for the barrel to touch him again before walking on, past a concrete plinth with rusty iron rings set into it.

Weeds are growing along the cracked edges.

Daniel has started to limp, and is walking more and more slowly.

'Just keep walking,' Flora says.

He holds one hand out and lets it slide through the tall weeds. A butterfly takes off and drifts up into the air.

'I was thinking we could stop here,' he says, and slows down. 'Because this was the old slaughterhouse, back when we kept cattle . . . do you remember the slaughtering mask, and the way they used to kill the animals?'

'I'll shoot if you stop,' she says, feeling her finger tremble on the trigger.

Daniel pulls a pink, bell-shaped flower from its stem, stops, and turns towards Flora to give her the flower.

She steps back, thinking that she has to shoot, but she's not quick enough. Daniel grabs the barrel and jerks the rifle towards him.

Flora is so taken aback that she doesn't even have time to pull back when he hits her hard in the chest with the butt of the rifle, knocking her flat on her back. She gasps for breath, coughs, fumbles with her hands, and gets to her feet again.

They stand there facing each other. Daniel looks at her with a distant expression in his eyes.

'You probably shouldn't have peeked,' he says.

With a languid gesture he lowers the barrel of the gun so it's pointing at the ground. She doesn't know what to answer. A surge of angst twists her stomach when she realises that she's probably going to die here.

Small insects are crawling among the weeds.

Daniel raises the rifle again and looks her in the eye. He presses the barrel against her right thigh, and it looks almost unintentional when he suddenly fires it.

The blast is so loud that it rings in her ears afterwards.

The jacketed bullet passes straight through Flora's thigh muscle, and she doesn't really experience any pain, more a sort of cramp.

The recoil forces Daniel to take a step back, and he watches as Flora falls, no longer able to support her weight with her right leg.

She tries to break her fall, but her hip and cheek hit the ground, and she lies there for a few moments, her nostrils full of the smell of straw and powder.

'Now cover your face,' he says, aiming the rifle at her face.

Flora lies there on her side as blood bubbles from her thigh. She turns to look at the large barn. Her vision fades for a moment. She feel sick, the landscape with the yellow fields and big red barn spin around her as if she were on a carousel.

Her heart is beating so fast that she's finding it hard to breathe. She coughs, and forces herself to take a deep breath.

Daniel is standing over her with his back to the sun. He pushes her in the shoulder with the barrel of the rifle, making her fall onto her back. A stab of pain from her thigh makes her gasp. He looks at her and says something she can't hear.

She tries to lift her head, and her gaze slips across the ground, past the weeds and the concrete plinth with the iron rings.

Daniel moves the rifle across her body, pointing it at her forehead, then moving down her nose to her mouth.

She feels the hot metal against her lips and chin. Her breathing is extremely fast. Warm blood is pumping out from her throbbing thigh. She looks up at the bright sky, then at the top of the barn, blinks, and tries to make sense of what she sees.

A man is running through the barn, behind the gaps in planks, through the striped light.

She tries to say something, but has no voice.

The barrel of the rifle moves towards her right eye, and she closes her eyes, feels the tentative pressure against her eyelid, and doesn't even hear the loud blast.

178

Joona has driven south from Sundsvall to Hudiksvall, before turning onto Highway 84 towards Delsbo. During the forty minutes the drive takes him, he hasn't been able to stop thinking about Daniel Grim and his box of photographs for a moment.

At first glance the contents seem almost innocent. Perhaps the opening phase had resembled flirtation, all kisses, longing glances, and passionate words.

But when the girls moved on, Daniel didn't hesitate to show his other side. He bided his time, then secretly visited them, and murdered them. Their deaths were rarely entirely unexpected. He gave them overdoses when that matched their medical history, and slit the wrists of those who had a history of cutting themselves.

Private care homes are run for profit, and have presumably done all they could to hush up the deaths in order to avoid the scrutiny of Social Services.

And no one has ever drawn any connection to the Birgitta Home and Daniel Grim.

But it was different with Miranda. He deviated from his pattern. Probably because he panicked when Miranda thought she was pregnant.

Perhaps she threatened to expose him.

She shouldn't have done that, because Daniel can't bear the

thought of witnesses. He's always taken care to get rid of them, one by one.

With a nagging sense of unease, Joona phones Torkel Ekholm, tells him he'll be there in ten minutes, and asks if Flora's ready to go home.

'Sorry, I fell asleep after tea,' the old policeman says. 'Give me a moment.'

Joona hears Torkel put the phone down, cough, then shuffle across the floor. He's already driving across the bridge at Badhusholmen when the old man picks up the phone again.

'There's no sign of Flora,' he says. 'And my rifle's gone too . . .'

'Have you got any idea where she might have gone?'

The line goes quiet for a moment. Joona thinks about the little cottage, the kitchen table covered with notes and photographs.

'Maybe to the manor house?' Torkel replies.

Instead of carrying on towards Ovanåker and Torkel's house, Joona turns sharply right onto Highway 743 and puts his foot down. He contacts the Regional Communications Centre, and requests police backup and an ambulance. On the short stretch of road beside the water he hits a speed of one hundred and eighty kilometres an hour before he has to brake, and turns right through the gateposts and into the narrow drive leading to Rånne Manor.

The gravel rattles beneath the car as the tyres thud across the uneven surface.

From a distance, the large white building looks like an ornate ice sculpture, but the closer he gets the darker it appears.

Joona pulls up sharply and leaves his car in the yard in front of the manor house. He's surrounded by a cloud of dust. He runs towards the main entrance, but suddenly catches sight of two figures some distance away, just as they walk around the end of a wall and disappear behind a large, red barn.

Even though he only caught a glimpse of them, Joona understands at once what he saw: Flora was pointing the gun towards Daniel's back. She's planning to march him across the field, the shortest route back to the road towards Delsbo.

Joona starts running along the gravel track, past the free-standing wing of the manor, and down the slope past the outhouses.

Flora's walking far too close to Daniel, he thinks. Her brother could easily take the rifle off her. She isn't prepared to fire, she doesn't want to fire, she just wants to know the truth.

Joona leaps over the remains of an old fence and slips on the loose gravel. He throws his hand out into the tall weeds, but manages to keep his balance.

He tries to see them through the slatted red walls of the barn. The black gates are open. Sunlight is flickering between the planks.

He runs past a rusty petrol tank, and is just heading into the barn when he hears the crack of the rifle. The echo bounces between the buildings and fades away across the fields.

Daniel must have overpowered Flora.

They're too far away. There's no time. Perhaps it's already too late.

179

Joona draws his pistol as he runs into the empty barn. The slats along the sides are shimmering as light streams in from all directions. The peak of the roof is something like seven metres high. The gaps in the sides shine, forming a huge cage of light.

Joona runs across the dry grit floor of the barn, sees the yellow field glint between the planks, then catches sight of the two figures behind the barn.

Flora is lying motionless on the ground, and Daniel is standing over her with the rifle aimed at her face.

Joona stops and holds his pistol out in front of him. The distance is too far really. Through the gaps in the planks he sees Daniel tilt his head and press the barrel of the rifle to Flora's face.

Everything happens very quickly.

The sights of his pistol tremble before Joona's eye. He aims at Daniel's torso, follows his movements, and squeezes the trigger.

There's a bang, the recoil jolts his arm, and the powder scorches his hand.

The bullet from the pistol passes between two of the planks in the wall. A small cloud of dust swirls in the light in the gap.

But Joona doesn't stop to see if he hit his target, he keeps on running through the barn. He can no longer see the two figures. The stripes of light flicker past. Joona kicks open a narrow back door, carries on through waist-high weeds, and emerges into the yard behind the barn.

Daniel has dropped the rifle on the ground, he didn't manage to fire it a second time. The bullet from Joona's pistol hit him before he could pull the trigger.

Daniel is walking across the yard towards the huge field, clutching his stomach with one hand. Blood is running through his fingers and down his trousers. He hears Joona behind him and turns around unsteadily, and gestures towards Flora, who's lying on her back gasping for breath.

Joona keeps walking towards Daniel with his pistol aimed at his chest.

The sunlight glints off Daniel's glasses as he sits down on the ground.

He groans and looks up.

Without saying anything, Joona kicks the rifle away, grabs hold of Daniel's arm, and drags him several metres across the yard. He cuffs him to one of the iron rings in the concrete plinth, then hurries over to Flora.

She hasn't passed out, but is staring up at him with a strangely fixed expression. She's bleeding heavily from her thigh. Her face is pale and sweaty. She's starting to slip into haemorrhagic shock, and her breathing is very fast and shallow.

'Need a drink,' she whispers.

Flora's trouser-leg is soaked with blood, and more is still bubbling out. There isn't time to apply a tourniquet. He places both hands around her thigh and presses his thumbs down hard just above the wound, right on her femoral artery. The warm flow of blood diminishes at once. He presses harder, and looks at Flora's face. Her lips are white and her breathing extremely shallow. Her eyes are closed, and he can feel how fast her pulse is.

'The ambulance will soon be here,' he says. 'It's going to be OK, Flora.'

Behind his back Joona hears Daniel trying to say something. He turns around and sees an old man walking towards him. The old man is wearing a black overcoat over a black suit, and his footsteps as he walks towards Daniel are strangely heavy. The man's solemn face is grey, and there's a desolate look in his eyes as he meets Joona's gaze.

'Just let me hold my son,' he says in a gruff voice.

Joona can't release the pressure on Flora's thigh. He has to stay where he is if he wants to save her life.

When the man walks past him, Joona can smell petrol. The old man's coat is drenched. He's soaked his clothes in petrol, and is already holding a box of matches as he walks on with numb slowness.

'Don't do it,' Joona calls out.

Daniel stares at his father and tries to crawl away, jerking and trying to pull his hand through the cuff.

The old man looks at Daniel as he struggles to get away. His fingers shake as he takes out one of the matches, closes the box, then holds the match against the side.

'She's lying,' Daniel whimpers.

His father barely has time to strike the match before he is enveloped in blue light. A ball of bright blue flame closes around him. The heat hits Joona's face. The burning old man staggers, leans over his son, and embraces him with his fire. The grass starts to burn around them. The old man holds on tightly. Daniel struggles, then gives up. Flames envelop the pair of them. Like a beacon in the wind, the fire twists upwards. A pillar of black smoke and glowing embers rises into the sky.

180

By the time the fire behind the big barn was put out, all that remained were two charred corpses. Blackened bones, meshed together and smouldering.

The paramedics drove off with Flora just as the old woman emerged from the house. The lady of the house stood completely still in the yard, as if she had frozen to the spot a moment before the pain hit her.

Joona is driving back to Stockholm, listening to the weekly book-club programme on the radio as he thinks about the hammer and the rock again, the murder weapons that have been troubling him so badly. Now everything seems much clearer. Elisabet wasn't killed because the murderer wanted to get hold of her keys. Daniel had his own keys to the isolation room. Elisabet must have seen him. He followed and murdered Elisabet because she was a witness to the first murder, not to take her keys.

Rain starts to hit the roof and windscreen, as hard as pellets of glass. The evening sun shines through the drops, and white steam rises from the tarmac.

Daniel probably went to see Miranda when Elisabet was sleeping soundly with her pills. And she did as he wanted, she had no choice. She would get undressed and sit on her chair with the duvet around her shoulders to keep her warm. But something went wrong that night.

Perhaps Miranda told him she was pregnant, perhaps he found a pregnancy test in the toilet.

And he panicked, his old panic from long ago.

Daniel didn't know what to do, he felt hunted and suffocated, he pulled on the boots that always stood in the hall, went out, and found a rock in the garden, demanded that she close her eyes, and hit her.

She mustn't see him, she had to be covering her face with her hands, just like little Ylva.

Nathan Pollock had interpreted the covered face to mean that the murderer wanted to remove the victim's face, to render her nothing but an object.

But in fact Daniel was in love with Miranda, and he wanted her to cover her face so that she didn't get scared.

He had had plenty of time to plan the other girls' deaths, but Miranda's was carried out in panic. He beat her to death without knowing how he was going to get out of the situation.

And at some point – while he was forcing Miranda to cover her face, beating her with the rock, moving her to the bed, and covering her face again – Elisabet saw him.

Perhaps he had already put the rock inside the stove, perhaps he'd thrown it into the forest.

Daniel chased after Elisabet, saw her go into the brew-house, grabbed a hammer from the store, followed her in, told her to cover her face, and hit her.

Only when Elisabet was dead did he get the idea of pinning the blame on the new girl, Vicky Bennet. He knew she would be asleep for the first part of the night because she was heavily medicated.

Daniel was in a hurry in case anyone woke up. He took Elisabet's keys and went back into the house, left them in the lock of the isolation room, then quickly planted the evidence in Vicky's room and smeared blood on her sleeping body before he left the home.

He probably sat on a bin-bag or newspaper in his car when he drove back to his house, and burned his clothes in the stove when he got there.

From then on he made sure he was never too far away, so

he could check if anyone had seen or knew anything. He was able to play at being both the helpful counsellor and the devastated victim.

Joona is approaching Stockholm. The radio programme is almost over. They've been discussing Selma Lagerlöf's novel, *The Story of Gösta Berling*.

Joona turns the radio off and thinks through the latter part of the investigation.

When Vicky was arrested and Daniel found out that Miranda had told her about the blind game, he realised that he would be found out if Vicky got the chance to talk through everything that had happened in detail. Just seeing a psychologist who asked the right questions would be enough, so Daniel did all he could to help get Vicky released from custody so he could arrange her suicide.

Daniel had spent years working with troubled girls, children who had no security, no parents. Consciously or unconsciously, he put himself into that environment and fell in love with girls who reminded him of the very first one. Daniel exploited the girls, and when they were moved, he made sure they could never tell the truth.

Joona slows down at a traffic light and feels a shiver run down his spine. He's met a number of murderers in his life, but when Joona thinks about how Daniel wrote reports and diagnoses and laid the ground for their deaths long before he went to see them for the last time, he can't help wondering if Daniel is the second worst of them all.

181

The air is full of cold mist as Joona Linna walks across Karlaplan from his car to Disa's flat.

'Joona?' Disa says when she opens the door. 'I almost didn't think you'd come. I've got the television on. They haven't stopped talking about what happened out in Delsbo.'

Joona nods.

'So you caught the murderer,' Disa says with a little smile.

'If that's the right description,' Joona says, thinking about the father's burning embrace.

'How's that poor woman who kept phoning you? They said she'd been shot.'

'Flora Hansen,' Joona says, walking into Disa's hall.

His head hits the lampshade, and the light starts to sway across the walls, and Joona finds himself thinking about the young girls in Daniel's box again.

'You're tired,' Disa says gently, pulling him along by the hand.

'Flora's brother shot her in the leg, and . . .'

He doesn't notice when he stops talking. He tried to clean himself up at a garage, but his clothes are still smeared with Flora's blood.

'Go and have a bath, and I'll get some food,' Disa says.

'Thanks,' Joona smiles.

Just as they're walking through the living room, the news

channel shows a picture of Elin Frank. They both stop. A young reporter explains that Elin Frank has been operated on overnight, and that her doctors are now optimistic. Elin's advisor, Robert Bianchi, appears on screen. He looks drained, and has tears in his eyes as he smiles and says that Elin is going to make it.

'What happened?' Disa whispers.

'She fought the murderer on her own, and saved the girl who—'

'Dear God,' Disa says quietly.

'Yes, Elin Frank is . . . she's . . . she's quite remarkable,' Joona says, putting his hands on Disa's thin shoulders.

182

Joona is sitting with a blanket around him while they eat chicken vindaloo and lamb tikka masala at Disa's kitchen table.

'Good . . .'

'My mum's secret Finnish recipe,' she laughs.

She tears off some naan bread and passes the rest to Joona. He looks at her with smiling eyes, drinks some wine, and goes on telling her about the case. Disa listens and asks questions, and the more he tells her, the calmer he feels inside.

He starts from the beginning, and tells Disa about Flora and Daniel, siblings who ended up in a children's home at a very young age.

'So they really were brother and sister?' she asks, refilling their glasses.

'Yes . . . and it was quite a big deal when the wealthy couple at Rånne adopted them.'

'I can imagine.'

They were just young children who played with the foreman's daughter in the manor house, on the estate, and in the church-yard by the bell tower. Daniel had a crush on little Ylva. Joona thinks back to Flora's wide-eyed account of Daniel kissing Ylva when they were playing the blind game.

'The little girl laughed and said now she was going to have

a baby,' Joona says. 'Daniel was only six years old, and for some reason he panicked . . .'

'Go on,' Disa whispers.

'He ordered both the girls to close their eyes, then he picked up a heavy rock and killed Ylva.'

Disa has stopped eating, and her face is pale as she listens while Joona describes how Flora fled and told her father what had happened.

'But their father loved Daniel, and defended him,' Joona says. 'He demanded that Flora take back her accusations. He threatened her by saying that all liars would be thrown into a sea of fire.'

'So she retracted?'

'She said she'd been lying, and because she'd told such wicked lies, she was sent away from the house for ever.'

'Flora took back her accusations . . . and lied about lying,' Disa says thoughtfully.

'Yes,' Joona says, touching her hand over the table.

He thinks about the fact that Flora was only a very small child, and soon forgot her previous life, her adoptive parents, and her brother.

Joona can see how Flora built a whole life around lies. She lied to keep other people happy. It wasn't until she heard about the murders at the Birgitta Home on the radio, about the girl with her hands over her face, that the past started to come back to her.

'But what about Flora Hansen's memories?' Disa asks, gesturing to Joona to help himself to more food.

'I actually called Britt-Marie on the way here to talk about that,' Joona says.

'Nils Åhlén's wife?'

'Yes . . . she's a psychiatrist, after all, and she didn't seem to think it was all that strange at all . . .'

He tells her that Britt-Marie had said there are many different explanatory models for memory loss linked to the concept of post-traumatic stress disorder. High levels of adrenaline, and stress-related hormones can affect the long-term memory. After particularly traumatic experiences, memories can be buried almost intact deep within the brain. They get hidden away and remain untouched emotionally because they were never processed. But with the right stimulus, the memory can suddenly pop up as physical sensations and images.

'To start with, Flora was just shaken up by what she'd heard on the radio, without knowing why, but thought she could make a bit of money by tipping the police off,' Joona says. 'But when her actual memories started to appear, she thought they were ghosts.'

'Perhaps they really were ghosts, in a way,' Disa suggests.

'Maybe,' he nods. 'Either way, she began to tell the truth, and Flora ended up being the witness who unlocked the entire mystery.'

Joona stands up and blows out the candles on the table. Disa walks up to him, makes her way inside the blanket, and embraces him. They stand there just holding each other for a long time. He breathes in her scent, and feels the vein pulsing in her slender neck.

'I'm so scared something's going to happen to you. That's what behind all this, that's why I've been keeping my distance,' he says.

'What could happen to me?' she smiles.

'You could disappear,' he replies seriously.

'Joona, I'm not going to disappear.'

'I used to have a friend called Samuel Mendel,' he says quietly, then falls silent.

183

Joona Linna walks out of Police Headquarters and up the steep path across Kronoberg Park, over the hill to the old Jewish cemetery. With practised hands he unfastens the wire holding the gate closed, opens it, and goes inside.

Among the dark gravestones is a more recent family grave bearing the words: 'Samuel Mendel, his wife Rebecka, and their sons Joshua and Ruben.'

Joona puts a small round stone on the top of the gravestone, then stands with his eyes closed. He can smell the damp soil and hear the park's leaves rustling as the wind blows through the treetops.

Samuel Mendel was a direct descendant of the Koppel Mendel, who, against Aaron Isaac's wishes, bought this cemetery in 1787. Even though it stopped being used in 1857, it has remained the last resting place for Koppel Mendel's family for all these years.

Samuel Mendel was a detective superintendent, and Joona's first partner in the National Crime Unit.

He and Joona were very close friends.

Samuel Mendel was only forty-six years old when he died, and Joona knows that he's lying alone in the family grave, even if the headstone says otherwise.

Joona and Samuel Mendel's first big case together also turned out to be their last.

Just an hour later, Joona is back at the Prosecution Authority's national department for complaints against the police. He's sitting in a room with Mikael Båge, who's in charge of the investigation, senior secretary Helene Fiorine, and senior prosecutor Sven Wiklund.

The yellow light from outside glints off the polished furniture, and reflects off the glass fronts of the bookcases containing handsomely bound law books, the police code, and volumes of judgements and test cases in the High Court.

'I now need to decide whether or not to press charges against you, Joona Linna,' the senior prosecutor says, putting one hand on a thick pile of papers. 'This is the material I've got to go on, and there's nothing in here that helps your case.'

His chair creaks as he leans back and meets Joona's calm gaze. The only sounds in the room are the rasp of Helene Fiorine's pen and her shallow breathing.

'As I see it,' Sven Wiklund goes on drily, 'your only chance of avoiding prosecution is a really good explanation.'

'Joona usually has an ace up his sleeve,' Mikael Båge says in a low voice.

Out in the clear sky the vapour trail from an aeroplane high above is slowly dissipating. Their chairs creak, and Helene Fiorine swallows audibly and puts her pen down.

'All you have to do is explain what happened,' she says. 'Perhaps you had good reasons to pre-empt the Security Police raid.'

'Yes,' Joona says.

'We know you're a good police officer,' Mikael Båge says with an embarrassed smile.

'I, on the other hand, am a stickler for the rules,' the senior prosecutor says. 'I'm the sort of man who crushes people for breaking the rules. Don't make me crush you here and now.'

That's as close to a plea that Helene Fiorine has ever heard Sven Wiklund make.

'Your entire future's in the balance, Joona,' the head of the investigation whispers.

Helene Fiorine's chin starts to tremble, and Mikael Båge's forehead is shiny with sweat. Joona meets the senior prosecutor's gaze and finally starts talking: 'The decision was mine, and mine alone, as you've already realised,' he begins, 'but I do actually have an answer that you might—'

Joona breaks off when his phone suddenly buzzes. He looks at the screen automatically, and his eyes turn as dark as wet granite.

'I'm sorry,' he says very seriously, 'but I really do have to take this call.'

The other three look on in bemusement as the superintendent answers and listens to the voice at the other end.

'Yes, I know,' he says quietly. 'Yes . . . I'll come at once.'

Joona ends the call, gives the senior prosecutor a lingering look, as if he'd forgotten where he was.

'I have to go,' Joona says, and leaves the room without another word.

184

One hour and twenty minutes later, the scheduled flight lands at Härjedalen Sveg Airport and Joona immediately takes a taxi to the Blue Wings care home. This was where he tracked down Rosa Bergman, the woman who was following him outside Adolf Fredrik's Church, the woman who asked him why he was pretending that his daughter was dead.

Rosa Bergman has adopted her mother's maiden name, and is now known as Maja Stefanson.

Joona gets out of the taxi and walks quickly up to the cluster of yellow buildings, through the main entrance, and straight to Maja's ward.

The nurse he met last time waves to him from the reception desk. The light coming through the blinds makes her curly hair shine like copper.

'That was quick,' she says. 'I've been thinking about you, and we've had your card pinned up behind the desk, so I called—'

'Is it possible to talk to her?' Joona interrupts.

His tone disconcerts the woman, and she brushes her hands on her pale blue tunic.

'Our new doctor was here the day before yesterday, she's a young woman, from Algeria, I think. She changed Maja's medication and . . . Well, I've heard about it, but I've never seen it myself before . . . The old dear woke up this morning and kept saying very clearly that she needs to speak to you.'

'Where is she?'

The nurse leads Joona to the cramped room with closed curtains, and leaves him alone with the old woman. Above a narrow desk hangs a framed photograph of a young woman sitting next to her son. The mother has her arm around the boy's shoulders, serious and protective.

Several heavy items of furniture from an affluent home line the walls: a dark bureau, a dressing table, and two gilded pedestals.

Rosa Bergman is sitting on a daybed with deep red cushions. She's smartly dressed in a blouse, skirt, and knitted cardigan. Her face looks swollen and wrinkled, but there's a completely new focus in her eyes.

'My name is Joona Linna,' he says. 'You had something you wanted to tell me.'

The woman on the couch nods and gets to her feet with an effort. She opens a drawer in her bedside table, and takes out a Gideon bible. She holds the spine and shakes the pages above the bed. A small, folded piece of paper falls onto the bedspread.

'Joona Linna,' she says, picking up the paper. 'So you're Joona Linna.'

He doesn't answer, just feels the migraine burn into his temple like a red-hot needle. 'How can you pretend your daughter is dead?' Rosa Bergman asks.

The old woman's eyes go to the photograph on the wall.

'If there was some way I could have had my boy here still . . . If you knew what it's like to see your child die . . . Nothing in the world could have made me abandon him.'

'I didn't abandon my family,' Joona says tersely. 'I saved their lives.'

'When Summa came to me,' Rosa goes on, 'she didn't tell me about you, but she was broken . . . It was worse for your daughter, though, she stopped talking, didn't speak for two years.'

Joona feels a shiver run all the way up his spine to his scalp.

'Were you in contact with them?' he asks. 'You weren't supposed to have any contact with them.'

'I couldn't just let them disappear,' she says. 'I felt so incredibly sorry for them.'

Joona knows Summa would never mention his name unless something was horribly wrong. There wasn't supposed to be any connection between them at all. Nothing, ever. That was the only way to survive.

He leans against the bureau, swallows hard, and looks at the old woman again.

'How are they?' he asks.

'This is serious, Joona Linna,' Rosa says. 'I usually see Lumi once a year or so. But . . . I . . . I've become so very confused and forgetful.'

'What's happened?'

'Your wife has cancer, Joona Linna,' Rosa says slowly. 'She called me and said she was going to have an operation, but that she probably wasn't going to recover . . . she wanted you to know that Lumi will be taken into care by Social Services if she . . .'

'When was this?' Joona asks through clenched teeth, his lips white. 'When did she phone?'

'I'm afraid it might be too late,' she whispers. 'I've been so forgetful and everything . . .'

She finally hands him the crumpled note with the address on it, then stares down at her arthritic hands.

185

You can only fly to two destinations from Sveg, so Joona has to fly back to Arlanda and change planes to get to Helsinki. The whole thing feels like a dream. He sits in his seat and stares through the veils of cloud at the rippled surface of the Baltic Sea. People try to talk to him and serve him drinks and snacks, but he can't bring himself to respond.

Memories are dragging him down into their murky ocean.

Twelve years ago Joona chopped off one of the fingers of the devil incarnate.

Nineteen people of all ages had disappeared from their cars, bicycles and mopeds. At first it just looked like a peculiar co-incidence, but when none of the missing people reappeared, the case was given top priority.

Joona was the first person to claim that the police were dealing with a serial killer.

Together with Samuel Mendel, he managed to track and catch Jurek Walter red-handed out in Lill-Jans Forest when he was forcing a fifty-year-old woman back into a coffin in the ground. She had already been in the coffin for two years, but was still alive.

The extent of the nightmare became apparent in hospital. The woman's muscles had atrophied, she was deformed by pressure sores, and her hands and feet had suffered frostbite.

After further examination, her doctors concluded that not only was she suffering from extreme psychological trauma, but that she was badly brain-damaged.

Joona usually thinks that if the devil is made up of humanity's very worst cruelty over the ages, then it must be impossible to kill the devil, but twelve years ago he and Samuel managed to cut one of his fingers off when they caught serial killer Jurek Walter.

Joona sat in the Court of Appeal in the Wrangelska Palace on Riddarholmen in Stockholm when the original sentence of the court was challenged and ultimately strengthened. Jurek Walter was sentenced to secure psychiatric care with very specific parole conditions, and placed in a secure unit twenty kilometres north of Stockholm.

Joona will never forget Jurek Walter's wrinkled face when he turned to look at him.

'Now Samuel Mendel's two sons will go missing,' Jurek said in a weary voice, while his defence lawyer gathered his papers. 'And Samuel's wife Rebecka will go missing, but . . . No, listen to me, Joona Linna. The police will search, and when the police give up, Samuel will go on looking, but when he finally realises that he's never going to see his family again, he'll kill himself.'

Joona had stood up to leave.

'And your little daughter,' Jurek Walter went on, looking down at the floor. 'Lumi will go missing . . . and when you realise that you're never going to see her again, you'll hang yourself.'

One Friday afternoon, a couple of months later Samuel's wife drove from their flat in Liljeholmen to their summerhouse on Dalarö. She had their two sons, Joshua and Ruben, in the car with her. When Samuel arrived at the house a few hours later, his wife and children weren't there. The car was found abandoned on a nearby forest track, but Samuel never saw his family again. One chill March morning a year, later Samuel Mendel went down to the beautiful beach where his boys used to swim. The police had stopped looking eight months earlier, and now he too had given up. He drew his service pistol from his shoulder holster, and shot himself in the head.

* * *

Far below, Joona can see the shadow of the plane on the darkly shimmering surface of the water. He looks through the window and thinks about the day when his life was torn to pieces. It was quiet in the car, and the world was bathed in an unusual light. The sun shone red behind thin veils of cloud. It had been raining, and the rays of sunlight made the puddles glow as if they were burning from below.

186

Joona and Summa had been planning a motoring holiday in gentle stages: up to Umeå, past Storuman, across to Mo i Rana in Norway, then back down the west coast. Now they were on their way to a hotel that lay in the middle of Dalälven, and were going to visit a wildlife park nearby the following day.

Summa changed the station on the radio and murmured happily when she found one playing pleasantly relaxed piano music, the notes all blending into each other. Joona reached back to make sure that Lumi was sitting properly in her child's seat and hadn't slipped her arms out of the straps.

'Daddy,' she said sleepily.

He felt her little fingers in his hand. She held him tight, but let go when he pulled back.

They passed the turning to Älvkarleby.

'You're going to love Furuvik Wildlife Park,' Summa said quietly. 'Chimpanzees and rhinocer—'

'I've already got a monkey!' Lumi cried from the back seat.

'What?'

'I'm her monkey,' Joona said.

Summa raised her eyebrows.

'It suits you.'

'Lumi's looking after me – she says she's a nice vet.'

Summa's sand-brown hair was hanging over her face, half

hiding her thick dark eyebrows. The dimples in her cheeks grew deeper.

'Why do you need a vet? What's wrong with you?'

'I need glasses.'

'Did she say that?' Summa laughed, and leafed through her newspaper, not noticing that he was driving along a different road, and that they were already north of the Dala River.

Lumi had fallen asleep with her doll pressed to her cheek.

'Are you sure we don't need to book a table?' Summa suddenly asked. 'Because I want to sit on the veranda tonight to see the whole river outside the window . . .'

The road was narrow and straight, the forest crowding in from behind the wildlife fencing.

It wasn't until he turned off towards Mora that Summa realised that something was wrong.

'Joona, we've gone past Älvkarleby,' she suddenly said 'Weren't we going to stop there? I'm sure we said we were going to stop in Älvkarleby.'

'Yes.'

'So what are you doing?'

He didn't answer, just stared at the road where the puddles glowed in the afternoon sun. A truck suddenly pulled out into the overtaking lane without indicating.

'We said we . . .' She fell silent, breathing through her nose, then went on in a frightened voice: 'Joona? Tell me you haven't been lying to me. Tell me.'

'I had to,' he whispered.

Summa looked at him, and he could sense how upset she was, but she still made an effort to speak quietly so she didn't wake Lumi: 'You can't be serious,' she said tersely. 'You can't just . . . you said there was no danger any more, you said it was over. You said it was over, and I believed you. I thought you'd changed, I really believed that . . .'

Her voice broke, and she turned away to look out of the side window. Her chin was trembling, and her cheeks turned red.

'I lied to you,' Joona admitted.

'You weren't allowed to lie to me, you weren't allowed to—'

'No . . . And I'm so, so sorry.'

'We can run away together, that would work, that would work fine.'

'You have to understand . . . Summa, you really have to understand . . . if I thought that was possible, if I had any other choice, I'd—'

'Stop it,' she interrupted. 'The threat isn't real. It's not true, you're seeing connections that aren't there. Samuel Mendel's family are nothing to do with us, don't you get that? There's no threat to us.'

'I've tried to explain how serious it is, but you won't listen.'

'I don't want to listen. Why would I want to?'

'Summa, I have to . . . I've arranged everything, there's a woman called Rosa Bergman. She's waiting for you up in Malmberget, she'll give you new identities. You're going to be fine.'

His hands had started to shake. His fingers were slippery with sweat on the steering wheel.

'You really are serious,' Summa whispered.

'More serious than I've ever been,' he replied heavily. 'We're on our way to Mora, where you'll be catching the train to Gällivare.'

He could hear that Summa was doing her best to sound composed.

'If you leave us at that station, you've lost us. Do you understand that? There's no way back after that.'

She looked at him with moist, stubborn eyes.

'You'll have to tell Lumi that I'm working abroad,' he went on in a subdued voice, hearing Summa start to sniff.

'Joona,' she whispered. 'No, no . . .'

He just stared ahead of him, out at the wet road, and swallowed hard.

'And in a few years,' he went on, 'when she's a bit bigger, you'll have to tell her I'm dead. You must never, ever contact me. Never come to find me. Do you hear?'

Summa could no longer hold back the tears.

'I don't want this, I don't want this . . .'

'Nor do I.'

'You can't do this to us,' she wept.

'Mummy?'

Lumi had woken up, and her voice sounded frightened. Summa wiped the tears from her cheeks.

'It's nothing to worry about,' Joona told his daughter. 'Mummy's just sad because we're not going to the hotel by the river.'

'Tell her,' Summa said in a louder voice.

'Tell me what?' Lumi asked.

'You and Mummy are going on a train,' Joona said.

'What are you going to do?'

'I have to work,' he replied.

'But I said we were going to play vet and monkey.'

'He doesn't want to,' Summa said harshly.

They were approaching the outskirts of Mora, passing scattered residential areas and a few industrial units. Shopping centres and car showrooms with a handful of cars parked outside. The dense, enchanted forest became more and more tamed, and the wildlife fencing disappeared.

187

Joona slowed down in front of the yellow station building. He parked the car, opened the boot, and lifted out the large wheeled suitcase.

'You took your things out of the case last night?' Summa asked in a subdued voice.

'Yes.'

'And added other things instead?'

He nodded and looked off towards the railway, with its four parallel tracks, rust-coloured gravel embankment, weeds, and dark sleepers.

Summa came over and stood beside him.

'Your daughter needs you in her life.'

'I haven't got a choice,' he replied, looking back through the car's rear window.

Lumi was pressing a big, soft doll into her pink rucksack.

'You've got plenty of choices,' Summa went on. 'But instead of fighting, you're just giving up. You don't even know if the threat is real. I can't get my head around this.'

'Can't find Lollo,' Lumi was muttering to herself.

'The train leaves in twenty minutes,' Joona said tersely.

'I don't want to live without you,' Summa said quietly, trying to take his hand. 'I want everything to carry on as normal.'

'Yes.'

'If you do this to us, you'll be alone.'

He didn't answer. Lumi climbed out of the car, dragging her rucksack along the ground. A red hairclip was dangling loosely from her hair.

'Are you going to lead a completely solitary life?'

'Yes,' he said.

The northernmost inlet of Lake Siljan glinted between the trees on the other side of the tracks.

'Say goodbye to Daddy now,' Summa said blankly, nudging her daughter forward.

Lumi stood still with a dark expression on her face, staring at the ground.

'Hurry up,' Summa said.

Lumi looked up for a couple of seconds and said: 'Bye, bye, monkey.'

'Do it properly,' Summa said irritably. 'Say goodbye nicely.'

'Don't want to,' Lumi replied, clinging to one of her mother's legs.

'Do it anyway,' Summa said.

Joona crouched down in front of his little daughter. His forehead was shiny with sweat.

'Can I have a hug?'

She shook her head.

'Here comes the monkey with his long arms,' he joked.

He picked her up, and felt her little body resist, then she started to laugh in spite of herself, even though she could feel something was wrong. She tried to kick and get down, but he held her tightly, just for a few moments, just to inhale the smell of her hair and neck.

'Silly,' she shouted.

'Lumi,' he whispered against her cheek. 'Never forget that I love you more than anything.'

'Come on, now,' Summa said.

He put his daughter down and tried to smile at her, felt like stroking her cheek, but somehow couldn't. It was as if his body was made of glass that had shattered and then been put back together again. Summa looked at him with a horrified, rigid expression, then took hold of Lumi's hand and pulled her towards her.

They waited for the train in silence. There was nothing more to say. Downy dandelion seeds drifted slowly across the tracks.

Joona recalls that the slightly scorched smell of the brakes hung in the air after the train had pulled away from the platform. As if in a dream he stood and watched his daughter's pale face through the window, and the little hand waving tentatively at him. Summa sat beside her like a paralysed black shadow. Before the train had disappeared around the bend down by the harbour he turned, and walked back to his car.

188

He drove for one hundred and forty kilometres without thinking. His head was full of noisy emptiness and frighteningly detached.

He drove without any memory.

Eventually he arrived.

In the darkness, the headlights shone on heavy, black metal silhouettes. He turned in to the large industrial estate in Ludvika, down by the deserted harbour next to the power station. There was already a large grey van parked between two huge heaps of sawdust. Joona stopped next to the grey van. He suddenly felt remarkably calm. So calm that part of him realised that he was in some form of shock.

He got out and looked around. Nils Åhlén was waiting in the darkness beside the van door. He was wearing white overalls, his face looked clenched and haggard.

'So, are they gone now?' he asked in the sharp tone of voice he always used when something upset him.

'They've gone,' Joona confirmed bluntly.

Nils Åhlén nodded. His white-rimmed glasses glinted coldly in the faint light from a streetlamp in the distance.

'You didn't give me a choice,' he said bitterly.

'That's true,' Joona said. 'You haven't got a choice.'

'We'll both get fired for this,' Nils Åhlén said, with an impassive face.

'Maybe,' Joona replied.

They walked towards the back of the van.

'There are two of them, I acted as soon as they came in.'

'Good.'

'Two of them,' Nils Åhlén repeated, almost to himself.

Joona remembers how he had woken up a couple of days before, next to his wife and daughter, because his mobile was buzzing in his jacket out in the hall.

Someone had sent him a text. When he got up and saw it was from Nils, he understood at once what it was about.

They had come to an understanding that as soon as Nils Åhlén came across two suitable bodies, Joona would set off with Summa and Lumi on the pretext of finally taking the motoring holiday they had talked about for so long.

Joona had been waiting to hear from Nils for almost three weeks. Time was starting to run out. He was keeping watch over his family, but knew that couldn't work for ever. Jurek Walter was a patient man.

Joona knew that Nils Åhlén's text meant he was going to lose his family. But he also knew that it meant he could finally give Summa and Lumi proper protection.

Now Nils Åhlén opened the two rear doors of the grey van.

Inside were two stretchers covered by cloths, one bearing a large figure, the other a smaller one.

'A woman and a girl, they died in a car accident yesterday morning,' Nils said, and began to pull one of the stretchers out.

'I've spirited them away,' he explained quickly. 'They don't exist, not a trace, I've deleted everything.'

He groaned as he pulled the bodies out. The stretcher's frame unfolded with a clatter as its small wheels touched the ground.

Without further ceremony, Nils unzipped one of the body-bags.

Joona gritted his teeth and forced himself to look.

Inside lay a young woman with her eyes closed and a perfectly calm expression on her face. Her chest was horribly crushed. Her arms looked as if they were broken in several places, and her pelvis was badly contorted.

'Their car went off a bridge,' Nils Åhlén said in his sharp, nasal voice. 'Her chest is so badly crushed because she wasn't wearing her seat belt. Possibly because she trying to pick something up for her daughter. I've seen it before.'

Joona looked at the woman. There was no sign of pain or terror. There was nothing in her face that gave any indication of what had happened to her body.

When he turned to look at the little girl's face his eyes filled with tears.

Nils Åhlén muttered something to himself and covered the bodies again.

'Well, then,' he said. 'Catharina and Mimmi will never be found, and will never be identified.'

He lost his train of thought for a moment, then went on angrily: 'The girl's father has been going around all the hospitals looking for them, all night. He even called my department. I had to talk to him.'

Nils Åhlén pressed his lips together.

'They'll be buried as Summa and Lumi . . . I'll organise fake dental records.'

He gave Joona one last probing look, but got no response. Together they moved the bodies to Joona's car.

189

It felt unreal to drive a car with two dead bodies as passengers. The roads were dark. Hedgehogs that had been hit by cars lay by the verges. A badger stared at him from the roadside with glowing eyes, hypnotised by the headlights.

When he reached the hill he had chosen, he began to arrange the bodies. As Joona moved the woman's body to the driver's seat and strapped the girl into Lumi's child's seat, the only noises were his own strained breathing and the soft sound of their dangling arms and legs hitting the seats.

He leaned in, released the handbrake, and set the car in motion. Slowly it began to roll down the hill, with him walking beside it. Every so often he would lean in and adjust the steering wheel. It gained speed, and he started to run. With a dull crunch the car crashed into a thick pine tree. There was a shriek of metal as the front folded around the tree. The woman slumped against the dashboard. The little girl's body jerked hard in the child's seat.

Joona took the petrol can from the boot and poured it over the seats, the girl's padded overalls, and the woman's shattered body.

It was starting to get hard to breathe.

He had to stop and calm himself down. His agitated heart felt as though it was trying to break into his throat.

Joona Linna mumbled a few words to himself, then pulled the little girl out again. He walked up and down with her in his arms, holding her tightly, rocking her, and whispering in her ears. Then he put her on her mother's lap in the front of the car.

He quietly closed the car door and emptied the last of the tank over the outside. One of the rear windows was open, and he set fire to the back seat.

Like a blue angel of death, the fire spread through the inside of the car.

He caught a glimpse of the woman's incomprehensibly calm face as her hair burned.

The car was wedged against the tree, and was now completely alight. The flames were loud, with ragged, shrieking cries and weeping sounds.

It was as if Joona suddenly woke up. He rushed towards the car to get the bodies out. He burned his hands on the door, but eventually managed to open it. The fire inside the car billowed out when he opened the door. He tried to get hold of the woman, but her jacket was burning fiercely. Her slender legs looked as if they were twitching in the flames.

Daddy, Daddy. Help me, Daddy.

Joona knew it wasn't real, he knew they were already dead, but he still couldn't bear it. He reached his hand in through the flames and held the girl's hand.

At that moment the heat made the car's petrol tank explode. Joona experienced a weird crunching sound as his eardrums burst. Almost in a dream he felt blood pour from his nose and ears as he was thrown backwards and his head hit the ground. His brain was flaring and roaring. Before his vision faded, he saw the burned embers of the leaves drifting slowly through the air.

190

Joona stares out through the window and doesn't hear the flight attendant announce that they will shortly be arriving at Helsinki International Airport.

Twelve years ago he cut off one of the fingers of the devil incarnate, and as a punishment he was sentenced to live alone. It's a high price, but he has always felt it wasn't enough, that the punishment has been too lenient, that the devil has just been biding his time before taking something else from him, waiting for him to think that everything has been forgiven and forgotten.

Joona hunches up in his seat, waits, and tries to calm his breathing. The man in the next seat looks at him anxiously.

Sweat is dripping from Joona's forehead.

This isn't a migraine, it's the other thing, the great darkness behind everything.

He caught serial killer Jurek Walter. That's not the sort of thing that gets forgotten, and it will never be forgiven.

He had no choice, but the price was too high, far too high.

It wasn't worth it.

His arms break out in goosebumps, he scratches his head hard with one hand, and pushes his feet down hard against the floor of the plane.

He's on his way to find Summa and Lumi. He's on his way

to do something unforgiveable. As long as Jurek Walter thinks they're dead, they're safe. He could be leading a serial killer to his family at this very moment.

Joona has left his mobile phone in Stockholm. He's using a fake passport, and pays cash for everything. When he gets out of the taxi, he walks two blocks before stopping in a doorway and trying to see any signs of life in the dark windows of their apartment.

He waits for a while, then goes to a café further down the street, pays ten euros to borrow a phone, and calls Saga Bauer.

'I need help,' he says in a voice that's on the brink of breaking.

'Did you know everyone's looking for you? It's absolute chaos here . . .'

'I need help with something.'

'OK,' she says, her voice suddenly calm and focused.

'Once you've given me the information,' Joona goes on, 'you have to make absolutely certain that you erase all traces of the search.'

'OK,' she says quietly, without any hesitation.

Joona swallows hard, looks at the little note Rosa Bergman gave him, then asks Saga to check if a woman called Laura Sandin at the address Liisankatu 16 in Helsinki is still alive.

'Can I call you back?' she asks.

'Preferably not, I'll wait while you search,' he replies.

The minutes that follow are the longest of his life. He looks at the dust on the counter, the espresso machine, the marks on the floor made by chairs.

'Joona?' Saga eventually says.

'I'm here,' he whispers.

'Laura Sandin fell ill with liver cancer two years ago . . .'

'Go on,' Joona says, as he feels sweat start to trickle down his back.

'Looks like she had an operation last year. And she . . . but . . .'

Saga Bauer whispers something to herself.

'What is it?' Joona asks.

Saga clears her throat and says with a hint of stress in her voice, as if she's only just realised that this is somehow extremely important: 'She underwent a second operation very recently, last week . . .'

'Is she alive?'

'It looks like it . . . She's still in hospital,' Saga says gently.

191

When Joona reaches the corridor where Summa's room is, it's as if everything slows down. The distant sounds of televisions and conversation get slower and slower.

Very gently, he opens the door to her room and walks in.

A thin woman is lying in the bed, facing away from him.

A cotton curtain is pulled across the window. Her frail arms are on top of the covers. Her dark hair is sweaty and dull.

He doesn't know if she's asleep, but he has to see her face. He walks closer. The room is completely silent.

The woman who was known in a different life as Summa Linna is extremely tired. Her daughter has spent the whole night sitting with her, and is now sleeping in the visitors' room.

Summa sees the weak daylight filter through the thin curtain, and thinks that human beings are ultimately alone. She has several good memories that she usually tries to find when she feels at her most lonely and afraid. When they gave her the anaesthetic before the operation she conjured up those moments.

The incredibly light summer nights when she was a child.

The moment her daughter was born, and held her finger in hers.

Her wedding on that summer's day, with the bridal crown her mother had woven from birch roots.

Summa swallows and feels that she is alive, feels the beat of her heart. But she's so horribly frightened of dying and leaving Lumi alone in the world.

The stitches from the operation sting when she rolls over. She closes her eyes, then opens them again.

She has to blink several times before she realises that her message must have reached him.

Joona Linna is leaning over her, and she reaches up and touches his face, then runs her fingers through his thick fair hair.

'If I die, you need to take care of Lumi,' she whispers.

'I promise.'

'And you have to see her before you go again,' she says. 'You have to see her.'

He puts his hands against her cheeks and strokes her face. Whispers that she's as beautiful as she ever was. She smiles at him. Then he's gone, and Summa is no longer afraid.

The visitors' room is simply furnished, there's a television on the wall, and a pine table covered with cigarette burns sits in front of a sagging sofa.

A fifteen-year-old girl is lying asleep on the sofa. Her eyes hurt from crying so much, and one cheek is striped from the pattern on the cushion. She wakes up abruptly with a strange feeling. Someone's laid a blanket over her. Her shoes have been taken off, and are standing neatly on the floor beside her.

Someone had been in there with her. In her dream there was someone sitting with her, very gently holding her hand in theirs.

192

The Löwenströmska Hospital is situated on the old trunk road, halfway between Stockholm and Uppsala. It was built by Gustaf Adolf Löwenström in the early nineteenth century in an attempt to atone for his family's guilt. His brother had murdered King Gustav III at the masked ball in the Opera House.

Anders Rönn is twenty-three years old, and freshly qualified as a doctor. He's slim, and has a handsome, sensitive face. He starts work today at the Löwenström Hospital. The low autumn light plays through the treetops as he walks past the main entrance.

Behind the modern main building of red-brown bricks is a remarkable second building. From above it looks like two adjoining Fleury crosses. This is the large psychiatric department, encompassing both forensic psychiatry and secure units.

On the hill is a bronze sculpture of a boy playing the flute. A bird is perched on the boy's shoulder, and another on his broad-brimmed hat.

On one side of the path, the pastoral landscape spreads out, with pasture that stretches towards Lake Fysingen, and on the other side, a five-metre-tall barbed-wire fence encloses a shaded rest area with cigarette butts surrounding a solitary bench.

No one under the age of fourteen is allowed to visit the psychiatric department, and photography and audio recordings are prohibited.

Anders Rönn crosses the concrete paving slabs, passes beneath a fading metal canopy, and walks through the glass doors.

His footsteps on the worn ivory-coloured linoleum floor are almost silent. When he reaches the lift, he notices that he's already on the second floor.

The first floor is below ground, and houses Ward 30, the secure forensic psychiatric unit.

The lift doesn't go any lower, but behind a pale yellow steel gate is a spiral staircase that leads down to Level 0.

That's where the isolated, bunker-like high security unit is located.

The isolated unit has a capacity for a maximum of three patients, but for the past twelve years it has contained just one, the aging Jurek Walter.

Jurek Walter was sentenced to secure psychiatric care with very specific probation requirements, and on his arrival he was so aggressive that he was placed in a straitjacket and forcibly sedated.

Nine years ago he was given the diagnosis 'Non-specific schizophrenia. Chaotic thinking. Recurrent, acute psychotic episodes with bizarre and extremely violent elements'.

It's the only diagnosis he has received so far.

'I'll let you through,' a woman with round cheeks and calm eyes says.

'Thanks.'

'You know about the patient? Jurek Walter?' she asks, apparently without expecting an answer.

193

Anders Rönn hangs the key to the steel gate in the cupboard of the security section before the woman opens the first door of the airlock. He walks in and waits until the door has closed behind him, before walking across to the second door. When a buzzer sounds, the woman opens that door. Anders turns and raises his hand in thanks before carrying on along the corridor to the staffroom of the isolation unit.

A thickset man in his fifties, with sloping shoulders and cropped hair, is standing smoking under the extractor fan in the small kitchen. He pinches the end of his cigarette off, tosses it in the sink, tucks the remaining half cigarette back in the packet, and puts it in the pocket of his white coat.

'Roland Brolin, senior consultant,' he says by way of introduction.

'Anders Rönn.'

'So how did you end up here of all places?' the consultant asks.

'I've got young kids, and wanted a job close to home,' Anders Rönn replies.

'You chose a good day to start,' Roland Brolin smiles, and starts to walk down the soundproof corridor.

The doctor takes out his card, waits until the lock in the security door clicks, then pushes it open with a deep sigh. He lets go before Anders has walked through, and the heavy door hits him in the shoulder.

'Is there anything I ought to know about the patient?' Anders Rönn asks, blinking away tears of pain.

Brolin gestures vaguely and recites: 'He must never be alone with any member of staff, he has never been granted leave, he must never meet other patients, he must never receive visitors, and he must never go out to the rest area. Nor—'

'Never?' Anders interrupts hesitantly. 'But it's against regulations to keep someone locked—'

'No, it isn't,' Roland says abruptly.

The atmosphere feels suddenly tense. In the end Anders asks tentatively: 'What did he actually do?'

'Nothing but nice things,' Roland replies.

'Such as?'

The consultant looks at him, and his puffy grey face suddenly cracks into a smile.

'You really are new, aren't you?' he laughs.

They pass through another security door, and a woman with piercings in her cheeks winks at them.

'Come back alive,' she says drily.

'Don't worry,' Roland tells Anders, lowering his voice. 'Jurek Walter is a quiet, elderly man. He doesn't fight, and he doesn't raise his voice. He keeps to himself, and we never go in to see him. But right now we have to, because the guys on duty last night noticed that he was hiding a knife under his mattress and—'

'How the hell did he get hold of that?'

Roland's forehead is sweating, and he rubs his face with his hand and wipes it on his coat.

'Jurek Walter can be pretty manipulative, and . . . We'll conduct an internal investigation, but who knows . . .'

194

The senior consultant runs his card through another reader and taps in a code. It lets out a bleep, and the lock on the security door clicks.

'What would he want the knife for?' Anders asks, hurrying through. 'If he wanted to kill himself, he'd have done it by now, wouldn't he?'

'Maybe he just likes knives,' Roland says.

'Is he an escape risk?'

'He hasn't made any attempts since he's been here.'

They've reached another sluice with mesh-covered gates.

'Hang on,' Roland says, and holds out a small box of yellow earplugs.

'You said he doesn't scream.'

Roland looks very tired, as if he hasn't slept for several days. He looks at his new colleague for a few seconds, then lets out a deep sigh before starting to explain.

'Jurek Walter will talk to you, perfectly calmly, perfectly pleasantly,' he says in a serious voice. 'But later tonight when you're driving home, you'll suddenly steer into oncoming traffic and crash into a truck . . . or you'll stop off at the DIY store and buy an axe before you pick the kids up from preschool.'

'Am I supposed to be frightened now?' Anders smiles.

'No, but hopefully careful,' Roland says. 'I've been in his room once before, last year, just after Easter, when he'd got hold of a pair of scissors.'

'He's an old man, isn't he?'

'Don't worry – it'll be fine . . .'

Roland's voice fades away, and the look in his eyes becomes vague and unclear. Before they walk through the first gate, he whispers to Anders: 'Act like you're really bored, as if being in his presence is utterly mundane, like changing the sheets on a bed in an old people's home.'

'I'll try.'

Roland's slack face now seems tense, and the look in his eyes is hard and nervous.

'We don't say what we're doing, we just pretend that we're going to give him his Risperdal injection as usual.'

'But—'

'But instead we'll give him an overdose of Mirtazapine,' the senior consultant says.

'We're giving him an overdose?'

'I tried it last time, and then . . . well, at first he became pretty aggressive, but only for a short while. Because then it starts to affect the motor functions . . . first the face and tongue. He couldn't talk properly. And after that he collapsed on the floor and just lay there. Then he had an attack of cramps, almost like epilepsy. That went on for quite a while, and left him tired and drowsy, almost out of it . . . That's when we take the chance to go in and get the knife.'

'Why not a sedative?'

'That would have been better,' Roland nods. 'But I think we should stick to the medication that he usually gets.'

They pass through the gates and into Jurek Walter's ward. Weak light reaches the corridor through the toughened glass in a white metal door with a hatch and a crossbar.

Roland Brolin gestures for Anders to wait. He's moving more slowly now, as if he wants to approach the toughened glass cautiously.

Perhaps he's worried about being taken by surprise.

He moves sideways, keeping his distance from the glass, then suddenly his face relaxes, and he waves for Anders to join him. They stand by the window in the door. Anders looks into a bright, fairly large windowless room.

195

A man wearing a pair of blue jeans and a denim shirt is sitting on a plastic chair in the isolation cell. He's leaning forward, with his elbows resting on his knees. Suddenly he turns his keen gaze on the door, and Roland Brolin takes a step beck.

Jurek Walter is clean-shaven, and wears his grey hair with a fringe and side parting. His face is pale and deeply lined with wrinkles, a network of pain.

Roland walks back to the gate, unlocks a dark cabinet, and takes out three small, broad-necked glass bottles. All three contain a yellow powder. He adds two milligrams of water to each bottle and rotates them gently to dissolve the powder, then draws the liquid from the bottles into a syringe.

They go over to window in the door again. Jurek Walter is now sitting on the bed. Roland puts his earplugs in, then opens the hatch in the door.

'Jurek Walter,' he says in a dull voice. 'It's time . . .'

Anders watches as the man gets up from the bed, looks at the hatch in the door, and walks towards it as he unbuttons his shirt.

'Stop and take your shirt off,' Roland says, even though that's what the man is already doing.

Jurek Walter continues walking slowly forward.

Roland closes the hatch and bolts it with movements that are a little too fast and nervous. Jurek stops, undoes the last buttons, and removes his shirt. He has three circular scars on his chest. His skin hangs loosely over his veiny muscles. Roland opens the hatch again, and Jurek Walter takes the last few steps towards it.

'Hold your arm out,' Roland says, and a tiny catch in his voice as he breathes in reveals just how scared he is.

Jurek doesn't look at him. Instead he is staring at Anders with great interest.

He pushes his old, pigment-mottled arm through the hatch. Three long burn marks run down the inside of his arm.

Roland inserts the needle into the thick vein and injects the liquid very quickly. Jurek's hand twitches in surprise, but he doesn't pull it back until he's given permission. The consultant closes and bolts the hatch quickly, then looks in. Jurek Walter stumbles towards the bed. He sits down with jerky movements. Roland accidentally drops the syringe, and they both watch it roll across the concrete floor.

When they look back at Jurek Walter again, the inside of the toughened glass is clouded over. He's breathed on the inside of the glass and written 'JOONA' with his finger.

'What does it say?' Anders asks in a weak voice.

'He's written "Joona".'

'Joona?'

'What the hell does that mean?'

The condensation fades, and they see that Jurek Walter is sitting on the bed just as before, as if he hadn't moved.